MILLENNIAL GLORY III

APOCALYPSE, *THE UNVEILING*

A novel about the earth's last days.

WENDIE L. EDWARDS

WITH TIM HARTMAN

Cover and book design
Ronn Raymond © 2005

Published by Seventh Seal Publishing, Inc.
Cedar Hills, Utah

Copyright © 2004 Wendie L. Edwards

All rights reserved. No part of this book may be reproduced in any form or by any means without permission in writing from the publisher, Seventh Seal Publishing, Inc.

This is a work of fiction. The characters, names, incidents, places, and dialogue are products of the authors' imagination, and are to be construed theoretical.

Library of Congress Catalog Card Number: 2004091708

10 ISBN 0-9712228-2-7
13 ISBN 978-0-9712228-2-3

Fifth Printing 2006
Fifth Edition
Printed in the United States of America

DEDICATION

Ted, I'll love you forever.

To my sweet children: Look up and live. Find your glorious place among the noble and great ones in preparation for His coming.

ACKNOWLEDGEMENTS

Thank you to all who have supported me in this endeavor. Thank you Tim, for sharing such a fantastic mind for both the future and the eternal. Thank you Terie, Darlene, Lori, and Kathryn my editors, for your enduring eye and your willing hearts. Thank you Lynn, for your undying service. Thank you Debby at Deseret Book for believing in me. Thank you Jolyn for your patience. And most of all, thank you Mother for your loving guidance.

Millennial Glory

Hidden Light,
Millennial Glory I

A strange plague breaks out among a rebellious segment of society. The sickness is related to a mysterious man who claims he is the resurrected Savior of the world. His intent is to hide the light of the truth as he stands in its stead. His words are hypnotic. His message is deadly. Corrynne Rogers is an Intensive Care nurse who cares for the dying. Through her hospital association she uncovers a destructive plan to implant computer chips under the skin in anyone who worships the false Christ in an effort to control the followers. Some followers are killed by a flesh eating bacteria as they turn away from the religious leader. Eventually, Corrynne exposes the deadly plan but not in time to protect one of her own from the lethal chip. The Zulu countdown has begun. Fire is prophesied to rain from heaven to punish those who refuse to accept the false Christ. But will it? Only time will tell.

Wars of Light,
Millennial Glory II

Bo is the father of the Rogers family. He learns that he and his eldest son, Braun, share a gift of dreams and are able to see mysterious things that often tell of the future. Through his dreams he realizes two of his children will soon fall prey to the mysterious Antichrist that is growing in power. Bo is painfully admonished by the Spirit not to interfere but to allow his children to face the evil man alone in fulfillment of agreements they made before their life on earth. How can he do this? Through his trials he learns that an unseen war comprising all of God's children, both good and evil, continues in the world from when it began in heaven. Bo comes to understand that there are greater powers than his own in charge of his life. He is expected to exercise true faith in God's power and to lean not unto his own understanding. Can he be brave enough to just sit back and trust in Heavenly Father's promises to save his children? It's a request almost too hard to bear.

A LETTER TO YOU, THE READER

Dear Reader,

It is my hope you will learn through reading as I have in writing. I believe the key to such learning lies in the endnotes for each chapter. The endnotes are jewels, revealing the book's true value in helping us all research the last days in an enjoyable and educational fashion—through story. It is up to you to study the endnotes or simply pass over them. However, for me, it has been extremely valuable to have many sources of revealed knowledge collected together in an organized fashion and has aided me in speeches, talks, missionary work and other research dealing with the church.

The story found within these covers, is not meant to tell the future, but to be similar to a parable for us in the last days. It is written to help us see deep into our reality and understand our potential in the future that unavoidably lies ahead of us. I pray each of us will read and take to ourselves the power of God that will make us a powerful people who will conquer all that stands in our way of eternal exaltation.

One last note: In my research, there were many quotes that I felt inspired to include in this story but could not find an economical way to do so without making this book over a thousand pages long, so I have included an introduction that expresses the spirit of the book. Endnotes are included to fulfill the perceptions of my heart to all who read.

I hope you love this work as I do.

Sincerely,

Wendie L. Edwards.

TABLE OF CONTENTS

INTRODUCTION

FUTURE UTAH

"Behold, vengeance cometh speedily upon the inhabitants of the earth...And upon my house shall it begin, and from my house shall it go forth, saith the Lord; First among those among you, saith the Lord, who have professed to know my name and have not known me, and have blasphemed against me in the midst of my house, saith the Lord...purify your hearts before me..." (D&C 112:24-26, 28).

Promised Land

It has been prophesied that before the coming of the Lord, there would be an accounting of God's people in the mountains.[1] Such an accounting has arrived and demands both the God fearing and the atheist to declare their hearts.[2]

Before Joseph Smith was martyred, he saw in vision the stark deserts,[3] lush riverbeds, and snow-laden mountains of Utah. He knew without a doubt that many prosperous cities would rise from the dust of a barren land. Work from faithful Saints and the blessings of the Almighty would build a heritage for their pioneer children.[4] It wasn't until later, when Brigham Young led his people to the Salt Lake Valley that Joseph's vision became a reality.[5]

The Lord drew the Saints to the mountains to protect them from the buffetings of Satan.[6] The land was meant to cradle God's people, allowing them to raise a righteous generation to serve him.[7] However, Brigham Young knew the Saints would not be isolated for long. He foresaw that many righteous people would move on to colonize other stakes of Zion. There they would mingle with the world,[8] just as the world would come to the Valley and mingle with the Saints.[9]

Utah became what Joseph Smith had seen and as Brigham Young expected it would become. Many people from all nations gathered spontaneously to the mountains,[10] enlarging its borders and filling its empty spaces.[11] Infiltration of money and commerce[12] caused Utah to expand, and the people grew successful.[13] High health vitality, low disease rates,[14] academic excellence,[15] and a safe, nurturing environment for family living,[16] was the natural outgrowth of a religious society. However, as in most successful societies, a false sense of security began to permeate the people.[17] Among many of the Saints worldly appetites and behaviors began to replace piety.[18]

Now, the prophesied day has come that Utah has taken to herself the ways of the world, and found herself in moral as well as financial bondage.[19] Many of the Lord's people have forgotten why success came so readily to them.[20] Many have become materialistic, prideful, judgmental, and ignorant of their covenants and blessings.[21] Those who emulate the world, claiming to be members of the Church of Jesus Christ of Latter-day Saints, blaspheme the Lord's name while sitting in his house.[22] A warning to the people: "*the Lord will not be mocked!*"[23]

Still—all is not lost! Not all have fallen! Faithful Saints, good and obedient people, seek to reestablish Zion. These are the people who will prove to be the core of the righteous, and will greet Christ as he comes to receive his keys at Adam-ondi-Ahman.[24] It is in behalf of these beloved people that the Lord will reach out to cleanse his house.[25] Through adversity and the elements the disobedient will be plucked out from among them and the righteous will be spiritually refined.[26] Through trial and adversity the Saints will discover their true identity and power.[27] They will become a beautiful and terrifying people that will cause the nations to shake in fear of them.[28] They will be beings of light in bodies of clay.[29] Through all this, they will—REMEMBER!

ξξξξξξ

From the northeast, out of the jagged peaks and the spring-snow covered mountains, flow countless streams and small rivers. The silvery threads of water cascade down rocky cliffs in luminous waterfalls. Each stream eventually finds and joins countless others in one seaward goal. Growing over miles of connections the streams feed the increasing volume of the larger Provo River. Gathering volume and speed, the river charges relentlessly downhill finding its way out of the hills and through the canyons southwesterly toward the quiet valley of Provo, Utah.

High above the peaceful valley, the force of the river is harnessed by many massive man-made dams, one being the Deer Creek Dam. The barrier causes the rocky ravine to support a vast, serene body of water between two mountainous formations. The enormous reservoir lies suspended sixteen miles northeast of the quiet family neighborhoods of suburban Provo.

Those living in the valley have only fleeting thoughts of the potentially deadly power of the giant sleeping serenely in the mountains above them. It would take a large, catastrophic earthquake to unleash its destructive power—but that would never happen....

Notes to "Future Utah"

Promised Land

[1] "Zion is not going to be moved out of her place. The Lord will plead with her strong ones, and if she sins he will chastise her until she is purified before the Lord. I do not pretend to tell how much sorrow you or I are going to meet with before the coming of the Son of Man. That will depend upon our conduct" (Wilford Woodruff, *Millennial Star*, 1889, Vol. 51, 547).

[2] "So then because thou art lukewarm, and neither cold nor hot, I will spew thee out of my mouth" (Revelation 3:16).

[3] Most of the land in Utah was a desert wilderness. Through faith and sacrifice, the barren land was turned into a blossoming, lush, garden, being one fulfillment of the scripture; "The wilderness and the solitary place shall be glad for them; and the desert shall rejoice, and blossom as the rose" (Isaiah 35:1). In the words of Brigham Young, "We prayed over the land, and dedicated it and the water, air and everything pertaining to them unto the Lord, and the smiles of heaven rested on the land and it became productive" (*Discourses of Brigham Young*, 483).

[4] "Mosiah Hancock, reported a visit by Joseph Smith immediately before his departure for Carthage: '...The Prophet came to our home and stopped in our carpenter shop and stood by the turning lathe I went and got my map for him. 'Now,' said he, 'I will show you the travels of this people.' He then showed our travels thru Iowa, and said, 'Here you will make a place for the winter; and here you will travel west until you come to the valley of the Great Salt Lake! You will build cities to the North and to the South, and to the East and to the West; and you will become a great and wealthy people in that land'." ("The Life Story of Mosiah Lyman Hancock," typewritten copy in Brigham Young University Library, 27-29, as quoted by Hyrum L. Andrus, "Joseph Smith and the West," *BYU Studies*, Spring and Summer 1960, Vol. 2, No. 2).

[5] "When President Brigham Young entered the Salt Lake Valley in 1847, he raised himself upon his elbow, in the carriage of Brother Woodruff, where he was reclining, and looked over the valley, from the mouth of Emigration Canyon, and said, 'This will do; drive on, Brother Woodruff; this is the place for the gathering of the Saints'" (Seymour B. Young, *Conference Report, Second Day—Morning Session*, April 1907, 40 - 41).

[6] The purpose of moving to the Rocky Mountains, according to Joseph Smith was, "to get up into the mountains, where the devil cannot dig us out, and live in a healthful climate, where we can live as old as we have a mind to" (*History of the Church*, 6:22).

[7] "We are blessed in these mountains; this is the best place on the earth for the Latter-day Saints. Search the history of all the nations and every geographical position on the face of the earth, and you cannot find another situation so well adapted for the Saints, as are these mountains. Here is the place in which the Lord designed to hide his people. Be thankful for it; be true to your covenants, and be faithful, each and every one" (Brigham Young, *Deseret Evening News*, May 1, 1861, Vol. 11, 1).

[8] "It appears that in August of 1845 the Mormon leaders were formulating plans to colonize the Pacific Coast, Oregon, Vancouver Island, and other proposed sites for 'stakes of Zion' but that the center would probably be somewhere near the Great Salt Lake" (Lewis Clark Christian, "Mormon Foreknowledge of the West," *BYU Studies*, Fall 1981, Vol. 21, No.4).

[9] "After a while the gentiles will gather by the thousands to this place…" (Heber C. Kimball, Deseret News, May 23, 1931, 3).

[10] "And it shall come to pass in the last days, when the mountain of the Lord's house shall be established in the top of the mountains, and shall be exalted above the hills, and all nations shall flow unto it"(2 Nephi 12:2).

[11] "For Zion must increase in beauty, and in holiness; her borders must be enlarged; her stakes must be strengthened; yea, verily I say unto you, Zion must arise and put on her beautiful garments" (D&C 82:14).

[12] "Each year the state of Utah receives thousands of calls from site selectors, facility planners, corporate executives, and citizens who want more information about Utah's business environment for possible business expansion or relocation" (Mike Leavitt, *Utah dot gov*, "All about Utah," 2003, Available: [Online] http://www.utah.gov/textonly/about/quickfacts.html).

[13] Clearly Utah is the "Zion" that has been established by the Lord and blessed to flourish in the hills (D&C 49:25). If there is any question of whether the mountains described in the above scripture refer to Utah see the following statistic: "Utah's peaks, on average, are the tallest in the country. That is, if you average the elevations of the tallest peaks in each of Utah's counties and compare that number with the average elevations of the tallest peaks in each county of every other state, you will find that Utah's peaks will be an average of 11, 222 feet taller" (*Utah Dot Gov.*, "All About Utah Interesting facts and demographic information" 2003, Available: [Online] http://www.utah.gov/about/quickfacts.html).

[14] "Latter-day Saints generally adhere strictly to their health code which prohibits the use of tobacco and alcohol. These practices have always shown up in national health data, which consistently rate Utah as having the lowest rates of smoking, alcohol use, lung cancer, etc. The National Institute of Mental Health ranked Utah as the second-lowest U.S. state in new inpatient admissions to state mental hospitals, and ranked Utah as having the lowest per-capita alcohol consumption. (Lauran, Neergaard, (Associated Press) *MMR Weekly*, July 28, 1989, 501-505).

"In 2000, Self magazine ranked Provo, Utah as the number 1 healthiest city in the country for women. The article said that the Mormon influence is the reason women in Provo experience such low incidents of cancer, smoking, drinking, violence, depression, etc." [Source: *MSNBC*], (Sampling of Latter-day Saint Demographics and Social Statistics from National Sources, site updated, July 25, 2002, Available: [Online] http://www.adherents.com/largecom/lds_dem.html).

[15] "Longstanding Latter-day Saint emphasis on secular education and learning, in addition to religious education, can be seen in federal education statistics. The American Legislative Exchange Council's (ALEC) Report Card on Education 1996 reported that Utah was ranked 7th academically in the nation, despite the fact that the state spent less money (49th in expenditures per pupil) than most other states. (Center for Education Reform, 1001 Connecticut Avenue NW, Suite 204, Washington, D.C.).

"Utah has one of the highest high school graduation rates in the nation, ranking third in 1990-92, with 93.9%, behind North Dakota and Iowa. Tennessee was ranked last. ("Graduation Rates in the United States," National Center for Education Statistics.) Utah is ranked 2nd in proportion of the population who are high school graduates. 85.1% of Utah's adult populations are high school graduates. Alaska is ranked 1st, with 86.6. Nationally the figure is 75.2%. (1990 Census, U.S. Bureau of the Census, Statistical Abstract of the United States 1997 (117th Edition), U.S. Dept. of Commerce, 161).

[16] "The 1999, Places Rated Almanac (IDG Books) ranked the Salt Lake City-Ogden metro area as the best place to live in North America. The quadrennial statistical study, first

published in 1981, rates 354 U.S. and Canadian metro areas on nine quality of life factors including cost of living, transportation, jobs, education, climate, crime, arts, health care and recreation. In four... categories -- transportation, jobs, the arts and recreation -- Salt Lake-Ogden placed in the highest 10 percentiles. A few years earlier, the Provo-Orem metroplex where 70%-90% of people are Latter-day Saints was ranked as the 'most livable' community in the United States. (Joel Campbell, "S.L.-Ogden best place to live in N. America," *Deseret News*, 4 Nov. 1999; Lori Buttars, "Salt Lake-Ogden Is the Place," *Salt Lake Tribune*, 5 Nov. 1999).

"In November 2000, Money Magazine ranked Salt Lake City as the 'West's most livable metropolis.' (Phil Sahm, Money Magazine and Salt Lake Tribune, 14 November 2000). According to the latest Bureau of Justice Statistics, Utah has fewer people per capita in prison (a lower incarceration rate) than all but six states. In 1998 Utah's incarceration rate was only 205 per 100,000 residents, compared to the national average of 423. The states with lower rates were all more rural than Utah: West Virginia, Vermont, New Hampshire, North Dakota, Maine and Minnesota. The states with the highest incarceration rates were: Louisiana, Texas, Oklahoma, Mississippi and South Carolina" (Sampling of Latter-day Saint Demographics and Social Statistics from National Sources, site updated, July 25, 2002 Available: [Online] http://www.adherents.com/largecom/lds_dem.html).

[17] "And others will he pacify, and lull them away into carnal security, that they will say: All is well in Zion; yea, Zion prospereth, all is well—and thus the devil cheateth their souls, and leadeth them away carefully down to hell" (1 Nephi 28:21).

[18] The Lord loves his people and has great patience for them, however there comes a time when a righteous people becomes wicked and they call upon themselves destruction.

"His people [Israel] finally did reject him through unrighteousness and rebellion. Then, true to the words of his holy prophets, the Lord suffered them to be scattered—the people of the Book of Mormon, the Lord's "other sheep" (John 10:16), whom he personally visited in the meridian of time, who at one time achieved for the space of 200 years a society of perfect peace and unity. Nevertheless, these too fell into disobedience and rebellion and wickedness and were cut off from the presence of the Lord, to be scourged, scattered, and "led about by Satan, even as chaff is driven before the wind, or as a vessel is tossed about upon the waves, without sail or anchor, or without anything wherewith to steer her" (Mormon 5:18).

"The title to the land of America is a conditional title, and only those who live the laws of God and serve him faithfully can inherit it. He wanted the Jaredites to come over. They found America. They lived for a long while here and ripened in iniquity before they encountered the people of Mulek. The land then was given to Lehi and to his sons and their families, but when a fullness of iniquity arose among these children of the land, they were swept off. Therefore, I want us to keep in our minds the fact that this land is ours only so long as we live the commandments of God. Whether it is Greeks or Italians or Norwegians or whoever is going to enjoy this land, they are going to serve God or they shall be swept off. There is much evil, much wrong, much wrongdoing in this land of ours. Many people break the laws of God, and the day will come when he just cannot tolerate it. He says he won't" (Spencer W. Kimball, "Our Paths Have Met Again," *Ensign*, Dec. 1975, 2).

[19] "Salt Lake City will be classed among the wicked cities of the world. A spirit of speculation and extravagance will take possession of the Saints and the results will be financial bondage" (Heber C. Kimball, *Deseret News*, May 23, 1931, 3).

[20] "Let any people enjoy peace and quietness, unmolested, undisturbed—never be persecuted for their religion, and they are very likely to neglect their duty, to become cold and indifferent, and lose their faith" (Brigham Young, *Journal of Discourses*, 7:42).

[21] "And inasmuch as they are not the saviors of men, they are as salt that has lost its savor, and is thenceforth good for nothing but to be cast out and trodden under foot of men" (D&C 103:10).

[22] "And upon my house shall it begin, and from my house shall it go forth, saith the Lord; First among you, saith the Lord, who have professed to know my name and have not known me, and have blasphemed against me in the midst of my house, saith the Lord" (D&C 112:25-26).

[23] "If the Latter-day Saints do not desist from running after the things of this world, and begin to reform and do the work the Father has given them to do, they will be found wanting, and they, too, will be swept away and counted as unprofitable servants" (Brigham Young, *Journal of Discourses*, Vol. 18, 262).

[24] The Lord identified Adam-ondi-Ahman in upper Missouri, as the site where the great gathering will take place when Jesus Christ comes to meet with Adam and his righteous posterity and receive keys (see D&C 78:15; 107:53-57; 116).

[25] "Zion is not going to be moved out of her place. The Lord will plead with her strong ones, and if she sins he will chastise her until she is purified before the Lord" (Wilford Woodruff, *Millennial Star*, 1889, Vol. 51, 547).

[26] "Because of our disobedience and our failure to keep the commandments of the Lord, the righteous, as in times past, may be called upon to suffer with the unrighteous among them" (Joseph Fielding Smith, *Conference Report*, April, 1937, 60).

[27] "But we believe that these severe, natural calamities are visited upon men by the Lord for the good of His children, to quicken their devotion to others, and to bring out their better natures, that they may love and serve him. We believe, further that they are the heralds and tokens of his final judgment, and the schoolmasters to teach the people to prepare themselves by righteous living, for the coming of the Savior to rein upon the earth, when every knee shall bow and every tongue confess that Jesus is the Christ" (Joseph F. Smith, *Improvement Era*, June, 1906, 654).

[28] "And the day shall come when the nations of the earth shall tremble because of her, and shall fear because of her terrible ones. The Lord hath spoken it. Amen" (D&C 64:43).

[29] "Man was also in the beginning with God. Intelligence, or the light of truth, was not created or made, neither indeed can be" (D&C 93:23).

CHARACTERS

ROGERS FAMILY

Bo Andrew Rogers	45	Father
Corrynne Rochelle Rogers	42	Mother
Braun Joseph Rogers	22	First Son
Conrad Ryan Rogers	20	Second Son
Brea Nicole Rogers	19	First Daughter
Dane Russell Rogers	17	Third Son
Carea Lorrell Rogers	16	Second Daughter
Jax William Rogers	11	Fourth Son
Ry Benjamin Rogers	9	Fifth Son
Rocwell Joshua Rogers	7	Sixth Son
Striynna Chandelle Rogers	1 yr.	Third Daughter First Twin
Strykker Adam Rogers	1 yr.	Seventh Son and Second Twin

PROLOGUE

BITTER WITH THE SWEET

"Q. What are we to understand by the little book which was eaten by John, as mentioned in the 10th chapter of Revelation?

"A. We are to understand that it was a mission, and an ordinance, for him to gather the tribes of Israel; behold, this is Elias, who, as it is written, must come and restore all things" (D&C 77:14).

92 A.D.
Island of Patmos

Memories of Translation

John nimbly dipped the tip of a thin bamboo stick into the inkwell and refilled his pen. He sat in the shade of a large bush and wrote a personal command given to him from the Lord Jesus Christ, *"Take the book and eat it up; and it shall make thy belly bitter, but it shall be in they mouth sweet as honey."*[1]

John remembered eating the little book in his waking-dream and just as Christ had described, the book was sweet upon his tongue but it made his belly ache. The burden of the words in the book was a hard one; yet he promised he would fulfill them.[2] Within those pages were written his sweet call to serve his Master, preaching to many in the world to help gather the Lord's lost.[3] He remembered a similar command given to him on another day as he sat on another shore.

The Sea of Galilee had been quiet, smooth, and clear—green as an emerald when Christ's disciples gathered at Tiberias. It had only been a short time since Christ's death and resurrection, and they all longed to be with the Lord again. He was coming to teach them, as he had promised.

During the meeting on the shore of Galilee, Christ spoke to John. He remembered him saying, "John, my beloved, what desirest thou? ...For if you shall ask what you will, it shall be granted unto you."

John had contemplated the desires of his heart. He would not ask for anything for himself; selfish desires were overshadowed by his love for his Savior. All he wanted to do was serve his Master. He remembered asking, "Lord, give unto me power over death, that I may live and bring souls unto thee."

John remembered the sublime smile that crossed Christ's face. He seemed pleased with John's request. He answered, "Because thou desirest this, thou shalt tarry until I come in my glory, and shalt prophesy before nations, kindreds, tongues and people."[4]

John had felt satisfied with Christ's statement, and when his body changed from mortality to a state of translation, he knew the letter of Christ's words would be fulfilled. He would live until Christ returned to the earth, but how long that would be, no apostle, prophet, nor man knew.[5]

Along with tasks aimed at gathering Israel, he was given responsibility from the foundations of the earth to reveal the future.[6] Through his words he would call to the lost tribes hidden throughout the world. It was his duty to reveal the Lord's plans to all who would seek them. The Greek word for his revelation would be *"apocalypse,"*[7] thus by that name, the mysteries of the last days would be known to help gather God's children home.

Sadly, John foresaw conspiring men would change his writings.[8] But due to the mercy of the Lord, in time, the righteous would still come to understand his words and recognize the signs of the Second Coming.[9] It would be a great time of *unveiling,* as those who were worthy would understand through the whisperings of the Spirit.[10]

John dipped his bamboo pen again and prepared to write more.

"You! *Prophet*!" A rough voice irreverently interrupted John's thoughts.

John looked up from the squirrel skin on which he had been writing. The voice was that of a grimy man twice John's size and three times uglier than anyone John had ever seen. Other men, similar to the first, grinned wickedly as they surrounded John, each harboring a threatening stick.

"What food are you hiding over there?" asked the leader, "During this famine, Christians get food last! The rules are the same here on this island!"

"I have no food," John said simply, knowing that many Christians suffered because of the boycotts and trade sanctions the government had passed upon them because they would not offer sacrifices to idols.[11]

The large man took two steps forward then waved his stick over John's head creating a wind that moved his hair. "You must have some food because you are sitting there as satisfied as if you just ate a roasted pig and drank the depths of a wine flask!"

John did not flinch but began to gather his belongings. He shook his head slightly as he stood, then said, "I have no need of food. The word of the

Lord is all I need to nourish my body. If you want the word of the Lord, I will give it to you until you too are filled."

The leader spat on the ground near John's feet, and yelled angrily, "*You speak crazy tales of foolishn*ess! No one can exist on prophecy—unless you are a *ghost*, instead of a *real* man as some say!" The man grinned and looked at his comrades who laughed menacingly at his comments.

"I speak only truth," John said standing tall and unafraid.

"What do you have in that bag?" asked one of the men. "Why do you hide it from us?"

"Is it chicken with drippings?" asked another.

"How about rabbit in herb sauce," joked a third.

"Yeah, we've all seen you drying skins. Where's the vermin that was inside them?" asked the leader, this time whipping his stick to the side of John's face.

"We're sure you have salted meat hidden in some rock around here!" said another crazed prisoner surveying the area.

"I say we torture him until he gives us what we deserve by the divine decree of Dominitan!" yelled the leader again, raising his arms and his stick high above his head.

"*Yeah!*" yelled the men in hostile unison, as they mimicked their leader and held up their heavy sticks also.

In the next moment, the men violently and hungrily rushed toward John. However, in simplicity of thought, and in the name of Christ, the apostle was gone from among them[12] and their sticks fell hard upon each other.

ξξξξξξ

Cold water lapped at John's feet. He was standing beneath the overhang of a rock in the sea on the opposite side of the island. He would stay here and write in peace for a time.

With a deep breath he sat down and balanced his belongings on an adjacent rock. Dipping his pen again in his black ink, he marveled at how much he must write. Despite that fact, nothing would stop his words. For this purpose was he preserved with the power of heaven coursing through his veins.

He would write for those in the end of days when all would be in commotion.

Notes to "Bitter With the Sweet"

[1] See Revelation 10:9 for the scripture in context.

[2] Richard Draper gives a theory of why the book that John ate was both sweet and bitter. "Just why his mission would contain bitterness is unknown. In Ezekiel's case, the parchment he figuratively ate contained woes, lamentation, and judgments (see 2:9-10). Because it was the word of God, it pleased Ezekiel, but because it was harsh it pained him...perhaps John's mission is somewhat the same.... By witnessing the gospel, John participates directly in the

damning rebellious nations. Therefore, their rejection of his message, in part, brings upon them the horrible judgments he saw while on the Isle of Patmos" (*Opening the Seven Seals*, 116).

[3] "...We are to understand that it was a mission, and an ordinance, for him to gather the tribes of Israel" (D&C 77:14).

[4] See D&C 7:1-3 for the quotes used in the text and compare with Revelation 10:11.

[5] But of that day and hour knoweth no man, no, not the angels of heaven, but my Father only" (Matthew 24:36).

[6] Although many prophets have seen the history of the earth and the events of the last days, all were forbidden to write them because John was given this stewardship. "And behold, the things which this apostle of the Lamb shall write are many things which thou hast seen; and behold, the remainder shalt thou see. But the things which thou shalt see hereafter thou shalt not write; for the Lord God hath ordained the apostle of the Lamb of God that he should write them" (1 Nephi 14:24-25).

[7] "John's vision is often called 'The Apocalypse.' This title is derived from the ancient Greek word apokalupto, which means to make bare, disclose, or uncover. In a religious sense it carries the idea of disclosing divine secrets and making known holy mysteries" (Richard Draper, *Opening the Seventh Seal*, 15).

[8] "...Thou seest the formation of that great and abominable church, which is most abominable above all other churches; for behold, they have taken away from the gospel of the Lamb many parts which are plain and most precious; and also many covenants of the Lord have they taken away" (1 Nephi 13:26).

[9] "And to them will I reveal all mysteries, yea, all the hidden mysteries of my kingdom from days of old, and for ages to come, will I make known unto them the good pleasure of my will concerning all things pertaining to my kingdom. Yea, even the wonders of eternity shall they know, and things to come will I show them, even the things of many generations" (D&C 76:7-8).

[10] "Are we expected to understand the book of Revelation? Certainly. Why else did the Lord reveal it? ...Most of the book—and it is no problem to count the verses so included—is clear and plain and should be understood by the Lord's people. Certain parts are not clear and are not understood by us—which, however, does not mean that we could not understand them if we would grow in faith as we should. The Lord expects us to seek wisdom, to ponder his revealed truths, and to gain a knowledge of them by the power of his Spirit" (Bruce R. McConkie, "Understanding the Book of Revelation," *Ensign*, September 1975, 87).

[11] During the 90's A.D. there was a struggle between the pagans, Jews, and Christians in Asia Minor. It was sparked by natural disasters. "About A.D. 92 there was an anti-Christian outbreak due in part of a serious famine blamed on the Saints because they refused to pay homage to pagan gods. Boycotts and trade sanctions were directed against the churches. Arrests, imprisonments, banishments, and even executions followed" (Richard Draper, *Opening of the Seven Seals*, 4).

[12] Because John has a translated body, he has capabilities that normal mortals do not have. One, as indicated by the scripture below is the ability to "appear" to whomever he wishes, or equally disappear from whomever he wishes.

"And they are as the angels of God, and if they shall pray unto the Father in the name of Jesus they can show themselves unto whatsoever man it seemeth them good" (3 Nephi 28:30).

CHAPTER ONE

QUAKE

"And the angel took the censer, and filled it with fire of the altar, and cast it into the earth: and there were voices, and thunderings, and lightnings, and an earthquake" (Revelation 8:5).

00:09:04, 18:10:17 Zulu
Friday, March 25th
10:50 p.m.
Provo, Utah

Words of Warning

Corrynne sat, seemingly relaxed, in front of her computer. She was randomly surfing the Internet while she listened to the October conference session.[1] Despite her calm exterior, there were a thousand knots inside, and her head hurt from worrying about her two missing children. She was trying to be strong, but Dane and Carea had been gone for more than four hours and it had been at least two since Dane had called to tell her that he could not find his sister.

Calmly, the prophet spoke to Corrynne, as if to reassure her. *"...Are these perilous times? They are. But there is no need to fear. We can have peace in our hearts and peace in our homes.*

"Life is fragile, peace is fragile, and civilization itself is fragile. The economy is particularly vulnerable. We have been counseled again and again concerning self-reliance, concerning debt, concerning thrift...[2]

Corrynne bit her lower lip. The words of the prophet seemed to float from the computer, initiating myriads of challenging thoughts. Oh, how she needed to find peace amid adversity right now! She prayed that listening to the prophet's counsel would help her heavy heart.

The talk continued. *"We have been continuously counseled for more than 60 years. Let us have some food set aside that would sustain us for a time in case of need...I do not know what the future holds. I do not wish to sound negative, but I wish to remind you of the warnings of scripture and the teachings of the prophets which we have had constantly before us..."[3]*

"I cannot forget the great lesson of Pharaoh's dream of the fat and lean kine and of the full and withered stalks of corn. I cannot dismiss from my mind the grim warnings of the Lord as set in the 24th chapter of Matthew. I am familiar, as are you, with the declarations of modern revelation that the time will come when the earth will be cleansed and there will be indescribable distress, with weeping and mourning and lamentation..."[4]

Corrynne had strong feelings about this particular discourse. She knew it wasn't time yet for the cleansing of the earth; however the awful Bat organization with the evil Imam Mahdi at its helm infiltrating their lives, made her wonder if the cleansing wasn't just around the corner.

"I believe that the Ten Virgins represent the people of the Church of Jesus Christ and not the rank and file of the world," the prophet continued. *"All of the virgins, wise and foolish, had accepted the invitation to the wedding supper; they had knowledge of the program and had been warned of the important day to come. ...Rushing for their lamps to light the way through the blackness, half of them found them empty. They had cheated themselves. They were fools, these five unprepared virgins. Apparently, the bridegroom had tarried for reasons that were sufficient and good. Time had passed, and he had not come. They had heard of his coming for so long, so many times, that the statement seemingly became meaningless to them. Would he ever come? So long had it been since they began expecting him that they were rationalizing that he would never appear. Perhaps it was a myth. At midnight: Precisely at the darkest hour, when least expected, the bridegroom came."[5]*

Licking her lips, Corrynne frowned as a question formed in her mind. The prophet had said Christ would come at the "darkest hour." When would that be? How "dark" *exactly* was it going to get before Christ came again? For her, life was pretty stressful already. Children disappearing, reappearing, and being threatened, acting strange...could it get worse?

Corrynne reflected on her ward and neighborhood. She couldn't help but conclude that her family seemed to be suffering more than all of them. Was there anyone in the world that was suffering as much as she? Immediately guilt for her selfish and myopic conclusions filled her. What about people who were sick with AIDS and living in constant hunger? AIDS had infected over 80 million people and was still consuming whole countries![6] What about the orphaned children in Africa? Millions of them left without protection, food or shelter. What about the rampant drug abuse? Nations were legalizing the use of harmful substances for recreation, destroying lives and families by the billions.[7] No, life for Corrynne was not that bad. She still had many blessings to count.

The talk continued, *"For us the "midnights" of life are the times when heaven comes to offer its joy for man's weariness. But when the cry sounds there is no time for preparation...Midnight is so late for those who have procrastinated."⁸*

"Procrastinated..." Corrynne wondered if she had procrastinated. Had she done everything in her power to prepare for the hardships that would come her way? Was she ready for what was around the corner? Was she strong enough? For the first time, these familiar questions were suddenly intimidating. She had been warned throughout her life, but now she knew she had been somewhat lax, perhaps even foolish, just like in the parable. She had been complacent and satisfied because of the good times. She found herself fearing her spirit had grown weak.

"We have had sufficient warning...while no man knows the day or the hour, yet if we are taken unawares, we will be without excuse, for the signs are ample and we now see them being fulfilled."⁹

Corrynne nodded in agreement, as she thought of the many signs she could name. No one could deny that statement!

"Now, brothers and sisters, we must do our duty, whatever that duty might be. Peace may be denied for a season. Some of our liberties may be curtailed. We may be inconvenienced. We may even be called on to suffer in one way or another. But God our Eternal Father will watch over this nation and all of the civilized world that look to him. He has said, 'Be still, and know that I am God.'

"May the God of heaven, the Almighty, bless us, help us, as we walk our various ways in the uncertain days that lie ahead. May we look to Him with unfailing faith. May we worthily place our reliance on his beloved Son who is our great Redeemer, whether it be in life or in death, it is my prayer in His holy name, even the name of Jesus Christ, amen."¹⁰

"Amen," said Corrynne.

She quietly contemplated the prophet's words—words she needed to take into her heart and make her own. Deep inside, she knew that if she followed the prophet's counsel, she would be able to successfully wade through the opposition no matter what transpired in her life. That knowledge was like a life raft in turbulent waters.

Corrynne dialed the phone that had been lying next to her monitor. *"Pick up, Dane, please pick up!"* she said as it rang without response.

It was Bo's voice on the other end, "I'm either on the other line or unable to take your call..."

Hearing Bo's voice startled Corrynne for a split second. She wondered if she had dialed the right number, but then she realized Bo had thrown Dane his own cell phone that night.

"Please leave a message and I'll get back to you," continued Bo's recorded voice.

Corrynne hesitated a moment until the beep cued her to leave a message, then she said, "Call me Dane. I'm worried. Tell me what is happening. I love you. Bye." Then she pushed the off button and disconnected the line. If Dane would check the messages, he would find hers.

Corrynne heard a door open, then quick little footsteps coming from the hall. Putting her thoughts on hold, she moved from her computer chair and walked around the corner into the kitchen. Roc burst into the room, his eyes wide as saucers.

"What are you doing up?" Corrynne glanced at the clock on the oven, *"It's nearly 11:30 at night!"* she continued in an intimidating tone. She intended for him to think twice next time about getting up after bedtime.

Roc stopped in his tracks and looked warily at his mother and his father in the adjoining room. Bo was sitting on the couch looking out the front window for his lost children. Corrynne could not see him, but from where Roc was standing in the hall, she could tell *he* could see both parents.

With a small, sheepish smile Roc stuck his tongue in his cheek and then said, "Well, I just wanted to tell you that Dane and Carea are on TV."

"*What?*" Corrynne felt a bolt of shock fill her body.

"What did he say?" asked Bo from the other room.

Corrynne, momentarily frozen in place, asked, "Dane and Carea are on TV? How could that be?" Corrynne wondered if she had heard her seven-year-old correctly.

"What? TV?" asked Bo, as he moved towards the doorway.

Roc hesitated, not knowing exactly which of their questions to answer first. Then he nodded as he pointed towards his bedroom and looked back and forth between his parents. "Jax said to come get you. They're on our TV right now!"

"How, but why…Roc, listen to me. Did you actually see them?" asked Corrynne, as she was irresistibly pulled toward the boy's room.

Roc attempted an explanation. "I couldn't sleep because Jax had his desk light on while he was doing his homework. I was going to play a video game until I got tired, but when I turned on the TV," Roc paused then smiled, "I saw Dane and Carea! They are in a big fight! It's cool! Come and see!"

"Fight?" asked Corrynne still wondering if she was hearing right.

"On what channel?" interrupted Bo who was already down the hallway.

"On every channel," said Roc with a smile as he followed his parents down the hall.

Corrynne and Bo rushed to the boys' room. Jax and Ry were intently watching the small television that sat atop their dresser drawers.

Corrynne moved closer so she could see the screen clearer. Her eyes searched the display and then settled on a familiar form. Yes, inexplicably, there was Dane, bent over and looking like a frail, old man. He was struggling to stand. She took a great, gasping breath. *"What's wrong with him? He was fine earlier today!*" Turning toward her husband, Corrynne grabbed his sleeve and said urgently, "*Bo! We need to get to him!*"

"I know Corrynne, but we don't even know where he is. Let's watch and see if the commentator will tell us what's happening." Bo returned his attention to the little twelve-inch TV screen.

The camera switched views to reveal a beautiful and angelic looking woman dressed extravagantly who was attending to their son.

"Who is that?" asked Bo.

"That's Carea!" said Roc pointing to the woman on the screen.

Jax also pointed. "She's dressed really fancy, but that *is* Carea."

"Yeah," said Ry. "We had to look really close, but you can tell that it's her. See?"

After studying the screen a moment, both Bo and Corrynne realized that their young sons were right.

"Why in the world is she dressed like that?" asked Corrynne, not expecting an answer. "This situation is becoming stranger by the moment!"

Bo shook his head indicating that he was equally astounded and then he hit the volume button on the TV, and heard the voice of a male commentator.

"This is CNN Live. We apologize for the interruption of the regularly scheduled programming. We interrupt to show you late-breaking scenes from a tragic battle. War is once again breaking out on the outskirts of Israel after three years of relative peace…"

"Israel? We can't be seeing Israel," said Corrynne emphatically and frowning even deeper. "What are they talking about?"

The commentator continued, "There are numerous civilian casualties as Israeli troops target terrorists and radical Islamic leaders in South Lebanon…"

Bo switched the channels back and forth on the TV, but every channel showed the same image of Dane and Carea standing in a great hall, as mismatched commentary about the distant war continued.

"I think the signals must be mixed up," said Bo. "I bet we're seeing a local broadcast feed instead of the conflict in Israel."

"A conflict in Israel?" asked Corrynne. "Oh, my goodness! When it rains it pours! What city did they say the fighting was in?"

Bo thought for a moment and said, "I think they said South Lebanon."

"Oh good," Corrynne said as she felt a slight relief. "I'm glad they didn't say Jerusalem. I know fighting has been threatening to break out there for a while…. At least Conrad's safe."

"I'm sure Conrad's safe," said Bo as he continued to switch the channels.

"Bo? Do you think everyone else is seeing the same thing we are?" asked Corrynne.

Bo shook his head. "I don't know. It's on all the local cable channels as well as the major networks, so I would think everyone is seeing it. There's no way of knowing what system they're sending these signals out on. The story about Israel most definitely would be a global broadcast, so maybe this is too."

The male CNN commentator continued, "Seemingly unprovoked cross-border attacks have been said to have come in reaction to alleged terrorist activities…"

A different voice then interrupted the first. "We apologize, but we are still having some technical difficulties. Your patience is appreciated. Please stand by."

Then without warning, a sudden explosive deep voice was broadcast into the room. "*I CHALLENGE YOU, IN THIS HALL TODAY TO SHOW THIS GOD TO US. GIVE US A SIGN!*"

"Oh that was loud!" exclaimed Corrynne as she quickly turned the volume down. "What's that screaming all about?" she asked no on in particular, and then she noticed that the sound from the broadcast had ceased. "We've lost the sound again," said Corrynne still messing with the volume dial. Suddenly a familiar memory piqued her mind. The man on the screen—she knew him! "Isn't that person—*Imam Mahdi*?"

"Yes, I believe it is," said Bo frowning.

Corrynne was thoroughly surprised. She watched, as Imam Mahdi stood tall upon a stage towering over a massive gathering.

"Bo! That's the same place we just saw the kids. He must have Dane and Carea there after all! They must be at another Rave! *What are they doing there?*"

Bo slowly rubbed the back of his neck. "I think I know what Imam Mahdi is doing. I think he is intercepting a global broadcast by hacking into it with his own signal. This show is intentionally being broadcast everywhere. In fact, I wouldn't be surprised if Imam Mahdi had something to do with that attack in Israel to lure the media onto one common broadcast signal to hijack the news for his own purposes. We already know he has enough money to pay a whole terrorist army, as well as an Israeli response if he wanted to."

"Really?" asked Corrynne. Things suddenly clicked in her brain. "That makes sense! I bet you're right. But what is he trying to do?" asked Corrynne.

"I don't quite know," answered Bo.

For the next few seconds, the group watched in stunned silence.

Filling the screen, and standing in front of a purple and gold banner, which read, "The Unveiling, the King is come!" Imam Mahdi's image was striking. His full-length, shimmering white robes billowed around him from a mysterious wind. The bright, iridescent cloth contrasted with his jet-black hair and deep, dark eyes. He looked stunning and powerful.

With a stern gaze, and a pointed finger, he gestured menacingly toward Dane who seemed to suffer with some sort of painful illness.

Corrynne took offence at the way Imam Mahdi gestured, presumably chastising Dane, who was looking upward from where he was standing in front of the stage.

"*He's such a bully!*" she said through clenched teeth. She knew he was trying to incite the viewers to join in his own feeling of contempt for her son.

"Why is Imam Mahdi being mean to Dane, Mom?" asked Jax.

"Yeah, what did he do?" asked Ry almost at the same time.

"*That man's not nice.* Is he, Mom?" asked Rocwell with an edge to his voice.

Corrynne abruptly turned to her sons and said, "No, he is not. He's a bad man." In the next breath, Corrynne said, "I'll bet Imam Mahdi has done something to Dane and he's trying to use him as an example!"

"That would fit that man's sick and deluded way of thinking," Bo said with a sneer.

Corrynne suddenly burst into tears. "Oh, Bo! I just can't bear to watch this!" With tears flowing down her cheeks, she cried, "Dane is in trouble because of me! He went after Carea because *I* told him to!"

"Why are you crying?" asked Roc, who was staring with concern into his mother's face as he patted her stomach with his hand.

"Shhh," said Jax to his little brother.

"She's just sad," Ry whispered to Roc.

Bo nodded to his sons and put his finger up to his lips to shush them. Then turning to Corryne he said, "No, Corrynne. Remember our conversation earlier. You *are not* to blame for this. Remember, we talked about how something like this was going to happen? Dane has something he needs to do and Imam Mahdi must be held accountable for his actions. All of this is only happening because the Lord is allowing it to."[11]

Corrynne shook her head and covered her face with her hands. "I don't care why this is happening! I just hate it! I don't think I can bear to watch any of this!"

"I know," said Bo, "but we must look at the end result! We must trust the Lord even now when things seem so dark.[12] We were warned and prepared for this through my dreams. I promise you Dane eventually will be OK, because the Lord promised me. He is in charge.[13] We must have faith in him."

Corrynne wiped away her tears, and with heaviness of heart pulled her emotions barely under control. Silently, she asked the Lord to help her endure the things that were happening.[14] As the family continued to watch the TV, it became obvious Imam Mahdi was growing dangerously more impatient with Dane. His anger seemed to boil, as he demanded some sort of answer.

Turning to Bo, Corrynne asked angrily, "*What does he want from him?*"

"I think he's asking Dane for—a sign?" questioned Bo. "I'm not exactly sure myself…we've missed a lot of the conversation, but that's what I gather so far."

"A sign, Daddy?" asked Jax.

"Yeah, what does he want, *a stop sign?*" asked Roc trying to be funny at the wrong time as usual.

No one responded to Roc. They were intently watching the television trying to get answers to their own questions.

Corrynne watched Dane respond to Imam Mahdi. He was gazing steadily, but it seemed that every breath he took was difficult. Suddenly, the commentator's voice came in full volume, this time the sound corresponded with the scene.

"OK! We have sound again," said Bo.

"Good. Maybe we can find out what's happening," said Corrynne.

Dane staggered a little. Then with a breathy voice he began, "…I know God's will must be done. If it so be that God would strike you down it would be because he wills it."

Corrynne felt a burst of energy. "*Tell him, Dane!*" she said as tears once again welled up in her eyes. She was both proud of Dane's strength and fearful of the backlash that could result from his defiance.

"Good answer, son!" echoed Bo.

"*Show me a sign!*" On the screen before them, Imam Mahdi seemed to lose all composure. Apparently, Dane's bold answer was neither what he wanted nor expected. Dane remained righteously defiant.

Despite Imam Mahdi's demand for a sign, Dane continued speaking, "God has all power, both in heaven and in the earth!" Then with visibly renewed energy, he stood a little taller and straighter, "Christ will come," he said, "and at that time, you will be thrust down to hell. Let that be a sign to you and to all who follow you!"

With what seemed to be the last draw of energy, Dane finished his powerful statement, "*The Lord's will be done!*" His voice cut through the air like a swift and mighty blade.

Corrynne thought she heard a sort of rumbling interference coming from the TV. "What's that noise?" she said to Bo.

Bo leaned closer to the TV speakers. "It sounds like thunder outside the building. Maybe there's a storm or something that the microphones are picking up."

Corrynne returned her attention to Imam Mahdi. She was certain that he was surprised by Dane's answer.

The evil man looked a little strange, and flinched ever so slightly. Then he bellowed, "*SHOW ME A SIG—*"

All of them watched as Imam Mahdi's words caught in his throat. He let out an awful gurgle as he grasped at his chest and formed words that looked like, *"help me."* With reddened face and bulging eyes, he looked frantically around the room.

"What's happening, Mom?" asked Roc.

"Yeah," said Jax. "Is he choking?"

Corrynne didn't answer, but a foreboding feeling overshadowed the scene before them. She reached out and covered Roc's eyes. "Don't look, guys," she warned her other two boys who were not quite within her arm's length.

Corrynne returned her attention to the screen, and noticed that the great hall, where Imam Mahdi's faithful followers had gathered to pay homage to him, was visibly trembling. The shaking was made worse by the bouncing of the cameras. She saw a tall pole sway then fall, and realized what was truly happening. "Bo, I don't think that's thunder, I think they're having an earthquake!"

Bo scratched his head and raised his eyebrows. "I think you're right!"

"Oh great! One more thing to put Dane and Carea in danger!" exclaimed Corrynne as she brought her free hand up to her forehead, not knowing if she could endure one more second of stress.

"Let me see!" Roc yelled, pulling away from Corrynne's grasp, and freeing his eyes.

Corrynne pulled Roc back into her arms, saying, "No, Roc, you may not see this. Now cover your eyes or I'll send you out of here."

Roc sneaked another quick peek at the chaos, and then in frustration covered his eyes.

The sound of a woman's scream came from the TV and on the screen a bright light exploded, causing a shower of sparks to fly and fall over the bewildered crowd standing before Imam Mahdi. Corrynne watched the hall shift, rising and falling as the low rumble increased in intensity.

Another tall pole with multiple hanging TV lights began to lean and fall, as its bulbs suddenly exploded causing another bright shower of sparks.

It was difficult to see center stage because of the jarring images, but it seemed to Corrynne that Imam Mahdi's face was turning a slight shade of blue. He began to stagger and grabbed his chest and throat. There was a loud clanking sound, and one end of a long piece of steel bracing rod broke loose from the staging. Imam Mahdi looked up, his eyes bulging wildly, and saw the rod swinging threateningly above his head.

Corrynne checked to see if Jax and Ry were watching, and of course they were. *"I told you to not look at this. It's too graphic!"* she said forcefully.

Jax excitedly pointed at the screen. "Mom! This is cool! Dane's winning! That guy asked for a sign and boy, is he ever getting one!"

"Yeah, Mom. This is way cool! I hope everyone all over the world is seeing this!" said Ry.

Corrynne frowned. "Cool or not, I want you to obey! I don't want you to see this violence."

"What violence?" asked Roc sneaking another peek behind his hand.

Corrynne reached out and rotated the TV so that only she and Bo could see what was happening on the screen.

"Hey! That's not fair!" yelled Roc who had taken his hands completely from his eyes.

On TV, a visible shock wave moved from the back of the large hall, and people fell to the floor as the wave swept toward the stage. They were weeping and looking about in helpless confusion. As the room bucked and swayed, the rumble grew to the roar of a full-scale earthquake, distorting the sound coming from the TV speakers.

The swinging steel shank suddenly broke loose, and with nothing more than a little "clink" sound, it dropped like a spear. Frantic screams were heard throughout the hall, as the sharp, sword-like rod pierced the top of Imam Mahdi's head and drove deep into his skull.

To Corrynne, the gruesome scene seemed surreal as the now defeated Imam Mahdi reached out, first to his people and then strangely to Carea. She wondered why he would look to her daughter for help!

Imam Mahdi rocked forward and backward, the steel rod jutting from the top of his head. Then he fell, and with a dull thud landed on the hard surface of stage floor. The TV cameras focused on the terrifying image of his face; eyes open in a sightless stare, mouth agape in a frozen shout for help.

"Oh! *I can't even look at this*!" said Corrynne as she ducked her head and, in abhorrence, covered her eyes.

"What happened, Mom?" asked Ry as he tried to step sideways and again sneak a forbidden peek, while poking his head around Corrynne's back.

"*Nothing! Now do what your Mother asks!*" Bo firmly ordered his sons.

Corrynne heard a low, almost inaudible, bass rumble fill the house, slowly at first, then steadily increasing. The TV rattled slightly on the dresser.

"What's happening? Bo, the TV is moving," said Corrynne with a worried voice. "Everything is shaking! Look at the pictures on the wall!"

Everyone looked worriedly at the increasing vibrations of the walls. The ominous rumbling motion caused them to stumble in their places.

"*Get into the doorway FAST!*" Bo commanded, "*We're having an earthquake here too!*"

"Hey, you guys!" called a voice. "What's going on? Is this an earthquake?" Brea asked, as she sleepily rubbed her eyes. "It feels like everything's shaking."

As the family rushed to find places of safety, Bo shouted, "Yes, it's an earthquake. Get into a doorway!"

The bedroom and hall shook and jolted in sudden escalating intensity. Corrynne called to Brea, "Go get the babies from their bed. Hurry! Stand in their doorway with them."

"Alright!" shouted Brea as she ran quickly into the adjoining bedroom. After a moment, she returned holding the sleepy-eyed twins tightly in her arms.

The dreadful sound of the earth's trembling energy was overwhelming as it was transmitted through the surrounding walls, floor and ceiling. No movie or story about earthquakes matched the sheer terror they were feeling. The younger kids cried and clung tightly to their parents while trying to brace themselves in the doorway.

The TV vibrated, then fell from the dresser and landed sideways on the floor, the screen facing the doorway where the family huddled together. Terrible vibrations amplified into a constant thunder around them, and everything shook and jumped as if the house itself was angry.

A large E.B.S. symbol replaced the graphic scenes on the television screen, and a high-pitched wailing tone squealing from the speakers was followed by an emergency broadcast message. "This is not a test. Repeat. This is not a test. This is an important bulletin from the Emergency Broadcast System. Utah, Idaho, Colorado, and Wyoming are experiencing major earthquakes. Please remain calm and stay tuned by radio or television for further instructions… "

"*This is a HUGE earthquake!*" exclaimed Brea. "*Mom! Dad! We have to get out of here!*"

Without a moment's hesitation, Bo and Corrynne said, almost in unison, "*Go! Go!*" They instantly rushed into the hall, urging the children towards the front door. The rumbling eased a little allowing the family to move in a tight, huddled group.

The house swayed as if made of cardboard, and the escalating vibrations caused the front door to swing open. Seeing the door open and sway back and forth and then up and down, Roc dug in his heels.

"*Roc, run!*" Corrynne yelled above the loud groaning of the earth. Then while continuing her effort to push her family out of the house, she shouted, "*We have to get out of the house!*"

"No, Mommy! I can't!" cried Roc, his eyes wide with terror. Without another word, Corrynne picked him up and stumbled past the others, taking the lead toward the open door. Brea followed next, holding the twins tightly in her arms. Finally, Ry and Jax jumped through the threatening open doorway and followed the others into the darkness of the night.

Corrynne led her children to the shuddering sidewalk, where they held tightly to each other. Despite their efforts to stay balanced, they fell to the ground when a violent, sideways jolt knocked them off their feet.

Together they helped each other stand back up as the twins began to cry hysterically.

Corrynne could still feel the earth shift and shake below them. In the darkness she saw the streetlights and telephone poles swaying and bending above them like fishing poles pulling in giant, live fish.

"*Where's Dad?*" yelled Jax above the roar.

Corrynne saw fear in his eyes. "*I'm not sure!*" she shouted back to her eleven-year-old. "*But stay here. Do not try and go back to find him. I'm sure he'll come out in just a minute. Maybe he's getting something.*"

"*What if the house falls in on him?*" asked Jax with effort. He looked back toward the rattling house, his face twisting in worry.

"*It won't,*" assured Corrynne. She took the twins from Brea, and holding their bodies tightly to her, tried to calm their fear.

A few seconds later, Bo bounded out of the house and joined his family on the undulating sidewalk with a transistor radio in his hand.

Notes to "Quake"

[1] The conference talk in this chapter is a compilation from several previous talks given by various prophets. In the future, it is logical to expect more of the same admonishments when perilous times come.

[2] Gordon B. Hinckley, "The Times in Which We Live," *Ensign*, Nov. 2001, 74.

[3] Gordon B. Hinckley, "The Times in Which We Live," *Ensign*, Nov. 2001, 73.

[4] Gordon B. Hinckley, "The Times in Which We Live," *Ensign*, Nov. 2001, 73-74.

[5] Spencer W. Kimball, *Faith Precedes the Miracle*, 253-254.

[6] The number quoted in the text, is a futuristic extrapolation taken from the numbers projected in a CNN article reviewing the AIDS epidemic. It says that by the year 2010, the amount of people infected in Russia, India, Ethiopia, Nigeria and China could climb to up to 70 million. When added to the amount of projected carriers in Africa, the total number could climb as much as between 80 and 100 million worldwide. For more information see: http://www.cnn.com/2002/HEALTH/conditions/09/30/hiv.epidemic/index.html.

[7] On a Google search using the words "drugs, legalization" over 65,000 sources can be brought up, demonstrating the movement of our society's perceptions concerning drugs. Although drugs have been found to be lethal as well as psychologically destructive, our global society seeks to make it more available. Eventual legalization seems to be the global trend.

[8] Spencer W. Kimball, *Faith Precedes the Miracle*, 253-254.

[9] Joseph Fielding Smith, *Church History and Modern Revelation*, 1:195.

[10] Gordon B. Hinckley, "The Times in Which We Live," *Ensign*, Nov. 2001, 74.

[11] Harsh as this scenario might seem, this is exactly what God the Father had to do with his only Begotten Son. He had to look on while the will of evil, tortured and killed Jesus Christ so that he might fulfill all righteousness. How awful it must have been to know the hearts of the designing evil, as they consorted and then carried out their plan to destroy the most perfect being that had ever set foot on this planet, and not do anything to intercede or protect! There is no other harsher reality. Bo and Corrynne taste a bit of this anxiety as they must sit back and allow evil to have its will with their son, knowing it will eventually fulfill a higher purpose.

[12] "You need the strength that comes from faith and trust in the Lord Jesus Christ if you are to fulfill your duty "to stand as witnesses of God at all times and in all things, and in all places"

(Mosiah 18:9). In times of trial you need the comfort offered in the holy scriptures, which assure you that when you have the shield of faith you will "be able to quench all the fiery darts of the wicked" (D&C 27:17). Faith in the Lord Jesus Christ prepares you for whatever life brings. This kind of faith prepares you to deal with life's opportunities—to take advantage of those that are received and to persist through the disappointments of those that are lost" (Dallin H. Oaks, "Faith in the Lord Jesus Christ," *Ensign*, May 1994, 98).

"But if ye will turn to the Lord with full purpose of heart, and put your trust in him, and serve him with all diligence of mind, if ye do this, he will, according to his own will and pleasure, deliver you out of bondage" (Mosiah 7:33).

[13] "Therefore, he giveth this promise unto you, with an immutable covenant that they shall be fulfilled; and all things wherewith you have been afflicted shall work together for your good, and to my name's glory, saith the Lord" (D&C 98:3).

[14] "Be strong and of a good courage, fear not, nor be afraid of them: for the Lord thy God, he it is that doth go with thee; he will not fail thee, nor forsake thee" (Deuteronomy 31:6).

CHAPTER TWO

SPIRITS[1]

"The light of the body is the eye: therefore when thine eye is single, thy whole body also is full of light; but when thine eye is evil, thy body also is full of darkness. Take heed therefore that the light which is in thee be not darkness." (Luke 11: 34-35).

00:09:04, 17:25:16 Zulu
Friday, March 25th
11:35 p.m.
Skull Valley, Utah
Between here and there

Dark Whispers[2]

The grand hall was rocking violently, but Imam Mahdi could not feel the jarring. He was standing straight and unaffected as he noticed the mass of his people on the floor swaying and falling as if they were on the deck of a great boat in a storm.

Looking down Imam Mahdi was surprised to see a lifeless body crumpled, face down by his feet, a metal shaft protruding from the top of the head.[3] What had happened? A shimmering white robe fanned out on one side of the body. Imam Mahdi recognized it as his own. Why was this person dressed in *his* clothes? Was this supposed to be him?

"What kind of gag…" began Imam Mahdi as he moved to push the form with his foot. "What?" he questioned as his foot passed right through the torso. Then he realized that the body must not be real. He was astonished! Who could have developed such an effective illusion?

In confusion Imam Mahdi took a quick look around, then to relieve his tension he nervously scoffed, "Hah! All of this is ridiculous! Good try!" He forcefully laughed at the thought that someone believed he could be clever enough to trick the great Imam Mahdi. Impossible! He stood straight and looked away from the figure on the floor as he tried to regain his composure. "Just a holographic image, I'm sure. An elementary effect." Despite his rationalizations, his stubborn spirit began to fill with anger and frustration. He *would not* be the brunt of an elaborate hoax, nor would he allow someone to best him at his own game. *He was in charge here!*

Imam Mahdi looked around in an effort to pinpoint the culprits who were bent on ruining his coronation. His people were in chaos, running and screaming hysterically throughout the grand hall. What was happening? It was then that he realized that he had lost control. *"This is a fiasco!"* he exclaimed in disbelief.

Gazing angrily at Dane and his sister in front of the stage who now were crouching together to keep their balance as the floor rocked. Imam Mahdi muttered angrily under his breath, *"I'll bet that boy and his impetuous sister had a hand in this disaster!"* They had fought and threatened him openly. They were trying to discredit him! *"How dare they!"*

A heavy woman suddenly crossed his view. She rushed towards the stage with her arms outstretched then fainted, falling upon the stairs leading up to the stage. Immediate anger flared in his chest, and he whirled about to see if the TV cameras had caught her collapse. He was embarrassed to see that all three cameras were focused on her.

Greatly irritated, Imam Mahdi shook his head and clenched his teeth. *This was not how things were supposed to be!* He flexed his fists open and closed. He had planned to emerge from this key event as the most influential religious figure of the world! He *had* to do something to regain power over his people!

The anger within Imam Mahdi grew hotter. ***"AAHHHHHCH!** Turn off the cameras!"* he yelled to his cameramen. There was no response as they kept filming. *"Turn them off NOW!"* No one paid attention to him. Cameras in two corners of the room and directly in front of the stage continued to greedily film everything that was happening in the hall. His plans to take advantage of the world's misguided faith in religion were toppling right before his eyes.[4]

"Fine! I'll give you something to film!" he threatened as he marched towards Dane and Carea, intending to kill them with his bare hands. Then, stopping short of the edge of the stage, he had second thoughts—*what was he thinking?* He couldn't attack the boy and girl in front of the cameras! He had to make their punishment appear to be a *miracle* of his power! Maybe he could salvage the situation by pretending that in his wrath he had caused this earthquake. That was it! In the recent past he had caused many of the strongest Christians to bow and worship him![5] What was to stop him now?

For a fleeting moment, Imam Mahdi searched his mind for options to make Dane and Carea pay for their part in destroying his plans. They needed to be punished. He remembered the remote that controlled the computer chip implanted in Carea's forehead. He could send her to her death with one flourishing magical gesture and a verbal curse—all with an unseen push of a button. Yes! That was the best idea yet! That would punish them both! *He was a genius! Let Carea join her brother in a painful death.* Imam Mahdi rubbed his hands together and smiled to himself. This chaos could work to his benefit after all!

With a murderous laugh, Imam Mahdi reached for the remote in the folds of his robe, but found that both the robe and the remote were gone. He was naked! How did he not notice? His anger exploded again. *"What? Where are my clothes? Where are my things?"* Imam Mahdi looked out at Carea. Frowning and growling he cursed and then yelled, *"Carea!"*

Carea did not look up, and he now knew he had been right all along. *She did do this to him!* She was the only one who had been close enough to him to pull off such treachery! She must have drugged him and taken his clothes! *Well, he would take care of her! He would not be made a joke in front of the world!*

Turning to his people, unashamed of his exposure, Imam Mahdi pointed and commanded as loudly as he could muster, *"SEIZE THE BOY AND GIRL THAT STAND BEFORE YOU! THEY ARE DEVILS!"* But no one moved to fulfill his will. It was as if they neither saw nor heard him. Indeed, his own voice seemed flat and thin and did not echo or reverberate the way he was used to hearing it boom with authority.

Again Imam Mahdi yelled at his people, *"Seize them! Seize them now! They are trying to make fools of us!"* But again not one person acknowledged his voice.[6] Instead, the followers continued to run helter-skelter, now towards the doors leading out of the hall.

"Where are you going?" Imam Mahdi questioned his people, but his question remained unanswered. *"Stop! Stop! I command you to stop!"* He took another step forward and pointed at the rushing crowd. "Do not run like *scared rabbits*! These people have no *real power*, they only have tricks, and…" his voice was diminishing. Now it was weak, flat, and falling quieter by the moment despite his efforts to shout. It was as though his voice was decreasing to a whisper in the back of his own mind.

A threatening memory assaulted Imam Mahdi's psyche and brought terror to his soul! He looked up and cowered as he remembered the horrible words that Carea's brother, Dane, had spoken. He had testified of a mighty "God of miracles" who could strike him down. *Could it be true?*

Imam Mahdi turned and moved back to the body on the floor. He reached for his robe to cover himself, but he could not grasp it. There was nothing to hide his bare body. At that moment he was forced to consider the form on the stage floor. Was that his corpse? No! It couldn't be! How could he be dead? He was rich and powerful! *He was invincible*! How could anyone take that away from him?

Imam Mahdi shook his head, and the truth crept into his being. *He was dead!* Both hands came up to his mouth. The sharp pain of recognition was too much! How would he exist? What would happen to him? How would he maintain his money, mansions, and power? How would he continue to command thousands without his body? What was he to do? Where should he go?

Imam Mahdi looked about and cowered. Could there actually be a God in heaven?[7] His mind raced, as for the first time he considered the possibility of the presence of a powerful being other than himself. Could that God have struck him down?[8] If there was a God, was he an angry God? Would he be unhappy that Imam Mahdi had tried to usurp his position and steal his authority on earth? The terrifying threatening thoughts frightened Imam Mahdi.[9] He wished the building would fall upon him that very second to cover him. He never wanted to meet the powerful being who had silenced his words. He would rather disappear, both body and soul, than to meet God and be held accountable for his deceit![10]

"*I should hide!*" whispered Imam Mahdi, feeling more and more aware of his nakedness.[11] He quaked in fear. "I should hide in a place so dark that no god could ever discover me!" He looked about and wondered where such a place might be. "Then I'll be safe!" he said to himself.

He heard voices whispering behind him. The sound was different than the loud, echoing voices of the people who were screaming and attempting to escape his mansion. Imam Mahdi turned towards the whispering voices. "Who's there?" he asked.

"Imam Mahdi!" It was a man's voice.

"Imam Mahdi!" called another who sounded like a woman.

"Yes? Who are you?" The voices seemed to be coming from the hall behind the stage. Imam Mahdi slowly took a few steps. "Show yourselves! I command you to show your faces to me!" he demanded, trying to sound confident.

No one came forward, but the whispers continued until Imam Mahdi finally understood the words. "Come with us, we will show you where to go."[12]

"Yes, come with us. Hurry," said other voices from the darkness.

"Are you here to take me where the eyes of God cannot see?" whispered Imam Mahdi hopefully, as he took a few more steps towards the hall.

"Yes," said the first voice.

"Yes, yes," answered many others.

"*Grant me safe hiding and protection!*" ordered Imam Mahdi.

Indistinct whispers answered, "Hiding..."

"Protection..."

"Escape—yes. Come with us."

Imam Mahdi was adequately satisfied. He looked once more at the chaos in the room and then cast a last look up at the ceiling. Yes, he had to get out of here! It was too open...and bright! He took a few cautious steps, and then slinked into the hazy darkness.[13]

Realms of Reality

Dane felt himself slowly slipping away. In his transition between the physical and the spiritual world, he felt relief as the painful ache of his mortal body diminished. A sense of belonging replaced mortal fear and apprehension, and a fullness of love encompassed him giving him deep and satisfying peace. He looked up and discovered a new light growing directly above his head. It came though the ceiling, and he was undeniably drawn to it. Turning to the light, Dane felt warm and happy. He was gently being pulled into the brilliance and he allowed himself to go.

As he moved into the light, a strange perception flowed over him. He felt as though his life had been only a brief, passing dream and now he was truly waking up into his *real* life and a pure state of being. He marveled at how his mind was free from fear, hate, doubt, prejudice, pain, and time, but yet full, as if wisdom of the ages was freely available to him.[14]

Dane looked back at his sister. Carea was sitting on the floor of the assembly hall. She looked lonely and sad. Was it right for him to be happy and free at a time like this? He wanted to hug her one last time and tell her that he was going to be OK. He loved her and wanted her to be relieved from her pain too.

Dane's progress into the light stalled for a moment as he considered his life. What about his family? He didn't want everyone to be sad like his sister. He visualized their faces. They were a good family. He didn't want to leave them...but he knew he would. The light was so inviting, so right and loving.[15] Finally, Dane gave in to the desire to be pulled away. "I love you...I love you all." Dane sent the silent message into the cosmos in hope someone would deliver his message to his family.

In an instant Dane was rushing through an infinite tunnel toward the source of the brilliant light. [16] He traveled at an amazing speed. As he moved through the brilliance, he saw his life unfold chronologically, beginning even before his birth.[17]

He remembered his joy[18] and great anticipation of finally being born into mortality. Dane had waited for eternity[19] for his physical body! He also remembered that he agreed to be subjected to opposites, learning the difference between right and wrong,[20] so that eventually, if he proved himself worthy, he could receive the fullness of eternal joy that Heavenly Father had promised him.[21] He yearned to prove to the Father that he would be faithful in all things,[22] so that he could be added upon.[23] It was an opportunity to gain glory and the likeness of the Father[24] that could not be obtained in any other way. As he contemplated his opportunities he felt overwhelming gratitude and a sense of abundant wellness flowing through him. Dane's emotions continued as he viewed the beginning of his life with his family, remembering every part except the times when he had repented of his mistakes. Those experiences had been edited and cast into the sea of eternal forgetfulness.[25]

Dane smiled when he saw himself, not much more than two years old, trying to teach his little sister Carea, eighteen months younger than himself, how to walk. He would take hold of her hands, pull her up to a standing position, and then slowly walk backwards, guiding her step by step. He remembered that his support gave her the confidence she needed to eventually walk on her own.

Dane retained perfectly the shocking sensation that shot through his toddler body when he jumped into cold water in the deep end of a pool. It was before he knew how to swim. He knew that his mother would save him—she always did.

He remembered his first lost tooth, his first day of school, and the time he was hit by a truck. He had been taken to the hospital, only to receive a blessing and go home that same day, miraculously uninjured except for some minor cuts and bruises. Even his first infatuation with Katie, the cutest girl in the eighth grade, was not spared. So many things flooded his memory—no, it was more. The memories flooded his being. They were a part of him. [26]

The recollections ended with his confrontation with Imam Mahdi. Those moments, as he stood in power for the Savior, felt good and right. He was thankful that he had not been a coward, but had the courage to say what the Spirit had directed…but there was something else. An unwelcome pain shuddered through him, as once again he perceived the heavy emotions of his family. They missed him and were worried about his welfare. Carea especially mourned for him from deep within her soul. He realized that she blamed herself for his condition. The sudden negative emotions were almost stabbing and he purposefully withdrew from the intensity. In an instant he made the decision to return to the earth. It was the only way he could eliminate his family's heartache and worry.

As he turned to go back, he became aware of a being of light standing beside him—no, two beings of light, one on the left and one on the right. Instinctively he knew they were male. [27] They were bright, white personages whose countenances burned like the sun. [28] They did not have physical bodies but were beings of spirit with forms of light in the likeness of bodies. [29] Dane looked closer, but could not recall having met them.

"Come with us," they beckoned.

"Where?" Dane asked.

"To paradise," the being of light on the right replied.

Dane moved away from the spirits, "But I need to go back. I can't stay. My sister and my family need me right now. I shouldn't have left them."

Both angels advanced, and gently taking Dane by his arm, [30] one of them spoke. "Yes, your sister and family have many trials to endure, but it is not in your calling nor capacity to relieve them of their experiences."

"Trials will come to them whether you stay here or return to earth. That is the purpose of life. Through their trials, they will receive wisdom and strength just as you have," [31] said the other spirit.

"However, the Father has spoken to us concerning you. If going back is what you choose, you will be able to do so at the proper moment. Right now you must follow us," said the first.

Dane considered their words. He knew these bright spirits told the truth and that all of heaven wanted only the best for him and his family.[32] Having faith in his new understanding, Dane changed his thinking. He would follow these two beings that had become his guides. With the speed of thought, Dane and the angels were somewhere else.[33]

A Hellish State of Being

Once out in the hall, Imam Mahdi expected to see three or four people waiting for him in the dark, but the place was empty. Frustrated, he looked both ways. "Hey! Wait! Who are you? You promised me a place to hide!" he yelled down the hall in his flat, shallow voice, then listened for a response.

"Come, Imam Mahdi," said a voice of normal volume. It seemed to come from the left. "Come into the darkness."

"Yes, I want to go where it's dark, then no one can see me!" Imam Mahdi began to run towards the left and down the hall where a gray haze floated in the air, filling the empty space of the long corridor.

"Come, yes, keep coming," appealed the voice again.

"I am! Wait for me, don't go so fast!" shouted Imam Mahdi. He rushed forward into the deepening darkness.

Imam Mahdi ran a considerable distance, sensing that many beings were leading him but not being able to see them.[34] After what seemed many hours, maybe even days, he stopped running and looked behind him. Stark blackness permeated everything.[35] After running so far, it dawned on him that he did not know his destination.

"Where are we going?" he questioned the people in front of him.

Suddenly, the voices fell silent.

"Answer me!" demanded Imam Mahdi.

Again there was only silence.

Imam Mahdi took a step or two backward; at least he thought it was "back." He was confused about his directions. Waving his hand in front of his face he realized he couldn't see even one inch in front of him. How could anyone find anything in such a deep void? "Maybe we should return to the mansion," he suggested aloud.

Silence.

"Hey! Whoever you are, show me a way out of here!" he yelled.

Silence.

"Hey!" he yelled again. *"Where did you go*? You can't just leave me here!"*[36]

"What do you want?" came a rough, rude voice that was nearer than he had expected.

Startled, he hesitated, wondering where the voice came from. Imam Mahdi had thought he was alone for a moment. The gruff voice seemed to be only inches from his ear. Was there someone that close? Shaking off his anxiety he answered, "I want to be lead out of here!"

"I thought you wanted to hide from God!" came a whiny female voice, also extremely near.

"I did, but this is no place for anyone," said Imam Mahdi. "Take me back."

"Back where?" said a third voice.

"To my mansion."

Suddenly he was surrounded by a thousand—no, millions of laughing voices. The volume terrified Imam Mahdi and he realized that there were not just three or four of them, but a quantity he couldn't comprehend. Were they looking at him? Could they see him even though he could not see them?

"What mansion?" asked the whiny female voice again.

"Yeah, who do you think you are? A king or something?" asked a fourth and totally different voice.

Again the laughter rang in his ears, mocking and demeaning him.

Imam Mahdi felt fear for the first time since his childhood. He gathered the small amount of courage he had left, and in an attempt to establish his authority he shouted, "*I am Imam Mahdi, the chosen one, the beginning and the end, the Messiah…*"

"Yeah, yeah, shut your trap! We have a lot of your kind here," said an angry voice, "I was once one of those too!"

"You 'god complex' people are always so full of yourselves!" shouted another unknown voice.

"*The Messiah—ach!*" came a voice with a tone so indignant, so hateful that Imam Mahdi was glad he couldn't see the person who had said it.

Suddenly Imam Mahdi heard a little sound near him, and a fist came from out of nowhere and hit him square in the face. He reeled from the impact and shock. He thought he couldn't be touched! He thought spirits were merely whips of smoke, a gaseous enigma incapable of interaction! How wrong he had been! These spirits had form and substance![37]

Another sharp jab caught his ear. He covered his face with his hands just as a barrage of insults came from all directions and hit his body.[38] Who were these people? Then without another thought, he realized that they were the angry and evil spirits of hell![39] He had been enticed into a trap!

Imam Mahdi began to run, trying to escape the crowd, but no matter which way he turned sharp fists pounded his body in a barrage of excruciatingly painful impacts. He swung back but there was only empty darkness.

The crowd grew more violent, ripping at his body and grabbing at his arms and hair. It felt like they were clawing him, digging into his skin with knife-like fingernails. In searing pain beyond his ability to endure, Imam

Mahdi screamed for the mob to stop the attack.[40] He gnashed his teeth[41] and wept for it to end, but the laughter and violence increased whenever he made any kind of noise.

After a grueling eternity, Imam Mahdi gave in to the violence. He stopped running and fighting and just let the spirits abuse him. Resistance was vain. He could not die. There was no escape, no point in defending himself. Imam Mahdi knew he was at the mercy of these people. They were punishing him for his crimes on earth.[42]

A keen memory of every second of his life rushed back to him. Between the blows,[43] he saw his lies, his trickery and his evil. He knew that because of his choices on earth, he had become prey to the same carnivorous evil that he had served while he fed upon the spirits of man. This was his justice.[44]

After the bashing insults were over, the spirits left Imam Mahdi and went to amuse themselves elsewhere.[45] He lay motionless and alone. In the stillness, an awful reality hit him. This was now his world. He was overcome with a horrible, endless weeping, and he knew he had done this to himself. Only one thought gave him solace. At least God couldn't see him.[46]

Notes to "Spirits"

Dark Whispers

[1] The fictional afterlife experiences in this chapter have been written after extensive comparative study of many "Near Death Experiences" (NDEs) combined with scriptural documentation.

According to our own scriptures, we believe there are different places that the righteous and the evil go after life. Spirit prison is a place of spiritual darkness that those people reside until they either accept the gospel or are resurrected. (Moses 7:57, D&C 88:99, D&C 138:8, 1 Peter 3:19) and spirit paradise is a place of light and joy that the righteous go to wait for the resurrection (Revelation 2:7, 2 Nephi 9:13, Alma 40:12, 14, 4 Nephi 4:14, Moroni 10:34, D&C 77:2, 5).

In near death experiences, reported in research studies, people report two different experiences; a positive near death experience, in which light is seen and love and acceptance is felt, and negative near death experiences in which darkness and evil is perceived or experienced. These reports are very similar to the scriptural description of what waits for us beyond the veil before the resurrection and according to our worthiness.

According to Kevin Christensen, from the Foundation for Ancient Research and Mormon Studies (FARMS, See NDE Research and the Book of Mormon" *FARMS Journal of Book of Mormon Studies*, Spring 1993, vol. 2, no. 1, 4 for complete article), he claims there are scriptural accounts that parallel reports found in academic research. Alma the younger, after he was visited by a heavenly being and was "nigh unto death," reports what is known as a "polar" experience containing both positive and negative near death experience elements. (See Mosiah, chapter 27 for account.)

Thus it is the goal of this chapter to demonstrate the experience of both an evil individual as well as a righteous one in their separate experiences after life, using both real after life experiences gleaned from select near death experiences and scriptural support. See the endnotes for all comparisons. All other storyline extrapolations are to be deemed fictional.

[2] The afterlife experience of Imam Mahdi depicted in this section is patterned after a factual afterlife experience taken from Howard Storm, a Professor of Art from Northern Kentucky

University who was an atheist. He was in a French hospital suffering from a deadly ulcer and peritoneal inflammation when his spirit was able to leave his body in what became a negative near death experience.

[3] The account of Howard Storm will be included in the endnotes for comparison with the fictional text.

"For a time there was a sense of being unconscious or asleep. I'm not sure how long it lasted, but I felt really strange, and I opened my eyes. To my surprise I was standing up next to the bed, and I was looking at my body lying in the bed. My first reaction was: "This is crazy! I can't be standing here looking down at myself. That's just not possible." (Arvin S. Gibson, *Journeys Beyond Life* True accounts of Next-world experiences. "A Remarkable Experience, Howard Storm," 214-218).

[4] Alma the Younger sought to destroy the church of God just as Imam Mahdi desired to destroy religion.

"And now it came to pass that while he was going about to destroy the church of God, for he did go about secretly with the sons of Mosiah seeking to destroy the church, and to lead astray the people of the Lord, contrary to the commandments of God" (Mosiah 27:10).

It would be logical that one who chose evil and designed to destroy what God had built, would suffer at least as much as Alma did during his three days "nigh unto death," insinuating that our after life experience is directly related to our worthiness.

[5] "In those days there shall arise false Christs, and false prophets, and shall show great signs and wonders" (Joseph Smith Matthew 1:22).

[6] Mr. Storm, at the beginning of his experience also tried to communicate with the people in the room with him, but no one heard him. "Not knowing what was happening, I became upset. I started yelling and screaming at my wife, and she just sat there like a stone. She didn't look at me, she didn't move—and I kept screaming profanities to get her to pay attention. Being confused, upset, and angry, I tried to get the attention of my roommate, with the same result. He didn't react" (Howard Storm as quoted by Arvin S. Gibson, *Journeys Beyond Life*, 214-218).

[7] "Behold, I am Jesus Christ, the Son of God. I am the same that came unto mine own, and mine own received me not. I am the light which shineth in darkness, and the darkness comprehendeth it not" (D&C 6: 21).

[8] The Lord loves his children and wishes for them to hear the gospel and have eternal life, however the Lord is bound by agency, thus he must allow the wicked to choose to do wickedly. Even though the worth of a soul is great, the Lord is willing to lose a soul to save many. "And now I say unto thee, Alma, go thy way, and seek to destroy the church no more, that their prayers may be answered, and this even if thou wilt of thyself be cast off" (Mosiah 27:16). "But behold, it is better that thy soul should be lost than that thou shouldst be the means of bringing many souls down to destruction, by thy lying and by thy flattering words;" (Alma 30:47).

We can see through history that there comes a point after which wicked people have condemned themselves that the Lord shuts their mouths because of the huge destruction that they cause among the innocent. This happens either through a flood in Noah's day, the destruction of cities as in Sodom and Gomorrah, or at the time of Christ's coming on the American continent, as it will be in the last days. Also, sometimes at the request of the 'antichrist' such as demonstrated in this text and in the Book of Mormon as in Jacob 7.

[9] Imam Mahdi hopes that now that he is in a world of darkness that he can avoid God and judgment. This is similar to Alma's feelings as he experienced the realm of darkness. "...The

very thought of coming into the presence of my God did rack my soul with inexpressible horror. Oh, thought I, that I could be banished and become extinct both soul and body, that I might not be brought to stand in the presence of my God, to be judged of my deeds" (Alma 36:14-15).

[10] "For our words will condemn us, yea, all our works will condemn us; we shall not be found spotless; and our thoughts will also condemn us; and in this awful state we shall not dare to look up to our God; and we would fain be glad if we could command the rocks and the mountains to fall upon us to hide us from his presence" (Alma 12: 14).

[11] "For behold, when ye shall be brought to see your nakedness before God, and also the glory of God, and the holiness of Jesus Christ, it will kindle a flame of unquenchable fire upon you" (Mormon 9:5).

[12] Howard Storm also heard his name being called by unseen beings. "Then I heard my name. In French there is no equivalent to 'Howard,' and they [the doctors and nurses] messed it up when they tried to use it. But someone was saying my name correctly. I heard "Howard, Howard—come here." Wondering at first where it was coming from, I discovered that it was originating in the doorway. There were different voices calling me. I asked who they were and they said, 'We are here to take care of you. We will fix you up. Come with us.' Asking, again who they were, I asked them if they were doctors and nurses. They responded, 'Quick come see. You'll find out'." (Howard Storm as quoted by Arvin S. Gibson, *Journeys Beyond Life*, 214-218).

[13] Again, this section is patterned after the negative near death experience of Howard Storm: "As I asked them questions they gave evasive answers. They kept giving me a sense of urgency, insisting that I should step through the doorway. With some reluctance I stepped into the hallway, and in the hallway I was in a fog, or a haze. It was a light-colored haze. It wasn't a heavy haze. I could see my hand, for example, but the people who were calling me were fifteen or twenty feet ahead and I couldn't see them clearly. They were more like silhouettes, or shapes, and as I moved toward them they backed off into the haze." (Howard Storm as quoted by Arvin S. Gibson, *Journeys Beyond Life*, 214-218).

We see here that the following scripture may be literal. "And they that will harden their hearts, to them is given the lesser portion of the word until they know nothing concerning his mysteries; and then they are taken captive by the devil, and led by his will down to destruction. Now this is what is meant by the chains of hell" (Alma 12:11).

Realms of Reality

[14] The scriptures state that now, in the mortal world our perception of reality is shallow, but as we progress, we grow in understanding.

"But we all, with open face beholding as in a glass the glory of the Lord, are changed into the same image from glory to glory, even as by the Spirit of the Lord" (Corinthians 3:13).

"For now we see though a glass, darkly, but then face to face: now I know in part; but then shall I know even as also I am known" (Corinthians 13:12).

[15] The afterlife experience portrayed in this segment is meant to reflect a positive NDE. It is derived from a compilation of many afterlife experiences reported from multiple sources; both from research material and personal interviews of actual experiences. (Interviews consisted of Bonnie Thomas of Seattle Washington and Katrina Appiah of Nagoya, Japan. Books included: *I Saw Heaven* by Lawrence Tooley; *The Message* by Lance Richardson; and *Journeys beyond Life* by Arvin Gibson, which is a compilation and analysis of thirty-two first hand accounts of life after death experiences).

[16] According to the research of the Near Death Experience Foundation (NDEF) and the International Association for Near-Death Studies (IANDS): 82.8% experience a separation between the consciousness and the body. 53.9% pass through a tunnel or an enclosure. 69.1% see a light. 73.7% see or meet other beings. 35.1% experience a review of their life events. 61.1% see other beautiful locations, levels or dimensions. 74.2% experience altered sense of space or time. 61.9% gain a sense of a special knowledge or purpose. 43.5% were shown the future. 61.7% were aware of a cognitive decision to return to their bodies. 53.5% experienced special paranormal or other gifts after their experience that they did not have before their experience. 91.2% experienced a change in attitude after their experience.

See: http://www.nderf.org/Research%20Breakthrough.htm for more statistics and other information concerning this topic.

[17] It is not unusual for a person to report remembering a premortal existence in a near-death experience. See the following example:

DeLynn, a subject of a near-death experience interview, reported that he asked when faced with heavenly beings, why he had to suffer with cystic fibrosis in mortality. He was told, "You chose your disease and the amount of pain you would be willing to suffer before this life— when you were in a premortal state. It was your choice." He understood then that he made that choice so that he could learn in the "fastest way possible" (Arvin Gibson, *Journeys Beyond Life*, 253).

[18] When we were given the opportunity to come to earth, Job tells it was an overwhelming joyful occasion.

"Then the LORD answered Job out of the whirlwind...Where wast thou when I laid the foundations of the earth? Declare, if thou hast understanding.... When the morning stars sang together, and all the sons of God shouted for joy?" (Job 38:1,4,7).

[19] Mankind went through an unaccountable amount of time to prepare for this earthly existence and has always existed.

"Man was also in the beginning with God...." (D&C 93:29).

[20] "For it must needs be, that there is an opposition in all things. If not so...righteousness could not be brought to pass, neither wickedness, neither holiness nor misery, neither good nor bad. Wherefore, all things must needs be a compound in one; wherefore, if it should be one body it must needs remain as dead, having no life neither death, nor corruption nor incorruption, happiness nor misery, neither sense nor insensibility" (2 Nephi 2:11).

[21] "For man is spirit. The elements are eternal, and spirit and element, inseparably connected, receive a fullness of joy. And when separated, man cannot receive a fullness of joy" (D&C 93:33-34).

[22] "...I have decreed in my heart, saith the Lord, that I will prove you in all things, whether you will abide in my covenant, even unto death, that you may be found worthy" (D&C 98:14).

[23] "...And they who keep their second estate [mortality] shall have glory added upon their heads for ever and ever" (Abraham 3:26).

[24] "God himself was once as we are now, and is an exalted man and sits enthroned in yonder heavens!" (Joseph Smith, *Teachings of the Prophet Joseph Smith*, 345).

"Man is the child of God, formed in the divine image, and endowed with divine attributes, and even as the earthly son of an earthly father and mother is capable in due time of becoming a man, so the undeveloped offspring of celestial parentage is capable, by experiencing through ages and eons, of evolving into a God" (Joseph Fielding Smith, *Improvement Era*, November 1909, 75-81).

"As man now is, our God once was; as now God is, so man may be" (Lorenzo Snow, *Improvement Era*, June 1919, Vol. 22, 660).

[25] "Behold, he who has repented of his sins, the same is forgiven, and I, the Lord, remember them no more" (D&C 58:42).

[26] "Now the Lord had shown unto me, Abraham, the intelligences that were organized before the world was; and among all these there were many of the noble and great ones" (Abraham 3:22).

The word "intelligences" is used synonymously with premortal spirits in the above scripture, giving insight into the potential of the spirit. For the Lord to use this word may insinuate that the whole spirit body is capable of holding and experiencing knowledge.

It is interesting to note that according to some near-death experiences, people describe the act of gaining or remembering knowledge as an experience that encompassed their whole being. For example, note the words used in the following reports: "Pure knowledge seemed to pour into me from Him. The knowledge was transmitted by…energy. Energy flowed into me and with it was knowledge. It was as if my entire being was a receptor of knowledge" (from an interview with "Roger" as quoted by Arvin Gibson, *Journeys beyond Life*, 248).

"…It's like you are an angel. It's like you can perceive and know all, and all is so unnecessary. It's like a free spirit, a knowing being…" (from an interview with "Jennette," as quoted by Arvin Gibson, *Journeys beyond Life*, 78).

[27] Often in a near-death experience, one will identify a personage that they come in contact with as both spiritual and with distinctive gender identity, thus insinuating that the spirit has a gender as well as a body. It is an assumption that man was created with gender from the beginning before his mortal state from the sources below:

"For I, the Lord God, created all things, of which I have spoken, spiritually, before they were naturally upon the face of the earth" (Moses 3:5).

"In the image of his own body, male and female, created he them, and blessed them, and called their name Adam, in the day when they were created and became living souls in the land upon the footstool of God" (Moses 6:9).

"All human beings—male and female—are created in the image of God. Each is a beloved spirit son or daughter of heavenly parents, and, as such, each has a divine nature and destiny. Gender is an essential characteristic of individual premortal, mortal, and eternal identity and purpose" ("The Family: A Proclamation to the World*," Ensign*, Nov. 1995, 102).

[28] In a near-death experience people sometimes describe spirit personages with light emanating from them. Often their descriptions are very similar to accounts found in the scriptures. Compare:

"Not only was his robe exceedingly white, but his whole person was glorious beyond description, and his countenance truly like lightning" (Joseph Smith History, 1:32).

"His eyes were as a flame of fire; the hair of his head was white like the pure snow; his countenance shone above the brightness of the sun…" (D&C 110:3).

"And I turned to see the voice that spake with me…I saw…the Son of man, clothed with a garment down to the foot…. His head and his hairs were white like wool, as white as snow; and his eyes were as a flame of fire; and his feet like unto fine brass, as if they burned in a furnace. … And his countenance was as the sun shineth in his strength" (Revelation 1:12-16).

"I think they were two men, from the tone of the voice of the one, and they were dressed in white. The white was as bright as…it was as bright as the snow when the sun hits it" (from an interview with "Eloise," as quoted by Arvin Gibson, *Journeys beyond Life*, 22).

"When I reached the edge of the light, I could see the shape of a human in it. A man in the light reached out His hand, and I reached to touch Him. …He was in a white robe…and He was very bright. Instantly, upon touching His hand, I knew it was the Lord. I was filled with peace, I felt calm…." (From an interview with "Mike," as quoted by Arvin Gibson, *Journeys beyond Life*, 36).

[29] "…That which is spiritual being in the likeness of that which is temporal; and that which is temporal in the likeness of that which is spiritual; the spirit of man in the likeness of his person, as also the spirit of the beast, and every other creature which God has created" (D&C 77:2).

[30] One might ask if a spirit body has arms and legs. Since we know that the body is created after the form of the spirit (D&C 77:2), and in Ether, the brother of Jared was shown the spirit body of Christ, (Ether 3:6-16), we can safely assume that it does. Then one can ask, does the spirit arms and legs have substance? The Lord tells us, (D&C 131:7) "There is no such thing as immaterial matter. All spirit is matter, but it is more fine or pure, and can only be discerned by purer eyes." Thus we can understand that the spirit body is matter of a fine nature.

In near-death experiences, accounts repeatedly report an interaction that resembles the physical experience of touching and perception. See the following account:

"To find out if I had substance, I rubbed my hands together and I felt my face with my hands. In both cases I found that I had form and substance. I could feel myself. Looking at my hands, I saw that they looked like my hands normally did, except there was a glow to them" (from an interview with "Delynn," as quoted by Arvin Gibson, *Journeys beyond Life*, 187).

[31] "But the God of all grace, who hath called us unto his eternal glory by Christ Jesus, after that ye have suffered a while, make you perfect, establish, strengthen, settle you" (1 Peter 5:10).

[32] It is impossible for God to lie. God is a god of truth. All those that will dwell with Him will have to be like Him, unable to lie or have any part of deceit.

"[God] is the Rock, his work is perfect: for all his ways are judgment: a God of truth and without iniquity, just and right is he" (Deuteronomy 32: 4).

"For he said, Surely they are my people, children that will not lie" (Isaiah 63:8).

[33] In a near-death experience, often people describe themselves as being able to travel from place to place by walking, floating, or just moving from place to place using thought.

"I felt as though I traveled more by thought than by anything else" (from an interview with "Stephanie," as quoted by Arvin Gibson, *Journeys beyond Life*, 98).

" I was aware of myself being there, not my body, but me, Joanne Jones. And I was kind of walking—floating, if you will—down this country road" (from an interview with "Joanne Jones," as quoted by Arvin Gibson, *Journeys beyond Life*, 102).

A Hellish State of Being

[34] See description from Howard Storm: "Walking for what seemed to be a considerable distance, these beings were all around me. They were leading me through the haze. I don't know how long…there was a real sense of timelessness about the experience. In a real sense I am unaware of how long it was, but it felt like a long time—maybe even days or weeks" (Howard Storm as quoted by Arvin S. Gibson, *Journeys Beyond Life*, 214-218).

[35] Imam Mahdi runs into intense darkness. Alma also reported such darkness existed in the spiritual realm until after he repented, "I was in the darkest abyss" (Mosiah 27:29). These are similar findings in NDE research, "In place of elation, the emotions of fear and panic; similar though less pleasant sensations of being out of the body; the plunging into a totally black void instead of an end-lit tunnel; and not least, a sense of an overwhelming proximity of the forces of demonic evil" (Kevin Christensen, "'Nigh unto Death': NDE Research and the Book of Mormon" *FARMS Journal of Book of Mormon Studies*, Spring 1993, vol. 2, no. 1, 4, quoting Wilson and Grey, The After Death Experience, 161).

[36] Howard Storm decided he had gone far enough and asked the spirits to take him back to his hospital room, but such a request caused the spirits to become abusive and violent; "Finally I told them that I wouldn't go any farther. At that time they changed completely. They became much more aggressive and insisted that I was going with them." (Howard Storm as quoted by Arvin S. Gibson, *Journeys Beyond Life*, 214-218).

The experience of Howard and the enticings of the evil beings cannot help but draw a close resemblance of this scripture: "And behold I say unto you all that this was a snare of the adversary, which he has laid to catch this people, that he might bring you into subjection unto him, that he might encircle you about with his chains, that he might chain you down to everlasting destruction, according to the power of his captivity" (Alma 12:6).

[37] "Joseph Smith absolutely shocked everybody when he said 'Spirit is a more refined form of matter.' We had spirit bodies. You don't just go around as a gas when you are a spirit, you see. The Christian world doesn't know how to handle that…you have to be made out of cellophane or something like that. You shake a lot and that makes you a spirit. (Hugh Nibley, "Teachings of the Book of Mormon--Semester 1" *Foundation for Ancient Religion*, 75).

[38] The author was intrigued by the report of what seemed like physical pain and torture reported by Howard Storm, thus perceptions of a physical-like encounter is included in the text because it can be found in many sources of negative near death experiences. See his account: "A number of them began to push and shove me, and I responded by hitting back at them. It seemed to be almost, a game for them, with me as the centerpiece of their amusement. My pain became their pleasure. They seemed to want to make me hurt—by clawing at me and biting me. Whenever I would get one off me, there were five more to replace the one. By this time there was almost complete darkness, and I had the sense that instead of there being twenty or thirty, there were an innumerable host of them. Each one seemed set on coming in for the sport they got from hurting me." (Howard Storm as quoted by Arvin S. Gibson, *Journeys Beyond Life*, 214-218).

[39] "And they were thrust down, and thus came the devil and his angels And, behold, there is a place prepared for them from the beginning, which place is hell" (D&C 29:37-38).

[40] In the text, Imam Mahdi's spirit body is not really being torn apart, but the evil spirits wish to terrorize him into thinking so. In some NDE's this kind of perceived "ripping of the spirit body" is reported by multiple negative NDE sources by evil spirits. It is clear that in the spirit form, one can feel when other spirits touch them. It would be logical that spirits could inflict pain on other spirits if desired.

[41] "These shall go away into outer darkness, where there is weeping, and wailing, and gnashing of teeth" (D&C 133:73).

[42] "If he has desired to do evil, and has not repented in his days, behold, evil shall be done unto him, according to the restoration of God" (Alma 42: 28).

[43] In a NDE, one has his life flash before him. Alma expressed this and the suffering attached to the memory, "Yea, I did remember all my sins and iniquities, for which I was tormented with the pains of hell" (Alma 36:13).

[44] "But the fearful, and unbelieving, and the abominable, and murderers, and whoremongers, and sorcerers, and idolaters, and all liars, shall have their part in the lake which burneth with fire and brimstone: which is the second death" (Revelation 21: 8).

[45] The notion of evil beings torturing a newcomer out of sheer amusement is an awful thought; however knowing the evil that exists and existed in this world and to think that all of them gather in the same place after this life, the thought becomes less foreign. Because death cannot come to one who is a spirit, it would be logical that after a while, the spirits would become tired of their game and stop their abuse out of boredom. This agrees with Howard Storm's account: "Fighting well and hard for a long time, ultimately I was spent. Lying there exhausted amongst them, they began to calm down since I was no longer the amusement that I had been. People were still picking at me, occasionally, and I just lay there all torn up, unable to resist." (Howard Storm as quoted by Arvin S. Gibson, *Journeys Beyond Life*, 214-218).

[46] "And if they be evil they are consigned to an awful view of their own guilt and abominations, which doth cause them to shrink from the presence of the Lord into a state of misery and endless torment, from whence they can no more return; therefore they have drunk damnation to their own souls" (Mosiah 3: 25).

CHAPTER THREE

DEER CREEK DAM

"For the time is come that judgment must begin at the house of God: and if it first begin at us, what shall the end be of them that obey not the gospel of God?" (1 Peter 4:17).

00:09:04, 17:18:11 Zulu
Friday, March 25th
11:42 p.m.
North of Provo, Utah
Deer Creek Dam

The Breach

"Hey! You'd better come take a look at this!"

"What is it? I'm busy bringing up the auxiliary power! This earthquake is wreaking havoc on our systems!"

"I know, but, John…" began Mark.

John interrupted abruptly, "Look, we need to be ready in case our main turbines seize!"

"Um, John, I think we have bigger problems than worrying about maintaining our power! You need to come in here right away, she's, well, it looks like—*she's breaking up!*" Mark shouted frantically.

Hearing that alarming news, Supervisor John Myers spun around, and steadying himself with his hands on opposite walls of the tiny room, yelled, "That's impossible! This dam was built to withstand a seven point five earthquake!"[1]

As the ground trembled beneath him, John slid his hands along the walls and moved briskly towards the blue flickering lights coming from the control room. "There is no way this is greater than a five—or six!" At that moment, the jarring escalated dramatically, casting a shadow of doubt over his mind.

Inside the control room, there were multiple computer screens, with a series of dials and metal toggle switches. Four video monitors allowed them to view the operation of the floodgates and the resulting flow of water. Mark Garvey, the night-shift control room operator, sat on a swivel chair and braced himself with both hands on the counter. The entire room seemed to rise and fall as he stared wide-eyed at the video monitor on the far right.

"Show me what you're talking about! I'm sure you're mistaken," came the dubious challenge from Mark's more experienced supervisor.

"Look right there, below the main floodgate," said Mark as he pointed to the monitor screen on the far right. "See the crack right there and that dark flowing movement just outside the lighted area?"

Mark slid his chair backward, making room for John to move in closer. John pushed his glasses higher on his nose and squinted to see the image before him. His face slowly turned from a scowl to a look of fear and dread.

"Oh no! Th—that's not supposed to happen!" John stammered, as he quickly reached for one of the four joysticks that controlled the cameras on the outside of the dam. Grasping the joystick he slowly twisted clock-wise, causing the camera to zoom in on the image. Then he focused on the crack in the dam. Black streams of water came into view in the center of the monitor screen. "*Oh no!*" he repeated. It was all he could say as he continued to study the dam. With his left hand, John held tightly to the countertop to keep his chair from rolling away in the sea-sway of the bucking control room. With his right hand still on the control he slowly widened the camera view. In continuing horror, he saw numerous cracks spreading outward from the main break.

Frozen in apprehension, John silently watched a chunk of concrete the size of a semi truck lean precariously from the wall, then fall...down and out of sight. A thunderous roar was heard, and with great force, a gushing wall of water gathered momentum and thrust through the bottleneck opening.

The continued motion of the earthquake caused huge sections of earth and rock, on either side of the dam structure, to simultaneously shift. The result was at first a loud, violent bending of the structure and finally a fracturing of steel and concrete, and then the irresistible force of water tore through the breach and slowly opened the gap even wider.

An intense tremor unexpectedly shook the building John and Mark were in. The ground rose in a hard and abrupt jolt beneath them and they were thrown backward. The back of John's head hit sharply against the floor. He blacked out briefly, then saw stars and heard loud ringing in his ears, as excruciating pain developed at the back of his skull.

John struggled to get his bearings. He was lying on his back on the shaking floor. He slowly rolled onto his stomach and pushed himself up on his hands and knees. Still dizzy from the blow to the back of his head, he tried to regain his footing. He straightened his glasses on his nose, and looked at the four bouncing monitor screens. Each displayed grim images of

⌐ dam breaking up and falling away all along the great wall. In shocked silence, John visualized the unsuspecting people in their homes and neighborhoods below, frightened by the uncommon earthquake, yet unaware of the inevitable wall of watery death that frothed toward them in the dark of the night.

John yelled over the roar of the water and the earthquake, "Mark! Call 9-1-1 and tell them what's happening! I'll get on the Emergency Services Hotline and talk to them myself. Tell the police we're going to call for an immediate evacuation of everything below us, NOW!!"

John searched the wall for the emergency dam breach plan, found it in a clear plastic sheath pinned to the bulletin board, and ripped it off the wall. In front of him, Mark was already yelling into a cellular phone to the local 9-1-1 Emergency operator.

"...Yes, that's right! Mark Garvey and Supervisor John Myers at the Deer Creek Dam! Yes, you heard me correctly, the dam is breaking up; we're asking for the immediate evacuation of all the cities below us!" After a brief pause, he said, "Yes, good, notify the National Guard and the Red Cross, too!" He thanked the dispatcher and then hung up the phone.

John searched for the antiquated red emergency phone that would activate sirens to alert those who lived near the Provo River. He pulled the phone from beneath a pile of books where it had landed when falling shelves ripped it from the wall. The cord was severed. John feverishly tried to reconnect the wires so he could make the emergency call. Having no success, he frantically looked for the cell phone. He would have to call the main number.

"Mark! Throw me the phone! We have to sound the alarm in the valley or thousands of people will be killed!"

Mark did not respond to him. Instead he turned his back on his boss and shouted into the phone, *"Honey? Can you hear me?"* he yelled. "Good, listen, don't ask questions, just get the baby and drive east. I'll meet you at Rock Canyon Park."

"Hang up! Mark! We need that phone!" yelled John forcefully, not believing that Mark would delay warning the thousands down river in order to warn his own family first.

Mark continued to ignore John's command as he spoke into the phone, "Go as fast as you can!" He listened intently for a moment and then shouted again, "Yes, I know we're having an earthquake," a brief pause. "Yes, I know you're scared, but listen to me. Please just do it! Don't bring anything..."

John ripped the phone out of Mark's hand and pushed the "off" button. Glaring at his trembling companion, he pulled apart the emergency hotline plastic cover to search for the number he would have to dial on a conventional phone.

Continuing in destructive intensity, the movement of the earthquake changed from an up and down motion to a side-to-side swaying.

Finally, after finding the number and dialing it, John steadied himself against the doorway. "This is Supervisor John Myers at the Deer Creek Dam. We have a code four! *Repeat, CODE FOUR!!*"

John couldn't believe the reality of his own words. Codes one through three went from bad to worse. Nobody, including himself, ever imagined that a code four could occur at the dam. A code of that level meant only one thing, the rushing tide of destruction and death would reach the housing developments in less than ten minutes.

John listened to a sleepy voice that had been jolted to cognition, "Code four? That means a dam breach!"

"*Yes! You heard me right!*" John yelled into the phone. "*The dam has been breached and a massive flow is moving into the valley.*"

"How much of the dam has breached?" asked the unknown person on the other end.

"*How much? ALL OF IT! I SAID WE HAVE A CODE FOUR!*"[2]

Flood

"Is everyone OK?" Bo spoke loudly over the rumble of the quake and the screams of his twin babies. Standing on the bouncing sidewalk, he glanced quickly from person to person to assure himself that his family was safe.

"No, Daddy," said Roc. With wide eyes and a drawn face, he looked around, "I'm scared!" he cried. "When is this going to stop?"

Ry nodded his head fast, agreeing with his brother's question.

"We're going to be just fine and this should be over in just a minute," said Corrynne as she eyed her husband hoping he would validate her comment

"Of course!" said Bo trying to be positive. "Earthquakes usually only last a minute or so."

"Hasn't it already been more than a minute, Dad?" asked Jax as he nervously watched the lampposts sway. "I think it's been like ten minutes already!"

"No, not ten. It just seems that way," offered Brea who was speaking to Jax but reaching out to hug Roc.

The sound of sirens wailed from somewhere in the west and echoed eerily through the valley. Bo, Corrynne, and the kids looked at each other, worrying about the meaning of the blaring sirens. Their silent questions were answered by the amplified voice of the emergency broadcaster, which rang from speakers mounted in the trees of their neighborhood. "There has been a total dam breach. Evacuate to higher ground immediately! Repeat—there has been a total dam breach, evacuate to higher ground immediately!"

Corrynne pulled the crying twins close to her chest, and in amazement asked, *"Are you serious?"*

An almost inaudible, distant screaming could be heard echoing in harmony with the sirens and over the rumble of the earth. A feeling of growing panic seemed to be infecting families who were gathered together in neighborhoods beyond their view, and it was quickly spreading toward them.

"What do we do, Bo?" asked Corrynne in restrained fear as she looked across the heads of her trembling and crying children toward her husband.

Bo and Corrynne stared at each other with unblinking eyes when they realized the meaning of the sirens and the sound of the screams. Since they lived in the Provo River bottoms, they knew the water was *rushing their way*!

Bo suddenly flew into action. "Kids!" he said, "Stay with Mom! Brea, help Mom keep everyone together! Jax, come with me! We'll be right back!"

Bo and Jax sprinted toward the rattling house. Bo grabbed hold of the front door jam to steady himself as the whole house rocked back and forth. He pulled himself in, swaying like a drunkard through the house. With Jax close behind, Bo nimbly grabbed the car keys from the hook as they moved toward the door leading into the garage. Throwing open the door leading from the laundry room to the garage, the door slammed back and hit him in the face. He opened it again and punched the buttons to open the garage door and turn on the light. Luckily, the electricity was still working.

With a shudder the garage door began to rise. It opened only half way, and then fell off the track. Bo ran under the crippled door, jerked the red cord that released the door from the motor, and with a flood of adrenaline strength, forced the door up the rest of the way.

Bo pushed the button on the car key to unlock the rear door of the Suburban, and the door swung open. Bo and Jax steadied themselves, and then staggered toward the storage shelves in the garage.

The quake seemed to ease a bit, and Jax and Bo looked at each other as if to ask if they had each felt the change. But the urgency of the moment demanded that they not stop.

Bo urged Jax into further action. "Jax, grab the flashlight and those two bundles of rope and throw them into the back of the Suburban!" yelled Bo, pointing as he reached the far wall.

Jax already had the flashlight and the rope in his hands and was careening around the Suburban toward the back of the car.

Bo knew there was a rubber raft and an air-compressor somewhere in the garage. He moved a bag of kitty litter and saw the plastic crate he had been looking for. He pulled it forward and checked the contents. There was the folded raft and two deflated inner tubes. Standing up quickly, he saw the battery-operated air-compressor and two telescoping oars on a shelf above his head. He grabbed the three items and dropped them into the crate. With a heft, he slid the crate and its heavy contents across the floor towards the back of the Suburban. Just as he reached the back of the car, the garage ceiling collapsed and he was thrown against the side of the car. His only thought was that he and Jax would surely be killed.

"*Dad! Are you OK?*" shouted Jax from somewhere beyond the rubble.

Bo hesitated and mentally checked himself for broken bones. "Yes, I think so," he said, as he looked at what had landed on him. Heavy boxes and bags stored in the attic above the garage had crashed down on him, causing him to hit his head hard on the car bumper.

"Dad, we've got to get out of here! Everything is falling down!" urged Jax.

"Yes, we will. Hold on," Bo said numbly, not yet thinking clearly.

Sitting in a daze on the floor, he looked about and saw various packets of food spilling out of a backpack. Bo was amazed! In a disguised blessing the big box containing their 72-hour kits of food and water rations had fallen from the ceiling and hit him on the head! Groggy and faint from the blow, Bo slowly but thankfully gathered up an armload of the food and water and stuffed it back into the bags. Still on his knees, he reached with one arm into the back of the Suburban and placed the pack inside the open door.

"Jax, grab the rest of the backpacks and get in the car!" Bo said as he grabbed one more backpack.

"Dad! These are our emergency kits!"

"Yes, I know. This is an emergency! I would have forgotten them if they hadn't fallen on my head! Grab them fast!"[3]

Jax climbed over boxes, and began heaving the other bags into the back of the car. But he stopped suddenly, "Dad! You're bleeding!"

Bo shook his head. "I'm fine, son, just get those packs and get in the car. *Hurry!*"

Blood trickled down into Bo's right eye as he grunted, lifted and finally pushed the crate of flotation devices, air pump, and oars into the back of the Suburban. Bo opened the driver's side door, momentarily stumbled backward from a sudden tremor, and then finally climbed into the driver's seat.

Bo turned the key in the ignition, and revved the engine hard as Jax climbed into the passenger side. He shifted into reverse and floored the gas pedal. The tires squealed and smoked as the car suddenly shot backward out of the garage, punching through wood and boxes that had fallen from the ceiling. With a loud crunch he pushed out into the driveway.

Bo turned the wheel hard to the right, which caused the Suburban to lurch backwards into the street. Artificial Christmas tree branches that had fallen out of the garage rafters and on to the roof of the car, were now sliding off the car onto the driveway. Bo hit the brakes, causing another squealing skid, and then he pulled the lever down into drive. Corrynne and the kids ran from the shaking sidewalk, opened the doors, and clambered inside the car.

Bo revved the engine, his left foot still firmly planted on the brake pedal. He looked down at his wristwatch. Eight and-a-half minutes had passed since they first heard the sirens and the radio-warning message.

"Hurry! Buckle up quickly! We have no time before the water's around our ears!" shouted Bo. *"This ride is going to be a bumpy one! Hurry! Please hurry!"*

"We're going as fast as we can, Bo!" came Corrynne's charged reply. She almost threw the babies into their car seats and latched them in as she stood on the pavement.

Brea quickly helped Ry and Roc into the car then followed them into the back seat. Finally seated, they fumbled with their seat belts.

An unexpected, powerful impact of icy black water hit Corrynne's ankles and shins with tremendous force, and nearly swept her off her feet. Then a sudden sound of rushing water heightened their fear and dread. Corrynne barely held on to the door handle as she pulled herself into the seat. *"Bo! Go! Hurry!"* she shouted.

Bo simultaneously released the brake and floored the gas pedal sending the big car into a forward lurch. He groped for the manual headlight knob in the dark and twisted it to turn on the headlights, but the "auto sensor" malfunctioned and left them in the dark. Bo tried again, turning the knob back and forth, but there was still no light. Bo hit the high beams but to no avail. They would have to drive without lights. He tromped on the gas pedal again, and as the car shot forward, he experienced the sickening feeling of slipping sideways to the left. Despite Bo's efforts to steer to the right, the car hydroplaned across the road with the force of the floodwater.

Escape

Panic filled the auditorium of the mansion as Carea sat on the floor, crying silently and gently rocking her brother's limp body in her arms. A heavy-set woman trying to escape the catastrophe tripped over Dane's supine form then fainted on the stairs leading to the stage. Carea was shocked into awareness of the commotion around her, and knew that in order to avoid further injury she must move Dane to a safer place. Carea gently rested Dane's head on the floor and rose to her feet. A violent aftershock hit the room, and she staggered for a moment before regaining her balance enough to grasp Dane's shirt. She pulled so hard that the fabric ripped. Dane was just too heavy to be moved that way. She secured her arms firmly around his chest just below his armpits, and inching backward, began dragging the heavy weight of her brother's flaccid body.

After only a few steps she fell over a toppled stage light pole and landed hard on her bottom. As the room continued to rock around her, she quickly got back up, moved the lamp and pulled Dane toward a side door near the stage.

Dane seemed to weigh a thousand pounds, and it was becoming harder and harder for her to move him. She was exhausted, and wondered how she could go another inch. She stopped to rest and looked around her. She would have to leave Dane and go find help. At that moment, she saw a wild-eyed and panicked man and woman running toward the door behind her. They rushed towards Carea as if they didn't see her. She suddenly realized that they were going to go through the doorway, whether she and Dane were there or not. A jolt of adrenaline flowed through her. With a burst of extra energy she managed to pull Dane's heavy body out of their reckless path.

Carea let Dane's arms fall to the floor just as the crazed people reached the doorway. Suddenly both the man and women fell down hard as if a heavy, unseen hand had knocked them to the floor.

"What? What is going on?" shouted Carea to no one in particular. Then a third person careened out of control, took a nosedive, and landed on the floor between the other two. The three of them lay as if dead. Carea froze for a moment, wondering if *she* would be able to get through the door, or if she would also drop dead on the floor too. Perhaps there was an invisible, deadly force field or something that Imam Mahdi had created to force everyone to stay inside the hall…she wouldn't put it past him. He was capable of almost anything.

Slowly, her eyes slightly closed, Carea approached the open door and reached forward. She took a few more steps, until her hand was beyond the door. "Oh this is ludicrous!" she said as she finally stepped through the doorway and stood intact on the other side. She looked down at her hands and feet. Nope, there was nothing holding *her* back.

The thought prompted her to move Dane. She took a deep breath. She would have to find more strength to move him further. Returning to Dane's body, she noticed that a fourth and fifth person had fallen on top of the other three, making a pile of human bodies.

Carea tried to lighten her mood with humor by yelling, "*Dog pile!*" although this pile wasn't very humorous, but the thought almost brought a smirk to her taut lips. Then for some reason, she felt like laughing out loud as some people do in reaction to overwhelming situations. "Come on, Carea. Keep it together," she said as she returned to the heavy task before her.

Carea noticed that the shaking under her feet had slowly subsided. She bent down again and began to drag Dane backwards. She grunted as she pulled him around the unconscious people to the doorway. Finally outside the door she continued backward, half step by half step dragging her brother's heavy body and moving ever so slowly down a long corridor away from the crazy jumble of human tragedy in the auditorium.

Finally Carea backed into a counter in what appeared to be a kitchen that serviced the auditorium. There on the wall was a telephone. She picked it up and heard a dial tone. "Thank you!" she whispered in reverent appreciation to her Heavenly Father as she dialed 9-1-1.

"*9-1-1 Emergency, please state the nature of your emergency,*" came a very tense male voice over the phone.

"This is Carea Rogers, we're at…" she stopped and looked around and realized that she didn't know how to tell the emergency people how to find her. Feeling stupid she continued, "Well, I'm not sure where I am, but there are a lot of people here who need help!"

"What kind of help?" the man seemed irritated.

"I don't really know that either. This might sound funny, but people are falling over as if they were dead all around me—and my brother…" Carea felt emotion filling up her chest again as a wave. She continued, "He may be dying too!" She began to cry again.

The emergency operator responded quickly and abruptly, expressing no empathy. "*Is your brother breathing?*"

Carea looked down at Dane and she could not see his chest rise and fall. "Maybe…if he is, he isn't breathing very well."

"*Is he responsive?*"

"What do you mean?" asked Carea becoming angry herself. This guy wasn't being very nice.

"Is he awake? *Responsive means 'awake!'*" the man stated briskly as if Carea was a kindergartner.

"No. I can't wake him."

"OK. Now listen."

"I am!" exclaimed Carea as she began to feel more rumblings pulse through her feet.

"Do you know CPR?"

"Yes—I mean no. I've been taught but I don't remember all the breaths and things. I don't want to hurt him more by doing it wrong."

"Well—" the man hesitated for a moment and then said, "*Change of plans….*"

"What does that mean?" asked Carea, just knowing this man thought she was an idiot.

"Our ambulance and police are already on their way to your location. Someone called us on a cell phone earlier. They should be driving up any minute."

"Yes! *That was my brother*!" said Carea excitedly. "Before he fainted he told me he called you guys!"

"Well, good. His call may have saved his life because we deployed cars before the earthquake began. We'll have guys there who can do CPR."

"Good!" said Carea but not feeling good. She felt like a useless, total failure.

"There are four squad cars and two ambulances pulling up to your location now. You should be able to hear the sirens."

Carea held the phone away from her ear and strained to hear above the low rumble of the earthquake aftershocks and the rattling house. "Yes, I think I hear them," she said dully but inside she was thankful, despite being frustrated.

"Good," affirmed the emergency operator. "Now, tell me what you're wearing."

"What?" Carea was instantly self-conscious and filled with guilt. She was still wearing the gold satin dress and white chiffon train with her ornate pearl crown. What would they think? She reached up and undid the clasp holding the train on her shoulders and let it fall to the ground.

"Tell us so we can find you and your brother."

Carea looked down again at her elegant dress then responded a little nervously, "Well, I'm wearing a gold satin dress with a crown—I know it sounds weird, but that is what I'm wearing."

"Fine. Go outside."

Carea shook her head. "I can't leave my brother! It's not safe here!"

"Listen, miss. There is nothing for you to do in there. Right now your job is to follow instructions. Just put him in a doorway away from falling debris."

Carea was already angry, embarrassed, and overwhelmed; now this guy was yelling at her over the phone! "OK, I'll try," she said in a defeated tone.

"Good," said the man and then the phone went dead.

Rising Tide

After recovering from hydroplaning in the rushing water, Bo sped the big Suburban down the flooded street. He stared into the darkness in an effort to see the road beneath the tires but he saw only black flowing liquid where the pavement should have been. Now he was driving from memory. A black, rising, tumultuous torrent of icy water flowed around them from behind and rushed on into the darkness as they plowed through it.

"Dad, go faster! Its getting deep fast!" shouted Jax as he gripped the dashboard with both hands.

Bo was already going faster than he knew was safe, and did not respond to his son's urging. They had to get the raft and inner tubes inflated in case the car couldn't make it through the deepening water. "Brea!" he shouted to his daughter.

"What, Dad?" answered Brea.

"I need you to climb into the back and get the air pump out of the crate."

Brea immediately unbuckled her seatbelt and turned toward the back of the car.

Bo turned and spoke reassuringly to Jax, "Climb all the way into the back and help your sister—first pump up the raft and then the inner tubes. You know how. You've done it before at Scout camp. Hurry, son!"

Jax quickly climbed through the car, stepping carefully between his mom and Strykker's car seat, then climbed into the back to help his sister.

Bo turned the car onto the main road outside their neighborhood, causing a wave of water to splash high off to the right side. Both Striynna and Strykker began to howl. Bo ignored the crying and the increased stress it was causing him, and tried to keep his mind on maneuvering the Suburban.

Feeling the water push against the side of the car, Bo knew that he and his family would soon have to abandon the vehicle. The distributor and vital ignition would foul out first and then water would get into the carburetor. In the mean time, he would drive as far as he could in order to get his family to the safety of higher ground. One positive aspect about a Suburban was that it sat higher off the road than most cars.

As Bo plowed through the rising water, he tried not to watch the myriads of frantic people run from their homes and struggle through the water where the streets once were. Men, women, and children, dressed in pajamas and robes were running in small groups, seemingly in every direction and not knowing where to go. Once in a while it felt like his heart would drop into his stomach, as he saw one of them being pulled under the rushing current of the black water. Others were scrambling to get back into their houses as the water rose to their front doors, quickly reaching mid-thigh. Some were climbing onto fences. Bo noticed that a few others had already climbed onto their roofs. Interestingly, he didn't recognize any of the people. That was either a good sign that his friends and neighbors got out before him or a bad sign indicating that the people he knew were trapped. Bo shook his head to stop his thinking. He didn't want to consider negative possibilities. The truth is, all he knew was what was happening right there around his car.

The automobile suddenly swerved uncontrollably as for one brief and terrifying moment the force of the rising water caused the rear of the Suburban to come up off the pavement. Bo instinctively, activated the four-wheel drive mechanism, and pressing the gas pedal all the way to the floor, regained control of the car.

"How's it coming with the raft and inner tubes back there?" called Bo over his shoulder.

"OK, Dad. The raft is inflating but it's going to get real crowded in here in a minute!" said Brea with worry in her voice.

"Oh yeah. Sorry. Here, I'll open up the top half of the tailgate and you can let part of it inflate out the back window, but *hold on to it*! It may save our lives!" Bo reached for the key fob dangling from the steering column and hit the button he knew would open only the top half of the rear door.

Jax helped push the half-inflated raft into position so it could continue inflating while they drove.

"Bo, how do you plan for us to get into the raft while we're speeding down the street—or river—or whatever this is!" asked Corrynne.

Bo looked at his wife through the rearview mirror. She was intently watching out the front window. He recognized the stress taking a toll on her face. Bo answered, "I don't know yet. But I'll bet you we'll soon find out."

"Oh good! Just let me know when you find out, because we're getting very worried back here!" said Corrynne nervously.

Bo smiled slightly at his wife and said, "I'm sure we'il find a way out of this. We're all going to be fine. I promise."

Bo began to pray silently and fervently. He hoped he could deliver on his promise. Adrenaline surged through his body as he flexed his shoulders and arms, and his knuckles turned white as he tightly griped the steering wheel. He would assure safe passage for his family, even if he had to die doing it.

"OK, Dad. The raft is done and now we're blowing up the tubes," shouted Brea from the back of the Suburban. Jax held the raft in the car with both hands, as instructed.

Looking to his left, Bo saw a familiar gas station. Beyond that, there was a main street. He knew the water would be deep and turbulent there as it rushed along unhampered by obstruction. He wanted to cross that road and go up the other side into the hills, but he was unsure if the Suburban would be able to grip the road enough to fight the growing current that was now pushing against the car door. He looked down briefly when he felt cold water pouring in from underneath the doors and rising up his ankles.

"Bo, you do know that the water is up to our shins back here," said Corrynne. "Maybe we should jump ship."

"No, not quite yet. I want to get across University first."

"*University?* I don't know, Bo. Are we going to be OK crossing that big open road? It looks pretty tumultuous. The last thing we need is for our car to roll over in this current."

"I know, but if we hurry, I think we can make it. It's better to go for higher ground now, rather than take our chances outside in the rising tide," said Bo.

"I think this car is a death trap," said Jax, abruptly lifting his feet out of the icy cold water.

"What?" asked Corrynne. "Why do you say that?"

"Because it's no good in deep water…"

"Everybody hold on!" interrupted Bo as he accelerated. They plunged into the deep tumult on University Avenue, creating a small wall of water in front of them.

Bo turned the wheel a little to the left to fight the strong current that was pushing them hard to the right. The car sluggishly obeyed his turning steering wheel and slightly turned to the left against the current. The rushing flow of water now climbed up and onto the hood of the car, and plowed into the windshield. Cold water poured through the open top half of the gate as well.

"*DAD!*" screamed Jax.

"The water is coming in really fast!" called Brea.

"I know, bear with me and *HOLD ON*!!" shouted Bo as he pushed the gas pedal to the floor. However, the Suburban did not lurch forward like it had before, instead it seemed to cough and stall mid-stream, hydroplaning and slipping once again out of control. Despite Bo's effort to steer left, the strong, deep current pulled the front of the car to the right. Then the whole car began to spin as the current pushed it down the street.

"Dad!" shouted Bo's frightened children.

"I know, just hold on! We'll be OK!" Not convinced of their outcome, Bo couldn't help but think that Corrynne had been right. He shouldn't have tried to drive across University after all.

The Suburban turned 360 degrees, traveled sideways in the current, and was once again facing toward the hills.

"Hey, I think we're going to hit a car that's under water back here!" shouted Brea, looking out the back window.

Brea's warning was answered by a dull sound and a jarring thud as the right rear side of the Suburban collided with the other car. The force of the impact rotated the Suburban back, a quarter turn, and then it came to a stop with the windshield facing into the rushing torrent, the front end was fully submerged; the back wheels rested half way up the sunken car so that the back end of the Suburban was sticking out of the water.

The once dead headlights flickered on as the water flowed over the hood and onto the windshield. Bo noticed that the dim beams of the headlights shining into the murky green depths of the water made it seem like they were in a submarine.

"*Bo, we have to get out of here!*" shouted Corrynne as she unlatched the straps on both car seats. Striynna and Strykker screaming in unison, scrambled to cling to their mother. The cold water was rising fast and was now halfway up their car seats.

"Go quickly! Out the back! Get everyone out and onto the roof, Corrynne! Grab Strykker and I'll take Striynna!" shouted Bo desperately. "Ry! Roc! Move to the back!"

The family began to climb single file out of the car and the icy grip of the rising water. One by one, they squeezed past the raft that was half in and half out of the car, and climbed through the window onto the roof of the Suburban.

Bo held Striynna under his arm like a football and crawled over the first row of seats to kneel on the second row. "Jax, do you remember the Bowline knot I taught you in Scouts?"

"Yes, Dad. Where do you want me to tie it?" Jax replied looking at the raft next to Bo.

"Undo a bundle of rope and loop one end through one of the inner tubes, then tie a Bowline! Do it fast!"[4]

"OK, Dad!" Jax leaned over the seat and fished in the crate that was now under water and found the rope. After a few moments he said, "I've done that, now what?"

"Let's push that tube into the middle of the raft, and then put it out the window."

With Bo's help, Jax pushed down on the edge of the raft then slid the inner tube over the edge and into the open middle riding area of the raft.

"Now loop the other end of the rope through the second inner tube and then through a grommet right there on the side of the raft, then tie a square knot."

"Oh, I get it. We're linking them all together," said Jax quickly as he threaded the rope and tied his knots.

"Yes, we are. Good, son," encouraged Bo as Jax finished his tasks. "Let's push that inner tube into the raft too."

"OK," said Jax as he manhandled the second tube.

"How are you guys doing in there?" called Brea from on top of the roof.

"The water is continuing to rise, Bo. Give me Striynna. You need to get Jax out of there," came Corrynne's voice from above Jax and Bo.

Bo precariously climbed over the last row of seats and moved to the window. Sticking his head and torso out the opening, he handed the wiggling, crying baby girl to her mother. "We finished tying the knots. Get ready to climb into the raft in a minute," said Bo to Corrynne. Turning and ducking back into the Suburban, Bo said, "Jax, now help me put all those backpacks and oars in the raft."

"They're soaked Dad."

"I know, but we need everything in them. Luckily, everything inside is waterproofed."

"Oh yeah. That *is* lucky!" said Jax, smiling as he worked. "Should I dump all the stuff out into the raft? The backpacks are super heavy when they are wet."

Bo abruptly shook his head. "No. We need the packs to carry everything. The water won't hurt the food," Bo instructed as calmly as he could while the icy water continued to rise to their chests as they bent over with their heads against the roof. It was causing their breath to come in short, half-gasps.

"OK," said Jax. Even though his jaw shivered and his teeth chattered uncontrollably, he helped his father lift the water-drenched backpacks one by one out of the deep water.

When all the backpacks were in the raft, Bo said to Jax, "Now, help me push the raft out into the water, but we can't lose control. Get a firm hold on the rope. If we're not careful, the water will take this raft away and we'll all be in huge trouble."

Working together, Bo and Jax braced themselves inside the lower half of the rear door, held firmly to the rope, and carefully pushed the raft out the window. "Now, everyone get into the raft," yelled Bo, "Brea you go first. Be careful though, there isn't much room to move around with all the backpacks and inner tubes."

"Do you want me to move them?" asked Brea as she peered down at her father and the raft from the roof.

"Yes. I would like you to throw the inner tubes out into the water, and arrange the backpacks around the inside of the raft to make room for the rest of us."

Quickly, Brea did as she was told, first climbing into the raft and then pushing the inner tubes out into the current. Once out in the heavy flow, the tubes began to sway left and right from the pull of the water.

"Now Ry and Roc, you guys carefully climb into the raft, too," instructed Bo.

One by one Ry and Rocwell carefully stepped into the wobbly raft as Brea held their hands to steady them.

"Now it's your turn Corrynne. Hand the twins to Brea, one at a time, then you get in, too."

Corrynne followed Bo's instructions, but the combination of the current, the increasing weight inside the raft and the inner tubes, caused the rope to slip in Jax and Bo's freezing hands. The raft started to drift away with incredible pull of the rushing water.

"Hurry!" Bo yelled as he winced. His cold muscles were becoming fatigued, his fingers numb from the strain and the cold. "We're losing our grip!"

After the babies were safely in Brea's arms, Corrynne scrambled and half fell into the raft, which gave the rope a good tug causing the rope to slip through their hands even more. Bo's arms began to shake as he gathered every ounce of strength to hold on. "Hurry, bud, it's your turn," Bo said to Jax with a forced smile, his face turning red with the strain.

"I can't let go, Dad. If I do, the raft will be too heavy for you," said Jax with a frightened look on his face.

"We don't have a choice! *Go, son... **Now**!*"

After a moment of hesitation, Jax let go of the rope, pushed through the water, and climbed through the open window.

The icy water was nearly to Bo's chin. The rope slipped again, and ripped into the flesh of his hands. The raft floated too far out for Jax to step onto it easily.

"Jump, Jax!" yelled Ry.

"Hurry! Jump!" yelled Rocwell.

Jax pushed off of the door of the Suburban and jumped, landing with his waist on the edge of the raft. Corrynne grabbed the back of his pants and hauled him into the raft. At that moment, the weight and motion was too much for Bo, and the rope ripped violently from his grip.

"Bo! Jump! Hurry! We're floating away!" yelled Corrynne.

"Daddy! Hurry!" yelled Roc.

"You're going to have to swim!" said Jax, as the distance began to grow between the car and the raft.

Bo climbed heavily and numbly out of the window, and stood teetering on the upper edge of the door, his limbs stiff and unresponsive from too much time and effort in the frigid water. He panted clouds of billowing breath into the night as he looked for a brief moment at the raft slipping away from him into the darkness. The water now rose up past Bo's numb, shaking knees, and completely covered the top of the car.

Bo took a big breath and dove headfirst into the black water. He swam with all his might in the direction of the inner tubes that were dragging behind the raft.

"Hurry, Dad!" yelled a child. Bo wasn't sure whose voice it was.

"Bo! Hurry! Swim fast! *We're moving too far away!*" he heard Corrynne call to him.

The cold quickly seized his chest and lungs. Needing another breath, Bo came up gasping for air as the freezing temperature sapped his strength and control. His arms and legs felt stiff and heavy as he tried to drive them harder.

The numbing affect of the cold on his body and mind drove a grave fear into Bo's pounding heart. Putting his head back down into the numbing water, he went into a full sprinting breaststroke. Trying to force his body into a streamlined machine, he pulled himself forward in powerful strokes as hard and fast as he could.

"Daddy! Faster! You can do it!" Bo heard someone say, but because of the cold he was beginning to lose touch with reality.

The world slowly began to spin into a cold whirlpool of detached thoughts and flashing images. With his strong body still swimming mechanically forward, his numb mind quickly began to wander. All of a sudden, Bo couldn't remember where he was or why he was swimming. Was he racing his son Braun at the pool? Or was it Conrad racing him in the Provo River? Was he even swimming at all?

"What's happening to me?" Bo wondered feeling very confused. The next moment, Bo found himself lying safely in his bed next to Corrynne as she gently ran her ice-cold fingers through his wet hair.

"It's freezing in here! Is the window open?" he asked in a dreamlike state, trying to awaken and pull the blankets and comforter up under his chin.

"Come on, wake up!" someone said to him.

In a dizzy haze his mind changed scenes. Bo found himself in the driver seat of their brand new Suburban; the glint of the sun reflecting off the hood burned his eyes. "Whew! The air conditioning is amazing in this car!" Bo said, shivering from the cold. He looked out the side window to his right and saw his family lined up, smiling and waving to him in slow motion. He smiled wide and waved goodbye as he slowly pulled away from the curb.

Corrynne and the kids continued to smile and wave goodbye from the sunny front lawn of their country cottage home. Bo wondered where he was going.

"Wake up, Bo!" came a familiar, far-off voice once again inside his numb mind.

Bo began to feel the presence of the same angel that had visited him in his dreams a couple weeks before.

"Angel! Where are you? Show yourself to me!" Bo called out in his mind, unaware that his body was still swimming for his life.

Suddenly, Bo heard words that seemed to shake his core, *"WAKE UP!!"* The message continued, *"You must fulfill your responsibilities! Be a leader in times of trial! Miracles will follow you because of your faith...wake up!"*

All at once, Bo came to and realized hypothermia was bringing shock and delirium to his brain. He forced himself to fight the urge to relax and float away into blissful slumber. Now kicking and pulling with the last efforts he could muster, he felt something brush his fingertips.

"Come on, Bo!" he thought he heard Corrynne yell through the rush of the cold water in his ears.

"Come on, Dad!" That was Jax, he was sure of it and it sounded very close!

He took another hard stroke and reached far out in front of him again. There it was again, his hand slipped across a slick, rubbery surface! Bo lifted his head up and took a loud gasp of air and saw he was just able to touch the last inner tube.

"Come on, Dad!" Bo heard Roc and Ry shouting and crying. With a big kick and a powerful stroke of his right arm, he brought his left arm up and over the edge of the shiny black rubber tube.

"That's it, come on, Dad!" came a tearful urge from Brea. Bo struggled to bring his other arm up and over the tube; then he just hung on for a moment, trying to catch his breath. Finally, with his last ounce of energy, Bo pulled his body up and rolled over backward onto the tube. He was completely exhausted.

Out of the corner of his eye, Bo saw Corrynne and Brea jump up and down with joy from their kneeling positions, as the boys laughed hysterically and the twins looked on in shock at the sudden movement.

"He did it, Mom! He did it!" yelled Roc and Ry.

Bo smiled and looked backwards to see his family cheering as they nearly capsized the boat in their excited celebration.

He was a blessed man indeed. Yes, he would stay and fulfill his responsibilities. It was a *pleasure* to do so.

Notes to "Deer Creek Dam"

The Breach

[1] The Deer Creek Dam is a real dam located above the city of Provo in the Canyons of the Wasatch front. The design for the Deer Creek Dam is designed to withstand an earthquake of

Richter scale magnitude 7.5. See http://www.usbr.gov/uc/feature/deercreek.html for more information.

[2] In researching the possible emergency evacuation plans for the unfortunate breach of the Deer Creek or the Deer Creek Dams, one Internet site that produced helpful directions was a plan created by Brigham Young University. See the following Internet address for information and tips to help recover from a flood caused from dam breach in Provo, Utah. http://fhss.byu.edu/adm/emergencyplan/individual%20annexes/annex1.html.

Flood

[3] "On a daily basis we witness widely fluctuating inflation; wars; interpersonal conflicts; national disasters; variances in weather conditions; innumerable forces of immorality, crime, and violence; attacks and pressures on the family and individuals; technological advances that make occupations obsolete; and so on. The need for preparation is abundantly clear. The great blessing of being prepared gives us freedom from fear, as guaranteed to us by the Lord in the Doctrine and Covenants: 'If ye are prepared ye shall not fear' (D&C 38:30)" (L. Tom Perry, "If Ye Are Prepared Ye Shall Not Fear," *Ensign*, Nov. 1995, 35).

Rising Tide

[4] Scouting can bless all the families of the Church by teaching the youth to be prepared for unforeseen circumstance with skills they wouldn't otherwise have, and serving others with that knowledge. "Every boy blessed by Scouting learns in his youth far more than that envisioned by Sir Tom of Warwick. He adopts the motto "Be Prepared." He subscribes to the code "Do a Good Turn Daily." Scouting provides proficiency badges to encourage skills and personal endeavor. Scouting teaches boys how to live, not merely how to make a living. How pleased I am that The Church of Jesus Christ of Latter-day Saints in 1913 became the first partner to sponsor Scouting in the United States" (Thomas S. Monson, "Run, Boy, Run!" *Ensign*, Nov. 1982, 19).

CHAPTER FOUR

ETERNAL PURPOSES

"And thus God bringeth about his great and eternal purposes, which were prepared from the foundation of the world. And thus cometh about the salvation and the redemption of men, and also their destruction and misery" (Alma 42:26).

00:09:04, 16:59:05 Zulu
Saturday, March 26th
12:01 a.m.
Skull Valley, Utah
Imam Mahdi's Mansion

Flight of Life

Carea ran through the enormous mansion, finding one winding corridor after another. At first she didn't know which way to go. How was she going to find her way back?

She turned a corner, and looked toward the end of the hall then glanced up at the vaulted ceiling. There was a balcony immediately above her head. "Yes!" she said aloud. It was the balcony she had stood on earlier in the evening! It was there that Imam Mahdi had made her faint! Now she knew exactly where she was!

Directly in front of her stood the massive double doors where she had entered the mansion with Steve… how long ago? It seemed like days ago. Throwing open the heavy doors, Carea ran out into the darkness but stopped in her tracks when she was suddenly blinded by intense light.

"Freeze! Police! Don't move!" shouted the amplified and fuzzy voice of a man.

Carea did what she was told, but she wondered what was happening.

Two police officers ran toward her from out of the darkness. They knelt in front of Carea with their guns drawn and pointing at her. "Are you a part of the Mahdi coronation?" one of them shouted.

Carea hesitated a moment. A thousand thoughts shot through her head. Something was wrong! They were pointing guns at her! "Oh, no!" she thought—*she still had the crown on her head* and they were asking about the *coronation*! What should she do? What should she say? Defiantly she shook her head. *"No! I'm not a part of the coronation!"* she said boldly, rationalizing that the only reason she was at the house was because she was being held against her will. She definitely was not *a part* of *anything* here!

"Where is Imam Mahdi?

"Are those your clothes?"

"Why were you in that building?"

A barrage of questions came from different directions. "It's..." Carea began, still not knowing what to say, and blurting whatever came to her mind. "It's a long story. I came here for a party, but when I wanted to leave they forced me to stay. The people inside took my clothes and put these on me." Carea held up one hand to block the light from her eyes, and then continued, "My brother came to save me and he is in there now, but he's very sick. I was trying to drag him out, but I'm not strong enough. I called 9-1-1..."

"Oh, you're the one that called," said someone behind the two officers, as the lights were turned away from her face. "Dispatch told us to look for this girl," said the same voice. "They said to look for a girl wearing a yellow dress and a crown. It sounded strange, but here she is. We'd better not let her get away; we need to hold her for questioning."

When Carea learned that the police knew about her call, she no longer cared that she might be in trouble. Dane was her priority. "Yes! I'm that girl!" she said, and her worry eased a little; she felt renewed hope for her brother's safety. "Come on! My brother—get Dane." Carea pointed back into the house. "He's in there and you have to get him to a hospital! *He's dying!*" she said forcefully, and then tears choked her voice.

"Tell us where he is!" said one of the policeman who had been kneeling in front of her. He put his gun away and stepped forward.

With great effort Carea tried to answer. She cleared her throat and said, "Follow the main corridor at first, then stay to the left. You'll come to a kitchen. He's lying on the floor by the counter in there." Carea turned to rush back into the house. *"I'll show you!"*

The other officer caught her by the arm, and held her with more strength than was necessary. "No, you stay here. We'll find him." He pointed to a man and a woman standing beside an ambulance; each had a stethoscope draped around their necks. "Go over there. A police officer will escort you."

The first officer waved his hands at an unseen audience and yelled, "OK, get the paramedics up here with a gurney!"

Within seconds two men dressed in white pushed a stretcher past Carea.

Another uniformed officer came out of the darkness, took her gently by her other arm and said, "Miss, please come with me. This way; I'll get you a blanket and some water." This man held eye contact with her a bit too long, as if he was trying to communicate something to her, but she didn't get it. She walked with him down the steps and out of the way. Together they approached the ambulance.

"Right over here," said the officer. He was kind to Carea as he helped her sit up on the edge of a gurney just outside the open back door of the ambulance. "Ah, there we go." He handed her a lightweight blanket and some bottled water. "Is there anything else I can do for you right now?"

Carea shook her head.

"You *stay* here alright?" the policeman looked at her pointedly. Again she got the impression he was trying to tell her something more than what he was saying. It was almost as if he was telling her he would help her escape. Was that right? Why would a police officer help her escape? Especially when it had been made clear to her that the police intended to question her!

"I'll be right back, OK?" The man said nodding and smiling. "I'll go find out what is happening with your brother."

Carea nodded, but was still confused. "Ah—thank you!" she called after the officer as he walked away.

The male paramedic to Carea's right quickly went to work. Within seconds, he placed a probe on her finger and a cuff on her arm. She assumed he was taking her blood pressure, pulse, and oxygen level.

The female paramedic had a device in her hand that Carea didn't recognize. It was the size of a plum, but thin, silver and sleek. The paramedic pointed it at Carea's hand and then her head. When it came close to her forehead, a high-pitched alarm went off.

"What does that mean?" Carea frowned and looked at the paramedic.

"We have a positive," said the woman to her colleague, ignoring Carea's question.

"What's a 'positive'?" asked Carea, but again no one answered her question.

The male paramedic pulled a small cell phone out of his pocket, and then pushed a button.

"Who are you calling?" asked Carea, becoming more and more worried as she watched the actions of the paramedics.

"Everything will be explained to you later," said the woman in a business like voice. Now she was holding another strange object. It was a black olive-like thing with a red light inside it. "Look up please and don't blink. I'm going to shine a light in your eyes," said the woman, then she held up the lit object and swiped a deep red, laser into her eyes.

"What does that do?" Carea asked.

"It maps your retina."

"Why does it do that?"

"Identification."

"Oh," said Carea dumbfounded, wondering why the paramedics needed to *identify* her?

The woman put the 'olive' in a holder that was attached to a screen, and then tuned away so Carea couldn't see what she was doing.

"Who does it say that I am?" asked Carea after watching the paramedic touch a computer screen lightly.

"It says that you are Carea Lorrell Rogers of Provo, Utah. Is that correct?"

Carea nodded stiffly, "Yes, that's correct."

"Do you live at 300 West 4250 North?"

"Yes. What is all this about? Are you worried about my insurance? I promise you'll get paid."

"No, ma'am, just protocol," said the woman as she closed her computer and took it into the medical van.

Thump, thump, thump, thump…

Carea turned her head to look behind her. A very loud and powerful noise came from above the mansion. The sound was growing nearer. A moment later, bright lights from overhead flooded the ground all around them as an enormous, dark green helicopter swooped in low out of the darkness. Carea watched over her shoulder in amazement as the chopper hovered above the ground just behind the row of police cars.

Swirls of dust flew all around the ambulance and the surrounding area. A strong wave of wind whipped up from the beating blades of the helicopter. Carea felt as if she might fall off the gurney. The male paramedic, who was still working with his equipment to her right, reached out to steady her and had to duck into the wind just to keep his balance.

"Is that Life Flight?" Carea yelled into the paramedic's ear.

"It's a military Medi-Vac unit, just like Life Flight."

I'll bet it's come for Dane, Carea thought to herself.

The kind patrolman came out of the house, and approached the gurney. He stood next to Carea, and the male paramedic joined the woman in the truck. It was as if he was being left in charge of her.

Carea decided to probe this officer to see if she could figure out what all the cloak and dagger stuff was about. "Excuse me…" she began, but before she could finish the sentence the officer pointed toward the house.

"Here comes your brother. They've intubated him so he can breathe better. That machine next to him on the stretcher is a ventilator."

Carea jumped off the gurney and the blanket fell to the ground. She stood on her tiptoes, and saw paramedics coming from the house. They were carrying a body strapped tightly to a gurney. As they approached the ambulance, the police officer walked away from Carea and left her standing alone.

Carea wondered what he was doing. There he went again. Was he leaving her alone on purpose? Did he want her to run away?

Carea looked into the back of the open ambulance and saw the two paramedics who had been attending to her. They were still busy inside. Yes, the coast was clear. She would accept the opportunity the officer had given her. Quickly, Carea reached down and picked up the blanket from the ground then pulled it tightly around her body. She didn't want to be a moving target, and the blanket was just long enough to cover the bright yellow gown. That done, she ran toward the helicopter.

Carea ducked beneath the whirling blades, just as a big door slid open on the side of the aircraft, then two people dressed in camouflage and helmets jumped from inside the door to the ground and moved quickly away from the chopper. It was as if they hadn't even seen her. A woman, also dressed in camouflage, poked her head out the door of the helicopter and looked directly at Carea.

Carea's stomach dropped. She felt as if she had been caught running on a red light in a game of "Red-light Green-light," and was going to be sent back to the ambulance.

"Carea Rogers?" asked the woman.

Carea gasped. This person knew her name! "Yes?"

"You are to come with us. We have a seat right here for you." The woman held out her hand to Carea. "Watch your head," she said simply as Carea accepted the help and climbed up the edge and into the main body of the helicopter.

Before Carea knew what was happening, she was strapped tightly into a high back seat against the opposite side of the helicopter. She was facing the open door and had a clear view of Dane in the stretcher.

Watching intently, she saw the men in white position Dane's gurney alongside the door. They folded the wheels down, and lifted him inside handing him off to the military medical personnel.

Carea stopped breathing for a moment when she saw Dane up close. He was so pale, and sweat was pouring off his face! She had never seen him so sick. "Please, Father, bless him!" she whispered below the roar of the engines as two army medical personnel slid the door closed. "Don't let him die."

Dane's gurney was taken to a column in the back of the helicopter and snapped into a flat area where there were several monitors. Carea watched as one of the people attending to Dane slipped a module into one of the monitors. Multicolored waves appeared. Carea recognized that one of the waves was tracking Dane's heartbeat.

Carea watched the rhythmic design pulse across the screen. She couldn't help but notice the lines as they peaked and curved as one beat connected to the next. She was mesmerized; struck with the beauty of the rhythm of life.

The pitch of the engines changed and Carea sensed that they were preparing to lift off. Carea exhaled a burst of air from her lungs. She felt a great weight of tension lift from her as the helicopter rose from the lawn. She was relieved that both she and Dane were finally leaving the mansion together.

Trial of Strength

The raft, heavily laden with Corrynne, Brea, the children, and their backpacks, drifted rapidly and unsteadily along the watery street leading straight into the heart of Provo.

"Dad! Are you OK?" shouted Jax. He leaned closer to the edge so he could get a better look at his father who was still recovering from his near-fatal swim. The sudden movement nearly caused the raft to capsize.

"*Jax!*" yelled Corrynne, "*Sit down!* You're going to tip us over! There are too many of us in here for you to be moving so quickly!"

Jax sat down, and with a sullen look said, "I'm just worried about Dad."

Corrynne's expression softened. "I know you are, but hang in there and just sit until we figure out what to do next. You'll be able to talk to him in a little while."

The raft's near capsize, brought to mind her own worries that the boat might tip over or fill with water. After all, it was only a four-man raft and there were seven of them in it.... Corrynne quickly changed her thoughts. It shouldn't matter that there was seven, because five of the seven were only children. What was wrong? Even though the backpacks were heavy and full of water, the raft should be more stable. Corrynne touched the air-filled sides of the raft and discovered that there was too much give.

"Jax, does this raft have a leak in it?" she asked quickly.

Jax turned his gaze from his father to his obviously concerned mother. "No. I don't think so. It worked fine last time we used it."

"Then we must have not filled it up all the way," Corrynne reasoned.

"No, we couldn't," said Jax in a matter-of-fact tone.

"Why not?"

"Because we pumped it up while it was still in the Suburban, there was only so much room."

"Oh," said Corrynne as worry began to grow in her chest. She wanted to get her family safely out of the raft as soon as she could. It just wasn't stable enough to trust. The depth and force of the water was rapidly increasing, and she wondered how far the raft would take them. She reasoned that if they continued straight down University, the water should get shallower as the street became wider, and they should eventually be able to get out of the raft.

Corrynne carefully turned around to survey what lay ahead. She realized that the level of the street was angled so that the water was rushing into the lower lying lands and flowing towards Utah Lake. They only had a minute or so before the wobbly raft would careen down a steep hill, then most likely throw her whole family into a torrent of deep water.

Sudden fear overcame her as she realized that she would never be able to swim while holding the twins above the water. And what was she going to do about Ry and Roc? They could barely swim in calm water let alone this threatening river!

"*Bo!*" she yelled to her husband who was still recovering from his swim. "The water is changing directions, and we're going to be heading down the hill! We have to do something now, or the boat will tip and we'll all go under the water!"

Bo abruptly lifted his head from the inner tube, turned over and stared up the street. "You're right. What do you want to do?" he asked, shouting back to her.

"*I don't know! What should we do?*" Corrynne felt totally helpless.

"I don't know!" said Bo. "You can grab the oars and try and steer the boat to the far side of the road away from the turbulence!" Then he pointed to a spot ahead of them. "Maybe you can get the boat to move up further toward that grassy bank."

Corrynne was taken aback. "*You want me to steer the boat?*"

"Yes, Corrynne, you and Brea! Jax knows how, he can tell you what to do."

"Bo! We're not strong enough!"

"You're going to have to be strong. I can't do it from back here!"

Corrynne carefully scooted over and handed one twin to Jax and the other to Ry. "Hang on to them tight!" Corrynne instructed firmly. "Don't let them squirm out of your grasp, no matter how loud they scream. *Do you understand me?*"

Both Jax and Ry nodded and wrapped their arms around the babies' waists. Both Striynna and Strykker began to struggle and yell, but the boys held them firmly.

Corrynne grabbed both oars and handed one to Brea. "OK, Brea," she said, "it's up to us now."

Brea looked worried but didn't say a word.

"Dig in deep, Brea! Let's try and slow down this raft," shouted Corrynne as she pushed her oar deep into the water.

Brea followed suit, but the raft didn't slow down…in fact, it increased in speed as the rushing water pushed it toward the hill.

"Mom, this isn't working! How do we turn the boat?"

Jax coached, "Mom, use the oar to paddle with the current!"

"Won't that cause us to move faster?" asked Corrynne as she glanced up at her son.

"No. Not if Brea keeps her oar in the water as a drag and you paddle on the other side with the flow of the water. That will cause us to turn to my left."

As if a light went on in her head Corrynne understood and began to paddle rapidly, pulling hard to leverage her oar in the water. Immediately the boat began to veer to the left and move up to the edge of the current, but the grassy area had passed, now there was a sheer rocky wall with nothing to grab on to.

The boat scraped along the wall then bounced, and began to rotate.

"Oh no, Mom! We're going to flip around!" cried Roc looking around with wide eyes.

"Use the oar on the wall, Brea! Push us away!" yelled Jax.

As Brea pushed hard against the wall, the boat changed directions turning to the right again. With great effort, Corrynne and Brea maintained control of the raft, keeping it on the highest point as the lay of the land began to turn down hill.

"Try to steer into that chain link fence!" yelled Bo.

Corrynne looked up and spotted the place Bo was talking about. "Brea! Put your oar in deep again and I'll try to move us close to that fence. When we get there, grab on to it with everything you've got!"

Brea dug her oar in, and as Corrynne pulled against the current the raft began to move along a chain link fence that stuck out about three feet above the water. When they were close enough, Brea attempted to grab the fence, but they were still moving too fast. "Mom! I can't grab hold!"

"Keep trying!" yelled Corrynne as she tried to keep the boat from veering too much to the right. "We should slow down a little as the water continues to turn!"

Brea grabbed a backpack, obviously having a new idea, and unzipped it. She emptied the contents into the center of the boat, and then she threw one of the shoulder straps over the top of a fence post alongside the raft and hung on tight. The boat tipped, and as it swung around almost 90-degrees, Brea became a stationary pivotal point.

Roc lost his balance and rolled momentarily towards his sister's feet. Ry and Strykker slid a little bit too. The uneven weight caused the left side of the raft to tip, allowing water to trickle over the edge, but Roc scrambled back, to his place and the raft stabilized.

Brea pulled the boat parallel to the fence. "I got it! I got it!" she yelled, as she struggled against the current. "Hurry everyone! I can't hold it for long!"

Corrynne dropped her oar inside the boat and unzipped another backpack. Repeating what Brea had done, she hooked it to the fence near the other end of the raft, making their docking secure. "Go, Jax! Go, Ry! Get the babies out! Rocwell, climb on the fence! Hurry!"

Rocwell scurried onto the fence but Jax and Ry hesitated.

"How, Mom?" asked Jax.

"The babies can't hold on themselves," said Ry with tears filling his eyes.

"Use their clothes!" said Corrynne. "Hook their clothes on the fence then support them with your body! Hurry!"

Jax unlatched a shoulder strap of Striynna's pajama overalls, threaded it through the fence then reattached it. Then he climbed onto the fence next to his little sister.

Ry looked around helplessly at Strykker's clothes. He was wearing plain footy pajamas. "Mom! I don't know what to do!"

"Just hook his neckline over the chain link fence, Ry!" yelled Brea. "Please hurry! I'm loosing my grip!"

Ry pulled the back of Strykker's pajama up to get some slack, and then tried to hook it onto the fence but it slipped off. "I can't do it, Mom!" Ry began to cry in frustration. "*I just can't do it!*"

Corrynne looked back at Bo and then to Ry again. "You've got to do it, Ry! Try again!"

As Ry tried again, Corrynne turned and watched Bo's inner tube slowly drift into the current. She realized that if it passed their raft and was caught into the downward rush of water, the rope connection would cause the inner tube to pull the boat away from the fence and down the hill. Thinking quickly, Corrynne yelled to her daughter. "Brea! Help Ry with Strykker! Hurry! I think I can hold the raft by myself while you help the kids!"

Instantly, Brea grabbed a child size backpack and put it on Strykker. She cinched the straps over his shoulders and slipped the loop of the backpack over one of the other fence posts. Strykker slipped a little when Brea let go of him, then his weight settled into the pack and he dangled from the fence a safe distance above the water. Next, Brea helped Ry onto the fence and took her place near Strykker to protect him from falling into the water.

"Hang on, Corr! I'm going to try to jump into the raft!" Bo shouted from the left.

Corrynne braced herself for the weight of her husband, but her muscles were shaking with fatigue. Within seconds she felt Bo jump into the raft, but the added weight was too much for her to control. The current swept the raft right out from under her feet and left her clinging to the fence chest deep. "*BO!*" Corrynne screamed as she squeezed her eyes tightly closed. She couldn't bear to watch her husband plunge over the hill with the raft.

In the silence of the night, only the tired whimpering of the twins and the rush of water could be heard. Corrynne returned her attention to her children. She needed to take care of them. She was all they had right now. With her last bit of strength, she pulled herself up out of the water. Then suddenly, she heard a noise behind her. She looked over her shoulder in time to see Bo come out of the water and grab hold of the fence right beside her.

When Corrynne realized that Bo had jumped off the raft and swam under water to her, she was so relieved that she was both laughing and crying as she held out one arm to embrace him.

Bo also held out an arm and hugged Corrynne tightly. "We did it." He managed to say in a breathy voice.

"I love you so much!" Corrynne said in gasps.

"And I love you," came Bo's kind reply. "I love all of you!" he said to his children who were either clinging to or hanging from the fence for dear life. "Tonight—we thank the Lord for the blessing of each other," he added, "because I know for sure the Lord helped us escape this water with our liv…" Bo did not finish his statement because Corrynne was kissing him full on the mouth.

"Hey, Mom! Dad!" came Rocwell's young voice. "Stop kissing and get us off this fence!"

Spirit World

Inside a sparkling white building, Dane was handed a brilliant robe. It was soft and warm, and shimmered as if it was made of a fabric that harnessed an unseen source of light. Dane put it on without a thought of why he had to wear it. Then he and his two guides walked through huge double golden doors into a new world.

As they exited the building, Dane stopped to take in the sights. The place where he and his two spirit guides had arrived was so beautiful—more glorious than anything Dane had ever seen on the earth! They stood on a golden road[1] and there were many shimmering, white buildings all around them.

Dane's eyes moved from one structure to the next. On some buildings there were tall golden steeples, on others, glorious broad, thick arches. There were balconies and pillars, and huge stately doorways everywhere. Buildings further away seemed to have jewels embedded into the walls, creating sparkling prisms of light.[2]

Dane was awestruck. Everything was bathed in vibrantly colored light. There were no shadows; the sky was clear and blue, the colors of the grass ranged from a brilliant green to a bluish-green and plants were endowed with thousands—no millions of blossoms![3]

"This is more beautiful than I would ever have guessed." Dane whispered, feeling warmth and light filter through him. He turned to one of the spirits, "Are we in heaven?"

"Yes," one of the spirits said. "It is *a* heaven."[4]

"You may know it as 'Spirit Paradise,'"[5] said the other, motioning with an upturned hand as if to present the new dimension to Dane.

Dane smiled widely as he remembered sitting in seminary, wondering what paradise in the spirit world looked like. Now that he was here, it was almost too good to be true! "Well, *this* is what I call *paradise!*" Dane said, smiling and nodding to his companions. "I feel like I've just won a trip to the Bahamas! This is *sweet!*" Dane's demeanor became more subdued. "Yes, I could live here!"

"Would you like to look around?" asked one of his guides.

"Yeah!" said Dane, continuing to take in every detail. "But to be honest, I'm kind of surprised there are buildings and grass here. I guess I expected clouds, harps, and lots of people milling around and singing hymns." Looking down the empty city road Dane asked, "Where are all the people? I don't see *anyone*. Did the dinner bell ring?"

The spirit on the right answered with a smile, "Everyone in the spirit world is very busy with work that takes him or her to other parts of the spirit world."

"What kind of work?" For some reason it was surprising to Dane that people *were doing something* in heaven.

The spirit on the left explained, "Some are serving missions, teaching truth to those who did not have it while in mortality,[6] others are administering to their loved ones on the earth.[7] Many have been called as angels in preparation for the Second Coming of Christ to the earth."[8]

Dane had serge of energy. "I had no idea. I guess there is no rest for the weary![9] No wonder the good die young!" Dane laughed, then hearing no response from the spirits, he changed the subject.

Dane looked down and studied the road again, stamping his foot on the gold bricks beneath his feet. "...So are gold bricks in heaven cheaper when they're made out of spirit gold?" Dane laughed loudly at his own joke. He was feeling more and more like his old self.

The angels looked at him blankly.

"Ah...never mind," said Dane, clearing his throat out of habit.

One of the spirit beings stretched out his arm, gesturing that they were to walk down the bright vacant street.

Dane nodded, "I see," he said, "you want me to 'follow the yellow brick road?'" Dane was sure he would get a laugh from that one.... "You know, Toto...and Dorothy?" He stood waiting for some kind of response.

The angels smiled politely.

Dane shook his head and began to walk, "You guys have got to get out more!"

As the three walked down the road together, the angel on the right introduced himself, "My name is David and this is Jonah."[10]

"David and Jonah. Those seem to be pretty normal names," commented Dane. "Why don't I know you?"

"You do." David and Jonah looked at Dane as if they expected him to recognize them.

Dane was confused, but as he tried to remember these two guys before him, a vague recollection of his two associates began to take form. Like light dew, a familiar feeling enveloped him; he felt as if these two were close, kindred spirits. "Are we related?" Dane asked, "Because, I think I'm beginning to remember you—both of you."

Jonah and David stopped walking. Dane stopped too, anticipating their answer. Jonah put his hand upon Dane's left shoulder and affirmed, "We are part of your family. We are sealed to your mother and your grandparents;

therefore, we're also sealed to you. Our earthly names were Ryan Douglas and Bryan Joseph. We were your uncles, but you never knew us on earth."

As Jonah released his grip, David nodded, "Indeed, we knew each other well before your mortality began on earth."

"Really?" Dane concentrated on the two spirits. He looked from David to Jonah then back to David. They were exactly alike in their appearance. Everything was the same, from the shape of their noses down to the toes of their feet. Their skin was perfect; there were no blemishes or marks such as moles or freckles. Their skin glowed with translucent brightness, almost like a white bulb glows through a white lampshade. Their hair was pure white, like fresh snow. Not like the graying of old age, but a soft, pure, healthy white. It was cut conservatively, just like missionary haircuts back on earth. They each wore a white loose fitting robe of exquisite glistening fabric, with an opening at the neck. The robes fell gently from their shoulders to their ankles. Their feet were bare and they did not wear jewelry or other dressings on their heads or bodies.

Dane's attention was drawn to the color of David and Jonah's eyes. He tried to recall what they reminded him of...they looked hot—like...fire! Yes, that was exactly it! They were a hot blue-white color found in the heart of the hottest fires.[11]

Wondering at their similarities, Dane couldn't resist asking David and Jonah the obvious question, "Why do the two of you look so much alike? Does everyone here look like you?" Dane stifled a laugh. It was obvious his humor wasn't working in this sphere.

David and Jonah looked at each other. David shook his head and said, "No—*you* don't look like us."

Dane looked down at himself and realized they were right. He still looked the same as he had on earth. He had the same large, sturdy hands, the big awkward feet (now sticking out from the hem of his robe), and the bulky body. Dane looked back up at the angels and asked, "What—do you have to pass some test to earn your 'alikeness' or something? Is it a club? When do I get a membership?"

David answered Dane as he turned to walk up the street once more, "We choose to look this way. We can appear as we might have appeared on earth, or change our appearance to match our spiritual maturity."[12]

"So this is not how you looked on earth? Why? Were you really ugly?" Again Dane laughed.

The spirits continued their serious attitude, "Maybe," Jonah replied. "We didn't get a chance to find out."

Dane began to worry that he was getting himself in more trouble with all the questions, but he was curious, "...Why?"

David answered, "We died as infants. Didn't your mother ever tell you about the brothers that her mother lost in childbirth?"

Jonah added, "We were identical twins."

Dane was sorry he had made light of their conversation. "Oh, I'm so stupid. That was so stupid of me to pry into your business. Yes, now that I think about it, she did tell me. I just didn't make the connection."

Jonah reached out and hugged Dane, filling him with a pure knowledge that they understood Dane's embarrassment, and that he had no need to be concerned. In the same moment, he received a flood of crystal clear memories. He knew who these two individuals were! Yes, what they said was true. They were the twins that his grandmother had lost in childbirth. Dane was elated. "Yes, I remember now! You are my uncles!"[13]

Jonah and David both bowed their heads in acknowledgement.

"It is so great to finally meet you—or re-meet you!" Dane reached out his hand.

Both spirits allowed Dane to shake their hands vigorously.

Dane looked at the two young men before him. "Hey, when you gave me that bear hug, I saw everything! I remembered everything. In an instant, I knew it all! That was a cool trick... How did you tell me all of that without talking?"[14]

"Soon you will relearn the ways of the spirit." David reassured Dane.

"So, I'll go around hugging everyone when I talk to them? ...Personally I think that's kind of weird."

David answered quickly, "No, soon, if you wish, you'll be able to communicate with your thoughts and emotions. The hug was for your perspective and familiar benefit."

"Oh good." Dane was relieved. "I was never good at the hugging thing."[15]

Notes to "Eternal Purposes"

Spirit World

[1] Joseph Smith was given a vision of the celestial kingdom in which he noticed not only the beauty of the kingdom, but also that the roads were paved with gold.

"The heavens were opened upon us, and I beheld the celestial kingdom of God, and the glory thereof, whether in the body or out I cannot tell. I saw the transcendent beauty of the gate through which the heirs of that kingdom will enter, which was like unto circling flames of fire; Also the blazing throne of God, whereon was seated the Father and the Son. I saw the beautiful streets of that kingdom, which had the appearance of being paved with gold" (D&C 137:1-4).

[2] Heber C. Kimball reported an account of the spirit world told by Jedediah Grant, a member of the first presidency of the church at that time, speaking of the beautiful buildings in the spirit world, after passing into the spirit world, having to return again to his body.

"He also spoke of the buildings he saw there, remarking that the Lord gave Solomon wisdom and poured gold and silver into his hands that he might display his skill and ability, and said that the temple erected by Solomon was much inferior to the most ordinary buildings he saw in the spirit world" (Heber C. Kimball, *Journal of Discourses*, Vol. 4, 135-36).

[3] President David O. McKay saw a vision of a celestial sphere testifying of foliage and a clear sky. "I...beheld in a vision something infinitely sublime. In the distance I beheld a beautiful white city. Though far away, I seemed to realize that trees with luscious fruit, shrubbery with

gorgeously tinted leaves, and flowers in perfect bloom abounded everywhere. The clear sky above seemed to reflect these beautiful shades of color" (*Journal of Discourses*, Vol. 14, 302).

Jedediah Grant also saw beautiful foliage in the spirit world. "I have seen good gardens on this earth, but never saw any to compare with those that were there. I saw flowers of numerous kinds, and some with from fifty to a hundred different colored flowers growing upon one stalk. We have many kinds of flowers on the earth, and I suppose those very articles came from heaven, or they would not be here" (*Journal of Discourses*, Vol. 4, 135-36).

[4] "This term [Paradise] has several meanings in the scriptures. It is first of all the place where God lives and the future home of the saints (Genesis 28: 12; Psalms 11: 4; Matthew 6: 9). It also means the expanse around the earth, as the heavens (Genesis 1: 1, 17; Exodus 24: 10). It is usually thought of as being "up," or above the earth (Alma 18: 30-32). In the sense of being God's home and the ultimate place for the faithful, it is clearly distinguished from paradise, which is the temporary abode of the faithful spirits of persons who have lived and died on this earth. Jesus visited paradise after his death on the cross, but on the third day thereafter, he informed Mary that he had not yet been to the Father" (see Luke 23:39-44; John 20: 17)" ("Heaven," Bible Dictionary).

[5] "And then shall it come to pass, that the spirits of those who are righteous are received into a state of happiness, which is called paradise, a state of rest, a state of peace, where they shall rest from all their troubles and from all care, and sorrow" (Alma 40:12).

[6] "...I perceived that the Lord went not in person among the wicked and the disobedient who had rejected the truth, to teach them; But behold, from among the righteous, he organized his forces and appointed messengers, clothed with power and authority, and commissioned them to go forth and carry the light of the gospel to them that were in darkness, even to all the spirits of men; and thus was the gospel preached to the dead" (D&C 138: 29-30).

[7] "Without question there are occasions upon which those from the other side of the veil reach out to bless and protect those of us in mortality. Numerous scriptural texts attest to such a thing. Of those who keep their covenant to magnify their priesthood, the Lord said, 'I have given the heavenly hosts and mine angels charge concerning you' (D&C 84:42). Of his missionaries he said, 'And whoso receiveth you, there I will be also, for I will go before your face. I will be on your right hand and on your left, and my Spirit shall be in your hearts, and mine angels round about you, to bear you up' (D&C 84:88). Of those who have been endowed in the temple and have received the promise of protection there, the Lord said they would go forth from his house armed with power, and his name would be upon them, his glory round about them, and, he added 'angels have charge over them'" (D&C 109:22) (Joseph Fielding McConkie, *Answers; Straightforward Answers to Tough Gospel Questions*, 113).

[8] The word "angels," refers to "...Messengers of the Lord, and are spoken of in the epistle to the Hebrews as 'ministering spirits' (Hebrews 1: 14). We learn from latter-day revelation that there are two classes of heavenly beings who minister for the Lord: those who are spirits and those who have bodies of flesh and bone. Spirits are those beings who either have not yet obtained a body of flesh and bone (unembodied), or who have once had a mortal body and have died, and are awaiting the resurrection (disembodied). Most often angels that administer in the flesh to the flesh are those that are resurrected beings" ("Angels," Bible Dictionary, 608).

The tasks of angels to the earth, to prepare the earth for the Second Coming, are many. Consider the following scriptures:

"Behold, verily I say unto you, the angels are crying unto the Lord day and night, who are ready and waiting to be sent forth to reap down the fields" (D&C 86:5).

"And the lesser priesthood continued, which priesthood holdeth the key of the ministering of angels and the preparatory gospel" (D&C 84:26).

"And angels shall fly through the midst of heaven, crying with a loud voice, sounding the trump of God, saying: Prepare ye, prepare ye, O inhabitants of the earth; for the judgment of our God is come. Behold, and lo, the Bridegroom cometh; go ye out to meet him" (D&C 88:92).

"And the four angels were loosed, which were prepared for an hour, and a day, and a month, and a year, for to slay the third part of men" (Revelation 9:15).

[9] All righteous spirits in Paradise are very busy doing the work of the Lord. See this statement from President Wilford Woodruff: "I will say here that in my dreams I have had a great many visits from the Prophet Joseph since his death. The last time I met him was in the spirit world. I met him at the temple. He spoke to me. Calling me by name, he said, 'I cannot stop to talk to you, for I am in a hurry.' I met Father Smith. He, too, said to me, 'I am in a hurry.' I met a great many of the Apostles and others who are in the spirit world, and they all seemed to be in a hurry. I marveled at this, and wondered very greatly in my mind why anybody should be in a hurry in the Paradise of God. I had an interview with the Prophet Joseph afterwards and asked him the question, 'Why are you all in such a hurry here?' I said, 'I have always been in a hurry in the world since I was born, but I thought there would be no occasion for it when I died and entered the spirit world.' He replied, 'Well, I will tell you: The Prophets and Apostles in this dispensation have had no time nor opportunity to prepare themselves to go to the earth with the great bridegroom when He goes to meet the bride, the Lamb's wife. We in this dispensation have not had time. We have first as much work to perform, to prepare ourselves, as in other dispensations.' He said the time was at hand for the coming of the Son of Man, for Christ to go forth in fulfillment of revelation and prophecy, to meet the bride, the Lamb's wife, the Church and Kingdom of God upon the earth. Says he, 'That is not revealed to us, nor never will be until the hour comes; but we have much work to do to prepare ourselves for the event'" (Wilford Woodruff, *General Conference*, October 4, 1890).

[10] "Spirits will be familiar with spirits in the spirit world—will converse, behold, and exercise every variety of communication with one another as familiarly and naturally as while here in tabernacles. There, as here, all things will be natural, and you will understand them as you now understand natural things" (Brigham Young, *Discourses of Brigham Young*, 380).

[11] The descriptions of the spirits match that of heavenly beings recorded in the scriptures. See Joseph Smith History 1:32, D&C 110:3, Revelation 1:12-16.

[12] "On the earth-plane, our rigid garment of clay makes it fairly difficult for us to change our appearance very greatly; but in the after-world, a spirit may, so it would seem, assume at will any stage of its previous earth life, with the very appearance of clothes worn at the time, including the peculiarities of personal bearing and mental traits" (Professor N. L. Nelson, "The Veil: Its Uses and Abuses", *Improvement Era*, March, 1929 Vol. 33, No. 5).

[13] "The spirits of our children are immortal before they come to us, and their spirits, after bodily death, are like they were before they came. They are as they would have appeared if they had lived in the flesh, to grow to maturity, or to develop their physical bodies to the full stature of their spirits. If you see one of your children that has passed away it may appear to you in the form in which you would recognize it, the form of childhood; but if it came to you as a messenger bearing some important truth, it would perhaps come as the spirit" (Joseph F. Smith, "The Salvation of Little Children," *Teachings of Presidents of the Church*, 128).

[14] Often in near death experiences, communication between spirits is managed through spirit to spirit exchange of information that can happen instantaneously.

"Communication was different—it was not English—it was communication of thought. When He spoke, words were used, but I can't tell you what they were. It was more a conveyance of knowledge. Later, I was able to recollect the ideas of the second coming the resurrection, and the redemption" (from an interview with "David," as quoted by Arvin Gibson, *Journeys beyond Life*, 166).

"...The voice persisted, not in my ears, but in my mind...I wondered how I could hear with my mind and not my ears, and I learned that it wasn't necessary for me to understand the process just then" (from an interview with "DeLynn," as quoted by Arvin Gibson, *Journeys beyond Life*, 188).

[15] "Spirits are just as familiar with spirits as bodies are with bodies, though spirits are composed of matter so refined as not to be tangible to this coarser organization. They walk, converse, and have their meetings" (Brigham Young, *Discourses of Brigham Young*, 379).

CHAPTER FIVE

BLESSINGS IN DISGUISE

"For the eyes of the Lord are over the righteous, and his ears are open unto their prayers: but the face of the Lord is against them that do evil" (1 Peter 3:12).

00:09:04 16:40:10 Zulu
Saturday, March 26th
12:20 a.m.
Provo, Utah
University Avenue

Prayers of the Righteous

The fence, which had saved the Rogers' lives, marked the perimeter of an office complex comprised of five large buildings standing end to end. The buildings lay parallel to the sheer side of a mountain, which rose abruptly out of the river bottoms. Bo, Corrynne, Brea, Jax and Ry were able to climb over the fence and then swim across a flooded parking lot. Bo, being the strongest swimmer, swam on his back with both twins on his chest, while Corrynne and Brea took turns coaxing and pushing Roc along as he struggled to make the distance. Ry and Jax swam independently for higher ground without a problem.

Up near the offices, the adults carried the smaller children as Jax and Ry worked hard to keep up with their parents. For the eleven and nine year-olds, the chest deep water caused every step to be a struggle; consequently, the going was extremely slow for everyone.

Strykker snuggled comfortably into Corrynne's neck and shoulder. Luckily, he was far from the threatening world, softly snoring in peaceful sleep. Rocwell had also fallen asleep. Bo carried him in one arm. Striynna rode in Brea's arms, fighting slumber and silently watching the dark world through wide eyes. It seemed she was on alert for any further danger.

They were heading south with the current. The street that would lead them east, up into the benches of Provo, towards BYU and the temple, was still a ways in front of them. Going up the mountain was an obvious choice, but to be close to the temple at a time like this struck Corrynne as symbolic. What better place could they be than at the temple? The Lord's house always offered shelter from the storms of life, but this time the safety was physical as well as spiritual![1]

Another benefit in going up the mountain was that BYU had an extensive emergency plan for not only the campus, but also for the community.[2] She had heard about it when she attended BYU for her nursing degree. It was comforting to know that just up the hill, her family would be well taken care of.

Corrynne smiled. She was still buzzing inside from the overwhelming feeling of thankfulness she had for the Lord because he had seen fit to save her little family. Even waist deep in water, without a home to return to, she looked up into the brilliantly star-lit sky and whispered a heartfelt "thank you" to the Father who knows all.[3]

Looking down, Corrynne noticed how brave her two sons were being. Jax carried the two empty adult sized backpacks they had used to stabilize the raft and Ry carried a child's 72-hour kit, the only one they had managed to salvage intact.

"How are you guys doing?" Corrynne asked both boys. "You're being very quiet."

"Fine," said Jax.

"Yeah, fine," said Ry.

"Are you cold?"

Jax nodded and then said, "I was really cold back on that fence, but once I got into the water I felt warmer."

Ry finished the thought, "Yeah, I think this water seems warmer than the water in the street."

Corrynne took inventory of her own hips and legs, and realized it was true. "What do you think, Bo? Is it possible this water is actually warmer here?"

Bo looked thoughtfully at Corrynne and shrugged. "Well, it's not bath water, but it's definitely warmer than that icy run-off I was swimming in a little while ago."

"Why do you think that is?" asked Corrynne.

Bo thought for a moment. "A few reasons—first, the water is stagnant here. We're in an artificial inlet and out of turbulent water, so any warmth left over from the sun shining onto the mountains and the buildings is transferred into the water. The water becomes warmer because it doesn't flow off."

"Ah," said Corrynne.

"And these buildings are heated," continued Bo. "The higher temperature would naturally radiate into the water too."

"Good point," said Corrynne, wondering why she hadn't thought of those things. She guessed she wasn't as mechanically minded as Bo.

"I also suspect these sidewalks and the surrounding parking lots have 'snow-melt' devices."

"What are those, Dad?" asked Jax.

"Antifreeze, steam, or water circulates and melts the snow so the sidewalks and parking lots won't be covered with snow and ice in the winter."[4]

"Wow! That's smart, Dad. Let's put those heating things in our cement at home so we don't have to shovel snow," said Jax.

"Yes, that would be a good idea wouldn't it? Maybe we will," said Bo. "We might need to rebuild anyway…."

The odd sound of Bo's voice caused Corrynne to look at him. She noticed that he had a faraway stare. He seemed to be bothered about something. She couldn't blame him though; he had much to be bothered about. She tried to be positive and help him see the bright side of things. They all needed to think positively for the sake of survival.[5]

"I'm so thankful we aren't freezing! We could so easily be somewhere else and be hypothermic!" Corrynne said, trying to encourage her family.

"What's hypo-ther…" began Ry.

"It means cold," interrupted Jax.

"You know what else?" said Brea catching on to her mother's optimism. "I was noticing that normally at the end of March, it's a lot colder outside than it is right now. Did you notice that too, Mom?"

"You're right," said Corrynne winking at Brea. "Often March is when we have snow, but it seems like a spring night." Turning to talk to her sons she said, "We'll have to thank Heavenly Father for helping us so much, huh guys?"[6]

"I already have!" said Ry. "I've thanked him a thousand times."

"You have not," said Jax to his little brother.

"I have too!"

"Hey guys, look!" said Corrynne trying to distract her sons from quarreling. "We're almost to the edge of the mountain. Then we'll finally get out of the water. That will be good won't it? Do you think you can make it that far?"

"Sure, Mom," said Jax.

"Now that I'm not so cold anymore, I bet I could walk all the way to the moon and back!" said Ry, nodding.

"You could not!" Jax repeated.

"Hey, that's enough! Stop picking on each other!" said Bo.

"But he always exaggerates! It bugs me!" said Jax as he hit the water with his hand, making a cold splash.

Corrynne reached out to Jax and Ry and touched each of them on the shoulder. "I'm proud of both of you guys. Tonight has been difficult, but you're both being very brave. Thank you so much!"

Relative silence bathed the group for a few moments as all were absorbed in their own thoughts.

Corrynne took advantage of the silence and prayed with a swollen heart. With every step she took, she thanked Heavenly Father for their safety, and added a plea for her son and daughter who were still unaccounted for; a prayer that she would repeat until she was reunited with them.

"I wish we had a cell phone," said Corrynne, reflecting her desire to talk to Dane and Carea.

"Mom, I have mine," said Brea as she reached toward the back pocket of her jeans. "That is if it hasn't fallen out of my pants."

"Really? Why haven't we used it to get help?" asked Corrynne.

"When did we have a chance?" asked Brea as she handed the phone to her mother. "I know I didn't have extra hands to open the phone while I was pumping up the raft, paddling for my life…or hanging from that fence back there."

Corrynne smiled and said, "Thank you, Brea." as she took the wet phone in one hand, switched Strykker's weight to her other arm, and then opened the phone. "I hope it will work. It's all wet."

Brea readjusted Striynna into a cradling position; she was finally beginning to sleep. "I don't know why it wouldn't, it's waterproof. All the phones are now," said Brea.

"I guess you're right." Corrynne dialed the phone number to call Dane. She put the phone to her ear and waited. "It's ringing!" she said excitedly. But then she heard a callous, recorded voice announce that all the lines were busy and to try again later. "No—it's busy. That's strange that it rang before I got a busy signal."

"The circuits are probably jammed from the earthquake and the flood," said Bo. "Everybody around here is trying to call family."

"I thought satellites solved that problem!" said Corrynne in frustration.

"Well, they did for satellite phones," said Brea. "This is not a satellite phone. Remember? We went with the cheaper family plan."

"Oh, what were we thinking, Bo?" asked Corrynne facetiously. "Boy, we are really cheap!"

"Yep, I guess we're up a *creek* without a *paddle*," said Brea teasingly.

"That's not funny," scolded Corrynne playfully, then she laughed. "I have to admit, that was a good one, considering the situation we're in."

Bo shook his head. "*We're fine.* I'm sure the phones will be working in a little while. We just need to be *patient*," said Bo, not going along with the humor of the moment.

"I'm being patient, Dad," said Brea. "Aren't you being patient, Mom?"

"Yes, I think we all are being pretty patient," said Corrynne.

"It was just a joke," added Brea. "I'm trying to lighten the mood around here."

Bo did not respond to Brea's attempt to involve him in idle chitchat. The obvious pause made all of them realize that he was in a serious mood.

Corrynne changed the subject. "Don't you guys think it was bizarre that Imam Mahdi's broadcast was shown on every channel, right before the earthquake hit?"

Brea suddenly turned to her mother. "What was on every channel?" asked Brea.

Corrynne looked at her daughter for a moment in the moonlight, remembering the sequence of events that had happened just a few hours ago. She had forgotten that Brea was not in the room with the family when they watched Dane on television.

"Oh, that's right, you didn't get to see the amazing performance of your brother and sister on TV, did you?" she asked Brea.

"Dane and Carea? Ah—no," said Brea with a puzzled look. "I was sleeping like a normal human being. It was late! What were they doing on TV?"

"Well, remember how Carea couldn't eat or sleep? Remember that she was looking very thin?"

Brea nodded. "Of course. I was worried about her. I wanted to ask you if you thought she was anorexic."

"No, she isn't anorexic." Corrynne shook her head. "At least not intentionally." She continued, "You did know that she had a tracking chip implanted under the skin on her forehead."

"What? No! *No one told me this!*" said Brea emphatically.

"Please don't go through the whole story!" interjected Jax. "All we've heard lately is about Carea and her *stupid* headaches."

"Jax, that was not a nice thing to say!" exclaimed Corrynne.

"I'm sorry, Mom, but I think she's faking everything to get what she wants."

"No, you don't know what you are talking about, so you need to be quiet," Corrynne warned her son.

"No really, Mom! I haven't seen any cuts on her forehead!" Jax continued defensively.

"Tell her the whole story later, Corrynne," said Bo in a monotone voice.

Corrynne stopped arguing with her son and looked at Bo. He seemed to be getting very tired. He looked like he was aging right before her eyes. Corrynne decided that for Bo's sake, she would abbreviate the detailed story. "To make a long story short, we believe the Bats implanted a computer tracking chip under her skin."

"That's crazy!" exclaimed Brea, "When did they do that?"

"During the time she disappeared."

"How do you know it was a chip that was implanted?" asked Brea.

"Because, despite Jax's conclusions, she *did* have a small incision near her hairline and a Bat tattoo on her back. It was the only conclusion that made sense."

"A tattoo?" asked Brea.

"A tattoo?" asked Jax. "Carea has a tattoo? Whoa! I didn't know that! Do those go with the tracking chips?"

"Yeah, that's so cool!" said Ry almost at the same time. "I didn't know that either!"

"No! It's not cool!" Corrynne snapped. "Tattoos are *not* cool, especially when someone puts them on your body without your permission!"

Brea shook her head. "Boy, I move right outside the door of the house, and suddenly everyone goes crazy and no one tells me anything about it!"

"I think it's because you were working so hard on your wedding plans," said Corrynne. "It isn't fair to burden you with extra family dilemmas. We've been trying to leave you alone."

"Mom! You know better than that! I'm always interested in what happens in your lives."

Corrynne looked lovingly at her daughter. "OK, I'm sorry."

"So she has a Bat tattoo on her back?" asked Brea, returning to the subject of her sister.

"Yes, she does. Your dad and I saw it."

"Hmmm," said Brea, thoughtfully hugging the sleeping Striynna closer. Then she relaxed. "Tell me why you think the incision on her forehead is from inserting a chip...you are talking about the same kind of chip inserted in Dane's hand right?"

Corrynne paused, then with the sound of relief in her voice continued, "We think so. However, we believe it is a much more advanced kind, capable of strong mental influence.[7] Ever since Carea came back to the house after it was implanted, she has been acting strangely. She hasn't been at all like herself."

"Is that like mind control?"

"Yes, similar."

"Hmmm," Brea paused. "That's very interesting. We haven't heard about those kinds yet."

"Who are 'we'?" asked Corrynne.

"The nurses at the nursing school."

"Oh," Corrynne nodded. "I see."

Brea continued. "It must be a larger chip than the ones I've seen, because the technology today is such that those tracking chips are injected with a needle. They are very small, so the kind Carea has must be a couple centimeters long."

"How do you know so much about this?" asked Corrynne.

"We've been studying that technology at school. In France and Germany, they are becoming the trend; I mean everyone wants one to track their loved ones. But in America, if the chips aren't embedded into an elderly person, or a child, or even a dog[8] for obvious tracking needs, the chips are a huge, red flag warning to the government. We, meaning the new nurses about to receive licensure, have even been given hand held instruments that sound an alarm when you wave them over someone who has a chip."

"Why?" asked Corrynne. She worried about the government's involvement. Knowing that two of her children had chips, she had an ominous feeling in the pit of her stomach. "Why do they want to know if someone has a computer tracking chip?"

"According to a U.S. Security Council Report we were given just last week, of those who have tracking chips between the ages of 12 and 65, 80% of them have been proven to be involved in destructive behavior. The FBI stated in the article I read, that an international terrorism campaign with Middle Eastern connections is powering the movement," said Brea.

"What? Terrorism? Are you sure?"

Brea nodded. "Well, yes, Mom. I'm sure."

Now things were beginning to fall together in a scary way. "I do know that on Imam Mahdi's Web site...." Corrynne's voice faltered.

"What, Mom?"

"The word BEASTS meant 'Break Everything After Striking Terror Systematically,' and Imam Mahdi has very strong Middle Eastern connections."

"Yes, that makes sense, Mom. The Bats were named in the report as one of the groups we should watch for. They've been directly linked to suicide bombers and sniper assassinations here in America."

"Doesn't that sound like what has happened in Israel?"

"Yes, car bombs and suicide bombers are cheap and effective. The report mentioned that point, too. That's why all hospital staff and policing agencies will soon need to have a sensing device to identify chips under the skin. That way, we can recognize and monitor those people before they do something deadly in our communities."[9]

Corrynne shook her head in an effort to rid herself of the thought she was having. She understood the logic behind the government's decisions, but she couldn't get over the idea that her children were in danger of being categorized as Bats and judged unfairly. "None of that sounds very good. I'm afraid of how this could play out for Dane and Carea."

Brea's eyes reflected sudden understanding. "Oh, I see what you mean. But Dane and Carea are not Bats. None of this should bother them."

"I hope not," said Corrynne. "It's easy for the government to make assumptions about strangers; especially when there's fear in the air."

"I really don't think it will go that far," responded Brea.

"I don't know. I've got a bad feeling about this," said Corrynne. "What do you think, Bo?"

Bo frowned. "I think we should just focus on the problems at hand."

"I agree," said Brea.

Corrynne forced a smile. "You guys are right. I've got to keep thinking positively."

Brea looked down and shook her head. "All I know is that to get my nursing license, I have to swear that I will report anyone with a chip for further evaluation, just as I have to turn in anyone who is involved in drugs or abuse."

"I'm sure I'll be hearing about this in the hospital soon if you're learning about it already," said Corrynne.

"I'm sure of it," said Brea.

"Do you have to turn in Carea and Dane?" Jax asked Brea.

Brea paused. "You, know—I didn't think about that. Do you think I have to, Mom? Both of them received their chips by accident and against their will. I don't think that really counts."

Corrynne laughed, although she wasn't at all happy. "Accidentally? Who is going to believe that excuse? That's exactly what I was talking about. Both Dane and Carea are from the same family, and in the high-risk age group. What else does the government need to know before they jump to conclusions?" She shook her head, frustrated that she had allowed herself an outburst at such a critical time. She didn't know how to answer Brea. It was true that Dane and Carea had appeared on international TV at a Bat meeting. How could they not be suspected of deeper involvement? The whole thing was ridiculous!

Corrynne wondered how they could keep their children away from government agencies and avoid the obvious potential entanglements. "Bo, I don't want to hammer this point into the ground, but do you think Dane and Carea, and Imam Mahdi, were really seen all over the world? I sincerely hope they weren't!"

Bo frowned more deeply, but remained calm. "Yes, I'm afraid there is no other conclusion. They were on every channel, both local and satellite. We'll know more after we see some media coverage about the whole thing."

"Tell me about this TV show," prompted Brea.

Ry tapped Brea with a finger. "Carea and Dane were on TV when the earthquake started. We saw them," he said with a smile.

"Yeah! We saw Dane totally kick Imam Mahdi's butt!" said Jax irreverently and then he laughed.

"What? Dane got into a fight?" asked Brea, looking back and forth between her mother and father.

"We're not sure what happened," said Bo shaking his head. "It looked like Imam Mahdi hijacked all the television station signals. He apparently intended to declare himself as the King, or the Messiah to the world, but things went very wrong for him."

"Really? So what happened?" asked Brea.

Corrynne answered for Bo. "His plans were sidetracked. He became extremely angry, and challenged Dane and Carea publicly because they called him a fake."

"Yes? Keep going," urged Brea.

"His plan backfired," said Bo simply.

"When the earthquake started, a metal beam fell from the ceiling and hit Imam Mahdi right in the head. It knocked him flat, and I don't think he'll be getting up any time soon, if you know what I mean," said Corrynne trying to be discrete.

"Is *that* what happened?" asked Jax. "I can't believe I missed it!"

"It's good that you missed it. I couldn't watch because it was so gruesome," said Corrynne.

"Cool!" said Ry as he snickered.

"Do you think the Lord intervened and caused that earthquake just to shut Imam Mahdi's mouth?" asked Brea.

"It's possible.[10] The earthquake seemed to begin right under Imam Mahdi, because *we* didn't feel it until a few minutes later."

"So, if the Lord caused the earthquake, do you think he caused Deer Creek Dam to break too?" asked Jax thoughtfully.

"No, the Lord didn't cause the dam to break. It just broke because of the earthquake," said Brea.

"But God knows everything. He would have known the dam was going to break," said Jax.

"Sure. I'm sure he knew it was going to break," replied Brea.

"So why didn't he protect us?"[11] asked Jax.

"He did!" said Corrynne. "We're here, and you're alive aren't you? Think about it, first, the television show brought us together…"

"Yes, but…" interrupted Jax.

"…Then the earthquake moved us out of the house. The sirens warned us to escape the flood," continued Corrynne.

"The Lord has programs to teach survival skills to boys so they can learn how to help in emergency situations," said Bo. "That's why you knew how to tie the Bowline and square knots that helped us escape the car…"

"And," added Brea, "The Lord also asked us to have 72-hour kits to help us…"

"Yes, but we lost them all," said Jax.

"Maybe we did, but we were able to use the back packs to help us escape drowning," continued Brea. "We wouldn't have thought of bringing the packs unless they held the 72-hour kits."

"Well, *I didn't think of them*, but they hit me on the head," said Bo sarcastically.

"Good thing!" said Corrynne with a smile. "Some say that men don't know a good thing unless it hits them on the head! Is that you, Bo?"

"Maybe! If the Lord thinks so, then I guess it's true!" said Bo as he rubbed his wounded head.

Corrynne turned back to Jax and continued, "But think what else helped us. Because of the heated sidewalks and parking lot, we were able to stay warm so we didn't die of hypothermia. Do you understand Jax? He helped us many times; in fact, I'd say that he has gone beyond helping us. Because of the things he asked us to do to prepare for an emergency like this, he *saved* us."[12]

Jax twisted his face in thought, then said, "But we almost died lots of times."

"Yes, but we didn't," said Corrynne, determined to help her son realize his blessings. "We could have died, but we didn't. We were prepared, obedient, and resourceful. The Lord helped us think of things that we wouldn't have ordinarily. Many decisions were made tonight that hinged on urgings from the Lord."

"I know why we didn't die, Mom," said Ry.

"Why, Ry?"

"Remember? Because I prayed the whole time."

"So did I," said Brea.

"So? I did too! What's the point?" said Jax to Ry. "You're not the only one that prays around here...."

Corrynne gave Jax a stern look as a warning about his rudeness then continued the conversation. "The point is that we *prayed* and the Lord listened to us and helped us.[13] We need to recognize that blessing and thank him."[14]

"But, Mom, I don't think dying is bad. Lots of good people die,"[15] said Ry out of nowhere.

Ry's comment surprised Corrynne. "Ry," she said, "you're right. When you believe in eternal life, dying is just another step.[16] However, we need to realize that we are alive because it was the Lord's will."[17]

"I'm glad he wanted us to live," said Ry. "I'm not ready to die."

Ry's simple statement silenced the group. Corrynne was especially touched by it. She realized how hard this night would have been for her if she had lost any of her children. Oh how dependent she was on the Lord! She hadn't realized it so poignantly until now.

They were approaching the end of the business complex and the road was very close. Soon they would be able to climb onto some rocks and get out of the water.

"Hey, Bo, what do you think of all this?" asked Corrynne, wanting to hear her husband's ideas.

"Oh, I'm just listening to you guys."

"You are normally very involved in this kind of conversation, and you've only said a few things. Is there something wrong? You seem kind of distant."

"Oh, I'm feeling a little inundated. I have many things to think about. Lots to prepare for. Lots to live up to."

"What do you mean?"

"I'm wondering, somewhere in this foggy brain of mine, if I could have done more to protect Dane and Carea, but at the same time, I know what I did was right. I know I was *supposed* to let them leave the house during dinner. Now I see that the confrontation between Dane and Imam Mahdi was meant to take place, and that only happened because Dane followed Carea."

"You're right, Bo." Corrynne assured him.

"Maybe the Lord was tired of the damage Imam Mahdi was causing." Bo paused before continuing, "I know I was."

"And maybe the Lord wanted the world to see his end," added Corrynne.

"Yes—maybe," said Bo. "I'm just trying to hold on to my faith that Dane will be OK. He didn't look good at the end. But I know I was promised he would be all right, so I'm trying to trust that he will be. Later, once we get back to a normal life, I'll be grateful that Dane was able to participate in such an amazing experience. What stories he'll be able to tell on his mission! But another part of me is frustrated with having my hands tied concerning their welfare. I'm not used to having zero options."

"Sweetheart, remember the lecture you gave me. This situation is totally in the Lord's hands. We have to lean on him and trust that he will take care of Dane and Carea. We have to have faith that he is in charge. Now, it would be different if we didn't know what to expect, but we do. Seeing Dane perform so well under pressure in front of all those people, and in the face of such adversity, just solidified our roles. This time we are to be patient and trust the Lord."

Bo nodded but didn't reply.

Corrynne continued, "We need to be satisfied with what we can do. That's what I'm trying to do. I know I'm helpless right now! I have no car, no money, no food, no house, but I'll tell you what I do have…."

"What, Mommy?" asked Ry.

Corrynne smiled down at her son. "I have you, Ry. I have Jax and Roc. I have Striynna and Strykker; I have Brea who is so wonderful, and a husband who is strong, worthy and powerful. I have two sons out in the world being great examples, and a son and daughter who were willing to give up their lives, if needed, to fight for the Lord. I am so proud of all of us! I have absolutely everything I ever wanted! I know that together we can get through anything. We'll put our heads together and find solutions that will surprise us… and you know what else?"

"What?" asked Jax.

"We'll look back someday and be amazed at how much this experience helped us grow."

"You are so right, Corrynne," said Bo.

"Bo, release this tension you're feeling," said Corrynne, "and know that I believe you are a great father, even if you can't rescue everyone! We need you to be full of wisdom and strength while we wallow up to our eyeballs in flood water!"

Bo bowed his head and took a deep breath. "You're right. I'll try."

Changing the subject, Ry looked at Bo and said, "When can we go home, Dad?"

Bo sighed, "Well, probably not for a while I'm afraid."

"Why?"

"Because even if we did, there wouldn't be anywhere to live," said Jax.

"Why?" asked Ry again. "Are we homeless?"

Bo looked down again. "No, son, not if I can help it."

"Duh! We have a home, but it's just submerged," added Jax.

"Hey! I don't want to tell you again to be nice. Ry was just asking questions," warned Corrynne.

"I know, but he knows what happened," said Jax. "He's just acting dumb for attention."

Ry ignored his brother's statement and suddenly pointed to a place in front of them. "Hey, Dad, look, there are some rocks and a path! Good thing too, because the water has made me just as wrinkled as you!"

Bo smiled for the first time that night. "What are you saying? I have wrinkles because I'm getting old?" said Bo, playing along with the joke.

"Well, aren't you?"

"I guess...if you say so. OK, let's get everyone out of the water and dry off a little," responded Bo.

Bo stepped up first, changing Roc from his right arm to his left, and held his hand out to Corrynne. She took his hand and climbed onto a boulder leading to a higher ledge, then Jax, Ry and Brea climbed up by themselves.

"Well..." said Bo. "I think right here, right now would be a great place to offer a family prayer of thanks. We can ask for help, too..." Bo leaned out and looked at the path that led toward the road above them.

Corrynne looked too, and her heart sank a little when she saw that the mountain jutted out sharply, cutting off their access to the road, and the little path ahead eventually curved back into the churning water below the edge of the mountain. They must have been walking at an angle toward the side of the mountain. But Bo was right, there was only one way around and that was back into the cold, black, turbulent water. There was no way the whole family could make it without a boat. "What are we going to do Bo?"

"I don't know. That's why I thought it was a good time for all of us to pray. The Lord knows how we can make it. He's going to have to solve this one."

"OK. Let's do it," said Brea, as she knelt down in the dirt that was quickly becoming spattered mud from dripping clothes.

The rest of the family joined her.

"I'll say it," said Bo.

Corrynne nodded.

"Our dear Father in Heaven," began Bo. "We come before thee as a family to thank thee for our blessings. We thank thee that thou saw fit to protect us in such deadly situations, as when the earth quaked and the water rushed from the broken dam. We know that at any moment our lives could have been lost, and it was by thy hand that we were protected. How thankful we are for that, we cannot express in words…"

Bo paused for a few moments. Corrynne opened her eyes to see if he was going to continue, then she realized that he was filled with emotion. After a moment, he regained his composure and continued his prayer. Corrynne closed her eyes again.

"Father, we thank thee for our gifts and talents. Help us know how to use them to help others and ourselves rebuild our lives. Help us all to have hope and faith in thy abilities and know that thou will visit us in comfort, peace, and enlightenment and help us know what to do."

"Father, at this time we ask thee to protect Dane and Carea. Help them in whatever way they need, and let them know that we love them. We are worried about them, and can't wait to wrap our arms around them again. We have to rely on thee to be their shield against evil. Protect them from evil, for we know that they are surrounded and must find a way out of their situation. Please bless them with wisdom and a way back to us."

"Now," Bo continued, "we find ourselves in a precarious situation. After all that thou hast done for us, we can do no more for ourselves. Because of the children, it is impossible for us to go back into the deep, swift water to get to safety. We need to be rescued, or be shown a way for us to get around the edge of the mountain, so we can preserve our lives and the lives of our little ones. We have little food and water to sustain us and soon all of it will be gone. We need to go up the hill to where there are resources to help us. Please, Father, make us aware of thy plan and our responsibility so we can bring our family to safety.

"Again we are so thankful for thy help and obvious intervention on our behalf. In the name of Jesus Christ, amen."

"Amen," echoed the rest of the family.

Now they were at the total mercy of the Lord. Together, they would wait. A voice inside Corrynne told her that help would come, and she believed it.

Jenessa

Dane looked ahead along the golden road where he was walking with Jonah and David. Someone was standing on the path as if waiting for them.

"Who is that?" Dane asked them.

"That is Jenessa. She is to be your teacher while you are here. She is waiting for us," said David.

"Why do I need another teacher? I thought that since you guys are family you would stay with me."

"No, we have other things that demand our attention. We were only to welcome you and introduce you into this world. We were to make you feel comfortable," answered Jonah.

"Jenessa will now take over and prepare you further," added David.

"Prepare me for what?" asked Dane with wide eyes.

"Your mission," said the two together.

Dane looked from David to Jonah and then back again. "I'm going to be called on a mission? Do I get to go to the dark side? Maybe I can shed some light on Imam Mahdi. Oh I would love to see his distorted face right now!"

David shook his head. "No. You will not be given a mission here. You are to be prepared for another work. You are to return to the world and serve a glorious mission, calling the inhabitants of the world to repentance and life, both day and night before the Second Coming of Jesus, the Christ."

"Are you serious? I *am* going back?" Dane began to smile. He liked that idea. Life on earth wasn't so bad, although this place was beyond amazing.

"If you choose to," said Jonah nodding.

Dane rubbed his hands together, "Bring it on! I'm ready!" he said enthusiastically.

"Alright, let's meet Jenessa," said David.

The three spirits moved together to meet the girl. She was dressed in a white flowing gown that caressed her ankles. She stood relaxed, her form leaning slightly as she waited on the road. A smile crossed her face as they came closer. "Well, hello guys. So good of you to come."

"Hello, Jenessa," said David as he and Jonah nodded in greeting.

Jonah held out his hand to Dane and said, "Jenessa, I'd like you to meet Dane."

"Hello, Dane." The words rolled off Jenessa's tongue in a leisurely way. "I'm very glad to meet you." She properly held out her delicate hand.

Dane was taken with Jenessa. He shook her hand gently as he studied her features. She looked to be about twenty or so, with blue eyes that glowed and sparkled like there was a light dedicated only to them. Her nose was small, pointed, and regal. Long silky brown hair, with auburn highlights tumbled over her shoulders. There must have been a breeze, because wisps of it were softly caressing her cheeks.

"Ah…hello," said Dane, he felt tongue-tied with this attractive tutor of his.

Jenessa released her grasp and pulled her hand back. Dane was surprised at his absent-mindedness. He didn't know whether to apologize for holding her hand too long or make a joke, so he just remained silent.

Jenessa broke the silence. "I'm going to teach you some truths that will make you very effective on the earth. Are you ready?"

"Sure. But...I'm sorry. Who are you? Should I know you from somewhere?"

"Me? What do you mean? Who am I now? Or who was I on the earth?"

Dane shrugged. "Ah—both, I guess."

"On the earth, I was a master's student in the 1940's. My name was Sara Jacobson. I was the oldest of seven children. Since I did not marry, and I had a knack for science, my father sent me to college to become a physicist. I never became one, since I died young of pneumonia. Here, though, my knowledge and natural ability has been put to good use."

Dane fidgeted with his hands. "Yes, but are we related? You know, like Jonah, David and I are?" He looked at the twins for a second than at Jenessa.

Jenessa stopped and looked at Dane. It was as if she were peering into his mind to clarify his question. Then she smiled. "Oh no!" she said, with a soft lilting laugh. "We aren't related, other than spiritually. I've been called to be your teacher while you are here. That's what I do. I educate certain individuals and empower them with knowledge, so they will be more effective servants."

Dane was instantly relieved. "Oh, good—so we aren't second cousins or anything." He had hoped there were no barriers to prevent him from getting close to this amazing person who stood before him.

Jenessa smiled and said, "Nope. We can become real—'chummy.' Is that how you say it on earth?"

"Chummy?" Dane blushed. He wondered what Jenessa was getting at. Was he so transparent? He pretended to not understand.

"You know, good friends—chummy," Jenessa explained.

"Oh, yes, I guess some people say that," Dane nodded.

Jenessa continued, "Anyway, you have been chosen by Heavenly Father to be taught today. So I'll ask you again, are you ready?"

Dane's eyes grew wide with comprehension. He was expected to spend time with this—angel. What a blessing! Who could ask for more? Dane smiled contagiously. "Can we start right away?"

"Yes," said Jenessa. She nodded slowly, hiding a smile.

Dane swallowed. He would accept any excuse to talk to Jenessa. Dane suddenly barked, "Right! Yes! That's so great...."

Jenessa stifled a giggle and tried to maintain her composure. Then she said, "Dane, a word to the wise. You shouldn't think so loudly. You might embarrass yourself again."

Dane was instantly humiliated. Oh, that's right. Thoughts could be read here. Had she heard everything he thought about her? He was mortified. He needed to figure out how to edit his feelings, or his rambunctious personality would get the best of him again.

Jenessa placed a soft hand on Dane's arm. "Relax. Your thoughts carry loudly when they are driven by emotion."

"Oh." Dane took a deep breath to calm his jitters. "Sorry."

"No problem," said Jenessa. "You'll get used to how things work here. Soon you will be able to shield your thoughts whenever you choose."[18]

"I hope so."

Jenessa turned to David and Jonah. "I believe I'll take it from here. Thank you."

"You are welcome," said Jonah.

"Good luck, Dane. Take it slowly," said David.

Dane nodded. "Alright. See you around."

Notes to "Blessings in Disguise"

Prayers of the Righteous

[1] There may come a time in various parts of the world in which safety *from* the world is in reality related to our worthiness to go to the temple, as well as go *in* the temple.

"Let them, therefore, who are among the Gentiles flee unto Zion. And let them who be of Judah flee unto Jerusalem, unto the mountains of the Lord's house," (D&C 133:12-13).

"The temples…are as a refuge from life's storms—even a never-failing beacon guiding us to safety," (Thomas S. Monson, "The Temple of the Lord," *Ensign*, May 1993, 4).

"It would be the deepest desire of my heart to have every member of the Church be temple worthy. I would hope that every adult member would be worthy of—and carry—a current temple recommend, even if proximity to a temple does not allow immediate or frequent use of it. Be strengthened by the sanctity and safety which is provided within hallowed and consecrated walls of the house of the Lord," (Howard W. Hunter, *Ensign*, July 1994, p. 4).

[2] This is a factual statement.

The state of Utah (http://des.utah.gove/training/courses/Emplanning.html), The Church of Jesus Christ of Latter-day Saints, through the wards, and BYU (http://fhss.byu.edu/adm/College.htm) all have emergency plans and resources set aside for disasters for the people of the community.

[3] Paradoxically, often, when we have the least is when we feel the most grateful because we realize the great blessings of the simple things in life.

"I am grateful to have lived long enough to have known some of the blessings of adversity. My memory goes back to the Great Depression, when we had certain values burned into our souls. One of these values was gratitude for what we had, because we had so little. We learned provident living in order to survive. Rather than create in us a spirit of envy or anger for what we did not have, it developed in many a spirit of gratitude for the simple things with which we were blessed, like hot, homemade bread and oatmeal cereal.

"A grateful heart is a beginning of greatness. It is an expression of humility. It is a foundation for the development of such virtues as prayer, faith, courage, contentment, happiness, love, and well-being," (James E. Faust, "An Attitude of Gratitude," *New Era*, Nov. 1993, 4).

[4] The technology described in the text is a factual invention and is becoming more utilized in areas where it snows. See http://geoheat.oit.edu/pdf/tp108.pdf for more information.

[5] "We can lift ourselves, and others as well, when we refuse to remain in the realm of negative thought and cultivate within our hearts an attitude of gratitude. If ingratitude be numbered among the serious sins, then gratitude takes its place among the noblest of virtues," (Thomas S. Monson, "An Attitude of Gratitude," *Liahona*, May 2000, 2).

[6] "The Lord has admonished parents to teach their children to pray and to walk uprightly before him. (See D&C 68:28.) This is our most important obligation to our children—to teach

them that they are the spirit children of their Heavenly Father, that he is real, that he has great love for his children and wants them to succeed, that they should pray to him expressing gratitude and asking for guidance, realizing that faith in him will bring them greater strength and success and happiness than they can receive from any other source," (N. Eldon Tanner, "Importance and Efficacy of Prayer," *Ensign*, Aug. 1971, 2).

[7] This fictional storyline is built around implantable devices capable of mind influence that are factual and do exist. Most are being used other places in the world. See the following Internet address for an actual lawsuit, U.S. v. Lambros, 65 F3d 698 (8th Cir. 1995). This suit was initiated   to   stop   such   a   product   being   produced   in   Brazil http://www.brazilboycott.org/BrazilByct/proctor6.html.

[8] Tracking chips are more than factual; they are being marketed in America as medical and safety devices for the elderly, children, and pets. See the following:

"The chip will also know if your child has fallen and needs immediate help. Once paramedics arrive, the chip will also be able to tell the rescue workers which drugs little Johnny or Janie is allergic to. At the hospital, the chip will tell doctors his or her complete medical history. And of course, when you arrive to pick up your child, settling the hospital bill with your health insurance policy will be a simple matter of waving your own chip — the one embedded in your hand.

"To some, this may sound far-fetched. But the technology for such chips is no longer the stuff of science fiction. And it may soon offer many other benefits besides locating lost children or elderly Alzheimer patients.

"'Down the line, it could be used [as] credit cards and such,' says Chris Hables Gray, a professor of cultural studies of science and technology at the University of Great Falls in Montana. 'A lot of people won't have to carry wallets anymore,' he says. 'What the implications are [for this technology], in the long run, is profound.' Indeed, some are already wondering what this sort of technology may do to the sense of personal privacy and liberty. 'Any technology of this kind is easily abusive of personal privacy,' says Lee Tien, senior staff attorney for the Electronic Frontier Foundation. "If a kid is track-able, do you want other people to be able to track your kid? It's a double-edged sword,'" ...(Paul Eng, "I, Chip? Technology to meld chips into Humans Draws Closer" *ABCNEWS.com*, March 1, 2002, Online,   available: http://abcnews.go.com/sections/scitech/DailyNews/chipimplant020225.html).

[9] This is a storyline extrapolation and should be deemed as fictional.

[10] Due to wickedness, there was an earthquake at the time of Christ's death both in Israel and in America (Matthew 27:54, 1 Nephi 12:4). There was an earthquake that freed Paul and Silas from prison, (Acts 16:26). There are multiple prophesies that detail earthquakes in the latter days in direct reference to the wickedness of the world, (Mark 13:8, Luke 21:11, Revelation 11:13, Mormon 8:30, D&C 45:33, D&C 87:6).

[11] In the last days, times of tribulation will come. They will come to all of us. They are prophesied to come. It is our job to weather them well and know that God is aware of our needs and is in charge. It is not his job to help us avoid adversity, but to give us the wisdom and the courage to deal with the adversity.

"God is in His heavens, and His promises are sure. "Be not troubled," He has said to us concerning the destructions that will precede the end of the world, "for, when all these things shall come to pass, ye may know that the promises which have been made unto you shall be fulfilled" (D&C 45:35). What an anchor to the soul in these troubled times!" (Dallin H. Oaks, "Give Thanks in All Things," *Ensign*, May 2003, 95).

[12] "There is a law, irrevocably decreed in heaven before the foundations of this world, upon which all blessings are predicated—And when we obtain any blessing from God, it is by obedience to that law upon which it is predicated," (D&C 130:20-21).

[13] "And whatsoever we ask, we receive of him, because we keep his commandments, and do those things that are pleasing in his sight," (John 3:22).

[14] "In all thy ways acknowledge him, and he shall direct thy paths," (Proverbs 3:6).

[15] "We need not look upon death as an enemy. With full understanding and preparation, faith supplants fear. Hope displaces despair. The Lord said, "Fear not even unto death; for in this world your joy is not full, but in me your joy is full." (D&C 101:36.) He bestowed this gift: "Peace I leave with you, my peace I give unto you: not as the world giveth, give I unto you. Let not your heart be troubled, neither let it be afraid," (John 14:27) (Russell M. Nelson, "Doors of Death," *Ensign*, May 1992, 72).

[16] "Death hath passed upon all men, to fulfill the merciful plan of the great Creator." (2 Ne. 9:6.) Where the true Saints are concerned there is no sorrow in death except that which attends a temporary separation from loved ones. Birth and death are both essential steps in the unfolding drama of eternity.

"We shouted for joy at the privilege of becoming mortal because without the tests of mortality there could be no eternal life. We now sing praises to the great Redeemer for the privilege of passing from this life because without death and the resurrection we could not be raised in immortal glory and gain eternal life," (Bruce R. McConkie, "The Dead Who Die in the Lord," *Ensign*, Nov. 1976, 106).

[17] "For there is a time appointed for every man, according as his works shall be," (D&C 121:25).

"Therefore, hold on thy way, and the priesthood shall remain with thee; for their bounds are set, they cannot pass. Thy days are known, and thy years shall not be numbered less; therefore, fear not what man can do, for God shall be with you forever and ever," (D&C 122:9).

Jenessa
[18] This is a literary extrapolation. It is unknown if spiritual beings have a need to shield their thoughts.

CHAPTER SIX

SEPARATED LIVES

"Trust in the LORD with all thine heart; and lean not unto thine own understanding" (Proverbs 3:5).

00:09:04 16:36:45 Zulu
Saturday, March 26th
12:24 a.m.
Provo, Utah
Regional Medical Center

Arrest

Carea looked through the window of the helicopter as it hovered above the hospital. Bright flood lights illuminated the area, allowing her to see that the building was surrounded by a wall of sandbags; a protection from the water that continued its rush down the streets toward lower lying areas. People milling around the hospital looked like multicolored ants as they moved between medical tents. It was obvious to Carea that the earthquake and the flooding had injured many people.

The helicopter landed in the parking lot, and Dane's gurney was rapidly wheeled towards the hospital. Carea moved to follow, but two officers dressed in different uniforms stood in the doorway, blocking her path.

"What's wrong?" asked Carea looking back and forth between the two.

"Please come with us, Miss Rogers," said a large police officer with a crew cut.

"Why?" asked Carea cowering. "I need to be with my brother. He's very sick."

"We're taking you in for questioning," said the other officer who wore a green Army uniform.

Carea shook her head. "What questioning? Am I in trouble? I didn't do anything."

"We need to ask you questions about Imam Mahdi's organization."

"But, I don't know anything. I told the officers back at the mansion that I was being held against my will. I *really* don't know anything!"

"Yes, you may return after we record your statement," said the policeman with the crew cut. He stepped into the helicopter and took hold of Carea's arm, but she gently raised it and the policeman released his grip.

"How long will this take?" asked Carea as she looked at the Emergency room door. Dane's gurney was already out of sight.

"It depends on how much trouble you give us," said the police officer as he unhooked a pair of handcuffs from where they hung on his belt. "If you come with us voluntarily, everything will take less time."

Carea eyed the cuffs. She did not want her hands restrained. "You don't have to use those, I'll come with you, but you need to call my parents. I'm not eighteen, you know."

"Yes, everyone will be called," assured the military officer.

Carea was not sure if he was telling the truth. "I want to wake up from this nightmare!" she said forcefully, but neither of the officers responded. They led her to a tall military vehicle that was parked near the Emergency entrance.

Hummer

"*Hey!*" a voice called faintly from the darkness.

Jax turned to listen, but heard only the sound of gurgling, rushing water. He was beginning to shake from the cold as the slight wind brushed his wet clothes. "Dad! I…I thought I heard something!"

"I heard it too," said Brea, as she looked into the blackness of the night. "I think it was a man's voice. It sounded like it came from the middle of the water."

"Hey! Do you need help?" There it was again…only this time the voice was louder.

"Yes!" shouted Bo. "Where are you? We can't see you."

An arc flashed from about fifty yards beyond them. As Bo studied the horizon the clouds moved just enough that he could see the shape of a man who seemed to be sitting on the surface of the water.

"I see him!" yelled Ry as he pointed and moved to the edge of the overhang so he could get a better view. "He-he's over there!"

"Stay where you are, and I'll be there in a minute," called the stranger, and then to their amazement, he disappeared beneath the water. The clouds moved across the moon, and once again they stood in darkness.

"Where did he go, Dad?" asked Jax as he moved closer to his father.

"He just disappeared!" exclaimed Ry. "Is he swimming?" He looked at his father then back out to the water.

"I don't know. Keep a look out for him," said Bo as he readjusted Roc's weight on his shoulder and looked out to the water. He was standing just behind Jax and Ry. "If he's under the water, he'll have to come up for air soon."

The family waited in silence for the mysterious man to emerge from the water. Too much time passed and it was obvious the man was *not* swimming.

Corrynne moved next to her husband and asked, "Could he be in some kind of vehicle?"

"What? *A car*?" asked Jax sarcastically.

Bo spoke gently to his son, "You never know, Jax. Your mom's pretty smart."

"It couldn't be a car, Dad," said Jax, shaking his head. "I think that guy got swept downstream. That current is wicked."

"He wasn't in the current, Jax," said Brea in a frustrated tone. "He was just right out there, in the calm water."

"Look again, Jax," said Bo, pointing at the faint glow of two submerged lights slowly coming closer to them. Rippling water fanned out behind the lights. "I bet you it is a car and it's coming right toward us."

Suddenly, Jax stood straight up. "Maybe you're right...if it is a car, I'll bet it's Brother DeVine's Hummer! He told me it had some sort of a snorkel so they can drive it almost completely under water through rivers and lakes!"[1] said Jax, crouching in anticipation.

Jax had barely finished speaking when the clouds once again moved away from the moon. Now they could see a dark gray roof, a black snorkel and about nine inches of windshield sticking out of the water.

"*See! I was right!*" shouted Jax. "*It is a Hummer!*" He thrust his arms and tightly clinched fists high above his head in celebration of his correct guess.

"Yeah! We get to ride in a Hummer!" sang Ry, jumping up and down, momentarily forgetting the cold.

The Hummer slowed its approach and eased alongside the ledge where they were standing. As soon as the car came to a stop, a large glass sunroof opened and a familiar face poked through the opening. "Is that Bo and Corrynne Rogers?" asked a friendly voice.

"Yes!" said Corrynne jubilantly. "Brother DeVine, I can't believe it's really you!"

"*Yes!*" said Jax beaming in excitement, "See! I was right!"

"What are you doing in this flooded parking lot?" asked Bo smiling.

Rocwell lifted his head from his father's shoulder and opened his sleepy eyes. The excitement had awakened him.

"I'm combing the area, looking for lost souls like you. The Bishop asked me to come out here and find people in need. The Lord blessed me with this Hummer, and it's about time it was good for something besides emptying my checking account."

"Well *I'm* glad you bought that machine!" said Bo, as he leaned over and held out his hand toward Brother DeVine.

Brother DeVine nodded, and shook Bo's hand. "Anything I can do to make a difference."

"We're freezing!" said Ry suddenly. "Does your car have heat?"

"Sure!" laughed Brother DeVine. "Come on in!"

Without warning Ry jumped onto the roof of the car. His wet shoes slipped, and he nearly slid off, into the deep water, but he caught himself and stood up.

"Be careful!" called Corrynne.

"Don't step on the seats!" added Brea.

Ry didn't hear his mother or his sister because he had already wriggled down through the opening past Brother DeVine.

"Sorry, Brother DeVine. He's a little anxious to ride in your car," said Bo with a shrug.

"Hey! It's like a spaceship down here! There are so many glowing lights! You guys have to see this!" said Ry from the inside the car.

Bo, Corrynne, Brea and Jax laughed.

Roc slid out of Bo's grasp and moved to the edge of the landing, and sleepily asked, "Can I ride in your underwater car, too?"

"Sure. Everyone gets a ride! Just get in line," said Brother DeVine with a smile.

"I'm next!" yelled Roc.

Falsely Accused

Inside the military vehicle Carea was placed firmly in a chair behind a table. She quickly realized that the vehicle was a mobile police station. Within minutes the officers had taken a picture of her, and had verbally entered her personal information into a computer system.

The police officer with the crew cut pulled a silver object from his pocket. It was similar to the one the paramedics had used earlier. He pointed it at her forehead and again, a light flashed and an alarm sounded. "I've got a positive identification. She's the girl from the mansion in Skull Valley," said the officer. "The frequency of the chip checks with the ambulance recording."

Carea was very disturbed. Things were not looking good. "Tell me what is happening right now. *I've got my rights you know*!" said Carea as firmly as she could without crying.

"Miss, we are going to ask you questions and you need to answer them truthfully," said the military officer who had been hanging back, watching his partner book Carea.

"Why am *I* in trouble? *I am the victim here*! You guys are supposed to be on *my* side!" said Carea looking back and forth between the two officers.

"How are you the victim? It looks to me like someone has been taking pretty good care of you," said the police officer, eyeing her satin dress and the crown that was still on her head.

In a fit of anger, Carea ripped off the crown and threw it on the table. "I was practically kidnapped to become Imam Mahdi's wife! It wasn't my idea, that's for sure! I'm still in high school! That man was crazy!" Neither officer replied, so Carea continued to defend herself. "It's not such a strange story! It happened to Elizabeth Smart! Stranger things happen every day!"

The military officer leaned back in his chair and asked, "How did he practically 'kidnap' you?"

"Just like Elizabeth, I was taken right from my own bedroom, only I was drugged. When I woke up the next day I had this chip under my skin and a tattoo on my back."

"Interesting. Have you noticed anything different since you received the chip?"

"Yes! The thing makes me do things that I normally wouldn't do!"

"Like what?" asked the military officer seeming very interested in this part.

Carea was growing more frustrated, but hoping to be freed, she said "It made me sick and depressed."

"How would it do that?" asked the Army officer.

Shaking her head Carea shrugged, "If I didn't obey Imam Mahdi, he wouldn't let me eat or sleep. He could just point at me and cause me to faint from pain—I can't explain it! But I think I would have died, if I hadn't escaped his house."

Both officers stared at her without expression.

"It's true!" complained Carea. "Check your own records! I was missing and my parents filed a report! That was when the chip was implanted."

The policeman with the crew cut pushed some buttons on his computer and pulled up a record. "Yes, you were reported missing, but it says you just showed up at home the next day a little tired but healthy. It says here that the Police Chief even went to your house and your parents did not report a kidnapping."

Carea remembered her parents' decision to not tell the authorities about the chip. They were trying to protect her, but now it was working against her. She was frustrated. "Well, I was kidnapped! I don't care what your report says."

"Anyway, miss, even if you were kidnapped it has no bearing on our questions," said the military officer who looked like he was getting tired of the bantering. "I'm going to ask the questions and you answer them as simply as you can. Do you understand?"

Carea frowned. She knew there was no other option. She had to cooperate. "OK," she replied.

"Tell us about the money that is collected from Imam Mahdi's followers."

"I don't know about any money."

"Where are Imam Mahdi's bank accounts?"

"I know nothing about money or bank accounts!" said Carea again.

"Is there a plan for more terrorist activities in the United States?"

"I am not one of them. I don't know anything about their plans!"

"What Middle East connections does Imam Mahdi have?"

"I told you! I don't know anything! I was just a pawn in Imam Mahdi's schemes to…"

The sudden buzzing of an alarm startled both officers. The military officer pulled out a headpiece from his pocket and put it on. "Scow here," he blurted, and then he listened for a moment. "No, sir. No, sir. Yes, sir, we have the girl, sir, but our agenda is…. Ah, no investigation? Yes, sir, I understand, sir," said Scow, his brow furrowed and his cheeks turned red. Scow removed the headpiece, walked down the stairs, and opened the door of the vehicle. "You are free to go, Miss Rogers."

"What?" asked Carea with surprise. "Really? I can go?"

"Yes. There will be no investigation," said the officer. He shot a glance at the policeman. He was thoroughly upset, but had to follow orders even if he didn't agree with them.

Carea hesitantly stood and smoothed her dress. Then looking at both officers, she stepped around the table where she had been sitting, then quickly walked the few steps to the door.

As Carea was moving down the steps, the policeman with the crew cut said, "Ah, miss?"

Carea turned around, "Yes?"

"Here's your crown," he said as he handed her the sparkling golden tiara with a large pearl in the middle.

"You can have it," she said as she stepped onto the pavement. "I've never been much for dress-up anyway."

Unity of the Saints

Corrynne basked in the warmth of the car's interior and the hot air blowing on her feet and face. She could feel the tingling sensation of her numb toes slowly thawing inside her shoes. She was tempted to take off her shoes and socks, like a little child. Corrynne was sure her sons had already taken their shoes off, but the sensibility of adulthood overpowered the urge. She would keep them on and show the wise restraint of maturity.

Strykker looked wide-eyed around the inside of the car. Corrynne, enjoying his expression, brushed his hair to the side and kissed his cheek. "How does that feel, baby boy? Isn't it wonderful that Brother DeVine saved us?" she asked soothingly, then she smiled at their rescuer.

Brother DeVine smiled, then reached out and softly caressed Strykker's cheek with his knuckle. "You guys are the… let's see, the twelfth family I've pulled out of the water tonight."

"Twelfth? Wow!" exclaimed Corrynne.

"Yep, packed in three on the first trip, two more on the second, rounded up two on the third, then four different families on the fourth."

"How did they all fit?" asked Corrynne.

"It was a squeeze—but then there's you guys." Brother DeVine glanced back to the full seats of his car. "I think your family counts for more than one. Your group fills this car almost like my last two or three big loads of adults and children put together!"

"I'm sure we do," said Corrynne, still smiling widely.

"Speaking of big families, aren't there some missing from yours?" asked Brother DeVine, looking at them through the rear-view mirror.

"Yes, a couple in fact. They were out when the earthquake hit." Corrynne didn't want to relate all the details of her son and daughter's absence, so she left it at that.

Brother DeVine cringed. "Boy, I hope they're alright. Many families are split up tonight. I'll try and keep an eye out for them."

"Thanks," said Bo.

"You're welcome," said Brother DeVine.

"Were all the families you rescued from our ward?" asked Corrynne.

"Nope, in fact none of them were," said Brother DeVine. He rubbed the windshield to remove the mist that had accumulated on it even though the heater and defroster were going full blast.

"Oh, no!" said Corrynne momentarily feeling her stomach drop.

"Some families from our ward are up the hill near the temple, but for the most part, we don't know where the rest are."

"Could they have gone west, up towards Orem?" asked Bo.

"Yes, that's what we think. Some of the two-way radio conversations we've heard indicate that many people are being sheltered in the church buildings. As you know, there are about five buildings up around Eighth South. After we finish our rescue efforts, we're going over to see who's there and what's happening."

"That's a good idea."

"Have you gone to rescue people in our neighborhood yet?"

Brother DeVine shook his head. "I haven't been able to make it out that far. I've just been picking up whoever I can find out here and taking them to safety. I'll probably go that way next."

Brother DeVine headed slowly up the hill. Finally plowing out of the water, he accelerated towards the temple.

"I'll bet people are up on their roofs," said Jax.

"You're probably right," said Brother DeVine. "If they're up there, and we can't get to them, then we'll find someone who can help them. The whole community is pulling together."

"Really?" asked Corrynne.

"Yes. When we get up the hill you'll be impressed to see the countless people who have already donated lamps, tents, and other shelters."

"Whose tents are they?" asked Bo.

"Everyone's! The Red Cross flew in some big army tents. But that's only the beginning, people from all over the lower east benches are bringing out blankets, tents, lamps, food, and other necessities for people who have been forced to leave their homes. It's really inspiring."[2]

"Wow!" said Corrynne, feeling a sense of pride well up inside her. She was grateful that she belonged to such a responsive community. "It's a good thing there are so many wealthy people in Provo who are able to contribute."

Brother DeVine glanced at Corrynne, and then returned his attention to the road. "Corrynne, it's not the wealthy that are contributing."

"It's not? How do you know?"

"Think about it. The wealthy are the needy this time."

"What? How?"

"Who lived in the river bottoms? Who lived up on the ridge where their big houses were demolished? Who lived in the areas most affected by the earthquake and the worst of the flooding?"

Corrynne thought for a second and then suddenly it hit her like a ton of bricks. Her mouth flew wide open as she gasped. "You're right! The wealthier families lived up on the ridges with the great views, right along the fault lines…"[3]

"And in the prime areas down in the river bottoms," added Bo.

"Oh my goodness!" Corrynne looked back at Bo.

"Hey, we aren't rich," said Brea. "I drive an old clunker to prove it!"

"Maybe we aren't," said Bo, "but most people around us are *very* well-off."

"What do you think it means?" Corrynne asked Brother DeVine and Bo.

Brother DeVine chuckled with what sounded more like an overwhelmed noise than a true laugh, and then said, "Well, I can tell you that it seems kind of odd to me. I'd like to think it isn't personal. My house is only a one story, and it's probably under water right now. But there might be a lesson in there somewhere."[4]

"I know," said Brea. "Don't build in high risk areas?"

Brother DeVine smiled and shrugged. "Maybe that too, but I don't think any of us thought the place where we chose to build was a risky one. Who would intentionally put their family in harm's way? I know I wouldn't."

"No, we didn't," said Bo. "We just found a great deal and liked the area. We didn't consider the thought that the dam might break someday."

"Right," nodded Brother DeVine. With a look of concern, he glanced at Bo in the mirror then suddenly changed the subject. "Bo, someone needs to look at that gash on your head."

"Oh, yeah, the gash," said Bo as he put his hand to the clotted wound.

"Don't touch it!" cautioned Corrynne as she turned around to look at him. "An infection is the last thing we need."

Bo moved his hand away from the wound. "Right. I *should* get that sewn up or something."

"Perhaps there isn't a lesson, Mom, maybe the earth just shook enough to break the dam," said Brea.[5] "I'm sure that not *all* the rich were affected."

"Maybe you're right. Maybe we're just jumping to conclusions," said Brother DeVine. "But I can tell you one thing, whether Godly lessons were intended or not, I'm sure we'll all learn something before we're through. I know I have already."[6]

"What lesson have you learned?" Corrynne asked Brother DeVine.

"Next time I should buy a *two* story house!"

Everyone laughed.

Notes to "Separated Lives"

Hummer

[1] A Hummer is a factual car that resembles a mini tank that replaced the Army tank in the 80's and hit the civilian market in 1992. It was first seen at Operation Desert Storm when it was called by its proper name: a High Mobility Multi Purpose Vehicle, or a Humvee. The universal nature of this car allows it to go most anywhere, in any terrain. It is famous for handling any off-road situation that can practically be imagined. The snorkel does exist for the described purpose. See the following web page to see the amazing things a Hummer can do in real life. http://www.lynchhummer.com/Hummer%20Tricks/StupidTricks2.html.

[2] Historically, whenever there has been a disaster the Saints have unselfishly helped those that were affected. See the following example:

"The Brisbane River crested at 21 feet 8 inches, nine feet above normal flood level. Rescue operations went on around the clock as portable floodlights lit up scenes of motorboats in flooded streets, and volunteers swimming from house to house, rescuing people and goods.

"Priesthood holders joined forces with the civil authorities in the rescue work and provided boats, trucks, trailers, and other necessary help. However, most of their energies were directed at evacuating ward members. Although many of the Saints were isolated, they were not directly affected by the rising water. Many were without normal supplies of milk, vegetables, bread, and power, but those participating in the Church food storage program suffered little hardship" ("News of the Church," *Ensign*, Apr. 1974, 70).

"When we love the Lord our God with all our hearts, might, and strength, we will love our brothers as ourselves, and we will voluntarily, in the exercise of our free agency, impart of our substance for their support" (Marion G. Romney, "Church Welfare Services' Basic Principles," *Ensign*, May 1976, 120).

Unity of the Saints

[3] This is not a commentary on the righteousness of the poor verses the rich. It is a description of reality. If an earthquake hit the Provo area, the damage would occur along the west side of the Wasatch mountains, which is the bench where many of the rich have built their homes, (see http://newsnet.byu.edu/story.cfm/44515), and if the dam broke, the River Bottoms would obviously be under water, (see http://www.usbr.gov/dataweb/dams/ut82912.htm) which also is an affluent area in Provo. This author couldn't help but see the coincidence of these two potentials underlining how true it is that wealth is fleeting.

It should be noted here that another area that damage would occur would be around the border of Utah Lake, in which a "liquefaction" of the ground would cause structures to sink (http://des.utah.gov/service/UTCountymap.html).

According to history, it is estimated that there is only a 14% chance of a large earthquake happening in the next 100 years in the Provo area. This number increases to 30% chance if earthquakes become more random rather than following the patterns set by history (see http://newsnet.byu.edu/story.cfm/44515).

[4] "Lay not up for yourselves treasures upon earth, where moth and rust doth corrupt, and where thieves break through and steal" (Matthew 6:19).

[5] Some devastation is not for wickedness, or righteousness. Some trials come by virtue of this mortal life…"It is a false idea that the Saints will escape all the judgments, whilst the wicked suffer; for all flesh is subject to suffer, and 'the righteous shall hardly escape;' still many of the Saints will escape, for the just shall live by faith; yet many of the righteous shall fall prey to disease, to pestilence, etc., by reason of the weakness of the flesh, and yet be saved in the kingdom of God. So that it is an unhallowed principle to say that such and such have transgressed because they have been preyed upon by disease or death, for all flesh is subject to death; and the Savior has said, 'Judge not, lest ye be judged'" (Joseph Smith, *History of the Church*, Vol. 4, 11, September 29, 1839).

[6] "We believe that his judgments are poured out to bring mankind to a sense of his power and his purposes, that they may repent of their sins, and prepare themselves for the second coming of Christ to reign in righteousness upon the earth…We firmly believe that Zion—which is the pure in heart—shall escape, if she observes to do all things whatsoever God has commanded; but in the opposite event, even Zion shall be visited 'with sour affliction, with pestilence, with plague, with sword, with vengeance, and with devastating fire.' (D&C 97:26) We believe that these severe, natural calamities are visited upon men by the Lord for the good of His children, to quicken their devotion to others, and to bring out their better natures, that they may love and serve him. We believe, further, that they are the heralds and tokens of his final judgment, and the schoolmasters to teach the people to prepare themselves, by righteous living, for the coming of the Savior to reign upon the earth, when every knee shall bow and every tongue confess that Jesus is the Christ" (Joseph F. Smith, *The Improvement Era*, Vol. 9, 653-654).

CHAPTER SEVEN

ENLIGHTENED

"The light which is in all things, which giveth life to all things, which is the law by which all things are governed, even the power of God who sitteth upon his throne, who is in the bosom of eternity, who is in the midst of all things" (D&C 88:13).

00:09:04 15:53:10 Zulu
Saturday, March 27th
1:07 a.m.
Provo, Utah
Regional Medical Center

Incognito

Carea hurried from the military vehicle to the hospital. Slowing her steps, she walked through the outside automatic doors as they opened for her. Carefully, she moved around in the lobby through the crowd of injured, keeping her eyes on the bold red words, "Emergency Room" displayed across a large, doublewide doorway. She assumed those were the doors Dane was taken through on his gurney.

Forcing herself through people in front of the entrance, Carea approached the intimidating doors that did not have handles. She pushed on them, wondering if the automatic mechanism was stuck, but to her surprise, a loud alarm went off. A thin nurse with gray hair and blue reading glasses perched on the end of her nose appeared out of nowhere.

"The ER is a closed unit, sweetie. You may not go in there!" the ER nurse said brusquely, as she held one arm out to bar Carea from entering. "Only doctors and nurses are allowed beyond this point."

Looking up with large eyes, Carea pleaded, "My brother was brought in here about twenty minutes ago! He's dying! I have to see where they took him."

The nurse's expression changed from stern intensity to soft empathy. Shaking her head and placing a hand on Carea's shoulder she said, "That's tough, kid...I'm sure it's hard to have someone so sick in your family," then she squared her shoulders and continued, "but you simply must stay in the waiting room like everyone else. The medical personnel need room to move around."

Carea had just about had it with people pushing her around that night. Before she knew it she blurted, *"For being a nurse, you're not very compassionate!* I don't care if the whole hospital is *falling apart,* you can't stop me from *seeing my brother!"* Carea put her hand to her eyes and began to cry uncontrollable, grief-stricken tears. *"Right now, he's all I have!"*

The nurse stood quietly for a few seconds and then put her arm around Carea's shoulders and moved her towards an empty place along the wall. "I'm sorry for being so stern with you. I just have to keep order in this ER, which is nearly impossible."

Carea nodded silently as she leaned against the wall.

"What's your brother's name?" asked the nurse.

Carea did not look up but stared at the floor. "Dane Rogers."

The nurse stood straight up and covered her mouth with her hand. "Are you Corrynne Rogers' daughter?"

Carea nodded, furrowing her eyebrows. "Why? Does it make a difference?"

The nurse looked around and then said, "I think I know where they took your brother. If you don't tell anyone, I'll show you where I think he is, but you have to follow me quickly and quietly!"

Carea stood up eagerly. "I won't tell anyone," she whispered. "I promise! I just want to know if he's alive!"

"They wheeled him into an operating room. Come with me!" The nurse moved to the opposite wall and touched an identification pad causing the Emergency doors to swing open.

With the nurse in the lead, Carea followed closely through a large busy room to another set of double doors. Bolting through the doors, both Carea and the nurse rushed down a long white hall to another part of the hospital she had never been in before. Turning to the right, the nurse put her finger to another ID pad and then pushed a square button. A third set of double doors opened, exposing an area where there were many nurses and doctors garbed in blue hats, gowns, and shoe coverings.

The nurse reached into a segmented shelf and she pulled out similar coverings for Carea. Then she took Carea into a women's bathroom. In a voice breathy from running, she looked Carea in the face and said, "Now my name is Carol and I want to make myself perfectly clear—I don't normally do this—but your mother and I are very good friends. I'm doing this for her."

"Oh, thank you, Carol!" exclaimed Carea.

"Shh!" said the nurse as she put a stern finger to her lips and looked around. Then, satisfied that no one was in the restroom with them, she continued. "I believe that everyone has a right to be with their loved ones before they die, even if only watching through a window. Your brother is very sick and might not make it, so go and see him."

"Alright," said Carea as she put blue coverings on both feet, and a mask on her face.

"Now, don't make waves. Be quiet and just watch and no one will bother with you. They'll think you're a medical tech and allow you to watch."

"Is this illegal?" asked Carea.

The nurse laughed, "Illegal? Oh, no! Not illegal—just bold. Nurses are very territorial and don't like spectators much. Just lay low and you'll be fine."

"OK! Thank you! I'll stay out of the way." said Carea, as she slipped the long cover gown over her yellow dress and put the hat on her head to cover her hair.

"Now let me take a look at you...." said Carol, scanning Carea slowly, stopping at the blue coverings over her high-heeled shoes and the yellow satin sticking out from the bottom of the gown. "First of all, take off your shoes, missy," she said with almost a snicker. "No one comes to the Operating Room with shoes like those."

Carea looked down. "What should I do?"

"Just take off your shoes and put the blue booties on your feet. You don't want to attract attention."

"What about my dress?"

"Yes, your dress is a problem, but I can't suggest you take it off and walk around in your skivvies! Maybe you could hike it up."

"Do you have any scissors?" asked Carea having an idea.

The nurse nodded. "Every real nurse always has scissors in her pocket." The nurse dug into the deep, waist pocket on her top and produced a small silver pair of scissors.

Carea took them and promptly cut off the bottom of the dress, at the level of the blue cover gown. "How's that?" she asked smiling.

The nurse winked at Carea then said, "You look good, kid, but you ruined your prom dress. It was a real nice one."

Carea shook her head, "Oh, I wasn't at..." but then she had second thoughts. This nurse didn't want to know the details of her awful night. It was too hard to explain anyway. "The guy was a real loser," Carea said abruptly. "I'd cut the whole thing up if I had extra clothes."

"Well then, no problem!" said the nurse with a smile and a hug. "Glad I could help you!" Carol patted Carea's back gently and said, "OK, cutie pie, go be with your brother. I'm sorry he is so sick. I hope he makes it."

"Me too," said Carea. Then she asked, "Which room is Dane in?"

The nurse, still smiling, shrugged. "Don't know, kid, you'll just have to look in the windows until you see him."

"OK," said Carea, dropping her shoes and the satin material into a trash can on top of a pile of paper towels. Then she left the bathroom and disappeared into a sea of medical personnel.

Carea, out in the hall, moved immediately to the wall, and walked quietly down a corridor. She noticed a bank of high windows, and realized that if she stood on her tiptoes, she might be able to see into them. She quickly peeked into two windows, and then stopping at the third, she saw two huge white feet sticking out from under a green paper sheet. There was no mistake. Those were Dane's feet.

Carea didn't blink an eye as she looked around the brightly lit, stark white room. The medical people in the room were moving quickly but methodically, as if moving to the same beat. One nurse in the far right corner of the room was unwrapping equipment; another one stood on a stool by the bed and handed surgical instruments to two men who looked like doctors. Carea looked to the left of the room and saw monitor screens that showed waves and numbers. Some of them were blinking. She wondered if that meant Dane was doing poorly. She wished her mother were there to tell her what was happening.

The nurse that had been standing in the corner moved close to the door. Carea debated whether it would be a good choice to open the door and ask for an update, but Carol had warned her to keep quiet.

After another moment, the nurse opened the door. Studying a small electronic, hand-held screen, she walked by Carea without noticing her.

Carea fidgeted and tried to stifle the impulse to talk to the nurse, but she couldn't help herself. "What's going on in there?" she asked much too loudly.

The woman was startled by the sound of Carea's voice, and then she looked up with a frown. "Who are you?" she asked.

Carea debated what she should say. "I'm a..." Carea couldn't lie. Expecting to be kicked out, but hoping for mercy she said, "I'm the patient's sister and I snuck in to see how he was doing," she said almost cringing at her own words.

The masked nurse relaxed and studied Carea. She must have assumed, as Carol had expected, that Carea was a medical technician, just looking in on a relative.

Carea's honesty was rewarded, as the nurse gave her an update. "His BP is 54/24 with a wedge of 20. We've tried pressors but he is not responding. There are multi-focal PVC's that look to me like we might 'tach' soon. I'm sorry," said the nurse in a matter-of-fact tone, "but I assure you that we're doing our best."

Carea looked deeply into the nurse's eyes, trying to understand what she was saying. All she could comprehend was the statement "I'm sorry."

Carea's heart sank, and she swallowed to keep back her tears. "Thank you," she said softly.

The nurse nodded her head and said, "You're welcome." She must have sensed Carea's true feelings, because in her next breath she said, "Try and think good thoughts. Miracles happen every day. We've pulled worse out of the grave." The nurse's eyes wrinkled, as if she was smiling from behind her mask, then she turned and walked back into the OR.

With that, Carea's mind was somehow satisfied. Yes, miracles did happen once in a while. She had forgotten that possibility. Maybe one would happen for Dane. She turned around, leaned on the wall, and slid down to a sitting position on the floor. She would wait…and pray for a miracle. It was the least she could do for her brother.

Blessings to Those in Need

The group, nestled safe and warm in the Hummer, was nearing the top of the hill. As they came over the bend Corrynne was indeed surprised at the hundreds of glowing, lantern-lit tents that were set up on the grass right below the temple. "Oh, my goodness! There are tents everywhere!" Corrynne turned back to Bo. "Where else in the world could there be one group of people with so many tents?"

"In Arabia?" asked Jax.

"Good thought!" said Bo, "But I'll bet they aren't tents like these! Look at all the tents! It looks like every family has at least one tent."

"This is amazing!" said Corrynne, marveling at the little tent city with people bustling all around, attending to the needs of each other. Even though it was dark, there were many people moving from tent to tent. They were obviously setting up camp.

"What a great place we live in; tragedy strikes, and everyone's ready. I love it!" she said optimistically.

The car eased to a stop right on the edge of the grassy knolls where an expansive city of tents was being erected.

"Well, here is your home away from home for a while," said Brother DeVine. "I'm off to save some more poor souls."

"Thank you, Brother DeVine! You were a godsend for us," said Corrynne as she opened the door and got out of the car. She closed the door halfway, but noticed a phone on the dashboard. "Is that a satellite phone?" she asked impulsively.

"Of course," said Brother DeVine.

"Does it work?"

"It worked last time I tried it," said Brother DeVine smiling.

"I hate to impose, but considering the circumstances, do you mind if I use it to try and reach my kids?"

"Not at all!" said Brother DeVine. He turned off the car then handed the phone to Corrynne.

The rest of the family filed out of the car. "Bo, can you take the children? I'll catch up with you. First, I'm going to call Dane and Carea to see if their phone is working yet, then I'll call Braun and Conrad to let them know we're safe."

Bo nodded and took Strykker from Corrynne. Then walking single file, he led the children towards a large, green tent with a big red cross on the top. It seemed to be the center of this tent city.

Corrynne dialed Dane and Carea's cell but once again, all she heard was a busy signal. "Darn it!" she said reflexively. "Still no service—stupid cell phones!"

Hesitating, she decided to go ahead and call her sons overseas. Looking up at Brother DeVine, she said, "I'll have to owe you for the long distance charges."

Brother DeVine smiled and shook his head. "There is no charge on my plan. All international calls at this time of night are free."

"Ah, that's great! You must have a *great* plan!" said Corrynne as she smiled, then dialed the operator.

"Operator," said a woman on the other end of the line.

"Please connect me to the Latter-day Saint Mission in Israel. I believe it is located in Jerusalem. This is an emergency."

A few moments passed, then Corrynne heard quiet clicking sounds; the phone was ringing. "You have reached the Israeli Mission for the Church of Jesus Christ of Latter-day Saints. Please leave a message after the tone."

Corrynne hesitated even after the tone. How does a mother leave a message when there has been such a catastrophe? She took a deep breath and said, "This is Corrynne Rogers, Elder Conrad Rogers' mother. We live in Provo, and, well the dam broke and we lost our home in the flood. Two family members are missing but we expect to locate them soon. Please tell Conrad not to worry, and that we will be fine. There are a lot of wonderful Saints helping in every way possible. Thank you. Good-bye." Corrynne clicked the off button.

"Is it OK to make one more call to Europe?" Corrynne ducked down to ask Brother DeVine through the open car door.

"Sure, go ahead. I'll just relax right here. No hurry."

"Thank you," said Corrynne. She dialed Braun's cell phone, luckily she remembered the number. The phone rang only once before Braun answered.

"Hello?"

"Braun?"

"Mom? Is that you?"

"Yes!"

"Mom! I've been trying and trying to get through to you. No one is answering any phones out there!"

"I know. All the cell phones are jammed."

"Are you guys OK?"

"Well," said Corrynne, suddenly feeling like crying. Braun's question brought to the surface all the emotion she had kept under control throughout the terrible ordeal. "Yes. It's been crazy but we're fine."

"I heard the news. They said the dam broke, is that true?"

"Yes, it's true."

"So the house—is it gone?"

"No. It's not gone. It's just underwater for now, probably totally flooded."

"Well then how, or what, are you guys doing?"

"We are up by the temple. Bother DeVine from the ward rescued us in his Hummer."

"Well, that's good!"

"They're assembling a huge tent city up across from the MTC. I guess we'll be staying here for a while."

"Should I come home?" asked Braun.

"No. We're fine. There are so many people here now, more would just add to the challenge. Stay where you are. We really are fine, OK? I'll keep in touch."

"Alright."

"I have to go. I'm using someone's satellite phone. I love you."

"Love you too, Mom. Stay strong."

"I will."

"I love you," said Braun simply.

Tears welled up in Corrynne's eyes from her son's words. "Love you too. Good-bye, son."

"Good-bye." The phone went dead.

Corrynne quickly wiped her wet eyes, sniffled, and then cleared her throat. Handing the phone back to Brother DeVine, she said, "Thanks again."

"No problem." Brother DeVine's eyes were soft and understanding. "You're a real trooper, Corrynne."

Corrynne looked down, then up again. She smiled. "Thank you. You are an angel.[1] We're blessed because of you."[2]

Brother DeVine shifted his car into drive. "See you soon." He winked at Corrynne then saluted with three fingers of his right hand.

"Good-bye." Corrynne smiled as she closed the door and walked towards the tents.

The square, bulky Hummer, with the snorkel sticking out of the hood near the windshield, moved back down the road towards the swirling water.

Corrynne turned and scanned the field to see if she could see her family. Not recognizing anyone, she headed for the main tent set up on the north side of the field.

Pushing open the heavy flap of the large tent, she took a second to look for Bo and the children. She stood on her tiptoes and saw them standing beside a table in the far northeast corner of the tent. It looked like each of them were holding sleeping bags. Bo had an oblong bag too that she thought might be a tent.

Long lines of wet and tired-looking people were waiting to get their sleeping bags. Corrynne walked quickly past them and approached her family.

"Hi, guys. Got everything?"

"Mom, they gave me *my own* sleeping bag!" said Roc, his eyes sparkling with excitement.

Corrynne looked down and smiled at him. "Wow! That's great, Rocwell! It looks like it will fit you perfectly!"

"Yep. And no one else is going to use it!" he said, hugging his bedding.

Corrynne looked at Brea and Bo. "If only we could all be so happy about something as simple as a sleeping bag."

Bo spoke to Corrynne, "What are you talking about? I'm ecstatic about mine! I just hope I can stay awake long enough to unroll it."

Corrynne looked at the bag Bo was holding and noticed the name "Anderson" written in ink on the tag. "Look, this bag belonged to someone named Anderson." She looked up at Bo. "I wish there were some way we could thank the people who donated all this wonderful bedding."

Bo smiled then said, "We'll give back. The Lord, in his infinite wisdom, has asked us all to consecrate everything we have to each other. Today it was someone else's turn to give to us. Tomorrow it will be our turn to give our things and talents to build up Zion."[3]

"I don't want to give away my sleeping bag tomorrow!" said Rocwell with worried eyes.

Brea laughed and then hugged him. "No, you don't have to give it away tomorrow, Roc."

"Dad means 'another day'-tomorrow, not *tomorrow* tomorrow," said Ry trying to clarify for his brother.

Corrynne continued, "Nope. You can keep it for a while. We'll probably use these bags longer than we want to."

Corrynne looked for the twins. They were toddling around, exploring things on the grass. "I'll bet those two won't want to sleep. We might have to take turns staying up with them, because I don't think I'm going to last as long as they will."

"I'll take care of them first," said Jax with a mature look on his face.

"Thanks, Jax. That will help," said Bo, reaching out to pat his son on the back. Changing the subject, Bo looked at his family and said, "Who knows how to set up a tent?"

"I do!" said Ry. "I'm good at it!"

"I am, too!" said Roc.

"No you guys aren't," said Jax. "You don't even know which poles go where."

"*Jax*," scolded Corrynne, rolling her eyes. "Be nice!"

"Well I guess its business as usual," said Bo as he looked at his quarreling boys.

Jax looked at his Dad with restrained irritation, "Well they think they know *everything* and they *don't*...."

Light of Discovery

"OK," said Jenessa, "It's time we begin your lessons. Look around you. Do you have any questions for me? Normally, that is the best place to start with a new student."

Dane squared his shoulders and followed his teacher's advice. He looked around at the glorious surroundings. He thought David and Jonah had answered most of his questions, but further down the road he saw a fountain of water, splashing over crystal shards. It stood in some sort of square in the middle of a hub of buildings.

The fountain sparkled brightly, emitting thousands of rainbows of light. It was breathtakingly beautiful. The brightness of the light seemed to feed him, filling him up like food used to fill him when he was on earth. Reflexively, Dane looked into the sky above him toward the sun, which he was certain must be the origin of the light. He thought the sun must be beautiful here, just like the fountain, but no matter where he looked he could not find a sun in the sky.

Dane formulated his thought. "This might seem stupid, but I'll start with a simple question. Where did the sun go?"

Jenessa looked into the sky. "You won't see the Son here..."

"Right, I don't see it. The sun isn't anywhere in the sky. What's up with that? How is it so bright around here without the sun?"

Jenessa looked at Dane for a moment, and then understanding overcame her momentary confusion. "Oh, you mean the sun of the physical world, not the Son of God."

Dane looked at Jenessa with narrowed eyes. "Normally the sun is in the sky. I don't think I've ever seen Christ in the sky, at least not yet."

Jenessa laughed, and pushed a lock of her hair behind her ear. "Forgive me, everything here centers around Jesus Christ. I'll have to adjust my answers back to how I perceived things when I first came here."

"No problem," said Dane smiling. It was good to see Jenessa pushed slightly off balance. This girl was really growing on him.

"Here we have no need of the physical sun," answered Jenessa.

"Why not? How do all these trees and flowers live if there is no sun? Where is all this light coming from? There has to be some source. Tell me the answer to that one, Teacher," Dane teased.

"There is an answer," assured Jenessa.

"What is it?" asked Dane.

"Before we get into this discussion, let's go sit by that fountain you have been admiring. Despite your desire to start with the simple, the answer to your question is not elementary."

"Alright," said Dane, and in a moment they were sitting on a ledge that encompassed the glorious fountain. Again Dane looked into the light that flowed from the fountain, it was so…delicious? Dane again marveled at his newly discovered perceptions.

Jenessa interrupted his thoughts. "Dane, the source of all light simply is the power and light of God. He is our sun, and because of that we have no need of a sun or any other physical light.[4] By virtue of his power, his brightness permeates our world and is the source of all life, just as he is the true source of light and life in the physical world."

Dane smiled sarcastically, still wishing to tease Jenessa. "I don't mean to disagree with you, but on the earth, the sun is the source of all physical life and the main source of light. I know that tidbit of knowledge from biology class. I'm not a scientist, but I do know the basics." Dane continued, "Maybe the Lord made the sun, but the light energy from the sun gives life to plants, which then allows animals and all life to exist."

Dane winked at Jenessa. "It must have been a long time since you lived on the earth because as I remember, God's brightness is not the earth's source of light. You must be getting our worlds confused again."

Jenessa smiled knowingly and shook her head. "No, I believe your thinking is too basic. Open your mind to truth. Truth is knowledge of things as they are, as they were, and as they are to come.[5] Peer into the light of what is reality, not what you think is reality."

Dane looked up into the brilliant sky and then shrugged. "OK, Teach, enlighten me—get it? …En-light-en me?" Dane laughed aloud, and slapped his knee with the palm of his hand.

Jenessa frowned at Dane's obvious attempt at humor. "Be serious, Dane. Consider the true nature of God. Why do you think it strange that I say that God's power is the same power that gives light to the physical world?"

Dane shrugged casually, "Because the sun does."

"And that means that God doesn't have anything to do with it?" Jenessa's eyes bore into Dane as her question hung in the air. Something seemed to be bothering her.

"No," said Dane. "I just mean, the Lord isn't standing by somewhere giving the sun its power to shine. He has better things to do. He made the sun self-sufficient, right?"

Jenessa nodded. "So he did, did he?"

"Sure." Dane didn't know why Jenessa seemed taken back by his words, but he sensed she was coming to some sort of conclusion.

Jenessa sat quietly looking at Dane. The silence was very uncomfortable for him. Finally she said, "Well, Dane, I can see that we need to reprogram your thinking."

"Why?" asked Dane. He wondered what was wrong. What did he do? He didn't know how to get out of this situation. Obviously their conversation had taken a wrong turn.

Jenessa held up her hand towards the sky. "Because, until you see the power of God in all things, you cannot bear witness of the true being that he is," said Jenessa. "Faith in God hinges on the knowledge of his true character and power."

Dane was becoming frustrated. He thought he had an adequate testimony. He thought he knew quite a bit about the Lord and his ways. After all, he had done pretty well against Imam Mahdi—but then again, he couldn't take credit for that one. The appropriate words had just come to him. The Lord had definitely helped him. He just wasn't smart enough to think of what to say. Remembering that experience, he thirsted to have that ability restored.

Dane's thoughts returned to what Jenessa had said. He began to analyze his personal perception of God. Was he really that far off base? He decided to probe Jenessa. "You know, I can see the hand of God in the creation, in miracles, and in conversions. I just didn't think God controls every little thing in the universe. So you think I'm getting this all wrong?" he asked, actually seeking an answer.

Jenessa nodded, "Absolutely. I have been sent to teach you the truth of all things. If you are not open to teaching, and are so connected to your preconceived notions, then maybe you are not yet ready for the mission God has in store for you."

Dane was alarmed. Did she just decide his future? Did she have the power to do that? Did that mean that he wasn't going back to earth? Who was this girl who thought she could judge him so quickly? Dane stood up and said, "Wait a minute. I'm just as ready to learn as the next guy."

Jenessa stood, too. "No, Dane, you are not the 'next guy.' You have been called to a work that only you and a select few have been given the gifts to perform. Many are called but few are chosen."[6]

Dane's eyes grew large. "What does that mean?"

"That means that the Lord extends calls to those who are worthy, but that doesn't guarantee that they will be faithful in that call. Each must decide the kind of servant he will be.[7] I'm here to teach you that alone you are nothing. As God's messenger, you act in his stead, as he would act. Remember that your power comes directly from him. You must use your priesthood, understanding that it is inseparably connected to heaven and righteousness.[8] This is why you must understand the truth of things. One cannot have faith in a false belief and be effective for God. Such attempts are vain and bear no power."[9]

Dane decided to backpedal. Maybe he was being difficult. He didn't want to be difficult; he wanted to learn. "Jenessa, please don't misunderstand me. Maybe I gave you the wrong impression."

"That's a difficult thing to do here. I understand your heart."

Jenessa's statement cut Dane to the core. She probably could understand his very intentions. She probably sensed he was being cynical and condescending. If so, he knew she was right. Those two attributes weren't 'learning friendly.' Maybe he wasn't valuing her knowledge. He suddenly felt remorseful. What a stupid jerk he was being to let his ego run rampant, here of all places. He should let Jenessa teach him; after all, she would not have been sent to him if she didn't know what she was talking about. He could see that his pride was getting in the way of his future.

"Jenessa, I'm sorry. Please forgive me for my arrogance. I want to be a good servant," said Dane.

"Sit down, Dane," She said as she patted the seat next to her. "Let me begin again. Maybe we can get it right this time."

Dane was relieved. Jenessa was giving him a second chance. "Alright. I'll listen. I'll be good this time."

Jenessa half smiled then took a breath. She looked thoughtfully toward the sky, then returning her gaze to Dane she said, "Try to understand. God's power is endless. The bounds of it are immeasurable. His power is in and through all things. All things are made by him and exist because of him.[10] Do you know what this statement means?"

Dane looked at the ground. He was unsure of his own knowledge. "I thought I did, but maybe I don't. Tell me what you mean when you say his power is 'in and through all things'."

"I'll try to clarify it for you. A creative and sustaining substance known as the 'light of Christ,' or the 'light of truth' emanates from the presence of God through the Son."[11]

Dane nodded. "I know of that power. All people are born with it, right? It helps those who don't have the Holy Ghost find the truth."

"I would clarify by saying that all people are born *of it*."[12]

"Really? I didn't know that."

"Yes. The Light of Christ is the power by which all life is quickened, but it also is the source of all truth, enlightening the physical and spiritual intellect to the recognition of truth,"[13] added Jenessa.

"OK," Dane nodded.

"However, this same light is also the power that permeates all nature and constitutes the immanence of God in the universe. At this moment, it is in every particle of matter and energy in all kingdoms and throughout the universe.[14] It is through this power, this light, that the laws of the universe maintain their boundaries and all things remain as they are, instead of spinning into chaos or simply dying off like a spent candle."[15]

Dane sat still for a moment and tried to understand the dimensions of what Jenessa had said. "Are you saying that because of this power, in all things and flowing through all things, everything exists from moment to moment? That life itself[16] and the universe depend on this power to exist even now?"[17]

"Yes. That is exactly what I am saying. Without God's influence, all things would vanish."[18]

Dane shook his head. "Wow, I had no idea. I had thought that the Lord created the earth, set it spinning, and then just watched it go. I didn't know that all the universe depended on his power for its very integrity."

"Yes, good. Now do you understand how dependent we are on God the Father and his Son Jesus Christ? Even the wicked depend on him for every breath."

"Yes, I see that's true now."

"Now let's go one step further," said Jenessa.

"OK."

"Just like matter receives its life through God, the earthly sun, like life, receives its power through God's will. It is made of his power."

"I think I can see that, too, now."

"Thus God, or his influence, actually *is* the light of the sun and the power by which it was made."[19]

"God is the light of the sun? Well, I know he made it, and it exists because of his power, but explain how he is the light himself."

"He, his power, and his light, cannot be separated. Together they are God. Let's talk about a subject with which you are familiar, it might help you better understand these truths. Let's talk about the laws of physics on earth."

"Alright. I was in a physics class before I came here, maybe I can relate to what you have to say."

"What is light?"

"Let's see." Dane wanted to get this one right. "Light is a wave of energy consisting of photonic particles," he said, sounding like a textbook.

"And what is matter?"

"It is substance. It has physical form and material dimension." Dane smiled, proud of himself for remembering the answers.

Jenessa nodded. "Right. Are they related?"

"I don't know. I guess they are because I remember that energy is released when matter is destroyed."

"Yes, you are on the right track. You see," said Jenessa, "it is an inescapable truth that throughout the universe, all matter and light are directly connected. Both are actually manifestations of the light of God and function according to his will. That is why matter can change to energy and energy to matter."[20]

"How can that be?"

Jenessa folded her hands together. "Well, what makes up the most basic elements of the physical world?"

Dane again tried to remember his physics class. Surprisingly, the knowledge came flowing back once more. He could recall everything perfectly. "Well, matter is made of atoms."

"All matter?"

"Yes."

"You mean gold, which is a solid, is made up of the very same particles as water?" asked Jenessa, obviously probing.

"Well, the atoms that make gold have a different number of protons, neutrons and electrons, than water does. Water is a mixture of two different atoms, but when you break them down into their most basic elements, protons, neutrons, and electrons, then yes, they are made of the same thing."

"So all matter is made of protons, neutrons, and electrons?"

"Right."

"What are *those* particles made of?"

"Well, electrons, I believe, are just pure energy. They run everything from light bulbs to human bodies in the Krebs cycle."

"OK, now what are protons and neutrons made of? They can be broken down further. ...Think and you'll remember."

The knowledge came easily to Dane. "Oh, yes, I believe they are made of strange particles called quarks and anti-quarks."[21]

"Right. What are quarks?"

"Essentially they are the most elementary particles of the physical world."

"Right, and do they have a charge?"

"They are particles that have strong interactions and a partial charge of an electron,"[22] answered Dane.

"So even the protons and neutrons, the essence of matter, are particles charged with energy?"

"I guess so."

"Can you see where I'm going with this?"

"You're saying that even in the physical world, everything is made of energetic relationships."

"Yes. Matter is actually made of energy. In the universe, energy flows into matter and matter into energy.[23] It is an eternal circle. As the Lord would say, when one world passes away another is born."[24]

"So, you're saying that the trees, the grass, the earth, and even my body was made of energy?"

Jenessa nodded. "You perceived the world as physical and solid, but in actuality, it was only a realm of electrical relationships between particles of energy."

"Wow. I never thought of it like that."

"So when Christ says he is the light and life of the world, he is telling you a scientific truth. Because of his glory that he gave freely to the world, it came into existence.[25] The physical world and all of its material was actually made from his light. Energy, or light which comes from God, dictates the dimensions of all the worlds and all the glories under God. It is through those laws that everything exists."[26]

"Whoa, this is deep."

"Once you understand this fact, then life itself begins to make sense. Through light, all of us exist. As beings of light we are made up of the very essence of God, and are given the opportunity to continue to grow in intelligence, which is the glory of God. As we grow and progress, it is really *his* dominion being expanded through us. In this way we give him glory by becoming more and more like God, who is our eternal Father."

"What is this 'intelligence'?" asked Dane.

"Intelligence is the eternal part of man which was not created or made, but born as an identity through God. This intelligence, combined with the spirit, constitutes the spiritual identity of an individual.[27] It is who you are and how you came to be an individual entity."

Dane was beginning to understand with a new perception. He felt like he was learning with every part of his being. "So in the scripture that says, 'The *glory* of God is *intelligence*, or *truth and light*,'[28] it is saying God our Father gains glory through our progression, because *we,* his children, are truth and light!"

"Yes, you've got it!"

"Wow. You're right. I wish everyone could know this. If people on earth knew who they really were, I think many would change their thinking and behavior."

"Exactly. That's exactly why the world needs to know."

Dane was filled with pure excitement. "All people are truly made from God's eternal elements and can become like their Father in whose image they were made."[29]

"You are so right. Satan has them thinking that they are accidents of nature,[30] or just some sort of wired bodies, meant for physical pleasures,[31] with no consequences for their actions. He has tricked the whole world into thinking there is nothing after death, that their whole definition is the present and what they can make of it."[32]

"I know. I was just there, remember?"

"Yes, so remember this lesson. It may serve you well in the future. People need to know their eternal worth, who they truly are, who they truly were, and who they yet will be."

Dane was amazed. Things *were* different than he had thought. "Wow, this is amazing."

Jenessa took a breath and smiled. "Well, Dane, we made it."

Dane looked at Jenessa. "What do you mean?"

"We got through the first lesson about the nature of God. It wasn't the easiest, I know, but you asked the questions."

"Yes, and did you notice, I listened to the answers?"

"Yes you did. You did very well."

"Are there more lessons to learn?" asked Dane.

"Oh, yes. More than can be imagined. In Celestial Glory there will be infinite lessons and room to grow as truth and light continue to expand. However, if you're asking for yourself, about here and now, then yes, but just a few more."

"When will I learn them?"

Jenessa smiled and nodded. "When you are ready."

"When will that be?"

"You will be ready when you ask the questions."

"Which questions?"

"You'll know them when they come to you."

Dane thought that was a strange answer. Suddenly he had run out of thoughts. "Oh...well—what do I do in the mean time."

"Ponder and pray."

"Alright. I'll do that." Dane closed his eyes, right beside the fountain and began to pray. After a moment, he looked for Jenessa, but she was gone. Dane was alone.

Notes to "Enlightened"

Blessings to Those in Need

[1] "...The message is that we should seek to overcome the selfishness we all seem to be born with, that we should overcome human nature and think of others before self. We should think of God and serve Him, and think of others and serve them" (James E. Faust, "A Pattern of Love," *Liahona*, Dec. 1999, 3).

[2] "...Ye are desirous to come into the fold of God, and to be called his people, and are willing to bear one another's burdens, that they may be light" (Mosiah 18:8).

[3] If we could all be unselfish and put the Lord's kingdom and its welfare first, how much easier the last days will be. The faithful promise to do just this, as many promise someday to live the law of consecration and give of everything they have to help others. "The law of consecration is a divine principle whereby men and women voluntarily dedicate their time, talents, and material wealth to the establishment and building up of God's kingdom." (See *Guide to the Scriptures*, "Consecrate, Law of Consecration").

Light of Discovery

[4] "The sun shall be no more thy light by day; neither for brightness shall the moon give light unto thee: but the LORD shall be unto thee an everlasting light, and thy God thy glory" (Isaiah 60:19).

[5] "And truth is knowledge of things as they are, and as they were, and as they are to come" (D&C 93:24).

[6] "Behold, there are many called, but few are chosen. And why are they not chosen? Because their hearts are set so much upon the things of this world, and aspire to the honors of men..." (D&C 121: 34-35).

[7] "If you do not magnify your callings, God will hold you responsible for those you might have saved, had you done your duty" (John Taylor as quoted by Hugh B. Brown, *The Abundant Life*, 37).

[8] "That the rights of the priesthood are inseparably connected with the powers of heaven, and that the powers of heaven cannot be controlled nor handled only upon the principles of righteousness" (D&C 121:36).

[9] "Faith is not to have a perfect knowledge of things; therefore if ye have faith ye hope for things which are not seen, which are true" (Alma 32:21).

"All true faith must be based upon correct knowledge or it cannot produce the desired results. Faith in Jesus Christ is the first principle of the gospel and is more than belief, since true faith always moves its possessor to some kind of physical and mental action; it carries an assurance of the fulfillment of the things hoped for. A lack of faith leads one to despair, which comes because of iniquity" (Bible Dictionary, "Faith").

[10] See D&C 88:41. "...[Christ is] in all things, and is through all things, and is round about all things; and all things are by him, and of him, even God, forever and ever" (D&C 88:41).

[11] "The light of Christ is just what the words imply: enlightenment, knowledge, and an uplifting, ennobling, persevering influence that comes upon mankind because of Jesus Christ. For instance, Christ is "the true light that lighteth every man that cometh into the world" (D&C 93: 2; John 1: 9). The light of Christ fills the "immensity of space" and is the means by which Christ is able to be "in all things, and is through all things, and is round about all things." It "giveth life to all things" and is "the law by which all things are governed." It is also "the light that quickeneth" man's understanding (see D&C 88: 6-13, 41). In this manner, the light of Christ is related to man's conscience and tells him right from wrong" (Bible Dictionary, "Light of Christ").

[12] "The light which is in all things, which giveth life to all things, which is the law by which all things are governed, even the power of God" (D&C 88:13).

[13] "And the light which shineth, which giveth you light, is through him who enlighteneth your eyes, which is the same light that quickeneth your understanding" (D&C 88:11).

[14] "...and all things are round about him; and he is above all things, and in all things, and is through all things, and is round about all things; and all things are by him, and of him, even God, forever and ever" (D&C 88:41).

[15] "It is also the doctrine of Joseph Smith that from the presence of these Divine Beings [God the Father and his son, Jesus Christ] proceeds an essence or substance...variously called "spirit," "light of truth," "light of Christ," corresponding somewhat to what other teachers regard as "vital force" or "energy" which permeates all nature and constitutes the immanence of God in the universe; through which the purposes of the Divine intelligences are impressed upon other minds and also upon matter, and hence the orderly creations and their maintenance—the cosmos" (B. H. Roberts, *A Comprehensive History of The Church of Jesus Christ of Latter-day Saints*, vol. 2, 399-400).

[16] "For behold, I am the Father, I am the light, and the life, and the truth of the world" (Ether 4:12).

[17] "All things were made by him; and without him was not any thing made that was made. In him was life; and the life was the light of men" (St John 1: 3-4).

[18] "... And if these things are not there is no God. And if there is no God we are not, neither the earth; for there could have been no creation of things, neither to act nor to be acted upon; wherefore, all things must have vanished away" (2 Nephi 2:13).

[19] "God is light, and in him there is no darkness. He is the light of the sun and the power thereof by which it was made...He says it is the same light that enlightens the understanding

of men. What, have we a mental light and a visual light, all proceeding from the same source? Yes, so says the scripture" (John Taylor, *Journal of Discourses*, 327).

[20] "It has been emphasized by scientists that if matter may be resolved into 'radiant energy' then said energy may be brought back to matter; thus constituting a cycle from matter to 'radiant energy,' and from 'radiant energy' back to matter; devolution to energy; evolution from energy to varied forms of matter and life. 'What a shock it would be to Lord Kelvin (1824-1907) if he should hear the modern astronomers talking about the stars radiating away their masses through the mere act of giving off light and heat! And yet this is now orthodox astronomy. And, again, if they do so in accordance with the Einstein equation, then is it not more than probable that the process is also going on somewhere in the opposite sense, and that radiant energy is condensing back into mass, that new worlds are thus continually forming as old ones are disintegrating? These are merely the current speculations of modern physics.' (B. H. Roberts, *A Comprehensive History of The Church of Jesus Christ of Latter-day Saints*, Vol. 2, 390).

[21] "Protons and neutrons, are each made of sets of three quarks..." ("Subatomic Particle Relationships," *Subatomic Particle Families and Relationships*, Available: [Online] http://members.aol.com/cclinker/sapfaml.htm).

[22] A quark is an "elementary particle having electric charges of a magnitude one-third or two-thirds that of the electron" ("quark," *Dictionary.com*, [Online] Available: http://www.dictionary.com/search?q=quark).

[23] "We get into quantum physics, you see. It's all forms of energy anyway; there's no real substance [on earth] at all, except we know it does exist. We are aware of it at various levels. (Hugh Nibley, "Teachings of the Book of Mormon--Semester 1," *Foundation for Ancient Religion*, 75).

[24] "And the Lord God spake unto Moses, saying: The heavens, they are many, and they cannot be numbered unto man; but they are numbered unto me, for they are mine. And as one earth shall pass away, and the heavens thereof even so shall another come, and there is no end to my works, neither to my words" (Moses 1:37-38).

[25] "I am the light and the life of the world. I am Alpha and Omega, the beginning and the end" (3 Nephi 9:18).

[26] "Because God is the creator of life, mortal and eternal, he is worthy of all honor and glory. But there is another dimension. He, at any moment, sustains all life. John saw streaming from the throne light—green light. It is this "which giveth life to all things, which is the law by which all things are governed, even the power of God who sitteth upon his throne, who is in the bosom of eternity, who is in the midst of all things" (D&C 88:13). Thus, he generates all life everywhere, even in the heavens" (Richard D. Draper, *Opening the Seven Seals*, 50).

[27] Joseph Fielding Smith, *The Progress of Man*, 11.

[28] "The glory of God is intelligence, or, in other words, light and truth" (D&C 93:36).

[29] "So God created man in his own image, in the image of God created he him; male and female created he them" (Genesis 1:27).

[30] Theory of Darwinism, or the theory of evolution is built on the belief that organisms originated on the earth as one-celled organisms. Through evolution, a genetic adaptation of organisms to the demands of their environment, all the creatures of the earth became what they are today.

[31] "And there shall also be many which shall say: Eat, drink, and be merry..." (2 Nephi 28:8).

[32] "And many more such things did he say unto them, telling them that there could be no atonement made for the sins of men, but every man fared in this life according to the management of the creature; therefore every man prospered according to his genius, and that every man conquered according to his strength; and whatsoever a man did was no crime" (Alma 30:17).

CHAPTER EIGHT

EXPANSION OF DARKNESS

"And I saw one of his heads as it were wounded to death; and his deadly wound was healed: and all the world wondered after the beast" (Revelation 13:3).

00:09:04 15:53:10 Zulu
Saturday, March 27th
1:07 a.m.
Skull Valley, Utah

The International Secret Service

Lights swirled in the dark night around the Mahdi mansion. The Skull Valley reservation was still alive with police and media. Sergeant Tony Spellman, the Native American Skull Valley Police Sergeant, searched the ambulance for the girl in yellow that had come out of the mansion earlier. When he didn't find her, he called into the back where the two paramedics were taking care of other people. "Hey! Where's that girl that I sent over earlier?"

The male paramedic came to the mouth of the truck. "She was released into the care of the police."

"Which police? *I'm the police* and I don't have her."

The paramedic stood tall and scanned the mammoth lawn, after a few moments he bent down and said, "I'm sorry, sir, but I cannot locate the officer I thought was in charge of the girl. He was just here a few moments ago."

"*Shoot!*" said Sergeant Spellman emphatically as he too scanned the area. "I needed to question her! There are just too many people taking things into their own hands around here. That's the problem! Too many chiefs on this reservation."

"Sorry, sir," said the paramedic. He shrugged then continued, "If I see her, I'll call you."

"Good. Thank you," said the Sergeant as he turned away from the paramedic.

Right then, another black, sinister looking helicopter appeared and hovered over the mansion.

"Now who is this?" Tony asked himself angrily.

Within seconds the craft had nimbly landed on the grass next to the others from the U.S. government that had come uninvited.

"I wish the U.S. would just stay out of this!" Tony murmured. "We are capable of handling our own situations!"

The side door of the helicopter slid open and four men in black suits, jumped out. One of them flashed a badge to an officer standing by.

"*CIA!*" Sergeant Spellman said forcefully under his breath. "*What in the heck are they doing here?*" he asked into the cold air causing a billowy steam cloud to encapsulate his head. He narrowed his eyes as he watched one of the men speak into a small handheld communicator, while two others in white jackets appeared from inside. They pulled a large stretcher out of the helicopter with them. As the wheels unfolded, the stretcher hit the ground in one motion; then the men hurried towards the mansion.

"That's it!" The sergeant took a deep breath, shook his head and walked forcefully toward the helicopter. It was time to figure out what was going on and stop this three-ring circus! But as he drew closer, an unexplained feeling of discomfort began to grow inside of him and he slowed his pace. Quickly shaking off the feeling, he spoke sternly to the man in black who was guarding the helicopter doors.

"*Who are you and what's going on here?*" he shouted over the thunderous roar of the chopper. The man responded coldly by flipping open his wallet and displaying his badge.

Officer Spellman stepped forward and looked closely at the badge. His eyes widened as he saw the United Nations Seal and the bold, black letters spelling out INTERNATIONAL SECRET SERVICE at the top.

"*What in the heck?*" he blurted. Now things were way out of control. Why was the ISS in Skull Valley? Knowing he had no power to stop the operation, he moved back a few steps and watched.

A U.S. SWAT lieutenant in fatigue gear marched up to Sergeant Spellman and yelled over the wind whipping in his ears. "Who are these guys?"

"They're ISS," said Tony.

"What?" questioned the lieutenant "What are *they* doing here?"

"Your guess is as good as mine!" yelled Tony. "Maybe the voodoo guy that owned this mansion offended people in high places!"

The lieutenant's face turned red with rage as he exploded angrily, "*Whether or not he did, those guys can't take anything out of this house!*"

Tony Spellman smiled sarcastically, having secret satisfaction in the lieutenant's frustration. "Looks to me like they *can* and they *are!* You and I both know that the International Secret Service can do whatever they want!"

The lieutenant swore loudly.

"*Hey, I don't like this any more than you*! Address your concerns to them, *not me!*" exclaimed the sergeant forcefully. He turned away from the lieutenant intending to leave, but then he stopped suddenly as he noticed the stretcher being brought from the mansion. It was heavily laden with an odd shaped object covered by a white sheet. The men from the helicopter carefully carried it down the wide, stone steps.

The stretcher jarred as it landed on the stone, and the sheet slipped down a little. Sergeant Spellman's eyes were drawn to a rigid, steel bar jutting straight out of the top of a human head covered with thick black hair. Tony realized it was the body of Imam Mahdi, the religious guru who owned the mansion.

The men in lab coats eased the stretcher into the chopper and rolled the door closed. The whipping whir of the black helicopter's blades increased as the engines roared. The sound was almost deafening and the brutal wind from the down wash of the whirling blades, cruel. Dust punished Tony for standing so close.

The SWAT leader moved from behind Sergeant Spellman, covered his face, and yelled to Tony over the deafening sound, "*President MacEntire will be interested in this one!*"

Sergeant Spellman shook his head slowly and took a breath. At least this lieutenant was being civil. He decided to engage in simple conversation to smooth things over as the helicopter pulled away. "Ever get the feeling something bad is going to happen?"

"Yeah! It's a constant in my job!" shouted the SWAT leader.

"Well, I have been having that gut feeling since those guys landed."

"Yeah, I swear those guys are nothing but trouble, badges or no badges," said the SWAT leader.

Tony nodded. "I think this time you got it right. The pot is boiling."

"Yeah, but who's turning up the heat?" asked the SWAT leader.

"Someone very, very high up, no doubt," said Sergeant Spellman, wondering if they would ever know.

3:05 a.m.
New York, New York

Discussions of Destiny

Cardinal Apollo Ramius[1] had just been summoned to an emergency meeting in New York City. He was called away from important church business in Rome when the Pope had suddenly died in the earthquakes that had rocked the earth.[2] The church was in commotion in an effort to select a new Pope. An influential American associate who went by the name "MD," had requested his presence at his mansion in America. The Cardinal immediately rescheduled all of his meetings and left the moment he received the message.

Although MD was calling a meeting in New York, he had many mansions in other countries. He was *the* mover and a shaker of *all* movers and shakers, rubbing shoulders often with the influential political icons of the world. It was common knowledge in political circles that the President of the European Union, the President of the United States, the Secretary General of the United Nations, and even the late Pope himself were personal friends whom he regularly entertained for festive weekend celebrations in his mansions.

MD had billions. He was powerful in every walk of life and one could tell he loved to have his hand in everything. With a nod of his head, he could sway the elections of entire countries by pouring money into support of the candidates sympathetic to his economic or political causes. With the wink of an eye his financial managers would withdraw his money from any market around the world. He could affect the world economy as stocks plummeted, beginning an avalanche of sell offs.[3]

The Catholic Church was no different. It too was affected by MD's religious whims. Cardinals who had not cared what MD desired of the church found their deepest secrets "leaked" to the media, causing great devastation.[4] Cardinal Ramius could not afford his secrets to be revealed. No, the truth was, no one fought against MD There was only one thing to do when he made a request, and that was to comply.

Apollo prized his progression within the Church's ranks. Currently he was the youngest and most elevated Cardinal in the history of the Catholic Church; well on his way to achieving his life's ambition to become Pope. His early progress was no mistake. Everything he did in life was geared to obtaining his dream. There was nothing on earth he desired more—and he would do *anything* to obtain it…*anything*….[5] Logically, however, despite his desires and careful designs there were many more senior Cardinals in line ahead of him. It was likely that the College of Cardinals would not elect Cardinal Ramius to that position.

Apollo eased into the plush, leather seat of MD's Lincoln that had picked him up from the airstrip in New York. He contemplated his meeting with one of the most powerful men on earth. The Cardinal didn't stifle his smile. He was confident that if he moved carefully and graciously, he would win MD's support. His influence could help Apollo in *many ways*. He could almost taste the prestige and honor calling to him from the Papal seat. It would happen…he would make certain of it.

The Cardinal closed his eyes. He needed to rest now, for he knew that when he reached MD's mansion, he would have to be calm, wise, patient, and as perceptive as a perfect Cardinal should be. The energy required for such perfection had to be conserved.

After an hour drive, the limousine finally turned off the main highway and pulled up to a tall, iron gate that stretched out in either direction as far as the eye could see. Once inside, the limousine proceeded down a long drive lined on both sides by mammoth bare trees. The full moon, still shining brightly in the dark early hours, thrust quick stabs of moonlight between the spear-like branches.

Cardinal Ramius was impressed with the vast lawns, hedge mazes, and castle-like mansion they were approaching. It occurred to him that MD's property could rival the Vatican itself.

The limousine slowed as it entered an enclosed, high brick and flagstone archway. The moment they stopped an attendant opened the door and extended two white-gloved hands to assist the Cardinal out of the car.

Once inside the two solid oak, twenty-foot-high doors, a highly refined butler approached, bowed and offered the Cardinal a sparkling glass of Perrier with a twist of lemon.

The Cardinal took the glass and raised it slightly. He rose subtly onto his toes as he said, "Thank you," then he rocked back and took a sip of the cold, sparkling water. The frosty temperature of the drink surprised him. It was always interesting to him how the Americans preferred their drinks ice cold.

"Your Eminence, MD is expecting you. Please follow me to his private library," said the butler. He bowed slightly, then turned and walked in stiff cadence down the great hall toward an adjoining foyer.

They entered a room that was more like a great hunter's lodge than a library. The paneling was solid mahogany, and no doubt came from one of the forbidden rain forests. Various heads of vanquished beasts ranging from African lions to tigers from India, adorned the wooden walls in snarling sneers, surely victims of countless safaris.

At the far end of the room a blazing fire burned brightly in a cavernous fireplace, which stood no less than seven feet high and ten feet wide. A Persian rug covered the floor, and a high-back chair hewn from burl wood and covered in animal skins and plush, thick leather faced the fireplace.

"May I present, His Eminence, Cardinal Apollo Damon Ramius of Germania," said the butler to the empty room, as he lowered his eyes and head in a slight bow.

Slowly a hand, adorned with lavish gems, appeared above the high back of the chair and gestured for the Cardinal to come into the room. "That will be all, Reginald," rasped the familiar, rough voice of MD from the chair as he lowered his hand again.

Without a word the butler bowed, reached out wide with both gloved hands and slowly pulled the double doors closed.

"Come sit with me, Your Eminence," choked the billionaire through a cough. He didn't move from the chair.

Cardinal Ramius moved a plush chair slightly to the side of the fireplace and facing MD

"Our deepest sympathies to the Church, friends, and family of his Holiness, the Pope," rasped the gravelly voice.

A look of grief crossed the Cardinal's face. Looking down he said, "Thank you, Mr...."

"MD, call me MD," said the gruff man in the chair.

"MD Yes, this tragic loss has been felt around the world," agreed the Cardinal.

"Yet—ahem!" MD coughed from many years of smoking. "Excuse me, Your Eminence."

"It's nothing," said Apollo smiling politely.

"Divine providence seems to have brought an opportunity for you to give a gift of great profundity to the world" said MD

The Cardinal wondered to which opportunity this man was referring. He folded his arms while still holding the glass of water in his hand. "It seems, you have me at a loss," he said, and then lifted the crystal glass of Perrier to his lips and drank deeply.

"Apollo...may I call you by your first name?" asked MD, his bushy eyebrows arched.

"Of course. I deem you a friend."

"Good. Apollo, times are desperate in this worn out world, and the hour is late, may I be frank with you?" asked the billionaire. He leaned forward for the first time and looked deeply into the Cardinal's eyes.

Taken slightly aback by the intensity of the conversation, the Cardinal lowered his glass and responded, "Certainly, uh, MD. Is there something you want me to do?"

"Apollo, I have been watching you."

Apollo swallowed self-consciously. What was MD getting at? "In what way?" he asked.

"In all the right ways," continued MD "I see a future for you, and without mincing words, let me just say that I can assure you unfathomable success."[6]

MD's statement captured Apollo's interest. Maybe this conversation would yield something valuable! "I am pleased to hear that," he said, maintaining a demeanor of stone. "Continue, MD," he urged calmly.

"I have sent an urgent memo to key leaders all over the world. Many will meet with us in my mansion in Germany. The meeting will include delegates from all the great nations of the world, such as the President of the United States, the Prime Minister of Great Britain, the leaders from the Arab League of Nations, the Prime Minister of Israel, and the Secretary General of the UN, and more. Also present will be the Chairman of the Tri-Lateral Commission, and leaders and high clergy from most of the world's largest organized religions," continued the billionaire in gravelly but grandiose tones.

The Cardinal was amazed. "That will be a powerful meeting—but how will it affect my future?" he queried as he shifted in the oversized chair.

"Apollo, you are no doubt aware of the demise of Imam Mahdi, a figure thought of by many to have been Christ himself?"

The Cardinal narrowed his eyes and took another sip of the bubbly water. Imam Mahdi was not a favorite subject with him. He had seen a considerable drop in membership because of the sudden appearances and many miracles he had performed all over the world. He nodded slowly.

"His death, along with that of His Holiness, the Pope, has lead us to a very curious juncture," rasped the billionaire.

"To what end?" asked Apollo.

"*Global peace and unity.*"

"You have my attention, MD, but I still don't follow," said the Cardinal. "I don't understand how the death of two of the world's most influential religious leaders could possibly bring peace."

"I'll explain," said MD, as his eyes widened and became more intense. "For the first time in history we are about to do something that will answer countless centuries of heartfelt prayers and the cries of the world."

"And what is that?"

"Apollo, we are literally on the verge of nothing less than uniting *all* the religions of the world under one church! Our church!"

Apollo was astounded. Such an attempt was surely fantasy. "Your statement cannot be true!"

MD leaned closer and whispered, "Not only is it true, *you*, my friend, hold the final key that will open the door."

"I have the key? Forgive me, MD, but how can this be possible? I know of no way global peace and unity could be a reality, especially if sponsored by the Catholic Church. Our world is angry, harsh, irreverent, unbelieving…"

The billionaire laughed loudly then patted the Cardinal's arm twice. "Yes indeed, it is! However, I promise you that with the honor and power you are about to receive, you will accomplish the impossible. Centuries of religious conflict will end,[7] and terrorism and war will be abolished. It is something you can do, and *I will help you*," said the harsh voiced billionaire with a smile, pausing long enough for the Cardinal to grasp the weight of his statement.

Apollo was speechless. He did not know how to respond to such promises. To be heralded as the one to give peace and unity to the world would put him in a powerful position. "What you say sounds nothing less than miraculous, MD Tell me how such a thing could happen. I am too simple a servant to understand the breadth and depth of your words," Apollo said with an outward appearance of humility.

"That's what I like to see, a man who is willing to submit to a good idea when he hears it." MD laughed as he paused to take a long, Cuban cigar out of the breast pocket of his smoking jacket. He lit the cigar with a shiny, gold lighter then inhaled deeply. "You see, many years ago my family, along with the Rothchilds, the Rhodes, the Rockefellers, and other powerful leaders united in one great cause. We had the hope of world unity and lasting peace," rasped the billionaire.

"That is an ambitious goal," acknowledged the Cardinal. "It's a goal we should all have."

"Yes. You're right," said MD, clinching the cigar tightly between his front teeth. After blowing several billowing puffs of dank cigar smoke into the air, he licked his lips and continued. "Now, here is the rest of the story— no one expected this Imam Mahdi to have such a meteoric rise in the religious world, but the fact is, he did. His charisma and believability were captivating. He persuaded the best of all religions; Catholics, Greek Orthodox, the Order of Islam, and the rest, to believe that he was their awaited leader, whether it be Buddha, Muhammad, or Jesus Christ himself."[8] MD looked up, worried that he might have offended the Cardinal. "Excuse me, Your Eminence," He said apologetically.

The Cardinal nodded once and held up a hand for MD to continue his explanation.

"Anyway, always at the center of this movement was the very charming, brash, and persuasive leader, Imam Mahdi. His devout and growing retinue ranged dramatically from conservative, peaceful religious groups to wild, zealous, and sometimes violent organizations throughout the world. Nevertheless, we were amazed at his accomplishments."

"I, too, was amazed. I felt he was a crook and a deceiver but still, I was amazed," admitted the Cardinal.

"We began to study him and his so called 'miracles.' The curses he pronounced seemed to be real. If anyone attempted to rebel against him, he would punish him or her with a flesh eating disease. It was as if they were being eaten alive by fire. Not only that, he could turn the most rebellious souls into obedient followers."

"How did he do this? Not even God can force a rebellious soul to be obedient."

MD looked up, took a lengthy draw on his cigar, then blew a grand billow of smoke above their heads. "Now that we understand how simple it was, I'm surprised that I didn't think of it myself."

"Tell me," urged the Cardinal.

"Mind control."

"Mind control?"

"Yes, a computer chip was used for the mind control through brain stimulation. We understand that Imam Mahdi successfully controlled several people. But he was a genius, he also embedded a virulent form of bacteria inside the chip, to be unleashed at a moment's notice if a harsher punishment was necessary."

"That is inhumane and insane!" The Cardinal was instantly offended.

The billionaire's wide smile exposed a single gold filling in one of his side teeth. "Exactly! It was perfect! And the most amazing thing was that because everyone thought this guy was God, no one suspected a thing!"

"That is blasphemous!" said the Cardinal.

"Yes."

The Cardinal's mind was almost numb with shock. "How did he implant the chips without being detected?"

"Oh, his follower knew about the chip. They were told it would be a protection to them when it came time for the world to be punished for rebellion."

"Rebellion?"

"Yes. Imam Mahdi took the whole 'end of the earth' rhetoric one step further. Since he had 'come again' as the supposed Christ, the world was going to burn…well, you know the story."

"Oh, I see…the chip was to ensure their protection. It was the mark that would make them his, as it says in the scriptures."

"Exactly."

"So everyone wanted it."

"Right," affirmed MD "Everyone who believed him."

The Cardinal nodded and then asked, "Where was the chip embedded?"

"Ah, just like it says in Revelation, it was embedded first in the palm and then in the forehead. Pretty cleaver, huh?"

The Cardinal studied the joy that emanated from MD "You think this chip is a good idea?" he asked with a frown.

"Absolutely! It was a fantastic idea! It *is* a fantastic idea. It will be the key to establishing peace and safety in the world!" exclaimed MD.

"How so?"

"In the last few hours we have analyzed everything that Imam Mahdi has done. We understand all of it, but we have mock ups of a plan that will improve his technology. Do you know what we call it now?"

"No," said the Cardinal trying to maintain an amicable attitude, but feeling disgusted inside.

"We call it the 'The Praetorian Guard'."

"Why the guard?"

"Because it will protect the people! Think of it. One little embedded chip will provide far-reaching security to millions. It will eliminate all rebellion of every kind."

"Why? Because you control their minds?"

"We will have that capability, but of course we wouldn't use it on the normal populations."

"Of course."

"We would use the chip for basic policing purposes. Think of it; all criminals could immediately be punished. Every citizen would know the price of lawlessness," rasped the billionaire. "All criminal activity would cease!"

The Cardinal was speechless. Searching for words of support, he said, "I didn't fathom that something of this caliber existed."

Apollo had misgivings about such an invasive system. There were too many ways a power hungry person could abuse it. His first impulse was to get up and walk out the door, but then he had second thoughts. It would do no good for him to oppose MD. Apollo concluded that if he left the house now, any possible benefit he might gain from this meeting would be lost. He would not progress in his calling, and he would lose everything! The Cardinal expelled a deep sigh. He knew that if he went along with MD's ideas, he would be given almost anything he desired. He would be on the old man's side. This was his chance. He asked himself what was so wrong with a system that punished criminals. That was not immoral, however, he wasn't sure about the mind control part.

Apollo hesitated, and then hoping his questions wouldn't be too obvious, he asked, "You mentioned that you wouldn't use mind control on the *normal* population. What does that statement mean?"

The billionaire blew another billow of smoke. "There are those who should be controlled."

"And who would they be?"

"You tell me, Apollo. Who would they be?"

Apollo searched his mind for an acceptable answer, "I don't know," he replied.

MD adjusted his weight in the chair and said, "Think about it. If there was a real, physical way you could stop, or even control evil men such as Stalin, Hitler, Osama bin Laden, or Saddam Hussein, wouldn't you be responsible, or perhaps accountable before God to do just that? If you could save the lives of millions of innocent people that those men would ultimately destroy, wouldn't you condone sacrificing those evil men? Surely you know that there is no difference between what I am proposing, and the death sentence."

"MD you make a powerful point, and of course I would wish I could protect millions of people from the predators of the world..."

"Yes! I tell you, you can and you should!"

The Cardinal was again surprised by MD's words. Why was he saying it was *his* duty?

Cardinal Ramius shook his head and said, "MD I'm sorry, but I believe these are the very dilemmas that have tortured the government of the Church for centuries. Sometimes God's divine will allows the destruction of human population, and who am I to intercede?" asked the Cardinal, his hands before him as if offering a prayer in respect of the Church's position.

"All right, yes, yes, that's a great line for the press and the general population, but Apollo, we are strictly off-the-record here. I want to ask you how you know that God does not *expect* you to use this technology? After all it is being handed to you. How, but through God's own will, could such a miracle occur? Could this not be the way the Lord will bring about the millennium spoken of in the book of Revelation?"

Apollo's mind reeled from the questions MD was throwing at him. As a man of the cloth, he needed to consider these things. He ignored MD's questions, and boldly stated, "You keep saying the technology has been given to *me*, when it has been made available to *you*. Please explain why you are repeatedly assuming my involvement in any of this."

"Because it is meant to be. I am who I am. I am *simply here to facilitate you*. All of it will happen as I have said."

"I don't accept that," said the Cardinal, shaking his head conservatively.

MD stuck his cigar in a holder on the table beside him and rubbed his hands together. Then he sat on the edge of his chair and cleared his throat. With a piercing look he said, "Look at your responsibilities. It's your job to protect the weak, the elderly, the mothers, fathers, women, and children!"

"Yes?" responded the Cardinal unblinkingly.

"What kind of humanitarian will you be if you deny this obligation?" scoffed the billionaire with obvious disgust.

The Cardinal hesitated. What was he doing? He had thought he was going to go along with MD, but now he was fighting him. He must stop cutting his own throat! He did believe in humanity! He did want world peace! Maybe he should just be patient and hear the rest of what MD had to say!

With determination the Cardinal tamed his own emotions and squared his shoulders. "I am sorry, MD, I have been unfair with you. You have me at a disadvantage. You know I have always been a passionate humanitarian. At the same time, I cannot easily and openly walk outside the boundaries and cannons of the Church without at least some measure of caution." Apollo sat stiffly in his chair, exhaled a sigh of stress, and somewhat remorseful but being honest to his personal beliefs, continued speaking. "So on one hand I fight your ideas, and on the other hand I am drawn to them."

MD was satisfied. He sat back in his chair, picked up his cigar, and said, "At last you have come to your senses."

Apollo continued, "I do believe, as you have said, that these *are* desperate times, the hour is late and the world is in dire need of healing and hope. Within that context, I suppose that identifying and stopping terrorists and bringing about world peace and harmony would be a good thing," conceded the Cardinal, hoping that he didn't sound too defeated.

"That's all we're saying, Your Eminence, and thank you for your humble honesty," affirmed the billionaire, a thin, wry smile playing subtly across his mouth. After taking another drag on his cigar, he pulled it out of his mouth, regarded it lovingly, and continued speaking. "It is my desire to give control over this system to you, *the sole mouthpiece and authority of God on earth.*"

The Cardinal furrowed his eyebrows. He suddenly understood that MD was offering him the very thing he had sought his whole life... the Papal seat! The Cardinal looked down at the floor. His stomach was tied in knots, and he wondered what he should do now. He needed to tread very carefully. He made eye contact with MD and nodded to let him know that he understood his offer. Then in a solemn voice that masked his anxiety, he asked, "So how would I control this system?"

"Good question—*Your Holiness,*" rasped the billionaire as he chewed and puffed on the slowly shrinking cigar.

Apollo tensed. MD had obviously attempted to flatter him. He didn't want to be controlled that way, but he couldn't deny that a part of him was drawn to MD's promises.

MD looked toward the ceiling and then back to Apollo, "The difficult words I'm about say require an open mind. I must insist that you listen carefully and withhold judgment until I have finished, Your Eminence."

Apollo flinched again. He knew weightier information was coming. This *was* going to be difficult. Despite that thought, the Cardinal nodded, but reminded himself that if he were to gain the Papacy, he would have to bite his tongue and be agreeable.

MD spoke. "You know me. I'm just going to dive right in. I don't like to mince words."

"All right," said the Cardinal apprehensively.

"We recovered the body of Imam Mahdi within twenty minutes of his death. We put him on ice and as we speak, he is being flown to the medical wing of the mansion in Germany."

"I see," nodded Apollo. Now he was really worried.

"Then there is *you.*"

"Yes? What about me?"

"Your Eminence," MD took one last puff on his cigar, then squashed the remaining one-inch tip of it in the ashtray. "Did you know that you are exactly the size, and have the same physical characteristics as Imam Mahdi?" teased MD, his gravelly voice clearing somewhat.

Apollo began to shake inside. Now, he sensed real danger. "What are you saying?"

"Trust me. You'll feel better after I explain," said MD. His eyes narrowed as he leaned forward to emphasize a point. "Apollo, I have always been aware of you. You have always been an amazing individual."

"Thank you," said Apollo hesitantly.

"Any student of ancient and modern history and sociology would recognize you as destiny's child. You are a direct descendent of the Caesars of Rome. I've watched you from your early years and have enjoyed seeing you advance in the Archdiocese of Germany. You are a man enjoying God's design and purpose."

"I would like to believe so," said the Cardinal honestly.

"I also believe it is no accident but rather a miraculous gift, that you have become remarkably fluent in so many tongues; German, obviously, but also English, and many others."

"Your knowledge of me is astounding."

MD continued, "The God of this world has placed his trust in you. You are his own very gifted, powerful icon in the world today. In fact, as we understand it, the Holy Catholic Church's College of Cardinals, the 'conclave,' has already chosen you to be the new Pope."

Apollo's mind was reeling. What was this? The conclave had chosen him to be the next Pope? He couldn't believe it! How could this be? It was impossible! "How do you know this?" demanded the Cardinal in great amazement.

"I just know these things," said MD coolly.

Suddenly Apollo's eyes narrowed. No, he didn't believe it. He knew MD was manipulating him. He was sure he had also manipulated the conclave…Apollo shook his head in self-disgust. It was happening again. His thoughts were pushing him to dangerous conclusions. The Cardinal cognitively stopped the avalanche of thoughts. No! Everything was turning out perfectly! How could he know if MD was manipulating anyone? After a moment the Cardinal relaxed, his face was expressionless. Maybe the conclave *had* chosen him. He was a good candidate for Pope…the *perfect* choice.

Apollo sat taller in the chair. Yes, all was well. MD was right, providence had brought him to this point. There was no other answer. He would listen and be open to his future.

MD stood, walked to a table, poured two glasses of red wine, and carried them back to the chairs. "I think it's time for a real drink. This wine is twenty years old and meant for this moment. Drink it. It will soothe your soul."

The Cardinal took the glass and looked at it. The liquid was as red as blood. He had always been both repulsed and tantalized by alcohol. At this moment the lure was strong. He took three long thirsty gulps. The fluid felt cold, yet warm as it drained into his belly.

"Your Holiness," addressed MD.

"Yes?" replied the Cardinal, looking lazily at the man seated before him. He wanted more wine. He wasn't drunk, but the stress of the day had taken a toll on him.

"I am prepared to support you in your greatest role, but it is much more than you think."

"What are you referring to?" asked Apollo.

"I am referring to the greatest position of power the world has ever seen. I am prepared to elevate you above the highest position of any religious leader on earth," rasped the billionaire, his voice rising to a crescendo near the end of his sentence.

"Higher than the Pope?" asked Apollo not really thinking ahead now.

"Yes. You see Imam Mahdi was the single most influential and powerful religious figure in the world, that is, for all religions other than the Catholic Church. He has successfully done the impossible by uniting many religions into one. That remains his current achievement despite his death."

The Cardinal nodded.

"Regardless of his personal idiotic behavior behind the scenes, we should thank him."

"Here, here!" said the Cardinal holding up his empty glass.

The billionaire stood and took the glass. As he moved to the decanter of wine on the table, he spoke over his shoulder, "Another good thing is that nearly all the world is completely unaware of Imam Mahdi's demise, despite the televised broadcast that seemed to mark the beginning of all the earthquakes."

"What broadcast?"

"Exactly!" MD refilled the Cardinal's glass. Then smiling, and turning back to the Cardinal he continued, "Imam Mahdi staged a sorry television broadcast to announce his official reign as the Messiah. It ended when he was speared in the head with a support beam."

"I see." It was all Apollo could say.

MD handed the wineglass to the Cardinal and sat in the chair beside him. "So from a global perspective, the Pope and Imam Mahdi hold the influence over most of the religious world. Our intent is to unite the two through an apparent 'miracle of God'," said MD, now leaning forward and staring intently into the pale gray eyes of the Cardinal.

The Cardinal silently considered what he had just been told. How could he and Imam Mahdi unite if he was dead? There was something missing here. The Cardinal slowly raised the glass to his lips, drank the wine, and said, "I continue to be at a loss. Are you thinking that we can invite all of Imam Mahdi's followers into the Church?"

"Yes, Apollo, that is exactly what we are going to do. One Church, one leader."

"I would give everything I have to see that happen," said the Cardinal, imagining such a grand day. It would be greater than any other day on the earth. What a gift to have so many souls giving honor to the Papal seat! Oh, if only it could be true! He would do anything—anything at all to make it happen. Then all would see that he, Apollo Ramius, was truly a great leader. "I would give everything to see that," said the Cardinal, this time to himself as he gave up his imaginations for reality.

MD smiled and said, "I was hoping you would say just that!"

"But alas," Apollo finally added, "it could never work."

"It will work. My plan is flawless," said MD, pointing his finger. "Let me ask you a question. What is the duty of the Pope?"

"To direct the people in the stead of God."

"All people?"

"Yes."

"Would God be happy if you were able to capture those that followed Imam Mahdi?"

"Yes."

"Does it matter what the Pope looks like?"

The Cardinal looked at MD with a puzzled look.

"Answer me, Apollo."

"Of course it doesn't matter what the Pope looks like."

"Just as long as he is the Pope, right?"

Cardinal Ramius frowned for a moment. What was MD getting at? "Right," he answered cautiously.

"And who do you serve?"

"The Holy Trinity."

"Yes, and as Christ sacrificed himself for the body of the church, could you sacrifice yourself in the name of righteousness?"

Cardinal Ramius answered quickly, "I could if called upon to do so."

"Then do it!"

"Do what?"

"Sacrifice yourself and you will gain yourself…isn't there a scripture like that one?"

"Yes, MD, there is…. Tell me how I would sacrifice myself to gain myself."

"Take on the appearance of Imam Mahdi."

"What?"

"We have the best surgeons and the most advanced technology to help you take on his appearance."

"And why would I do that?"

"To serve God, to sacrifice yourself, to lead the world. To take those that followed Imam Mahdi, the Messiah, and the Pope and bring them all into one! The Lord would be pleased with your ultimate selflessness to bring people to him!"

Although stunned, the Cardinal couldn't stop the smile that came to his face. That would be a great sacrifice, but he could see how such a plan could work! *It was pure genius.* He visualized the thronging nations, all giving praise and honor to him. The thought of it was intoxicating! Oh, the power it would bring. The Cardinal silently listened to his new associate.

"Cardinal Ramius, let me give you a greater perspective. The Catholic Church is the largest and wealthiest religious organization on the planet, yet numerically, she is vastly outnumbered by the combined memberships of all other religions."

"That is true," said Cardinal Ramius. He understood where MD was going with this line of thinking.

"There are approximately three-billion religious people in the world in addition to those who belong the great Catholic Church."

"You are right."

"Nearly two billion believers are looking for Imam Mahdi, and believe they found him in our departed friend. Another eight-hundred-million-plus devout Hindu's believe Imam Mahdi is their great, 'Vishnu' who is bringing Nirvana to the world. We haven't even mentioned the vast and growing New Age movement and various Religious Science groups that have hailed him as the long awaited Enlightened One."

"Yes, I understand."

"We mustn't forget the billions in China and India who do not embrace the Pope. Their leaders are looking for a state religion that will inspire the people to be satisfied with their government. We have their answer. It is you!"

The Cardinal, now comprehending the potential of the plan couldn't help being swept into the fervor of hope that it might work. He had only one more question. "What about the Church…" the Cardinal paused mid sentence and twisted his face in deep thought for a moment before continuing.

MD interjected, not allowing the Cardinal to finish his question. "My grandfather's contemporary, Albert Einstein, said the true definition of insanity is doing the same thing, the same way, over and over, and expecting different results. The world knows that the Holy Catholic Church and her Popes have had good intentions in bringing peace and healing to the world, but they have not yet been able to do it. This plan is a brilliant reach into the extreme; the greatest opportunity we'll ever have for real change."

"But how do we get around the truth?"

"I assure you, everyone will be told the truth. We will not hide your identity. You will still be the Pope, but you'll lead the whole world instead of only a part of it."

"But it doesn't make sense. It can't work. How would the Church still be able to…"

"Well, I'm glad you asked," interrupted MD "You see, that part is fairly simple and completely uncontestable, my friend. First, we will film the whole operation for replay to the conclave, the leaders and ruling governmental body of the Church. Second, you will choose two or three trusted clergy, from the Church hierarchy, to witness the operation and confirm under oath, both before and after, that you are indeed still *you*. It is essential that there be no doubt that you are still the man God has chosen to be Pope, regardless of your new good looks," teased the billionaire.

"I see, then the Catholic Church will be under obligation to honor me as the Pope, since I will still be me, the one chosen by the conclave in a irrevocable decision."

"Yes, exactly. It will be in answer to prayers that you will have the power to lead the whole world—this is the greatest opportunity ever given to any mortal man..."

"MD, please. You clearly are a gifted orator and persuader, but, please do not 'sell' me further on this plan."

"I will stop if you would like, but I must remind you that we have only a small window of opportunity. We must act now, while Imam Mahdi's tissues are viable for transplant, or this chance will be lost forever."

"I must meditate over night and think upon our conversation. I will have an answer to you by morning."

"Fine. You will not be alone in this decision. I have arranged the resources you will need to fulfill our plan. There will be a host of answers for every question you have."

"You're selling me again, MD."

"All right." MD stood and extended his hand to the Cardinal. "Enough said for today."

The Cardinal stood and accepted MD's handshake. MD knelt and kissed the Holy rings on the Cardinal's hand. Apollo suddenly understood the growing vastness of his own power, and how necessary *he* was to MD's plan. He didn't know the whole plan, but it must be grand if this powerful man would humble himself to honor the Cardinal. He could tell compliance was MD's greatest desire. Energy surged through the Cardinal's body and he felt empowered and strong. "Have your man show me to my quarters," commanded Apollo Ramius, almost too strongly.

MD looked up at the Cardinal. "Of course, Your Eminence," he said politely as he stood and pushed a button to summon his butler.

"I will see you in the morning," said the Cardinal.

"Yes, I will be looking forward to it," said MD as he opened the double doors.

The Cardinal nodded and with renewed strength, moved toward the doors. He was not the same man he had been when he arrived. The world had changed. He could feel it. Soon, *he* would be in charge, and *life would be magnificent.*[9]

Notes to "Expansion of Darkness"

Discussions of Destiny

[1] In an effort NOT to offend. It is the author's desire to clarify a notion in relation to the terms "Church of the Devil" and "Catholism."

A Cardinal from the Catholic Church is selected for this storyline, NOT to represent "the Church of the Devil." Although many have insinuated, even in one of the first editions of the Mormon Doctrine, such a relationship existed. Now, however, in the *Mormon Doctrine,* Bruce

R. McConkie defines the "Church of the Devil" as "all churches or organizations of whatever name or nature-whether political, philosophical, educational, economic, social, fraternal, civic, or religious which or designed to take men on a course that leads away from God and his laws and thus from salvation in the kingdom of God" (*Mormon Doctrine*, 137).

It needs to be clear that a Cardinal was chosen for this storyline purely to answer the question "How could one religion emerge on the world scene?" It is in this author's opinion that such a huge happening would have to include the cooperation of the Catholic Church because of their vast influence, power, and reach in our world today.

[2] Although it is true that the amount of significant earthquakes vary from year to year, the general trend is that earthquakes are increasing in number per year. The greatest example is to compare the earthquakes that happened in 1980 verses 2002. In 1980 there were 105 earthquakes of 6-6.9 compared to 130. The amounts of serious earthquakes that measure 7.0-9.9 have increased at a slower pace but have increased nevertheless. See http://neic.usgs.gov/neis/eqlists/graphs.html for up to date graphs that depict global statistics.

[3] The character, MD, is intended to symbolize the secret combinations of the earth that will threaten civilized society in our day as it did in ancient societies. "Secret combinations...are built up to get power, gain, and glory of the world. (See Helamen 7:5; Ether 8:9, 16, 22-23; Moses 5:31.)...Secret combinations brought down both the Jaredite and the Nephite civilizations and [have] been and will yet be the cause of the fall of many nations. (See Ether 8:18-25.)" (Ezra Taft Benson, Conference Report, Oct. 1989, *Ensign*, May 1989, 6).

[4] Secrets leaked to the world about Catholic priests' immoral activities were a true event. In reality there was a rash of sexual abuse claims that hit the media in 2002. An article found at http://www.cnn.com/2002/WORLD/europe/04/24/cardinals.communique/index.html reviews the Catholic declaration of their position concerning the many priests who had allegedly abused young boys under their influence. It is a fictional extrapolation that these news events are related to one source as portrayed in the text.

[5] The thought of an esteemed man of the cloth having such worldly desires of power, wealth, and prestige through his calling in the church is not a new idea. The Catholic Church has had similar difficulties of their clergy in the past. See the following excerpt from the Catholic Encyclopedia concerning the clergy of the fourteenth century during the Reformation.

"Gradually a regrettable worldliness manifested itself in many high ecclesiastics. Their chief object -- to guide man to his eternal goal -- claimed too seldom their attention, and worldly activities became in too many cases the chief interest. Political power, material possessions, privileged position in public life, the defense of ancient historical rights, earthly interests of various kinds were only too often the chief aim of many of the higher clergy" (J.P. Kirsch, "The Reformation" *Catholic Encyclopedia volume XII*, Available through New Advent, [Online] http://www.newadvent.org/cathen/12700b.htm).

[6] The notion of a factual political secret combination moving about in the political circles of the world, is not a new idea in our society. As brought up before, Ezra Taft Benson spoke a great deal about the threat of the world as well as America losing their freedom to designing and powerful people. On the back of "None Dare Call it Conspiracy" written by Gary Allen and Larry Abraham written in 1971, it outlines "an international conspiratorial drive for power on the part of men in high places willing to use any means to bring about their desired aim—global conquest." In reference to this book Ezra Taft Benson said, *"I wish that every citizen of every country in the free world and every slave behind the Iron Curtain might read this book"* (*None Dare Call it Conspiracy*, 21, back cover). The storyline found in this book has many similarities to the premises presented in the book quoted above.

[7] The UN views religious conflicts as one of the primary sources of violence in the world today. "Religious intolerance and discrimination on the basis of religion remain as one of the root causes of a number of conflicts, wars and ongoing violence in the world. Furthermore it is often a major motivation for attacks by extremists, against a minority group in the region. When religious discrimination is embedded in laws and social structures, this often leads to a victimization of minorities, as well as killings and assassinations" ("UN Commission on Human Rights, Sub-commission on the promotion and protection of human rights," *Ref. AP.11.E.03*, July-August, 2003, Geneva Switzerland, Available: [Online] http://www.paxchristi.net/PDF/AP05E03.pdf).

[8] Imam Mahdi is a factual expected leader of the Islamic people to come in the last days. The following was taken off the Internet site that proclaims his coming, as well as other religions expectations of a Savior. "The followers of all religions and traditions maintain such a belief and are awaiting the appearance of such a commanding figure under the divine protection Each tradition recognizes this figure with a different name and specific title. The Zoroastrians call him Saoshyant (meaning the 'savior of the world'); the Jews know him as the Messiah, whereas the Christians regard him as the Savior Messiah" ("Al-Imam al-Mahdi, The Just Leader of Humanity, Mahdi, in Other Religions," Chapter 3, Available: [Online] http://www.al-islam.org/mahdi/nontl/chap-3.htm#two).

[9] The Apostle Paul saw our day. He...warned that 'evil men and *seducers* would wax worse and worse, *deceiving*, and being *deceived*' (2 Timothy 3:13)." (Ezra Taft Benson, *The Teachings of Ezra Taft Benson*, 88; italics added).

CHAPTER NINE

INQUIRY

"And if thou wilt inquire, thou shalt know mysteries which are great and marvelous; therefore thou shalt exercise thy gift, that thou mayest find out mysteries, that thou mayest bring many to the knowledge of the truth, yea, convince them of the error of their ways" (D&C 6:11).

Paradise
Without time

Questions

Dane walked along the soft blue-green grass in his bare feet, out of the city and into what looked like a grove of trees. He had been wandering in this spirit world a while, how long he wasn't sure. There was no way to tell how much "time" had passed. He didn't even know if time existed in this realm without a sun and all. That thought made him wonder how anyone knew when to do things? David and Jonah had told Dane that everyone was busy with their "stewardships," but didn't the word "busy" indicate that there was a certain amount of "time" in which to be busy instead of being lazy?

These thoughts were overwhelming. He suddenly felt plagued with questions. Where was Jenessa? He needed to ask her some of these things. Wasn't that her job? Dane looked around. Where could she be? How was he going to find her? Maybe he should go back to the fountain. She might be looking for him there.

Just as Dane began to turn around, a sweet familiarity filled his being. The feeling was almost like breathing in the treasured scent of someone you love. He knew then that Jenessa was coming. In the next moment she stood before Dane. She was smiling—and those eyes, those eternal eyes, were looking into his.

"Hello, Dane," Jenessa said softly and confidently.

Dane felt a surge of energy, as if he was being strengthened by her presence. "Hello, Jenessa, I..." Dane stopped mid-sentence when he realized that he had almost said that he missed her. That would have been a huge mistake. He had met her only moments ago, or was it days? Who could know for sure?

Jenessa bowed her head and demurely said, "Yes, I know. I missed you, too."

Dane frowned. What? Did she say...? Remembering how communication was different between spirits he said, "Oh yes, you know what I'm thinking. Now I'm *really* embarrassed."

Jenessa smiled and tucked a stray hair behind her ear. "Don't be. You're being so sweet."

"Sweet, nothing, how is a guy supposed to court a girl if she always knows what he's thinking?"

Jenessa cocked her head to one side. "Are you courting me?" she asked with wide innocent eyes.

"Well..." he started to say, but then he stopped. He had to think things through. He was getting frustrated with himself. After all, was he crazy? Hello, insert foot in mouth for the third time, or was it the fourth? "...No, of course not," Dane answered quickly. "You're my teacher. I respect you as my teacher."

Jenessa smiled again and tucked some more hair behind her ear. Dane loved it when she did that.

"Good. Dane, I have to tell you that I am very pleased with your progress. Your willingness to learn has dramatically improved. You will be a very good missionary on earth."

Dane felt greatly encouraged. Wow, she thought he was doing something right! He didn't know what it was, but he was certainly glad he had done it. "Well, golly-gee-whiz, yes-sir, I think we should get to it— teacher. I'm starving for information." Dane smiled and tried to contain his excitement.

Jenessa returned the smile, but hesitated as if waiting for Dane to say something. Finally she said, "Did you have a question for me?"

What? What question? What was she talking about? Dane shook his head and shrugged. "No, you just go ahead and teach me whatever you want. I'm easy."

The smiled disappeared from Jenessa's face. "No questions? Not even one?"

Dane's mind went blank. He had questions before Jenessa appeared, but right now, he couldn't think of them. "No, Jenessa. Let's just learn."

Jenessa's countenance fell. Then she shook her head. "I guess you aren't as ready as I thought."

Dane frowned, what was happening? Why was he so clueless? Quickly, almost frantically, he asked, "What's wrong, Jenessa? I'm telling you to go ahead. *I want to learn.*"

Jenessa looked up, there was obvious disappointment in her eyes. "Dane, I thought I taught you this lesson. The desire to find answers must be accompanied by a willing heart."

"I have desire! Come on, Jenessa."

"No, your desire is not complete."

"Why?"

"Because you aren't searching for specific answers to specific questions."

"But I am!" Dane insisted.

Jenessa shook her head. "No, you were. Moments ago you were. You were so interested in finding answers that you called me here, but once I came, your interest disappeared."

"What?" Dane was flabbergasted. What was happening?

"Don't you remember that you asked me when you would be ready to learn?"

"Yes," said Dane as he nodded.

"What did I say?"

"I think you said, 'when I was ready to ask the questions'."

"Yes, exactly. Don't you remember the scriptures that say, 'Ask and ye shall receive. Knock and the door will be opened unto you'?"[1]

"Sure," Dane remembered a couple of examples.

"That is the way of learning. If I were to begin spouting off right now, about a subject that I choose, then do you know who would learn?"

Dane thought for a second. The answer snuck into his mind. He knew what she was expecting. "You?" he asked.

"Exactly. Me. Not you, but me. I would be focused on the subject I was teaching because it would be mine!"

Dane didn't know what to say. "Oh, I'm sorry, I…"

Jenessa interrupted, "Dane, I wasn't sent to teach myself, I was sent to teach you. You must want the truth as much as I want to give it to you. That is the only way a person truly learns."

"I see." Dane held up his hands. "OK, now I know. I'll do better."

"So what is it that I can help you with?"

"Ah," Dane tried to open his mind so he would know what he was supposed to be learning. It wasn't working.

Jenessa took a deep breath and shook her head. "I'll be back later."

"No! Don't go. I'll ask you a question. Just wait!" Dane frantically tried to retrieve a token question that would keep her there until he could think of other things to ask. "Umm, what do I need to know to be the best missionary I can be?"

Jenessa looked at Dane with furrowed eyebrows. "Come on, I know you can do better than that."

"OK, let me talk to myself for a minute. Ah, I think I need to be patient, long suffering, and all that kind of stuff it says in the Doctrine and Covenants, right?"[2]

Jenessa shook her head.

"No?" asked Dane.

"No, I don't mean 'no,' I'm shaking my head because you still don't get it. You are asking questions only to second-guess what I want. Again, that is not how it works here. This is not about me." Jenessa heaved another sigh and walked away from Dane.

Dane sensed great despair. He wanted to take Jenessa in his arms and comfort her, but he didn't, instead he said, "Maybe you're right. Maybe you should go. I don't want you to be this sad."

Jenessa shook her head again. "No, it's my fault. If I were someone else, you would be on the right track. I think I'm distracting you. I don't know why the Lord called me to this job. He should have called someone big, hairy, and male, instead of me."

Dane was alarmed. He didn't want someone big, hairy, and male. He wanted Jenessa! He bolted forward and took Jenessa's hands. "No," he blurted, "I know why he chose you! I love *you*. Jenessa, I promise, I will listen to you. I don't know why, but I need *you* to teach me..." the words barely crossed his lips when he was overcome with shock. He let go of Jenessa's hands and turned away from her. "I'm so sorry. That was uncalled for. I'm going on a mission. What am I thinking? My priorities are totally in the wrong place."

There was a moment of charged silence before he felt a tap on his shoulder. "It's alright," she whispered. "Life is a continuum. Many things will come to pass. Our future could be one of them. We will see."

"No. I don't deserve a future like that," answered Dane angrily. "If I can't control myself here, who's to say I can control myself back on earth. I can't control my thoughts. I can't control my actions. I'm a failure! I just got here and already I'm a failure!"

Jenessa gently took hold of Dane's shoulders and turned him around so he was facing her. She touched his face with the tips of her fingers and looked into his eyes. "You have great passion. You didn't realize it before because you were still sleeping. But now you have awakened. The new 'you' is emerging, and you are full of emotion and desire. This newfound energy will give you great power that will convince people on earth of the truth. We just have to figure out how to channel it, that's all."

Dane stared deeply into Jenessa's eyes, finally understanding her urgent need for him to want to find the truth. He knew she was right. It all made sense now, if he desired truth, it would be his, but he had to want it. He had to want it as much as he wanted Jenessa to be his forever. In Dane's mind, both desires were one. He would do whatever it took to have both in his future. "OK, I'm ready now. I understand fully. It's time."

Jenessa sat down on the grass and Dane sat beside her. They would begin this lesson with a complete understanding of what they were to accomplish.

4:30 a.m.
New York, New York

The Visitation

Apollo had changed into a pair of comfortable, loose cotton lounging pants, tee-shirt, and slippers. He moved to a large window that overlooked pools and vast lawns. "Such opulence and wealth!" he said to himself covetously. He opened the heavy curtains wider. What would it be like to live like this, surrounded by the finest things of life day after day?[3] His circumstances were not shabby by any sense of the word, but they were nothing compared to this.

Scolding himself for his petty thoughts, the Cardinal shook his head and walked over to the bed; he would sleep now. He ran his hand indulgently across the thick comforter. It was inviting to the touch. He pulled the comforter from beneath the pillows, and crawled between the silk sheets beneath it. Apollo relaxed and sank deep into a feather mattress that settled around every curve of his body. He could get used to this!

Lying in tantalizing comfort, the Cardinal realized he had forgotten to say his prayers. Rather than move from the deliciousness of ultimate bliss, he decided to repeat the Rosary in the warmth of the bed. He fell asleep before he uttered a single word of prayer. Fatigue had stolen his mind, and he drifted into the misty void of dreaming....

The Cardinal sat atop a high pedestal. Far below, he saw millions of people, their eyes focused singly upon him as they obediently worshiped him. He knew he must say something, for they waited so patiently.

Apollo stood to speak but was distracted by the weight of the priceless jewels that adorned his robes. He became acutely aware he was also wearing a hat. He reached up and felt the edges and dimension of his headpiece. He gasped when he realized that he was wearing the tall white iconic headpiece known all over the world as the Papal crown. The moment had come! He had obtained the highest office known to mankind. He was the Pope!

Looking again into the faces of the people, Apollo saw the admiration of the throng. They loved him! He knew it! As the crowd cheered, he lifted his hands high in a humble wave appropriate of a Pope.

Without warning, something in the distance appeared in the sky. An enormous red ball traveling towards him from the East, struck inexplicable fear in his heart. What was it? Might it be a sign? If so, he, God's mouthpiece, should be able to understand it. As he sought to discern the meaning of the sign, the ground began to heave. The people below him screamed and ran for protection, abandoning him.

The pedestal, upon which Apollo stood rocked violently, then toppled and sent him falling to the ground. He screamed for help, but no one stayed behind to protect him![4]

The earth shook and ripped apart, gapping open as if it were a hungry red mouth, ready to consume him. As he plunged into the darkness of the great hole, he heard a deep rumbling voice, saying, "*...ye are cast alive into a lake of fire burning with brimstone....*"[5]

The Cardinal woke with a start. Cold sweat poured from his face and wet his shirt. He threw back the now offending layers of coverings, and sat on the edge of the bed. What a horrifying nightmare! He must not read apocalyptic scripture any more! He was sure they were the source of his horrendous dream!

Looking out the window, he saw it was still dark. Slouching, and breathing hard, Apollo ran his fingers through his thinning gray hair. He glanced around and thought he saw a dim light glowing in the corner of the room. He blinked repeatedly, wondering if he was still dreaming. The light brightened, and soon became blinding.

Apollo instinctively raised one hand to shield his eyes then sighed in awe. What was this? He bounded out of the bed and flipped the light switch. He turned it on and off, but even when the bulb was on, there was no difference in the brilliance of the light that filled the room.

A man clothed in white robes stepped out of the dazzling luster. Apollo noticed he was comely and strong, a beautiful specimen of a man, but he sensed in his heart a mysterious darkness that he could not see with his eyes. Apollo squinted and rubbed his eyes in an attempt to understand the conflicting messages his heart and head were giving him. After a few moments, he consciously replaced the strange feeling in the pit of his stomach with the thought that it was nothing more than the aged wine MD had given him. His misgivings could be leftover emotions from his nightmare.

With renewed interest, Apollo took note of what surely must be an angel. His hair and eyes were black, a striking contrast to the shining countenance of his face. The man resembled the pictures he had seen of Imam Mahdi, yet his face was super-imposed over...who was it? The Cardinal squinted and rubbed his eyes again. He forced himself to see deeper, beyond Imam Mahdi's face, into the face of the angel. As he did this he recognized his own image! The vision was horrifying—yet exhilarating! What did it mean?[6]

"Who are you?" Apollo asked, almost in a whisper, patting his chest and face to assure himself yet again, he was not dreaming.

"I am he," said the figure in a voice both harsh and soft.

"What does that mean? Are you my Lord?" asked the Cardinal in anticipation.

"Yessss…"[7] came the voice. "I am *your* Lord."[8]

"Are you—" the Cardinal's voice faltered, for some reason he could not name Jesus Christ. In fact the words seemed to sting his mouth. He tried again. "Are you my Master?"

"Yes," came the voice. "I am the Son of the Morning."[9]

The Cardinal's eyes widened as the white figure held out his hands as if to take Apollo to himself.

The Cardinal responded by reaching out to grasp his Lord's hands, but he felt no flesh. Falling to his knees, Apollo attempted to kiss this man's feet, but his lips met only air. Looking up Apollo asked, "Master you hold out your hand, but I cannot take it.[10] I want to worship you, but I cannot touch you. Have I offended you?"

The man shook his head, "Why do you seek for me to have a body? According to your own Articles of Belief, I have no body, parts, or passions. I am the maker and preserver of things invisible and visible. I am eternity.[11] Doest thou not know me? I put out my hand to show you that I accept you as my servant."

"Oh!" said the Cardinal feeling ashamed and foolish. He bowed low to the floor and said, "I thank you! I knew you did not have a body as frail and as elementary as mine." Looking up slightly he said, "Please do not be offended by my simple assumptions!"

"I am pleased with your worship, Apollo,"[12] laughed the spirit.

"Thank you, my Lord."

"Rise and give your mind to me. There is no more time for petty thoughts. There is a work for you to do," said the glowing figure. Then the two transparent and overlapping faces smiled.

The Cardinal was relieved. "Yes! I am ready!" he exclaimed.

"I want you to take the place of Imam Mahdi in representing me."

The Cardinal was shocked. "Imam Mahdi? But he was a pagan imitation!"

"*DO YOU QUESTION ME?*" roared the being, with the voice of an angry wind.

Apollo cowered in absolute terror and rapidly shook his head. "Never! You know all! Who am I to tell you…"

"*I am the Son of God, I am the God of this world. Worship me and give me your will!*" yelled the being that continued to grow in size and fury.

"Yes, yes. I will obey," promised Apollo, timidly wondering what was happening. The figure's duel face contorted into an ugliness that he recognized, but in self-preservation fought to deny the obvious. He pushed his horrifying conclusions out of his mind. He was thinking the impossible. He shook his head and tried to appease the personage before him. "Please, Lord, let me serve you in a way that will please you."

The being returned to its previous calm state, and with a light that seemed to grow even brighter, said, "You are to take on Imam Mahdi's appearance, which is my appearance, and sit in his stead. I will give you power to lead the nations. They will follow you. Bring them to worship me. Reclaim them, for they have gone astray. They seek after an unknown God."

"Forgive me, Lord," said Apollo, "but I still don't fully understand how the nations will believe that the Papal seat and Imam Mahdi have become one? Where is the logic that will lead them to that belief?"

There was a glint in the eye of the snow-white being as he spoke, "The people will believe and they will follow you. Today is the day of my power[13] and you are to lead them in my paths. I cannot come to the world as myself, but am sending you in my stead. You are to stand in my place in fulfillment of the scriptures and the world's expectations of a Savior.[14] Even now, the leaders of the world look to you to unify the people into one. Claim the miracle of the transition, and the people of all nations will follow you."

Apollo bowed his head. "I will do as you say."

"Stretch out your hand in my name, and you will be able to perform mighty miracles in the sight of the world."[15]

"I've never done miracles before."

"As my servant, you will do many new things."

"Alright," agreed Apollo.

"Many will attempt to get in your way…"

"Yes, Lord?"

With almost a vicious smile, he hissed, "*Kill them!*"[16]

Apollo abruptly stood up from the floor, "Kill them?" he asked aghast.

"Yes, shut their mouths. Send them to the world of the dead, that they may not speak against me."

"How?" said Apollo not knowing how to do the thing this being was commanding him to do.

"Hide your deeds carefully from the world. Control those who follow you with a tight reign. Legions will help you maintain control over all, especially those who oppose you—and me."[17]

"Yes, Lord."

"This is your duty."

Apollo contemplated the words this great being spoke. Yes, there were many times in the history of the world when the church killed those that rebelled against the truth.[18] "It is thy will that I kill?"

"Yes. It's the ultimate peacekeeper. You will do this for the good of the nations."

Apollo nodded. Although killing would be an unsavory task, he knew it would be necessity to keep order in the worship of this being. "I understand."

"If you do these things, I will give you the power of the nations, the riches of the earth, and the honor of mankind."

Apollo had been offered these things twice in just a few hours this time by the most powerful of all beings. He knew that a glorious future would be his. A part of him felt liberated, and he answered zealously, "Yes, Lord. I will be thy servant and bring souls to thee, my God in heaven."

The room began to shake, and the being grew angry and pointed a finger at Apollo. The Cardinal could not breathe; it was as if his lungs had collapsed.[19] He struggled to take in a breath and clutched at his neck

"I am the God of the earth! I am the greatest of all! You will bring souls to ME! Do not become confused about whom you serve!"

The vice on Apollo's lungs released and he drew in a deep breath. Looking up he was forced to admit that this was not Christ. Now, he understood why there had been no sense in anything the being had said. He cowered in the corner of the room. This must be Satan! What were his options? How do you fight someone with such great power and no body? What should he do? Believing that he needed to obey the angry spirit or suffer death, he slowly nodded and prudently rose to his feet. "I understand everything now," he said.

The being came closer, closing in on Apollo. He reached out and touched Apollo, causing extensive sores to cover his body, and his skin to burn with fiery pain.[20]

Apollo screamed as he saw his flesh melt away and pain overtook his ability to think.

"You will give up all to me! I own your soul! You sold your pious office years ago when you loved yourself and power more than God! You love me! You gave up everything for what I can give you![21] You turned your back on your beliefs and reveled in secret plans of manipulation! You became my son a long time ago! You have been supporting my goals and thus have already become a son of perdition."[22]

The sores disappeared from Apollo's flesh and the pain ceased. In sadness he looked down at his hands. He knew that this being, which must certainly be Satan himself, told the truth. He searched his heart, and realized his own hypocrisy. He had never truly represented the Lord Christ. Everything had been done in his own best interest, and he had done it through lying, cheating, and manipulating. Great tears began to flow down his cheeks as he looked truth in the face. His breath heaved within him. It must be too late for him. He was too far-gone, and now Satan believed him to be his…well, maybe he was right.[23]

Apollo raised his head to look at the being, and saw darkness. All of a sudden, a new vision opened up to him. He was shown the world. He was shown his place among the most successful Popes who had ever walked the earth. He was shown the great palace in which he would eventually live, and the opulence that would be his. He saw himself reach forth his hand and strike people dead with a mere thought, or cause lightening to strike at his word. Despite his sadness, the visions called to him. He wanted what they promised. He had worked the whole of his life to ascend to power, and he would be foolish not to take the opportunity that was before him...even if he had to become as Judas to accomplish it. All he knew was that Satan's power was too great, and his hunger too fierce for him to fight. He wasn't strong enough to endure any more of the dark, evil wrath.

His body weakened, the Cardinal climbed into bed and fell fast asleep in a fetal position. At the moment, it was his only solace.

In My House There Are Many Mansions

Dane and Jenessa took a break from their lessons.

"Jenessa?" asked Dane. He tentatively touched her hand. Then with a gentle brushing motion traced her fingers. Her arm was extended and she supported her body by pressing her hands into the grass.

Jenessa looked down at her hand, and then smiled at Dane. "What?"

"I was wondering..."

"What were you wondering?" asked Jenessa, smiling as she pretended to pluck a piece of grass and throw it at Dane.

Dane flinched then smirked as he realized Jenessa was teasing him. Shrugging his shoulders he looked up through the branches of the tree above him. "Where is everyone?" he asked, absentmindedly.

Jenessa raised one eyebrow and looked at Dane. "Who is 'everyone'?" she asked.

Dane perused the majestic branches above him. "You know—the other people—are they OK? I mean, do they live in a nice place like this?"

"I hear your thoughts Dane. Thank goodness, because without that extra help I wouldn't know what you were talking about. You mean, people who die without the gospel, right? Is that what you're talking about?"

"Yes," said Dane, looking into her eyes. With Jenessa by his side, he was feeling pretty good about asking hard questions like this one. "My cousin died without the gospel," Dane continued. "He was a great guy. We were like brothers. I thought I would see him but he isn't here. I'm sure he must be in a good place."

Jenessa nodded. "If he was good, and I'm sure he was, there are many beautiful places in spirit prison."

"Prison?" Dane sat taller. He hadn't even considered that his cousin could be in prison! The thought stung his emotions.

"Oh, don't worry!" said Jenessa, sensing Dane's concern. "The word 'prison' sounds sort of harsh, but it really isn't. It's called prison simply because people like your cousin, the spirits that have not received the gospel, cannot progress until their ordinances have been done."

"So they have their fountains of light and broad oak trees?" asked Dane.

"Sure.[24] Hey, at one time, the whole spirit world was a prison, until Christ died and came here to reorganize it.[25] When he paid the price for all our sins, the righteous spirits were released.[26] Here they experience the happiness, peace, and rewards that came from living a righteous life."[27]

"What about evil people? I thought they were the ones that went to spirit prison."

"Yes, they do, but that is a different part of the spirit world."[28]

"So there are different segments of spirit prison?"

"Many different segments."

"I didn't know that."

"In fact, there are infinite levels of everything in the universe.[29] Wherever there is one kingdom, spirit, earth, or heaven, there is always one above and below it until you either reach the depths of hell, which is outer darkness, or the place of God's dwelling, which is the highest degree of the celestial kingdom."[30]

"So, who decides which people go where?"

"They do; the people themselves. It just depends on their heart."[31]

"Their heart?" asked Dane as he sought Jenessa's eyes for understanding.

"The Lord looketh on the heart,"[32] said Jenessa. She smiled and there was a twinkle in her eye. "Here, I want to show you something," she said as she stood and extended her hand toward Dane.

"Are we going somewhere?" asked Dane.

"Yes. You need to see the field and understand the work. It is the work you are called to do."

Dane touched Jenessa's hand, and suddenly they were in a new place.

Notes to "Inquiry"

Questions

[1] See Matthew 21:22. The commandment to ask in order to receive of God is given in the scriptures at least 35 times. It is proper procedure to show desire through asking, in order to receive.

[2] See D&C 121:41-45.

The Visitation

[3] "O how foolish, and how vain, and how evil, and devilish, and how quick to do iniquity, and how slow to do good, are the children of men; yea, how quick to hearken unto the words of the evil one, and to set their hearts upon the vain things of the world!" (Helaman 12:4).

[4] "And thus we see the end of him who perverteth the ways of the Lord; and thus we see that the devil will not support his children at the last day, but doth speedily drag them down to hell" (Alma 30:60).

[5] "And the beast was taken, and with him the false prophet that wrought miracles before him, with which he deceived them that had received the mark of the beast, and them that worshipped his image. These both were cast alive into a lake of fire burning with brimstone" (Revelation 19:20).

[6] This scenario is meant to represent Satan's ability to appear as an angel of light in order to deceive. "And no marvel; for Satan himself is transformed into an angel of light" (2 Corinthians 11:14).

[7] Satan often attempts to claim Christ's personage and authority. He came to Moses stating he was "the only begotten" indicating his attempt to trick Moses and appear to him as Christ. Satan must have done a good job at imitating the appearance since Moses had to think through his knowledge from previous appearances of Christ to decipher if the being standing before him was Christ or Satan. See Moses, chapter 1 for the account of this confrontation in context.

[8] "And thus we see how great the inequality of man is because of sin and transgression, and the power of the devil, which comes by the cunning plans which he hath devised to ensnare the hearts of men" (Alma 28:13).

[9] "How art thou fallen from heaven, O Lucifer, son of the morning! How art thou cut down to the ground, which didst weaken the nations! (Isaiah 14:12).

[10] "There are two kinds of beings in heaven, namely: Angels who are resurrected personages, having bodies of flesh and bones—For instance, Jesus said: Handle me and see, for a spirit hath not flesh and bones, as ye see me have. Secondly: the spirits of just men made perfect are they who are not resurrected, but inherit the same glory. When a messenger comes saying he has a message from God, offer him your hand and request him to shake hands with you. If he be an angel he will do so, and you will feel his hand. If he be the spirit of a just man made perfect he will come in his glory; for that is the only way he can appear—Ask him to shake hands with you, but he will not move, because it is contrary to the order of heaven for a just man to deceive; but he will still deliver his message. If it be the devil as an angel of light, when you ask him to shake hands he will offer you his hand, and you will not feel anything; you may therefore detect him" (D&C 129:1-7).

[11] The following is an excerpt of the Catholic Article I. It is a statement of belief originally taken from the 1517 copy from the Church of England. This Article is meant to teach those who are considering baptism the Catholic perceptions of God. "There is but one living and true God, everlasting, without body, parts, or passions; of infinite power, wisdom, and goodness; the maker and preserver of all things both visible and invisible. And in unity of this Godhead there be three Persons, of one substance, power, and eternity; the Father, the Son, and the Holy Ghost." To find more information about further Articles of the Catholic and Protestant religions, one site is http://members.tripod.com/~gavvie/39 articles/articles.html.

[12] It seems that worship is the foremost desire of Satan. He desired the honor of God in the pre-existence, which is the worship of the hosts of heaven (Moses 4:1), requested worship from Christ during his mortal ministry (Matthew 4:9), and commanded Moses up on a mountain to worship him (Moses 1:19).

[13] "Today you are witnessing the fulfillment of a prophecy. Today is the day when the devil has power over his own dominion" (Harold B. Lee, *Decisions for Successful Living*, 221.)

[14] "Satan is irrevocably committed to countering and overcoming the influence of the Spirit of Christ upon men. He is the representative, promoter, and advocate of that 'opposition in all things' referred to by Lehi in his instructions to his son Jacob. (See 2 Nephi 2:11, 14-18.) Satan's methods are various, devious, and countless. '... by every possible means he seeks to darken the minds of men and then offers them falsehood and deception in the guise of truth. Satan is a skillful imitator, and as genuine gospel truth is given the world in ever-increasing abundance, so he spreads the counterfeit coin of false doctrine. ... [As] 'the father of lies' he has ... become, through the ages of practice in his nefarious work such an adept 'that were it possible he would deceive the very elect.' (Joseph F. Smith in Daniel H. Ludlow, *Latter-day Prophets Speak*, pp. 20-21.)" (Marion G. Romney, "Satan—The Great Deceiver," *Ensign*, June 1971, 35).

[15] "And he doeth great wonders, so that he maketh fire come down from heaven on the earth in the sight of men, And decieveth them that dwell on the earth by the means of those miracles which he had power to do in the sight of the beast..." (Revelation 13:13-14).

[16] Murder has been a tactic of Satan to remove the righteous influential servants of the Lord from the beginning. Often murders are committed by a secret combination in hopes to benefit by the removal of people who work against them. "Wherefore, the Lord commandeth you, when ye shall see these things come among you that ye shall awake to a sense of your awful situation, because of this secret combination which shall be among you; or wo be unto it, because of the blood of them who have been slain; for they cry from the dust for vengeance upon it, and also upon those who built it up...[they] seeketh to overthrow the freedom of all lands, nations, and countries; and it bringeth to pass the destruction of all people, for it is built up by the devil, who is the father of all lies; even that same liar who beguiled our first parents, yea, even that same liar who hath caused man to commit murder from the beginning; who hath hardened the hearts of men that they have murdered the prophets, and stoned them, and cast them out from the beginning" (Ether 8:24-25).

[17] "There is a conspiracy of evil. The source of it all is Satan and his hosts. He has a great power over men...His evil influence may be manifest through governments; through false educational, political, economic, religious, and social philosophies; through secret societies and organizations; and through myriad's of other forms. His power and influence are so great that, if possible, he would deceive the very elect, (see Matthew 24:24)." (Ezra Taft Benson, *The Teachings of Ezra Taft Benson*, 404).

[18] The history of the Catholic Church is littered with violence, from the times of Constantine, to the wars erupting now in Ireland.

[19] Satan has the power to bind the physical body in efforts to intimidate. See Joseph Smith's account: "After I had retired to the place where I had previously designed to go, having looked around me, and finding myself alone, I kneeled down and began to offer up the desires of my heart to God. I had scarcely done so, when immediately I was seized upon by some power which entirely overcame me, and had such an astonishing influence over me as to bind my tongue so that I could not speak. Thick darkness gathered around me, and it seemed to me for a time as if I were doomed to sudden destruction. But, exerting all my powers to call upon God to deliver me out of the power of this enemy which had seized upon me, and at the very moment when I was ready to sink into despair and abandon myself to destruction—not to an imaginary ruin, but to the power of some actual being from the unseen world, who had such marvelous power as I had never before felt in any being..." (Joseph Smith History 1:15-16).

[20] If it is the will of God, Satan can also afflict men with physical adversity. "So went Satan forth from the presence of the Lord, and smote Job with sore boils from the sole of his foot unto his crown" (Job 2:7).

[21] "It is very important to know that Satan has power to deceive men and to blind men and to lead men captive at his will, even as many as will not hearken unto the voice of the Lord. Sin and evil come from Satan, and godliness and eternal life in the kingdom of God are from the Lord. 'And he became Satan, yea, even the devil, the father of all lies, to deceive and to blind men, and to lead them captive at his will, even as many as would not hearken unto my voice.' (Moses 4:3-4.) The apostle John said, 'He that committeth sin is of the devil; for the devil sinneth from the beginning. ...'(1 John 3:8)" (Bernard P. Brockbank, "Hearken Unto the Voice of God," *Ensign*, May 1974, 113).

[22] The statement that Apollo is a son of perdition is a lie. Elder Bruce R. McConkie has written that a son of perdition "commits murder by assenting unto the Lord's death, that is, having a perfect knowledge of the truth he comes out in open rebellion and places himself in a position wherein he would have crucified Christ knowing perfectly the while that he was the Son of

God. Christ is thus crucified afresh and put to open shame" (Doctrines of the New Testament, Vol. 3, 161). It is obvious that Apollo has never had enough knowledge to make him a son of perdition, but Satan says this to cause Apollo to think that he is already condemned so he will lose hope of anything else.

[23] This statement is also a lie. The truth is that Satan only has power over people who give him that power. So many in this world believe, as this Cardinal did, that they are too far-gone and are not candidates for the atonement. There is nothing that this Cardinal has done that has barred him from the atonement. The path he is on can be changed; however if he listens to Satan, he will tell this lie to lead him further using depression and the belief that punishment is just and deserved and cannot be avoided. All of God's children have the opportunity to bind Satan. We bind him through Christ and through our righteous choices. "Yea, verily, verily I say unto you, if all men had been, and were, and ever would be, like unto Moroni, behold, the very powers of hell would have been shaken forever; yea, the devil would never have power over the hearts of the children of men" (Alma 48:17).

In My House There are Many Mansions

[24] "It seems unjust to consign to a place of torment those of a terrestrial spirit or, more particularly, those who are of a celestial nature but who have not yet had the opportunity to hear and accept the gospel. Should such be consigned to a place of suffering? To so suppose obviously does not accord with the justice of God…the scriptures assure us that our works will follow us after death. Men and women of goodness here will be of the same nature there and enjoy the fruits of their labors even as they await the day when they will be taught the gospel" (Joseph Fielding McConkie, *Answers: Straightforward Answers to Tough Gospel Questions*, 107).

[25] "And also they who are the spirits of men kept in prison, whom the Son visited, and preached the gospel unto them, that they might be judged according to men in the flesh" (D&C 76:73).

[26] "And as many of the spirits as were in prison came forth, and stood on the right hand of God; and the remainder were reserved in chains of darkness until the judgment of the great day" (Moses 7:57).

[27] "And then shall it come to pass, that the spirits of those who are righteous are received into a state of happiness, which is called paradise, a state of rest, a state of peace, where they shall rest from all their troubles and from all care, and sorrow" (Alma 40:12).

[28] "And I said unto them that it was an awful gulf, which separated the wicked from the tree of life, and also from the saints of God" (1 Nephi 15:28).

[29] "If two things exist, and there be one above the other, there shall be greater things above them; therefore Kolob is the greatest of all the Kokaubeam that thou hast seen, because it is nearest unto me. Now, if there be two things, one above the other, and the moon be above the earth, then it may be that a planet or a star may exist above it; and there is nothing that the Lord thy God shall take in his heart to do but what he will do it. Howbeit that he made the greater star; as, also, if there be two spirits, and one shall be more intelligent than the other, yet these two spirits, notwithstanding one is more intelligent than the other, have no beginning; they existed before, they shall have no end, they shall exist after, for they are gnolaum, or eternal. And the Lord said unto me: These two facts do exist, that there are two spirits, one being more intelligent than the other; there shall be another more intelligent than they; I am the Lord thy God, I am more intelligent than they all" (Abraham 3:16-19).

[30] "Such language is simply figurative [concerning spirit prison]. Certainly some will be in a state of eternal torment, but not everyone will be. [Sprit prison] is simply the nation of departed spirits. Its cities have their ghettoes but also their pleasant suburbs. Kindred spirits by

nature gather together. Where honorable men and women have gathered, honor prevails. Where people of peace, virtue, and goodness choose to assemble, there such attributes will also be found. Others unlike them would be unwelcome and would seek society among those of like spirit" (Joseph Fielding McConkie, *Answers: Straightforward Answers to Tough Gospel Questions*, 107).

[31] "Death, which must come to all men, brings with it an inheritance in paradise or the consignment to hell. It is a judgment...for those who sought light will be united with children of light; those who knew naught but darkness will inherit the same. Truly our works follow us" (Robert L. Millet and Joseph Fielding McConkie, *The Life Beyond*, 61).

[32] "...For the LORD seeth not as man seeth; for man looketh on the outward appearance, but the Lord looketh on the heart" (Samuel 16:7).

CHAPTER TEN

ALL THINGS BECOME ONE

*"For verily I say unto you, Till heaven and earth pass, one jot or
one tittle shall in no wise pass from the law, till all be fulfilled"
(Matthew 5:18).*

00:09:04 05:45:25 Zulu
Saturday, March 26th
8:15 p.m.
Jerusalem, Israel
Mount of Olives

Jerusalem

Conrad adjusted his weight forward in the padded seat and placed his
elbows on his knees. He clasped his hands and rested his head on his fingers
and thumbs, like he used to do in sacrament meeting when he was young. He
could still hear his mother's voice in his head telling him to "sit up and
listen." This memory brought him comfort as he sat thousands of miles away
from his family. In response to the memory of his mother's words, Conrad
noticed that even though he didn't sit back, he was still listening intently, and
he remembered that he always whispered to his mother "*I am listening.*"

Conrad was at a missionary conference in the Jerusalem Center. They
were in a room right outside the main auditorium. The missionaries called it
the forum. His eyes were closed, and the words from the podium spilled out
of the amplifiers, filling his head. The voice of a senior sister missionary,
Sister Hall, filled him with symbolic spiritual imagery that lightened his soul.

"Israel, the Holy Land, the Promised Land,[1] a land of many names given
throughout time. This location, the geographical mother of Muslim, Jewish
and Christian religions, the chosen mother[2] of the twelve tribes,[3] has been the
central vortex of spiritual belief on this earth. When she became desecrated
through wickedness in the face of knowledge, she lost her stature and place

nigh to God through powerful kings and their unyielding swords.[4] Her fall from grace was devastating. Israel, a lamb full of beauty and grace, became a forlorn woman who had lost her children.[5] But that was not all that she lost. She also lost her husband, a prized marriage above all other marriages, to Christ himself.[6] What a sad transition. What a waste. What a terrible fall from a position of godly favor.

"With her innocence ravaged and her life blood spilt she lay trampled, ripped apart, and destroyed. Desolate from years of war and bloodshed,[7] those who were not of the covenant took her to wife. Uncomely and unholy marriages they became.[8] She longed for her previous place, but in torture, anger, and hatred her existence continued mercilessly. Finally, one day, a ray of hope once again began to shine upon her.

"Through wondrous miracles,[9] her gentile husbands were sent away, and with their leaving, returned her lost children.[10] In joy she opened up her land to the worn and homeless little ones. She nurtured them and fed them, loving them and remembering them. It was the beginning of a dream come true, one longed for for almost two millennia.[11]

"Today Israel is still an object of violence. She struggles to return to the ways of her covenants. She struggles to remember the oaths she had taken. She prays for her true husband and her other lost children to return to her. We are told that someday she will have been scourged long enough and her suffering for her unfaithfulness will have been complete. At that time Christ, her husband, and the remaining lost ones will return to her. God will then take her to his bosom forever, never to be abandoned again...."[12]

Conrad meditated and drank in the words of Sister Hall. He contemplated how Israel's fall from grace was a warning to the world. All who were in a choice position with blessings and authority could fall.[13] *Anyone could fall*, and it was prophesied that many in the last days would.[14]

Conrad thought about Elder Martin, his first companion in the mission field. He had seemed to be a rock, yet a couple days ago, he left the mission, left the church, and no one knew where he was. His family had written Conrad, but there was nothing he could tell them. Elder Martin didn't leave any clues other than a note that said, "The Lord expects too much. I'm gone." Conrad found Elder Martin's nametag, his "white bible," the nickname for the missionary rulebook, ties, his signed Books of Mormon, various pamphlets and other religious articles in the drawers of their dorm.

It disturbed Conrad to see someone so strong just fall away and leave everything that had been important to him. He often wondered if he too might just up and leave some day. He certainly hoped not.

In the time he had been in the violent environment of Jerusalem, he had already been spit upon, hit in the head and back by rocks, sworn at, and threatened, but still, none of that made him want to leave the church and the truth that it contained. Conrad rubbed his temples with his thumbs; he didn't even want to contemplate the mourning and sadness that would occur because of such a loss of privilege and potential. *That would be too much.*

Conrad knew his weakness all too well. He was aware of his quick temper and his impatience with other's shortcomings. He knew that he was prideful, judgmental, and slow to forgive. He fought daily to control his flaws. Some days he was successful in his efforts to change, other days he was not. But every person on the planet had similar trials,[15] and he was sure if he continued to plead for help, the Lord would protect him from himself.

Conrad's thoughts returned to the speaker. He slid forward in his chair, and then leaned back and relaxed, crossing his ankles in front of him.

Sister Hall was finishing her talk. "I wish, as we all should wish, to be a tool in the hands of God. Together, we can chisel the countenance of Christ back into the stone that is Jerusalem's heart, and in that work, be chiseled ourselves.[16] I know this can happen. Through the mercy, grace and love of Heavenly Father, we can be purified and feel his will strongly in our hearts and clearly in our minds.... Can you sense the hand of God hovering over us? We are not alone in this work. Angels surround us to aid us.[17] All will come to pass—when he comes."[18]

Sister Hall finished in the name of Jesus Christ. At that very moment, Conrad felt a low, subsonic rumbling below his feet that lasted only a second. His heart beat increased and his senses keenly searched for more shaking. The thought of another earthquake was tiring. Jerusalem had experienced a series of quakes that had rumbled in excess of ten times in the past 24 hours. Conrad hadn't felt all of them, but he worried about the possibility of a large one that could topple the entire city. He would lie awake at night, wondering if he could find a quick escape route out of the Jerusalem Center.

"Ahem. Excuse me, Elders," said their mission president as he leaned into the microphone. "I know you felt that quake, but there is no need to be alarmed. Just sit back and breathe deeply. The shaking has stopped, and everything is OK now."

The president looked toward someone just off stage, then he spoke, "I have brought someone here to speak to you concerning the earthquakes we've experienced here, as well as those happening throughout the world. Please give a warm welcome to Professor Graff, who is a seismologist from Brigham Young University."

Applause filled the forum.

"Hello, Sisters and Elders. It is good to see you young women and men. I want to tell you that the service you are giving is historic. Take courage and preach with strength. The Lord loves you and will protect you.

"Elders, you are especially a strength to us *older* guys, and an inspiration to all the girls who are waiting for you to return home!"

When the laughter had subsided the professor turned to Sister Hall who was sitting, expressionless, on a chair behind him.

"Oh sorry, Sister. I'm sure you and the other sisters in this room are an inspiration to many young men both here and at home." Turning again to face the audience, he continued, "One can't underestimate the power of women! My wife has encouraged me in righteousness for thirty years. I give credit to her for everything that I am."

Conrad watched for a response from Sister Hall. She smiled and nodded appropriately.

The professor took a breath and continued, "I have come to you today to discuss the increasing number of earthquakes that are occurring all over the world. It is no different here than in other places that lie along fault lines. There are incidents of earthquakes in Alaska, Japan, and even in Utah, and they are growing in number and intensity. This knowledge should not bring you fear, but rather cause you to see the wisdom in being prepared. It should give you a vision of the day when Christ will return to his people—for that day is coming soon, thus your mission here. The signs of his coming are all around us...many are happening even now, and he calls to his children through the voice of earthquakes...." Professor Graff paused, then smiled and said, "May they get the hint soon so we can stop all this shaking!"

After a few seconds of courteous laughter, the Professor pushed a button and a large colored map of Israel was projected on a screen behind him. "This chart depicts the risk of earthquakes along various fault lines," he said. Then using a pointer, he traced the eastern border of Israel. "Notice that the Dead Sea fault line runs along some of the most populated areas."

The professor looked into the audience... there was no sign of a response. "Do any of you realize the significance of a fault line that borders not only Jerusalem but also the Dead Sea?"

Conrad leaned over to his companion and whispered, "The Dead Sea is supposed to be healed by an earthquake."

The professor must have seen Conrad speaking because he said, "Elder, I believe that you have something to say, what do you think?"

Embarrassed, Conrad adjusted his weight in his chair. "I was just saying that the Dead Sea is going to be healed by an earthquake."

The professor's eyes lit up. "Yes, exactly! Is there anything else, Elder?"

Conrad thought for a moment and then said, "I think the Mount of Olives is going to split in two."

"Again! Very good! Yes, we can see now how prophecy will be fulfilled. Someday, an earthquake will actually save many of the Jewish people from total annihilation as they run through the new passage that will form when the Mount of Olives parts asunder. This should demonstrate that although earthquakes seem like events of destruction, the Lord is in charge and has control. Inevitably he will use the quakes to fulfill his purposes. In Jericho, for example, can anyone tell me how the Lord used a well placed earthquake to help Joshua?"

An Elder sitting on the other side of the room raised his hand. "Yes, Elder?" invited the professor.

"The walls-came tum-bling down," sang the Elder uninhibited.

A laugh rumbled through the forum.

"Yes! When Joshua fought the battle of Jericho, the walls definitely came tumbling down. I believe those walls fell because of an earthquake ladies and gentlemen.

"According to the estimates of Israeli experts, including some from the Geophysical Institute of Israel, the Jordan Valley segment of the Dead Sea Rift lies exactly where Jericho was located. They say that about every 1,000 years, it generates a major earthquake with a magnitude of approximately seven on the Richter Scale. Furthermore, we see from historical data that the last earthquake of that magnitude was in 1033, telling us that as we approach the year 2033, we should expect another big one. Doesn't that seem a little coincidental to the timing of the last days?"[19]

The professor shook his head and said, "I am here to testify to you that the Lord is in charge. He knows what he is doing. His purposes will be fulfilled."[20]

Another Elder raised his hand when the professor paused.

"Yes?" responded the professor, "The Elder in the back."

An Elder with fire-red hair thought for a moment and then said, "If it's true that we are expecting a big earthquake, and we are right along a fault line, and we have been having many smaller earthquakes—shouldn't we get the *heck* out of here?"

The Elders and Sisters laughed in agreement.

The professor smiled and said, "You'll have to talk to your ecclesiastical leaders about that one. However, having been on the committee that built this fine work of art, I mean the Jerusalem Center, I can tell you that it is built to withstand large earthquakes. I can pretty much guarantee that you are standing in one of the safest places on earth.[21] With the Lord's added blessing of protection, I believe it will withstand any earthquake as long as it is kept a holy place.[22]

"Stand in holy places, brethren and sisters of the gospel, and when the winds and hailstorms come, you will not be moved. When the earth shakes and moans, you will be protected. When plagues and illness come upon the earth, you will be spared."[23]

The mission president moved to the professor's side and whispered something into his ear. Then, with a look of seriousness, the professor moved to the middle of the stage. He took a deep, serious breath, and then said, "On the subject of earthquakes, ironically, it has been brought to my attention by your good mission president that a major earthquake, originating from the Skull Valley area in Utah has affected the Wasatch Front."

Conrad suddenly felt sick. That was where his family lived.

The professor continued, "Now I don't know the details, but I can get them. I just need to log in on my computer. I'm sure we'll have another opportunity to talk." The professor looked at the mission president who nodded his head.

"I'll fill you in on the details later this evening."

The mission president came to the microphone and said, "Any of you who have family in the area from Provo to Springville are to go to room 211 immediately."

Conrad stood up and walked to the aisle. His stomach tightened, and he felt queasy. He knew that the news could not be good.

Hearts Set on Riches

After sitting through an emotional meeting in one of the tents with other LDS members, Corrynne was more than ready for some food and then a nap. The meeting, a service provided by the BYU Psychology Department, was meant to "debrief" the victims who felt the need to discuss the events of the night before and deal with the realities of tomorrow. She had gone to the meeting more out of voyeurism than self-need, and was surprised when she was caught in the emotion of the meeting. Corrynne had thought she understood what she was feeling, and that her emotions were in check, but during the meeting she felt a flood of emotions that rivaled the flood that had stolen their home from them. She had cried more than her share because she didn't know where Dane and Carea were, or how they were doing. Tears of thankfulness also had fallen because she, Bo, and the other children had escaped the terror of the previous night without serious injury…or death. Never had she experienced such opposing yet poignant emotions. She wished she had some paper and a pen, just to record it. Maybe she would find some later. No matter what the outcome, this experience was definitely a central topic for their family history.

It was nearing lunchtime and concerned, selfless people from all around the city were delivering casseroles, fresh breads, desserts, fruits and vegetables to the people in the tent city. Her stomach growled at the thought of all that wonderful food, but her emotions still had control over her appetite. She didn't think she would be able to eat for a while, however she was thankful there was plenty for her children to eat. Brea and Jax were feeding the younger ones while she attended to the head wound Bo had received the night before.

Corrynne searched through the first aid supplies that had been provided to treat minor injuries. She gathered what she needed, and moved back to where Bo sat waiting for her. With sure movements she numbed his skin around the wound, but was distracted by a sudden outburst.

"What do you mean the building sites were uninsured! They are insured! We have all the insurance we need! Call AAMI. …What? …The dam

breaking WAS a sudden event! We're covered for that! ... I can't believe what I am hearing!"

"Sir?" said a young man with a sling on his arm as he tapped the red-faced businessman on the shoulder. He was the next person in line waiting for the phone.

Corrynne watched the two men from the corner of her eye as she slid a strait needle through Bo's numbed skin and secured a second stitch. "You doing OK, Bo?" she asked her husband.

Bo grimaced and closed his eyes tight. "Yes, but hurry. I hate needles."

"Stop squinting, Bo, or I'll sew your wrinkles in place."

"Oh, sorry," said Bo as he straightened out his forehead.

Corrynne continued to listen to the conflict over in the phone line, and even though she and Bo were a good ten feet away, she could feel the tension.

The red-faced businessman turned to look at the young man, pointed to the phone as if to tell him not to talk to him while he was on the phone, then he covered his other ear with his hand and yelled into the phone. *"The flooding was not from a water bed, it was from a dam breaking! Are these people idiots? Yes, I know the houses were located in the river bottoms but that is just a term used to refer to that area...."*

"Sir?" The injured young man tapped the businessman on the shoulder again. "This phone is for short calls. You've been on the phone for fifteen minutes already. We're all waiting to use the phone. Could you call those people back later?"

The angry man ignored the tapping. *"Yes, it used to be a river bottom before the dam was built. No! I don't have any other flood insurance! We weren't in a flood zone! I don't care what they say! I have twenty million dollars locked up in those housing developments! Fix this problem, or you're FIRED!"*

"Sir! All of us have emergencies. Please get off the phone!" insisted the injured man, now raising his voice.

Without warning, the large angry man took the phone away from his ear and with his other hand pushed the young man. As the injured man fell to the earth the man on the phone bent down and growled through clenched teeth, "Shut up! If you know what's good for you, you'll wait until I'm good and ready to get off the phone!"

Corrynne left the thread and needle dangling from Bo's face, and trudged over the matted and muddy grass to the businessman. "Calm down!" she said firmly to the man. Then she and two others helped the young man to his feet. "We're all in the middle of tragedy. We need to be supportive and patient, not angry and violent."

"Keep your nose out of this, *lady!*" shouted the man disrespectfully. "Don't be calling me violent. I'm not the one jabbing shoulders!"

In an instant, Bo was standing beside Corrynne. "What's the problem here?"

Corrynne looked at Bo, his barrel chest seemed larger and his shoulders broader than she had remembered. She marveled that he filled the space around her as he came to her defense. Looking up at him, she realized that the needle and black thread were casually swinging from his forehead. His wound gaped partially open like an extra mouth over his eyebrow. She gasped and covered her mouth with her hand. The effect was intimidating.

"Ah, nothing," said the man, gaining control over his temper as he looked up at Bo. "I'm under massive pressure. I just lost a fortune."

"I'm sure you did, but I think this young man deserves an apology for your abusive behavior towards him," said Bo, ignoring the needle that was swinging in front of his eyes. "We don't act like that here, no matter *what* the circumstances."

The wealthy man looked down at the ground as if weighing his options. It was obvious he didn't want to apologize.[24] He looked at the long line of people waiting for the phone, then hit the off button and handed the phone to the man he had pushed and headed towards the tent door. "*Self-righteous...*"[25] he grumbled, loud enough for everyone to hear, though the barbed statement was obviously directed at Bo.

The man backed toward the door with his hands out to his side. With a wicked glint in his eye he addressed the crowd, "A word to the wise. All you Mormons should be like me and get out of this religion now.[26] I've realized that people around here are only nice to you when you're rich and can give them a big tithing check. *Believe me*, I know."[27]

Corrynne watched the angry man leave the tent, and then she glanced questioningly at Bo. "What is his problem? No one here wants his money."

Bo shrugged, then turned and walked back to his chair. "Poor guy. He's got it rough."

"What?" asked Corrynne catching up to Bo. "He's the bully here! How can you feel sorry for him?"

"I'm not feeling sorry for him, but watching that much money go down the tubes can send a man over the edge. I can tell he's very close to losing it completely."

Corrynne pulled the rubber gloves on tight and made fists as Bo sat down. "Well, he needs to get over it! We've all lost a lot. What makes him so important that he can take his frustrations out on strangers?"

"Nothing. He can't. But just because I don't agree with him, doesn't mean I don't feel for the guy. People deal with catastrophe differently. Some people are humbled while others get angry. I can relate."

Corrynne raised her eyebrows and nodded. Bo was right. He used to get angry when things didn't go his way, but he was much calmer now. "So why is that?" she asked as she picked up the needle and poked Bo's skin. "Can you feel that?"

Bo raised his eyebrows up and down and then said, "No. I think the pain killer is still working." Then after a long pause he answered her first question. "I don't know. I'm easy. I guess I realize there isn't much I *can* control. Life's too short. I don't have enough energy to get angry any more. I'd much rather count my blessings. I guess I'm a lover now, not a fighter."

Corrynne smiled privately to herself. That was one good thing about adversity; it seemed to bring out the best in some people.[28]

Piercing the skin above Bo's eyebrow just below the wound, Corrynne pushed the needle through and then supported the skin on the other side with the fingers of her other hand so she could puncture the skin from the inside. Drawing the thread through the wound she tied a knot and then impulsively kissed the top of her husband's head.

"What was that for?" asked Bo.

"Because you're my hero. Have I told you that before?" Corrynne said with a straight face.

Bo looked up at Corrynne. "Awe, stop it—some more. Quit it—again," he said, and then he wrapped his arms around her waist and gave her a hug.

"OK, Bo, no public affection," said Corrynne chiding her husband as she held her gloved hands up to keep them from being contaminated by Bo's hair or clothing.

"Hey, that's my line," said Bo resuming his position so Corrynne could finish stitching his wound.

"I know but it seemed to fit," teased Corrynne as she resumed her stitching.

"OK, I'll be good," said Bo.

There was silence between the two, and as Corrynne continued to close the day-old wound she thought about all they had been through during the last 24 hours. It was amazing how lives could change in such a short time. Although her emotions were running amuck, reality still hadn't set in. She was sure she would notice when it did.

Corrynne's thoughts turned to her home, now half-submerged in floodwater. Surprisingly she didn't feel too remorseful about the things they had lost. Most of their possessions needed to be replaced anyway because they were worn out or beaten up through overuse. The only thing that nagged at her heart was the image of the children's baby books and the scrapbooks she had pieced together over the years, warped and falling apart from water damage. Luckily, a couple of years before they had scanned all the pages and put most of them on DVD so the kids could take discs with them when they left home instead of the bulky books. All but the most recent articles were permanently recorded. She was sure that since the DVD's were made of plastic the water would not destroy them. And they were in a closet upstairs in her bedroom, not on the first level where most of the damage would be. Technology had saved them this time, but losing the originals would still be difficult for her.

Corrynne's mind drifted to the idea of rebuilding, and the sting of remorse was gone. There was something inviting about the thought of starting over. She was secretly excited to have the chance. She knew they had insurance coverage, unlike the angry man who had left the tent earlier. Even though the cost of insurance had increased because of the natural disasters happening around the United States lately, she and Bo had chosen to keep the coverage. Looking back, she could see the value of that sacrifice! It had been a temptation to cancel it and take their chances…that would have been their ruin for sure.

As she made the last stitch in Bo's skin then tied the last knot, Corrynne wondered if the insurance company would allow them to demolish their 25-year-old house and build a new one. That would be fun! Maybe she'd get the large kitchen and extra bedrooms they had needed for a long time. In the next moment, Corrynne wondered if the insurance company would need receipts in order to replace everything that had been lost. That would be a problem. The receipts had been thrown away a long time ago. Maybe they would just give them an allowance to replace the furniture. Oh well, it didn't matter. Anything new would be an improvement over their old things.

"Excuse me," said the nurse who had been busily attending to people in the first aid corner of the tent just moments before.

"Yes?" asked Corrynne.

"You're obviously a nurse, too. What's your specialty?"

Corrynne looked at the kindly older woman and weighed her desire to reveal her abilities just yet.

"She's an Intensive Care nurse," said Bo without restraint.

"Oh good!" the portly woman exclaimed rubbing her forehead with the back of her wrist.

"Bo!" Corrynne exclaimed in astonishment. *"Maybe I didn't want anyone to know that!"* she said as she pushed Bo's shoulder abruptly. "They might expect me to go to the hospital."

Bo's expression was quizzical. "Corrynne? What are you saying? Of course they'll want you to go to the hospital."

"Yes," said the woman nodding her head. "The armed services are looking for nurses with intensive care experience. I guess the hospital staff is overwhelmed with serious injuries and they are asking any who can to help out," said the woman, "only if your own family has been taken care of."

"Of course," said Corrynne, contriving a smile. She really did not want to go. She wanted only to be surrounded by her family, if only to assure her that they were all accounted for. She was sure no one could blame her. Family always came first.

"How would the nurses get there? The hospital is a ways away on foot," asked Bo.

"The first aid helicopters are making trips back and forth."

"OK, well I'll have to think about it," said Corrynne suddenly wanting to run and hide.

"Who do we talk to?" asked Bo.

"Bo!" Corrynne giving her husband a warning glance. "Why are you so anxious? We just got here last night. I think we should take it easy for a little while."

"Well, I don't want to interfere," said the woman, beginning to eye Corrynne with reservation. "But I just thought I'd tell you. All the nurses that go will receive hazard pay."

"Great. Thank you for telling us," said Corrynne obviously ending the conversation.

The woman nodded again and returned to her work.

"A little touchy, Corrynne?" asked Bo.

"No! I'm a little protective of my right to be with my family during a disaster instead of being separated from them. We already have family members missing and I would rather keep us together than start taking off in the name of 'community service.' There will be a lot of time left for that." Corrynne waited for Bo to agree with her but he just raised his eyebrows and looked at her. "What, Bo?"

Bo tipped his chin up to Corrynne and then said, "Do you want to find Dane?"

Instant anger flared in Corrynne's chest. "Of course I want to find Dane! What kind of question is that?"

"Well, he isn't going to come here. He's going to be taken to the hospital! You saw him. He was sick!"

Corrynne reflected on the last time she saw her son. He was on the television screen, bent over like an old man. She bit her lip. She saw where her husband was going with this. "I know what you're getting at, you think I'll find him there."

"Yes, I do. Don't you?"

"Yes, I guess it is logical that he would be taken there. It's the nearest level-four hospital around. All the critically injured will be taken there as long as there's room for them."

"Exactly! Corrynne, this is your ticket to get over there. I've been trying to figure out how one of us could get to the hospital without a car. Someone needs to go over there and look for Dane and Carea."

"Do you think Carea would have gone to the hospital, too?"

"Of course she would. She would want to stay close to Dane."

Corrynne thought for a moment. Yes, Carea wouldn't let anyone drag her away from her brother if he was hurt. She was ferociously protective. "You're right," she said to Bo. "But what about the children? What about the twins? I need to take care of them. I need to be with them."

"What about them? You're talking to a dad here, and a darn good one!" Bo lifted his hand to Corrynne's cheek, "We'll be fine. I'll take good care of them, and Brea will help me. You go do what the rest of us can't do. You can get into all areas of the hospital. If Dane and Carea are there, you'll be able to find them"

"And if they aren't there?"

"They'll come," assured Bo with a knowing look.

Corrynne noticed Bo's confidence and decided she had better follow his advice. When he said things with that look it meant he knew something she didn't.

Corrynne studied the matted, muddy grass at her feet as she shifted her view about going to the hospital. She shivered a little, feeling her toes inside her shoes. They were still damp. Her clothes were grimy from the waist down! Oh how she longed to take a shower and sit in front of a hot fire and cuddle with each of her children…she didn't want to go to the hospital! If she went they would work her until she dropped. What about the nap she needed?

Corrynne closed her eyes tightly and tried to shake the negative thoughts from her mind. There would be no shower, no hot chocolate, no cuddling, and definitely no nap for a while. She had to be tough, unselfish and brave and just go. It was the right thing to do. She felt more confident, and became keenly aware that Dane and Carea needed her. Renewed hope of finding them began to replace her reluctance to leave Bo and the children.

"We'll be waiting for you."

"OK."

"In the mean time, you can do some good. Many people need what you can offer."

"Alright."

"Mom!" said Brea over the low noise inside the tent. "Mom? Where are you?"

"I'm over here!" called Corrynne.

"Oh good! There you are!" Brea had broken away from the mass of people going in and out of the tent, and was walking towards them. She carried a twin in each arm and Rocwell tagged along hanging onto her shirt.

"Tired of wrestling little ones? Did everyone eat well?" asked Corrynne, smiling slightly. She looked at each of the four children. Rocwell had something all over his face and the twin's sleepers were filthy. They must have been crawling around on the ground. It would be so good to find something to change them into and clean them up.

"Yes, Mom, there was so much food that we ate like it was Thanksgiving!"

Corrynne smiled brighter. "Good. That's very good. Where are Jax and Ry?" asked Corrynne, but her thoughts were diverted as she noticed there was something different about Brea. She was smiling contagiously. That was odd. Earlier she had looked so tired and spent. The change of mood piqued her interest "What's going on? Why are you so happy?"

Brea adjusted the twins as they struggled to get to their mother. "They're starting a fire out in the middle of the field with some other scouts."

"Is an adult with them?" interjected Bo, obviously not seeing Brea's face.

"Yes, they're fine," Brea quickly answered her father, then with wide and smiling eyes she spoke to her mother. "I've got something to tell you," she said excitedly.

"What is it?" asked Corrynne.

"Mom, *Matt is coming,*" said Brea smiling even wider than she thought possible.

"Matt? Where is he?" asked Bo getting up from his seat and taking Strykker from Brea.

"He's in a helicopter. He's coming to get me—if it's OK with you..." Brea added.

Corrynne knew Brea was just trying to be polite. She got the impression that her mind was made up and there was no chance of her staying.

"Helicopter? Whose helicopter?" asked Bo as he brushed loose debris off Strykker's sleepers.

"I'm not sure, but he sent a text message on my cell. He'll be here any minute," answered Brea.

Corrynne was disappointed. She had thought Brea would help Bo while she was gone. She took a deep breath and gave into another thought that she didn't want to accept. Brea needed to have her own life. Corrynne took Striynna from Brea's arms and said, "Of course it's OK with us. It's your decision. He can probably help you get showered and find some fresh clothes."

"Yes..." said Brea with a far-away look.

"What, Brea? Is there something else?" asked Corrynne.

"Yes, Mother, we're going to go get married."

"I know you're going to get married...what are you talking about?"

"No, now, Mother, right now. We're going to go find a temple that will allow us to get married now."

Corrynne couldn't believe what she was hearing! "What do you mean?"

"He's coming to get me today. We're going to walk into the nearest temple that will take us."

"Tell me why you've had such a sudden change of plans," said Corrynne trying to hold in the added emotions.

"Well, we were going to send out the invitations for the reception, but realistically, most everyone we would invite has been affected by the flood—so..."

Corrynne nodded. Suddenly she knew where this was going. "So you wonder why you need to wait."

"Exactly! Mother, there is no reason to wait. I'm worthy. I have a temple recommend."

"Where? In your socks?" asked Corrynne.

"It's on file, Mom. Remember now they have them in the computer systems at the temples?"

Corrynne nodded, and said, "Oh, yes."

"We've already been interviewed by the Bishop. Matt has found a sealer that has agreed to perform the ceremony..." Brea gave her mother a hug and then pulled away to look into her eyes. "I don't need a big wedding. I don't need a reception. I just need Matt, do you understand?"

Corrynne studied her daughter's glowing face, remembering her own engagement and how awful it had been waiting for the wedding day to arrive. Still, she wanted to attend Brea's wedding. It was her right to see her children get married and enjoy that time with them. She wanted pictures and memories.

"Oh, sweetheart!" Corrynne began, "I know you want to get married right now, but can't we wait for a few days until Dad and I can come? We want to enjoy your happiness, too." A thought suddenly came to her head. "Hey! Brea! Get married in this temple, here! We are sitting practically on the temple grounds!" Corrynne forced a smile.

"Mom, it's closed."

"It is?"

"Yes. Until the disaster is cleaned up it will be. There's a sign up on the door."

"How do you know?"

"I checked. It was the first thing I did."

Corrynne shook her head. "Please, Brea. Figure out something so I can be at your wedding, too."

"Come then!" said Brea with excitement. "Come right now! I'm sure we can work things out!"

Corrynne was enticed by the idea of being whisked away out of the mud and cold, but she refused to entertain those thoughts. "I would love to go with you but we need to be here for Dane and Carea."

"Well," said Brea as she reached out and lovingly pulled her mother's hair in front of her shoulder like she used to when she was a child. "We'll take pictures and come back soon—as long as you truly think it's OK."

Corrynne didn't think it was OK, but who was she to stand in the way of love. Smiling, she hugged Brea, and then with great effort, added, "Congratulations, sweetheart. I'm so happy for you." She nodded towards the tent door. "Go get married and be happy. We'll see you soon. Don't worry about us. Now go!" ordered Corrynne, pushing Brea away from her. "Maybe we can still have a small reception later, if not for you, then for me."

Brea stood in front of her family for a few moments. They heard the sound of a helicopter coming closer. Brea looked back towards the door.

"Mom! Listen!" said Rocwell, excited. He pointed to the sky. "I hear another helicopter coming! I'm going to go out and see if it's Matt—OK?"

Corrynne nodded and smiled. Rocwell loved Matt. "Yes. Go see it and take Brea with you. I'll be out in a minute."

Bo took a step closer to his wife and wrapped his arm around her shoulders.

Roc took Brea by the hand and led her out of the tent. Brea turned and smiled at her parents, and then in sudden excitement shouted, *"I'm finally getting married!"*

"Yes you are, sweetheart! Yes you are!" said Bo smiling.

"We love you so much. See you soon," said Corrynne as she nodded again.

Broadened Understanding

Conrad and four other Elders walked down the stairs to room 211. The Jerusalem Center was built on a mountain, so the second floor was actually below the forum. Room 211 was an empty dorm room. Conrad chose to stand while the other elders sat on the two beds and two desk chairs.

The mission president entered the room holding a piece of paper in his hand. "Thank you for coming down here," he said nervously. "We thought this would be a good place for you to make phone calls away from the other Elders." The President handed a satellite phone to each Elder.

Conrad took his and looked at the keypad as if the numbers were foreign. It seemed strange for the President to give him a phone. Mission rules didn't allow them to call home. This situation was obviously an exception.[29] A feeling of dread grew within his chest. Now he *knew* the news was bad.

"You may have as much time as you wish to contact your loved ones," continued the President. "We understand cellular phones in the area are still out for the most part. If your family has cellular phones, it may take you a while to get through to them so take as long as you wish."

Conrad frowned. It was taking a long time for the President to explain what had happened. He raised his hand. He needed to know what he was dealing with, so he could prepare himself emotionally.

"Yes, Elder Rogers?"

Conrad searched for an explanation of what had happened. "President Johnson, am I correct in assuming that you gave us phones because, something cataclysmic happened to the Orem-Provo area that may have affected, or even wiped out all of our families."

The President's forehead glistened with sweat. He looked down and then up again. "Well—we are unaware of what level of destruction that area sustained…"

"Destruction?" asked Conrad. "What happened?"

"Ah," the President looked around and then said, "Elders, the earthquake that hit Utah, caused the Deer Creek Dam to break and some others to sustain significant damage."

"The dam broke?" asked Conrad not believing what he had heard.

"Yes, Elder Rogers, it did."

"Did it just crack, or did the whole thing break apart?"

The President quickly looked from Elder to Elder then said, "I understand the whole thing broke apart."

"*Crap!*" said Conrad emphatically. His mission president and some of the other missionaries looked surprised at Elder Rogers' outbreak.

"I'm sorry," said Conrad as he shook his head.

"That's alright, Elder Rogers. Believe it or not, I've heard worse," said President Johnson as he patted Conrad on the back.

Conrad quickly walked out the door and up to his room on the third floor. He had to look up phone numbers on his laptop. There were too many to remember. His family had at least six cell phones.

"Ah, Elder?" yelled the President from the hall, "Your mother called us at nine this morning and told us that your family was OK."

Conrad stopped on the stairs and turned around. "My mother called here? At nine?"

"Yes. She did," the President answered. "She said she had to borrow a satellite phone because their cell phones weren't working but she didn't want you to worry."

Conrad's knees seemed weak as he was filled with intense relief. "OK— thanks," said Conrad hiding his emotions. He turned back toward the stairs and took a deep breath to release his anxiety. He wondered why the mission president had waited so long to tell him that his mom had called. He continued climbing the stairs to his room. He guessed that the president had his reasons for not notifying him, and that was fine with him, but he wished he had been told. Now he had an increased desire to talk to his family. He wanted to hear their voices with his own ears. He hoped there was a chance he could get through to someone.

Conrad powered up his computer and clicked on the file of phone numbers. The numbers popped up, including Braun's new one at the UN. He had received it by e-mail just a few days ago.

Conrad knew that the President wanted him to use his satellite phone downstairs, and he would eventually. First he had to see if he could contact anyone. Dialing his mother's phone first, he waited as it connected, but he got a recording. Next he tried his father's. Again all he got was a recording. Then he tried Brea's phone. This time he got a busy signal. He decided to try his own phone number, maybe someone had adopted his phone, but this time he got a disconnected message.

"*Forget this!*" He would call Braun at the UN. Braun would have first hand reports about what was really happening in the world. Maybe his mother had called him too. Conrad dialed the number and waited. It rang four times and then a message came on saying that Braun was unavailable.

"*Crap! Crap!*" said Conrad, losing all composure and hitting the disconnect button. "*I hate stupid phones that don't work!*" he said and then he threw the phone onto the bed. It bounced and landed face down on his pillow.

Conrad walked over to the sliding glass door that opened onto the patio that overlooked the city of Jerusalem. He felt helpless. He wished someone would answer a phone! Silently he began praying that someone would know he was trying to call, and...he didn't know what. If the phones weren't working, that was that. There was no way to communicate with anyone.

Conrad heard a buzzing noise, but ignored it. He heard it again and looked to see what it was. It seemed to be coming from under his bed. He knelt down and lifted the bedspread. He heard it again, and realized it was actually coming from on top of his bed. The phone was ringing! Conrad hadn't recognized the sound. Feeling foolish, he snatched the phone from the pillow. The caller ID said "United Nations."

Conrad quickly pushed the button. "Hello!" he said quickly.

"Hello?" came a woman's voice. "Who is this?"

"You called me," said Conrad in a frustrated tone.

"Forgive me, but this phone number showed up on a cell phone here, and we thought it might be an emergency," said the woman. "We're expecting some calls."

"I called Braun Rogers. He is an assistant to the Secretary General."

"Yes! I'm Chenille. I work with Braun. His phone is out of power. He needs a new battery, so he asked me to call you."

Conrad was energized. "Is he there? I have to talk to him. This is his brother. Tell him Conrad, or, Elder Rogers, needs to talk to him."

"No problem, Elder Rogers. Braun is in a meeting with Secretary Klump, but I'll go get him. He'll call you at this number."

"OK," said Conrad. "Thanks."

The phone went dead. Conrad flexed his fists and audibly thanked Heavenly Father. He felt the need to repent of the short temper tantrum he had pitched a few minutes earlier.

With elation, Conrad rushed down stairs to room 211, where other Elders were talking with their families.

"Did you get hold of anyone?" asked the president.

"Yes, my brother. He'll call me back in a few minutes. I think he'll know something about my family."

The president patted Conrad on the back then shook his hand. "I'm glad, Elder Rogers. You can find some privacy out on the patio."

"Thank you, President," said Conrad.

Conrad walked out to the cement pad that was dimly lighted by a single lamp. High walls built of red-clay brick surrounded the patio. Curving stone stairs led from this patio to others on the side of the mountain. He couldn't see the city from where he stood and he was thankful for the view from his own dorm room.

Conrad sat down on one of the steps and leaned his head against the cool brick. After a few minutes the phone buzzed and he quickly pushed the "on" button.

"Hello? Braun?"

"Hey, Elder Rogers! How are you?"

Conrad half smiled; it was good to hear a familiar voice. "I was doing great until I heard the news about the dam breaking."

"Yeah, that is a tough blow! But everyone's OK," said Braun in an upbeat voice.

"You sure?" asked Conrad, wondering if his brother was shielding him from the truth because he was on a mission.

"Yeah! Don't worry. Mom and Dad and the kids are being taken care of by everyone in the community. They are staying in tents up by the temple."

"So the house is demolished?"

"No. Mom says it's just flooded."

"So they'll be able to salvage it?"

"Probably. Mom didn't tell me all their plans, she had to get off the phone."

"So all the kids are OK?"

Braun hesitated. "You know, she said that 'everyone' was 'OK' so I assume that the kids are fine."

"Good," said Conrad. "So, Braun, since you're at the UN do you have maps that tell you what is happening in the world?"

"Sure. We have everything. Our satellite systems are better than crystal balls. You know the book about 'Big Brother' watching?"

"Yeah, was it *1984* by George Orwell, or something like that?" asked Conrad retrieving trivia from his memory.

"Yes, that's the one."

"I can't believe I remembered that book."

"Well we are 'Big Brother.' We see and monitor all."[30]

"That sounds a little intrusive."

"World security of course."

"I see," said Conrad, then he cut to another subject. "We're having earthquakes here too, do you show any connection between ours and the ones in Utah?"

"Are you thinking the Lord is mad at the Saints?" asked Braun in jest.

"No, I just think it's strange that the ground is moving on opposite sides of the earth at the same time."

"Well, let me explain. Earthquakes are happening all over the world. The one in Utah happened first, and it was a doozy. I think it measured 7.5 to an 8. The epicenter was west of Salt Lake in an Indian Reservation called Skull Valley."

"That is a strange place for an epicenter. That isn't even on a fault line," said Conrad.

"I know," said Braun. "It is strange. It seems that the moment the one struck in Utah others, of varying degrees of intensity, started happening all over the world."

"That reminds me of that scripture that says that the cleansing of the earth will begin at his house."[31]

There was a pause then Braun said, "Wow. You're right. Isn't that in the Doctrine and Covenants?"

"Yep," answered Conrad. "Section 112."

"...Well, I don't know if that scripture is referring to this moment though," said Braun after a pause.

Conrad reached for his scriptures and flipped to section 112. "I'm beginning to think that it does. I mean, think about it. Utah and Jerusalem are both the Lord's houses. You know, the Lord's people."

"Yes, but the earthquakes are all over the world," said Braun.

"I know, but you said yourself that they began in Utah."

"Well, the first one did."

"I think there is some significance in that."

Braun could be heard flipping some pages also, then he said, "Funny you should mention something like that, because right at the exact point of the epicenter there was a mystic man called Imam Mahdi that stole some CNN broadcasting time to announce to the world that he was the Messiah."

"What?" asked Conrad, closing the Doctrine and Covenants. "In Utah?"

"Yes. I didn't see it myself, but I'm told that the earthquake began during his meeting and that a steel shaft fell from the ceiling, pierced his head, and killed him."

"That sounds like an appropriate death for a blasphemer. I'm sure it made great news."

"Yes, you should have seen the media go crazy on that one. Newspapers and television broadcasts all over the world showed a picture of this guy being shish-kabobbed. His death should disprove rumors that he was the Messiah."

"God moves in mysterious ways. I like his style...I think," said Conrad with a smile, then he said seriously, "I don't know, maybe I don't like his style after all."

"What do you mean?" asked Braun.

"Well, if it is true that the earthquake was in response to this flaky fake Christ," began Conrad. "Why did the Saints have to suffer by losing their homes and putting everyone in danger?"

"Well I don't know for sure that the earthquakes started because of that Messiah-guy, I was just joking—kind of pointing out an interesting tidbit of information. Maybe it's only a coincidence, like earthquakes happening on both sides of the earth at the same time."

"Hmmm," said Conrad.

"What are you thinking?" asked Braun.

"The Lord promised in D&C 97 that if his people do not honor him after all that he has given them, that they will suffer afflictions, pestilence, plague, sword, vengeance and then fire.[32] Do you think that promise is being fulfilled? Do you think some of the Saints in Utah have mocked the Lord long enough and his anger is being unleashed?"

"Not all the Saints in Utah are bad, Elder Rogers."

Conrad shrugged. "I know, but I also know there is a good portion of them that are no longer righteous either. Neither hot nor cold so the Lord will spew them out of his mouth?"[33]

"OK, I was a missionary not long ago, so I understand the feeling missionaries have when they see things that seem like scriptural fulfillment, but you can't get too crazy with these ideas," Braun warned.

"I'm not crazy, Braun. I know what the scriptures and the prophets say. I know that throughout all time, whenever the Lord's people begin to rebel against him, they are not blessed anymore and bad things tend to happen...just look at the Nephites. They were completely wiped out!"[34]

"Conrad—I mean, Elder Rogers—we both know that the Saints will never be wiped out. We are promised that the gospel will not be taken from the earth again,[35] but that it is going to fill the earth."[36]

"I know, but we are also told that whoever does not observe all of the Lord's commandments will be visited with destruction."[37]

"Yes, I know the scriptures say that, but what are you going to do about it? We can't control everyone; we can't even remind them. We can't spank the Saints who choose to be naughty."

"I know. I can't, but I think the Lord can, and *is*."

"What?"

"Yes. I think the dam broke as a warning. Do you know if lots of people died?"

"Actually, I don't believe many did. I'm sure you remember that they have a great warning system. Those sirens are loud. I'm sure the warning was sounded in time for people to get out of the flooded areas. Don't get me wrong, there were some fatalities, but according to the data we have gathered here at the UN, relatively few died."

"See?" said Conrad.

"See what?"

"See? The Lord is calling to his people. He is calling attention to the finger of his power so that all might take warning and repent! If they repent now they won't burn at his coming. He is trying to save his people by chastising them."[38]

"I don't know. Many places have earthquakes, tornadoes, and fires. I don't necessarily think the Lord is calling to all those people. Sometimes bad things just happen to good people. We deal with them and go on."

"I think you have mingled with the world way to long,"[39] said Conrad with an edge to his voice. "You are starting to sound like them."

"Like 'them'? No, you're mistaken. I'm just thinking logically and not giving in to hysteria."

"So you're saying that I'm hysterical?"

"No, you've just experienced some traumatic news and it has you shaken up. Just step back and take a deep breath in through your nose—and out through your mouth," Braun condescended.

"I think our conversation has come to an end," said Conrad.

"Maybe it has. Have a great day, Elder Rogers."

"You, too." Conrad clicked the off button, then stood up and walked to the glass door. He set the phone on the desk and walked out of the room. He returned to his dorm and lay down. He had to cool off.

Conrad hated the way that conversation had ended. Why did he have to fight with his brother? Especially since he was on a mission and should have control over his temper. Conrad rolled onto his side and thought about his family living in a tent. At least they had escaped death. He was thankful for that. "*Let your hearts be comforted; yea, rejoice evermore, and in everything give thanks*"[40] the scripture came to his mind with force. Conrad closed his eyes and took a deep breath. He needed to relax and put all things in the Lord's hands.

Braun was right about one thing…no one had control over anyone else. Everyone had the ability to make his own choices.[41] Sometimes the righteous had to suffer with the wicked,[42] that was one sad consequence of this world. Righteous and wicked lived side by side…at least right now they did. It was the way of opposition.[43] Someday the wicked would not live among the Saints.[44] Then the Saints could be rewarded for their good works. He guessed that was what the millennium would be all about.

Why do we have to go through such hard times to get to the good life, wondered Conrad, pleading for an answer.

The answer came ever so quietly, "*Because this is the time to prepare to meet God.*"[45]

Notes to "All Things Become One"

Jerusalem

[1] Israel is known as the "promised land" because it was given to the Lord's covenant people as they were faithful to their promises. "And the LORD said unto Abram…Lift up now thine eyes, and look from the place where thou art northward, and southward, and eastward, and westward. For all the land which thou seest, to thee will I give it, and to thy seed for ever" (Genesis 13:14-15).

[2] Often the land is called "mother," due to its ability to give and sustain life. One can see this reference in the scriptures as well as in other religions.

"And it came to pass that Enoch looked upon the earth; and he heard a voice from the bowels thereof, saying: Wo, wo is me, the mother of men; I am pained, I am weary, because of the wickedness of my children. When shall I rest, and be cleansed from the filthiness which is gone forth out of me? When will my Creator sanctify me, that I may rest, and righteousness for a season abide upon my face?" (Moses 7:48).

[3] Israel was the name that "was given to Jacob at Penuel (Genesis. 32: 28) and at Bethel (Genesis 35: 10). It also applies to his descendants and to their kingdom (2 Samuel 1: 24; 2 Samuel. 23: 3). After the division of the kingdom, the northern tribes, as the larger part, retained the name Israel, while the southern kingdom was called Judah. The land of Canaan is also called Israel today. And in another sense Israel means the true believer in Christ, as explained by Paul (Romans 10: 1; Romans 11: 7; Galatians 6: 16; Ephesians 2: 12). The name Israel is therefore variously used to denote (1) the man Jacob, (2) the literal descendants of Jacob, and (3) the true believers in Christ, regardless of their lineage or geographical location. Israel was the home of the twelve tribes that came from Jacob whose name was changed to Israel" (Bible Dictionary, "Israel," 708).

[4] "While the children of Israel obeyed the Lord their God, the land abounded in wine, corn and oil, and they vanquished their enemies. When they departed from God and disobeyed his laws, those calamities, which were promised them through disobedience, fell upon them to the very letter even to this day. Their temple was destroyed, not one stone left upon another, as the Savior told, and the ground upon which it stood was plowed up by the Romans in search for gold which they expected to find there" (John Taylor, *Journal of Discourses*, 11:165-166).

[5] Ten tribes of Israel were removed from their land by the Assyrians in 721 B.C. and made slaves. Eventually they were released and both scattered and relocated to an unknown spot not to return to their land until near the second coming of Christ. The Babylonians removed the remaining two tribes from their land in 587 B.C. The Jews were allowed to return to rebuild their city but then were destroyed and scattered once again in 70 A.D.

[6] The scriptures represent Christ's relationship with his people like a marriage covenant (Isaiah 54:5-7; Jeremiah 3:14, 31:32; Hosea 2:19-20) depicting the church as the bride and Christ as the Husband (2 Corinthians 11:2; Revelation 21:2).

[7] "Once the Romans subdued the entire city, Titus ordered all the walls to be torn down and the city, including the buildings on the temple mount, to be razed. The troops systematically pushed all the rubble of the temple and its courts over the sides of the hill. They even ripped up the flagstones, so that the top of the hill was laid bear down to bedrock and dirt. Those portions that had soil, Titus ordered plowed and salted so that nothing would grow there. When he was done, not one stone remained on the hill" (This account was taken from the works of Eusebius as described by Richard D. Draper, *The Savior's Prophecies*, 106).

[8] The history of the land that was called Israel was conquered multiple times. The Romans held control until 630 A.D. at which time the Arabs took over the land. In 1099 the Crusaders captured the land and then it was passed back and forth between the Crusaders, Turks and the Arabs until 1832 when it was taken by Egypt, then Germany. In 1917, the British Empire entered the land and began to modernize it. In 1948 it was made a legal state by the British Empire. It was set aside for the return of the Jews in 1950 (See Eastern New Mexico University's site for further information on the history of Israel. http://www.enmu.edu/%7Erollinsh/history.html).

[9] Orson Hyde was given the stewardship of setting apart the land of Palestine for the gathering of the Jews. In 1841 he was able to perform the priesthood ordinance to do just that. Theodur Herzl, the founder of modern Zionism, 56 years later, began the process of establishing Israel as Zion for the return of the Jews.

"The Jewish return to Palestine is an astonishing phenomenon which cannot be divorced from the events that prophecy has foretold will transpire there. We need only think for a moment about the sheer improbability of the whole thing to begin to see its miraculous character" (Daniel C. Peterson, *Abraham Divided, An LDS Perspective On the Middle East*, 357).

[10] The land was made a legal Jewish state in 1948, and set aside for the return of the Jews in 1950.

[11] 1880 years passed between when the Jews lived in Jerusalem before it was destroyed the last time and until they were able to live there again.

[12] "And I saw a new heaven and a new earth: for the first heaven and the first earth were passed away; and there was no more sea. And I John saw the holy city, new Jerusalem coming down from God out of heaven, prepared as a bride adorned for her husband And I heard a great voice out of heaven saying, Behold, the tabernacle of God is with men, and he will dwell with them, and they shall be his people, and God himself shall be with them, and be their God. And God shall wipe away all tears from their eyes; and there shall be no more death, neither sorrow, nor crying, neither shall there be any more pain: for the former things are passed away" (Revelation 21: 1-4).

Even though this verse talks about the "New Jerusalem" it is referring to the celestial city of Jerusalem. At that time there will be a new heaven and a new earth and new city of Jerusalem, which will be the abode of God.

[13] "And thus we can plainly discern, that after a people have been once enlightened by the Spirit of God, and have had great knowledge of things pertaining to righteousness, and then have fallen away into sin and transgression, they become more hardened, and thus their state becomes worse than though they had never known these things" (Alma 24:30).

[14] "For in those days there shall also arise false Christs, and false prophets, and shall show great signs and wonders, insomuch, that, if possible, they shall deceive the very elect, who are the elect according to the covenant" (Joseph Smith Matthew 1:22).

[15] "Because God wants us to come home after having become more like Him and His Son, part of this developmental process, of necessity, consists of showing unto us our weaknesses. Hence, if we have ultimate hope we will be submissive, because, with His help, those weaknesses can even become strengths (see Ether 12:27). It is not an easy thing, however, to be shown one's weaknesses, as these are regularly demonstrated by life's circumstances. Nevertheless, this is part of coming unto Christ, and it is a vital, if painful, part of God's plan of happiness" (Neal A. Maxwell, "Hope through the Atonement of Jesus Christ," *Ensign*, Nov. 1998, 61).

[16] "...The light of the glorious gospel of Christ, who is the image of God, should shine unto them. For we preach not ourselves, but Christ Jesus the Lord; and ourselves your servants for Jesus' sake. For God, who commanded the light to shine out of darkness, hath shined in our hearts, to give the light of the knowledge of the glory of God in the face of Jesus Christ" (2 Corinthians 4:4-6).

[17] Angels are promised to missionaries for protection. "Behold, I send you out to reprove the world of all their unrighteous deeds, and to teach them of a judgment which is to come. And whoso receiveth you, there I will be also, for I will go before your face. I will be on your right hand and on your left, and my Spirit shall be in your hearts, and mine angels round about you, to bear you up" (D&C 84:87-88).

[18] "For verily I say unto you, till heaven and earth pass, one jot or one tittle shall in no wise pass from the law, till all be fulfilled" (Matthew 5:18).

[19] The data quoted here is factual. See the following: "The Dead Sea Rift fault system is the most important contributor to earthquake risk in Israel, running from north to south along the eastern edge of the country. The Jordan Valley segment of the Dead Sea Rift is particularly

relevant because of its proximity to major cities and the high probability of generating a major earthquake. "Based on what we know from the historical catalog, the Jordan Valley Fault generates earthquakes of magnitudes as high as 7 approximately every 1,000 years," said Dr. Fouad Bendimerad, vice president of RMS. "The last major earthquake on this segment occurred in 1033, increasing the current probability of a major event." ("Risk Management Solutions, (RMS) Releases First High Res Earthquake Model For Ins. Risk in Israel" *Insurance Journal*, July 15, 2003, Available: [Online] http://www.insurancejournal.com/news/newswire/international/2003/07/15/30672.htm).

[20] "For the eternal purposes of the Lord shall roll on, until all his promises shall be fulfilled" (Mormon 8:22).

[21] "Watch, therefore, for ye know neither the day nor the hour.... Let them who be of Judah flee unto Jerusalem, unto the mountains of the Lord's house" (D&C 133:11, 13).

[22] "When ye therefore shall see the abomination of desolation, spoken of by Daniel the prophet, stand in the holy place, whoso readeth, let him understand" (Matthew 24:15).

[23] "And thus, with the sword and by bloodshed the inhabitants of the earth shall mourn; and with famine, and plague, and earthquake, and the thunder of heaven, and the fierce and vivid lightning also, shall the inhabitants of the earth be made to feel the wrath, and indignation, and chastening hand of an Almighty God, until the consumption decreed hath made a full end of all nations; Wherefore, stand ye in holy places, and be not moved, until the day of the Lord come; for behold, it cometh quickly, saith the Lord. Amen" (D&C 87:6,8).

Hearts Set on Riches

[24] "How hard is it for them that trust in riches to enter into the kingdom of God! It is easier for a camel to go through the eye of a needle, than for a rich man to enter into the kingdom of God" (Mark 10:24-25).

"With men that trust in riches, it is impossible [to be saved]; but not impossible with men who trust in God and leave all for my sake" (Joseph Smith Translation, Mark 10:26).

"As we analyze the world around us, it becomes obvious that having wealth can easily divert a person's attention from righteousness toward the accumulation and care of those possessions. People thus distracted become preoccupied with providing for their own pleasure, neglecting service to others in order to better serve themselves. The Savior referred to this temptation when He gave the following explanation of what happened to some of the seeds in the parable of the sower: 'And that which fell among thorns are they, which, when they have heard, go forth, and are choked with cares and riches and pleasures of this life, and bring no fruit to perfection'" (Luke 8:14) (William R. Bradford, "Words of Jesus: Riches," *Ensign*, Feb. 2003, 52).

[25] "If the Latter-day Saints do not desist from running after the things of this world, and begin to reform and do the work the Father has given them to do, they will be found wanting and they too, will be swept away and counted as unprofitable servants" (Brigham Young, *Journal of Discourses*, Vol. 18, 262).

[26] "I am thankful that God allows those who do not keep his commandments to fall away, so that his Church may be cleansed, and, in this respect, this Church is different from any other that is upon the earth. ... The sifting or weeding process has been going on from the commencement of this Church until the present time" (George Q. Cannon, *Journal of Discourses*, vol. 18, 84).

[27] "The worst fear ... I have about this people is that they will get rich in this country, forget God and His people, wax fat, and kick themselves out of the Church. ... My greater fear ... is

that they cannot stand wealth" (Brigham Young as quoted by Joe J. Christensen, "Greed, Selfishness, and Overindulgence," *Ensign*, May 1999, 9).

[28] "How can we fortify ourselves against the [trial] in our lives and cope better when it comes? By being more like Jesus, such as by loving more. "And the world, because of their iniquity, shall judge him to be a thing of naught; wherefore they scourge him, and he suffereth it; and they smite him, and he suffereth it. Yea, they spit upon him, and he suffereth it, [Why?] because of his loving kindness and his long-suffering towards the children of men." (1 Ne. 19:9.) There are other significant keys for coping. "And he said to them all, If any man will come after me, let him deny himself, and take up his cross daily, and follow me." (Luke 9:23.) Wise self-denial shrinks our sense of entitlement. Another cardinal key is to "live in thanksgiving daily, for the many mercies and blessings which [God] doth bestow upon you." (Alma 34:38.) Life's comparatively few ironies are much more than offset by heaven's many mercies! We cannot count all our blessings every day, but we can carry over the reassuring bottom line from the last counting" (Neal A. Maxwell, "Irony: The Crust on the Bread of Adversity," *Ensign*, May 1989, 62).

Broadened Understanding

[29] "Do not telephone parents, relatives, or friends. In case of an emergency, contact your mission president" (*Missionary Handbook*, 29).

[30] Today, our satellite systems are extremely sophisticated. Microwave energy is beamed to earth to pick up weak electrical signals through clouds, fog and in the dark. Radar technology allows satellites to see objects as small as three feet tall or across from space. See the following Internet address for more info on satellites. http://collections.ic.gc.ca/satellites/english/function/reconnai/lacrosse.html

[31] "Behold, vengeance cometh speedily upon the inhabitants of the earth, a day of wrath, a day of burning, a day of desolation, of weeping, of mourning, and of lamentation; and as a whirlwind it shall come upon all the face of the earth, saith the Lord. And upon my house shall it begin, and from my house shall it go forth, saith the Lord; First among those among you, saith the Lord, who have professed to know my name and have not known me, and have blasphemed against me in the midst of my house, saith the Lord" (D&C 112:24-26).

[32] "For behold, and lo, vengeance cometh speedily upon the ungodly as the whirlwind; and who shall escape it? The Lord's scourge shall pass over by night and by day, and the report thereof shall vex all people; yea, it shall not be stayed until the Lord come; For the indignation of the Lord is kindled against their abominations and all their wicked works. Nevertheless, Zion shall escape if she observe to do all things whatsoever I have commanded her. But if she observe not to do whatsoever I have commanded her, I will visit her according to all her works, with sore affliction, with pestilence, with plague, with sword, with vengeance, with devouring fire" (D&C 97:22-26).

[33] "So then because thou art lukewarm, and neither cold nor hot, I will spew thee out of my mouth" (Revelation 3:16).

[34] "And this testimony shall come to the knowledge of the Lamanites, and the Lemuelites, and the Ishmaelites, who dwindled in unbelief because of the iniquity of their fathers, whom the Lord has suffered to destroy their brethren the Nephites, because of their iniquities and their abominations" (D&C 3:18).

[35] "Daniel, who foresaw and foretold the establishment of the kingdom of God in the latter days, never again to be destroyed nor given to other people" (D&C 138:44).

[36] "The keys of the kingdom of God are committed unto man on the earth, and from thence shall the gospel roll forth unto the ends of the earth, as the stone which is cut out of the mountain without hands shall roll forth, until it has filled the whole earth" (D&C 65:2).

[37] "That they may bring forth fruit meet for their Father's kingdom; otherwise there remaineth a scourge and judgment to be poured out upon the children of Zion" (D&C 84:58).

[38] "Verily, thus saith the Lord unto you whom I love, and whom I love I also chasten that their sins may be forgiven for with the chastisement I prepare a way for their deliverance in all things out of temptation, and I have loved you" (D&C 95:1).

[39] "And in nothing doth man offend God, or against none is his wrath kindled, save those who confess not his hand in all things, and obey not his commandments" (D&C 59:21).

[40] "Verily I say unto you my friends, fear not, let your hearts be comforted; yea, rejoice evermore, and in everything give thanks" (D&C 98:1).

[41] "...Every man may act in doctrine and principle pertaining to futurity, according to the moral agency which I have given unto him, that every man may be accountable for his own sins in the day of judgment. Therefore, it is not right that any man should be in bondage one to another" (D&C 101:78-79).

[42] "Because of our disobedience and our failure to keep the commandments of the Lord, the righteous, as in times past, may be called upon to suffer with the unrighteous among them" (Joseph Fielding Smith, *Conference Report,* April, 1937, 60).

[43] "It must needs be that there was an opposition; even the forbidden fruit in opposition to the tree of life; the one being sweet and the other bitter. Wherefore, the Lord God gave unto man that he should act for himself. Wherefore, man could not act for himself save it should be that he was enticed by the one or the other" (2 Nephi 2:15-16).

[44] "Therefore, let the wheat and the tares grow together until the harvest is fully ripe; then ye shall first gather out the wheat from among the tares, and after the gathering of the wheat, behold and lo, the tares are bound in bundles, and the field remaineth to be burned" (D&C 86:7).

[45] "For behold, this life is the time for men to prepare to meet God; yea, behold the day of this life is the day for men to perform their labors" (Alma 34:32).

CHAPTER ELEVEN

ENCHANTMENT

"And said, for this cause shall a man leave father and mother, and shall cleave to his wife: and they twain shall be one flesh? Wherefore they are no more twain, but one flesh. What therefore God hath joined together, let not man put asunder" (Matthew 19:5-6).

Without Time
Spirit Realm

Oh If I Were An Angel

Dane released Jenessa's hand and looked about him. He was in a large, dimly lit room. Harsh music blared irreverently; so loudly that Dane quickly covered his ears.

Jenessa looked over at Dane and smiled. She gently pulled his hands off the sides of his head and said, "Covering your ears won't help you any more. You hear with more than your ears now."

Realizing that she was right, Dane dropped his hands to his sides. The music pulsed through him in abusive waves of spiritual pain. He cringed and said, "Let's get out of here! I can't stand this! The sound waves are too much!"

Ignoring Dane's plea, she pointed to a place behind him and said, "Look."

Dane turned, and saw a group of people sitting at a long counter. Many of them were holding a glass of liquid in their hands. "What do you want me to see?" he asked.

"Look," She repeated.

Dane looked more closely at the people, and perceived that some of them were silently suffering a yearning sort of pain. He moved closer and focused on a gentleman seated at the end of the counter next to a female who was drinking something. At first Dane thought the man was being distastefully forward with the woman, but as he watched, he realized that wasn't the case at all. The man was actually focusing all of his energy on her drink!

Dane watched as the woman lifted the half-filled glass to her lips and sipped some of the liquid. The man leaned forward in anticipation, and his eyes traced every detail of her motion as if to record her every sense, perception and reaction as she consumed the liquid.

Dane frowned at Jenessa. *"Are we in a bar?"* he asked turning back.

"Yes," said Jenessa.

"What? Why did we come here—hey! I didn't know they had bars in the spirit world," said Dane with astonishment. Many thoughts were racing through his mind.

"They don't," said Jenessa simply.

"Then where are we?"

"Still on the earth."

"What do you mean 'still'?"

"The spirit world is on the earth[1] and we can move back and forth between the land of the living and the spirit world. We can also visit any place, in any time we choose, to see events first hand.[2] If you were to stay with me longer, I'd show you how you can do it on your own."

"I had no idea we could do all that! I think I've been missing out."

"Spirits can come and go as they please. Often when people die, they like to go back to visit their families to see how they're doing."[3]

"Well, if that is the case, why come here? I'd like to see my family too. Let's go...." Dane began to walk toward the door of the building.

Instantly, Jenessa was at his side pulling on his arm. "Turn your attention back to your lessons. I want you to see these people—here." Jenessa gestured back to the people drinking at the bar.

"Which ones?" asked Dane looking up and down the sad lot.

"All of them who are staring intently. The ones with an insatiable thirst."[4]

"I've already seen enough. This is depressing. Someone get those guys a drink already! They look parched," said Dane.

"They cannot drink," said Jenessa.

"Then tell them that it's rude to stare! I'd backhand someone if they watched me like that. I need my space."

Jenessa smiled then grew serious. "The people drinking do not know they are being watched. They cannot see people of spirit."

"Oh, I see," said Dane. He knew that, he just hadn't processed the fact that some of the people at the bar were spirits without bodies. When he looked again, he noticed the difference between the physical and spiritual beings.

Jenessa continued. "Those who are watching are the ones who have died but linger here.⁵ They cannot partake of liquor now that they have lost their bodies, so they watch intently as if to re-live their memories through the living."⁶

"Really? Why don't they move on? Where is the fun in watching other people drink?"

"They choose not to move on. They don't know where else to go. Their knowledge of higher things is sometimes non-existent. Many of these spirits do not believe there is a God. They forsook the truth and chose wickedness while they were in the body. They are blind to even the most simple truths."⁷

That explanation seemed illogical. "Why?" asked Dane. "Can't they look at their own spirits and realize they are more than—that?" Dane gestured toward the dismal bar.

Jenessa paused then smiled and said, "How, Dane? Do you know you 'are more than that'?"

"Yes, I do!"

"How?"

"I don't know..." Dane looked down at his hands then he blurted out, *"It's just obvious!"*

Jenessa nodded. "You have a testimony, Dane, that's why. The spirit has born witness of marvelous things.⁸ Those truths are a part of you, and you are right, it is obvious—to you."⁹ Jenessa moved smoothly to the spirit Dane had been studying. "This man doesn't have the knowledge that you do."

"Why not?"

"Because he was not ready for it in the flesh, and he is not ready for it now. As one spiritually prepares, he receives more and more understanding, but the opposite is also true. As one ignores truth, eventually he will know nothing of God.¹⁰ You know what you know because you sought goodness and light and found the truth. You were ready. You have been blessed with certain memories of your premortal life because of your faithfulness.¹¹ This poor man has only darkness where you have light."

"So what can he achieve sitting here?"

"He is trying to find relief from the pain he carries. He's confused and angry. He's still who he was on the earth before he died."¹²

"Why doesn't anyone come in here and rescue these guys?"

"Someone needs to. These people need to be shown the light. They need to be shown how to escape this sad existence and know that there is help for them."

"Well I'll tell him myself!" said Dane. He marched over to the man who was still staring as if about to expire of thirst.

"Hey, guy!" said Dane.

The man ignored him.

Dane tapped him on the shoulder. "Hey! I've got some great news! You'll want to hear what I've got to say!"

The man continued to watch the drinker. *"Leave me alone!"* he growled.

"No," said Dane. "You're going to be so amazed—come out of this dingy dungeon and see a great world where everything is made of light! There are trees and flowers and beautiful buildings, and there never is a night. No one is ever hungry or thirsty…"

Suddenly the man jumped from his seat and shoved Dane. "**SHUT UP!**" he screamed. "You tell whoever is sending you busybodies over here that we aren't interested in your fairy tales of lights and blasted blue skies![13] Such a thing doesn't exist anywhere in my universe except in a bottle! And all's I got is memories of that…." [14]

"But you can be happy again—without alcohol! There is a whole world just waiting for you! I've been there," said Dane, more subdued now, but still anxious to help this stranger.

The man eyed Dane up and down, then reached out and touched his bright white robe and said, "I can't go where you can. I'm damned to sit here and covet what I can't have. It's the hell that I earned.[15] I destroyed my marriage, hurt my children, ruined my life and now I'm reaping what I deserve."[16]

"No! It doesn't have to be that way! There is a way…"

"Yes! It does! Now go away and leave me in peace!" [17]

"Mister, you *need* to come with me," said Dane, trying one more time to convince the man.

The man's face contorted into an awful look of misery and anger. "See here! I *want* to suffer! I *don't want* to be rescued,[18] especially by a *snot-nosed-kid* that got lucky because he died before he knew how vodka made him feel! *Now get out of here! The mere sight of you offends me!"* [19]

Dane backed up and Jenessa touched his shoulder. Next thing Dane knew, he and Jenessa were standing in a new place teaming with myriads of people. It was a brighter place, like a city square on a Saturday afternoon when many people were running errands.

Various people standing on elevated platforms were giving sermons, or talks to groups of people. Some of the people were moving back and forth between the pulpits as if comparing what each speaker was saying.

"These people don't seem half as angry as that other man," said Dane as he watched the people milling about him. He was still rattled from his encounter with the man in the bar. "Why was that guy back there so angry?" asked Dane. "I was only trying to help him!"

Jenessa smiled and gently touched Dane's cheek. "Because he's so miserable. Don't let it bother you. He would have treated any good person the same way."

"I can't stand the thought of him just wasting his last opportunities to change! Why can't the Lord just force him to see a vision or something to show him what he could have if he would change?"

Jenessa shook her head. "Dane, you know that answer."

"No, tell me! I know that God wants *every* soul.[20] Why can't he do a simple miracle to shake that kind of people to their senses?"[21]

"Miracles, signs, visions—all gifts of the Spirit come only by virtue of faith."[22]

"I know that, but…"

"No, Dane, the thing is, if that man were to receive a vision he wouldn't take it seriously or even understand it because of his unbelief."[23]

"So what can save him?"

"He must choose to save himself.[24] He must acknowledge the existence of God and turn to the light.[25] He must repent just as you and I must, and accept the ordinances of life.[26] We can preach, plea, and encourage all day long, but if he doesn't seek the light and change, all of our effort is for nothing. It will do that man no good. All the rules are the same here and on earth."[27]

Shaking his head, Dane said, "The thing that gets me is, how can people accept truth if they refuse to learn it in the first place?"

"That problem has existed forever. With agency comes the ability to choose spiritual life or spiritual death.[28] Whatever one seeks, they find. That man seeks both punishment and relief. He finds both in the bar. To stay there is what he wants."

"That is so crazy!" exclaimed Dane as he began to pace.

"Yes, maybe. Now, shhhh," said Jenessa, as she put her finger to her lips.

"What?" asked Dane looking around.

"Be quiet now, and learn more. Look and see." Jenessa raised her arm and pointed to a man who was lecturing from a pedestal near them.

"I say unto you, my children, do not heed the Christians that speak endlessly to teach you of a resurrection. Look and see that there is no such thing! We have all died but still exist in this spiritual state. It is your responsibility to accept what is reality. This is now our new existence! The physical is a lower form of living. Look! We have evolved into a higher state of being and put off the physical…"[29]

"What is that guy talking about?" asked Dane.

Jenessa pointed to another pedestal from which a man was speaking. "God is a spirit like us. Being perfect, he is everywhere but nowhere…"

"That is so wrong! I know what God is like! He has a body. These people are confused!"

Jenessa nodded. "Yes they are. They are badly in need of the truth just like the man in the bar. All must have the truth to progress. These people are looking for something that makes sense!"

"Why are those preachers allowed to teach untruths?"

"Allowed? Everyone is allowed to act as they choose. No one is going to force truth on anyone, even here in the spirit world. Those preachers are preaching what they think is the truth.[30] They have parts of the truth, but they have not received the whole truth."

"Isn't it time that they are told how it really is?"

"It is, but even if they are taught the truth, many still reject it."

"Why?"

"They're familiar with what they know. New information threatens their perception of reality. They have listened to the precepts of men far too long. The reasons go on and on. Remember they are the same people they were on earth. They are no different here, they just don't have their bodies anymore."

"So how do people find the truth, if they are confused and are being taught things that are not true?"

"It is same here as it is on the earth. They must seek it.[31] They must pray. Through prayer, each person who seeks the truth will find it because they will see the difference between falsehoods and brightly burning truth."[32]

"That seems simple. Why don't these people pray?"

"Many have not been taught; many others believe they will not be answered. If one does not believe answers come because of their desire to find them, they will wander the earth as well as the spirit world without direction, looking in vain for truth when it is only an honest prayer away from them."

"Someone needs to help these people! It would be such a shame that so many would be lost just because they didn't pray for truth."

"Yes it would be. Like you said, 'the worth of a soul is great.' The field is ripe and ready to harvest."[33]

"I'm ready! Let me loose! I will build a pedestal taller than any of these guys! I will yell from the mountains until all listen!" exclaimed Dane, ready to go to work.

Jenessa put her hand forward and caught Dane's clenched fist. Again they were whisked to yet another place.

Dane was surprised when he saw what Jenessa had done, yet again. "I thought you were going to let me try to convince those people back there. Why didn't you?"

Jenessa nodded toward a place behind Dane. He turned, and saw hundreds of groups of people sitting on a great gorgeous carpet of blue-green grass. It was a brighter place, with flowers and trees, just like the place where he first met Jenessa.

He saw in the distance a shining edifice with high arches atop a mountain. Piercingly bright light escaped from openings in the walls, and shot directly into his body. He felt drawn to it. What was it, he wondered?

"Are we almost home?" asked Dane as a warm loving feeling poured over him. "I'm beginning to feel very happy inside."

Jenessa smiled and said, "Not yet. Look around you. These are the fruit of the harvest, and you are feeling the great joy that abides here among those who are studying and realizing the beauty of the true gospel."[34]

Everywhere Dane looked he saw joyful people talking and smiling. "Yes, these people are happy! Finally, someone is looking for the truth!"

"And finding it!" added Jenessa.

"Yes! And finding it!" Dane closed his eyes and basked in the bliss of his surroundings. "Now this is how things should be! How can anyone refuse this feeling?"

"It's great isn't it?" said Jenessa closing her eyes to share the goodness that surrounded them. "Everyone who desires this feeling should have it," she said smiling and nodding.

"No," said Dane. "*Everyone should have it.* I don't care if they want it or not. I don't care who they are. I just want to shake everyone and show them their potential!"[35]

Jenessa opened her eyes and looked at Dane then asked, "Even Imam Mahdi?"

Dane paused, but he was feeling so good that he didn't have to dwell on the thought. "Yes, if he repented adequately and was sorry, I think he should have this feeling too."

Jenessa smiled and hugged Dane. "You are beginning to love as God loves. Congratulations! This is why he gives everyone the opportunity to repent and change. Everyone has an invitation to come unto him and partake of his feast of eternal life!"[36]

Dane felt a jolt of immense excitement. He was getting it! He could now see that there was no work in the whole universe that was more important than to teach everyone the truth! It was truly a matter of life and death!

"OK, who do I teach? *Let me try, Jenessa, I know I'll be good!*"

Once again, Jenessa took Dane's hand and began leading him towards the beautiful building on the mountain.

"Where are we going?"

"There is one more lesson you should learn here."

"What?

"You shall see."

Ties of Eternity

Brea allowed Roc to lead her out of the tent. Looking up, she saw helicopters circling. She studied each one individually; trying to identify which one might be the one to bring Matt to her. The distinct white lettering on the side of one identified it as a Life Flight helicopter. She recognized another one as the Channel Two News "Chopper 2," and a third as belonging to Fox News. She couldn't discern the writing on two other helicopters. They were heading north out of the area, so she knew neither of them carried Matt.

She had never seen so many helicopters in one place at one time. They flew overhead as if they were buzzards over prey. She guessed their tent city must be the media "prey" today.

Brea moved toward a large rock. "Let's sit here and wait for Matt, OK?" she said to Roc as she pulled him to her side.

"Alright," Roc said looking up in the sky intently with his tongue in his cheek. He took a quick breath and asked, "Is Matt in that one?" he asked as he pointed straight above them.

"No. I don't think so," said Brea. "The helicopter Matt's flying in is not up there yet, but it will be coming soon."

Roc sat quietly for maybe a minute, then he began to look around. Suddenly he stood up and moved over to an area where the grass had been pulled up leaving dirt hole. "I'm going to look for worms over here. Tell me when you see Matt coming."

"OK," said Brea, as she passively watched Roc find a stick, and begin digging in the hole.

Brea looked again into the sky. It was overcast and from the way the air felt, she thought it was about 60 degrees; not too cold, but not quite warm enough. She unconsciously rubbed her arms hoping to warm them up with friction.

Smiling to herself, Brea pulled up one knee, hugged her shin, and cocked her head to gaze at the temple that stood above them on the hill. Although the Provo temple was closed, all the others were open and she was going back. Brea had recently received her temple endowment and had a deep yearning to return only this time to be sealed to Matt for time and all eternity. Tingles flowed through her. The day she had dreamed about for years had finally arrived!

Looking into the sky she remembered another day, not long ago, when she was in the mountains dreaming about her wedding day and waiting for Matt to join her for a picnic lunch. She wanted to remember that day in minute detail...it had been so beautiful—lazily swaying dry cattails stood waist high in the mountain meadow as the autumn leaves painted the mountain side creating an elaborate patch-work pattern. Brea remembered the huge diamond on her hand sparkled brightly as it reflected the golden rays of the mid-day sun.

She recalled Matt's car winding up the road towards their spot and how she had run to hide behind a boulder. She knew he wouldn't suspect that she had arrived first, and she wanted to surprise him. She sat in the cool shadow of the boulder to wait for him.

Her heart beat a little faster as she listening with anticipation for his footsteps. She hadn't seen him in such a long time, and she wished he didn't have to be away so much as he completed his doctoral studies.

Although Brea waited in silence, she couldn't hear Matt approaching. Slowly, she peeked around the corner of the rock and saw him rummaging in the trunk of his car. She liked the way he looked; his thin but muscular physique, his brown hair stylishly tousled. He wore Levi's with a loose, oversized dark blue, knit pullover, unbuttoned at the top—and sunglasses. He always wore sunglasses. Even if it wasn't sunny he carried them with him. Brea closed her eyes and breathed in through her nose. In her mind she could imagine the smell of Drakkar and Ivory soap. She loved that. He always smelled so clean and wonderful. Her stomach tensed knowing that he would soon be in her arms.

Brea eagerly leaned out a bit further to catch a glimpse of what Matt was looking for in the trunk. Tilting her head at just the right angle, she was able to see that he was holding a basket in his right hand. She could see a bottle and a bright arrangement of flowers sticking out of the basket. A cotton quilt, much too nice for a picnic, was draped over his arm. Brea also noticed Matt was carrying long stemmed crystal goblets in his left hand. Brea scooted back behind the rock again to wait. His thoughtfulness tickled her and she laughed to herself covering her mouth with her hand.

Finally she heard him coming up the slope to where they had agreed to meet. As Matt trudged up the hill, Brea bolted playfully from her hiding place and began running up the incline.

"Hey! What are you doing here so early?" Matt called to her.

Brea continued to run without turning back to answer.

"Come back here!" Matt demanded.

Brea rounded a bend and then dove into the tall grass, hoping that Matt would not see her and run past. She quietly held her breath. Soon Matt came around the turn but slowed dramatically as his eyes searched the horizon for her. Brea tried to stay quiet as her body screamed for oxygen. Finally, unable to hold her breath any longer, she gasped for air. Matt must have heard the sound because his eyes turned to where she was hiding.

Moving in her direction Matt took cautious steps coming closer with each one. Brea knew it was just a matter of seconds before he would find her. When he was a few feet away from her, she shot out of the grass. Brea had only taken a few steps when she felt Matt's firm grasp around her waist pulling her back down.

In a breathy voice Matt asked, "Where do you think you're going?"

Brea, still out of breath, inhaled heavily into the grass and didn't answer until a tiny insect leaped onto her upper lip. Spitting violently she rolled over to get her face away from the ground. She was inches from Matt's face.

Matt laughed softly then said, "That was attractive. It's nice to see you too. Was the spitting a response to the environment or me?"

Brea laughed too and then shook her head. "Hello, Matt! Imagine seeing you here!"

"Yeah, imagine!" Matt answered smiling sarcastically.

"Sorry, did I get you wet? I don't normally spit on those I love, but a bug tried to commit suicide by jumping into my mouth. I don't like bug parts caught in my teeth."

Matt adjusted his grip on Brea and said, "So what's a girl like you doing in a place like this?"

Brea eyed Matt, smiled coyly, and then looked away from him. "Well," she said softly, "I have a plan."

"Oh, so you're conspiring, are you? I should have guessed," said Matt smoothly. "So what plan is this?"

"I learned a long time ago that anything worth having is worth working for. I began to think I was too 'convenient'."

"What does that mean?"

"Well, you go away, and I wait. You go away again, and I wait again."

Matt flinched a little. "I'm glad that you wait. What else would you do?"

"Exactly! Boring! Predictable! I need to keep you guessing." Brea narrowed her eyes and deepened her voice. "I need to make you *worry*."

Matt shook his head and scoffed, "No, believe me, I have enough of that."

Raising her eyebrows Brea said, "No actually, I don't think you do. Everything is just how you want it. It's too perfect. We need to have a little chaos, or you'll think that's how our life together will be!"

"So you'll be running off every so often?"

"Maybe, just enough to encourage a little pursuit."

"Pursuit, huh?"

"Yep, I think that's the ticket. But it didn't quite work right this time. You caught me too fast. I don't think you worked hard enough to keep me yet, so we had better try this again."

Brea struggled to get free, but Matt's grip tightened. She thrashed about, peeling Matt's hands off her waist as she rolled away and got to her knees. Matt poked her sharply in her ribs then scooped her into his arms.

Brea collapsed in laughter. "Hey, no fair!" she said emphatically, once again face down in the grass.

"What's not fair?" said Matt as he rolled Brea over, being sure to secure both of her hands in one of his.

She furrowed her brows, and scolded him teasingly, "One thing you have to get straight in our relationship is that you need to fight fair. I'll have no gender advantages because of mere strength and ticklish tendencies. The ribs are strictly off limits."

Matt shook his head and shrugged. "They can't be."

"But they are," said Brea, "and let me tell you a secret…from now on, if you want to catch me, you have to *entice* me—not *hog tie* me."

Matt shook his head again and said, "Nope, I know that isn't the secret. Peter says that *enticement* isn't enough. *Control* is the answer."

Brea stopped struggling and her face twisted into a confused look, "Peter?"

"Yes, Peter. I hear that Peter had this exact problem over his wife."

"Peter? Who's Peter?"

"You know, he grows pumpkins."

"What?"

"He kept his wife in a pumpkin shell, and it seemed to work for him. Maybe I should get one too."

Brea looked at Matt for a few seconds, but still did not understand what he was saying.

"Come on, Brea, 'Peter, Peter Pumpkin Eater?'"

"Oh." Brea smiled, embarrassed that she hadn't caught on faster. "Now I understand. I know what you're talking about. I used to play that song on the piano."

Matt laughed teasingly. "You're slow in more than one way today."

"Matt!" If he hadn't had her hands tightly confined she would have hit him.

"Just kidding. You're just perfect." Matt leaned closer and whispered, "This view is especially exquisite."

Brea smiled. She knew he was trying to entice her to kiss him, but she wouldn't give him that satisfaction. There were some things she still had control over, plus he didn't deserve it yet.

"So, let's start again. What exactly were you doing up here all by yourself?" asked Matt as he teasingly inched his face even closer to hers.

Despite her resolve, she looked deeply into his chestnut eyes. They seemed to bore directly into her soul. She swallowed hard as she felt the familiar surge in her heart rate. She could smell Matt's sweet breath as it caressed her lips. She temporarily lost her train of thought. She couldn't remember for a moment why she wanted to arrive early. She could think only about his nearness.

"Brea."

"What?"

"I asked you what you were doing up here."

"Ah—nothing," Brea finally said, clearing her throat and trying to pretend that she was under control.

Matt nuzzled her right ear, and shivers spread out across her scalp and down her neck. In defense, Brea immediately covered her ear with her shoulder.

"Nothing?" Matt whispered directly into Brea's exposed ear, "That is not an answer. Tell me something that makes sense."

Matt's breath tickled her left ear now. "What?" asked Brea softly, not paying attention to his questions anymore.

"When you tell a lie, you have to be convincing, or it doesn't work," said Matt.

"Right," said Brea, still not hearing him.

Matt softly caressed Brea's cheek with warm, silky kisses. "Brea?"

When Brea didn't answer, Matt stopped and looked at her abruptly. "Having problems focusing today?"

Brea smiled. She knew Matt was very aware of both her state of mind and the cause of it. She decided to humor him. "Just a little."

Matt continued, "Tell me what you were doing. I'll keep kissing you until you do."

Brea exhaled a slow controlled breath. "You're asking me to do something that is very difficult right now."

"That's OK. Try."

"Umm, I was just up here sorting things out."

"Like what?" Matt's lips were only millimeters away from her mouth and coming closer.

"Like us," said Brea quietly, as she slightly turned away from Matt.

"What about 'us'?" asked Matt hesitantly stopping his advances.

Brea was unsure if she wanted to divulge her thoughts just yet. "What do you have in that basket I saw you carrying?" she asked, suddenly changing the subject.

Matt scowled, "So you don't want to tell me?"

Brea gazed blankly into his eyes. She didn't quite know what to say.

Matt obviously got the hint and accepted her attempt to change the direction of their conversation. Matt withdrew his attempts at romance and asked with a frown, "What do I have in my basket?"

"That's what I asked," said Brea.

"Don't pretend with me. I bet you could tell *me* what I brought, you beautiful spy you."

"Who me?" said Brea innocently and batted her eyes, "spying—on you? Never!"

"Honesty, Brea," Matt scolded as he released his grip and allowed her to sit up.

"OK, *spoil sport*! Yes, I saw that you had flowers in the basket," Brea reached out and plucked a daisy that was bowing low over her in the grass.

Matt stood up and held out his hand to help her to her feet. "Good. Then I don't have to surprise you. Come on, let's go eat." They turned and walked together back to where Matt had left the picnic supplies when he began to chase her.

"He loves me, he loves me not," Brea said as she pulled petals from the daisy.

Matt turned and studied Brea for a moment. "What are you doing?"

Brea continued as they leisurely walked, "He loves me, he loves me not." Then she looked up at Matt demurely and plucked two more, "He loves me, he loves me not."

Matt looked at the ground and shook his head. "Brea, what happens if the last petal tells you that I don't love you?"

"He loves me, he loves me not—I don't know what I'd do." Brea said as she playfully bumped Matt with her hip and continued to pluck. Finally, Brea held up the bare head of the flower with the last two petals hanging loosely from the head and exclaimed, "Oh no!"

"What's wrong?"

"You jinxed me!"

"What?" Matt looked credulous.

"He loves me, and he *loves-me-not,*" she said as she plucked the last petal. "Well, there we go. I can already see the writing on the wall."

"What do you mean? It's just a silly, childish ritual. It has no meaning."

Brea looked at Matt in contrived shock. "It's a *love* ritual! When you find your true love, the daisies are supposed to magically tell the truth. Every girl knows that."

"Well, mathematically, it would have if you had started with the phrase, 'he loves me not,' instead of 'he loves me.' You should have counted the petals first."

"No," Brea shook her head. "That would have been cheating. Every girl starts with hope. We all hope that the man of our dreams loves us."

"Well then, I don't know what to tell you," said Matt.

Brea shrugged her shoulders and raised her eyebrows; "Obviously our life together will be fraught with trials."

"Why do you say that?"

"Because I can't even get a stupid daisy to work out," said Brea.

"Oh, Brea. You make me laugh. Here drown your sorrows." Matt bent down and pulled a dark colored bottle from the basket.

"What did you bring me?" asked Brea.

Matt peeled off the foil and unscrewed the lid.

"What is that? Tell me!" said Brea coaxing Matt.

"It's sparkling raspberry juice."

"Ohhhh, yum."

Matt nodded satisfactorily, "I thought you would like it." He poured a crystal glass two thirds full of the bubbling maroon liquid, handed it to Brea, and then poured a glass for himself. "To us," he said, as he gently clicked his glass against hers.

"Yes, to us," she replied happily.

Brea was still smiling, basking in her memory as her thoughts were forced back to the tent city by the loud sound of helicopter rotors. Brea looked towards the sky and studied the machine that was coming closer. The name "Daimler" was painted on the bottom of the gold colored helicopter that seemed to catch the light just right.

"I wonder who this is," Brea said to herself, wondering who the Daimler's were.

The helicopter landed on a street that was blocked off from traffic, and to her surprise, Matt waved from the open door.

Brea stood up and waved back. "Roc, Matt's here!" she exclaimed calling to her brother while trying to contain her sudden excitement.

"He is?" asked Roc. His eyes widened as he looked for Matt.

"Yes, he's in that helicopter that just landed."

"*Yes!*" Roc said enthusiastically. "I've got to tell Mom and Dad!" he shouted as he ran toward the large tent to find his parents.

"OK," said Brea as she patiently walked toward the helicopter; her stomach suddenly full of butterflies.

Brea couldn't help but notice Matt was dressed in a black tux, and had a present in his hands. She loved presents! It was wrapped in dark blue delicate paper, gold and white ribbons lavishly adorning the surface. She couldn't wait to see what it was!

"Brea!" It was her father's voice.

She turned to see her family exiting from the tent to join her. She rushed into their midst and hugged and kissed each one of them. Tears began to flow freely down her cheeks. They each embraced her firmly and smiled at her.

"We're so happy for you," said her mother again.

"I know, Mom."

"Enjoy this day," said her father.

"I will."

Then Brea emerged from the huddle and began to walk towards Matt. It took a while to cross the field, and she became self-conscious as people poked their heads out of their tents to see what was happening. She didn't look to the right or left but concentrated on where she was walking, and periodically looked to where Matt was waiting for her.

Her walk turned into a conservative trot as she fought the embarrassment that was growing inside her. She didn't like public displays, but this time, she would swallow her discomfort and excuse Matt. She knew he was just trying to please her. She wouldn't let him down.

Picking up the pace, now she was running. Dodging people and weaving around children she ached to be in the arms of her fiancé. Off the curb and in between cars, then finally into Matt's firm embrace.

The crowd abruptly began clapping and cheering. Somehow they knew what was happening. People smiled and wished her well as she passed them. Matt kissed her sweetly and then smiled, lovingly pulling her into the doorway of the helicopter. A moment before disappearing into the helicopter, she turned and waved at her family who enthusiastically returned the gesture.

As they lifted off the ground, Brea smiled shyly at Matt as if they were school children. "Hello," she said. She was shaking slightly. "Whose helicopter is this?" she asked as she eyed the pilot behind the heavy darkened glass.

"Hello, Brea," said Matt smoothly as pulled a dark colored bottle out of a bucket of ice. He didn't answer her question.

Brea recognized the bottle. It was the same sparkling raspberry juice they drank together up on the mountain months before. She lost interest in the ownership of the helicopter. "Oh! You brought our favorite!" she said, realizing she was very thirsty. Her mouth was so dry! She looked at the sparkling liquid with great interest as Matt began to pour.

"Yes," said Matt, handing a glass to her. "To us," he said softly.

All of a sudden emotions bubbled up inside of Brea. Oh what joy she was feeling! Joy in the midst of the chaos that was happening on the ground below them. Calming her erratic emotions and slowing her thoughts, she took the glass, touched it gently to Matt's, took a sip, and waited a moment before swallowing the delicious juice. "Yes, to us," She said. She took another sip and indulged in the sweetness of the sparkling raspberry fruit drink, and then quickly, her thoughts turned to the gift Matt was holding. "What's in the box?"

Matt ignored Brea's question and said, "You are so beautiful."

The statement almost offended Brea since she knew that she was covered in damp, muddy clothes and in need of a shower. She self-consciously touched her hair, tucking the stray pieces back in the bun that she had managed with a single rubber band. "Matt, don't lie to me on our wedding day."

Matt stared at her steadily, "No, I mean that you are truly beautiful, Brea. Inside and out you are beautiful."

Brea looked down at her dirty jeans and shoes, and then at Matt who was perfectly groomed. "You must be going somewhere with this, because I just don't see what you mean. You're the beautiful one in here," she said managing a smile. "Let me get all fancy for you and then you can tell me that I'm beautiful...."

Matt leaned over and kissed her on the lips before she could say more. Then he bent over and picked the gift from off the floor and handed it to Brea.

"Matt, you always do things so well," she said, smiling as she slipped the ribbons off the corners of the box. "Thank you for being so nice to me."

Brea half expected it to be a wedding dress; hers was most likely underwater or water damaged. Instead she saw an envelope and two small boxes.

"What is this?" asked Brea.

"Read the note aloud," said Matt, contemplatively.

"OK," said Brea as she opened the envelope and took out the card inside. Opening it she began to read.

> *"All this time, you've been mine*
> *Without judgment or disdain.*
> *I want to reveal myself right now,*
> *And make all things quite plain.*
> *The first item in the boxes, dear,*
> *Describe me in total truth I fear,*
> *I pray that you, after seeing how I stalled,*
> *Will still agree to wed me after all."*

Brea looked up. "You're such a poet, Matt. I love how you write poetry for me, but your words make me a little nervous. Should I be nervous? Are you a serial killer or something?"

Matt laughed and said, "Open the small box."

Brea opened the box to reveal a small silk jewelry sachet with a large crest embroidered in gold on the side. "*This is beautiful*," said Brea holding it up.

"It's my family crest," said Matt.

"Really? My family doesn't have a crest. What? Are you royalty?"

"Not exactly." Matt looked at Brea for a moment and then coaxed, "Look at it carefully."

Brea studied it. The design looked like a shield being supported by a vicious looking dragon. Upon the shield was a red cross that divided the shield into four parts. A decorative "D" adorned the upper left corner, and there was an eye in the upper right. In the lower left corner there was a picture of the world, and in the lower right, a sword.

"What does it all mean?" asked Brea.

Matt pointed at the letter D. "Well, that 'D' stands for Daimler. My last name is really Daimler, not Garrett."

A shock went through Brea. She remembered the name Daimler on the helicopter and thought Matt had just been resourceful. Suddenly, she realized that this helicopter was *his*. "Daimler?" Asked Brea as she swallowed thickly. So many thoughts hit her head at the same time. "Why haven't you told me this before now? Where did you get the name Garrett?"

Matt put one finger to her lips, "Shhh, let me tell you. My family is very wealthy, so when we go out into the world, we all assume aliases. We do this to protect ourselves and our associates."

"Why? Is your family mixed up in something dangerous?"

"Let's just say that we are—influential, and such influence can be hazardous."

"How?"

"I can't tell you right now, but I will in time."

"Why show me this crest if you can't tell me now?"

"Because I wanted you to see who I was. I have wealth and responsibility that goes along with being a Daimler, and sooner or later I might have to act on behalf of my family business. Are you willing to stand by me in such a position?"

"I'm sure that I can, but tell me what business are we talking about? Drug trafficking?" Brea was joking, but worried that she might be right.

"International finance."

Brea was relieved. "That doesn't sound so dangerous. So what is so secret?"

"I'm not allowed to tell you the fine details. My family forbids it. As soon as you prove to my family that they can trust you, as I trust you, I promise you will know everything. They'll want to test your loyalty before you know more."

"What?" asked Brea with sudden apprehension, "Test me? That's ridiculous!"

"I know, I know," said Matt sadly. "Really, it's to protect you. Please don't get upset, Brea. Just listen and try to understand."

"I am," said Brea.

"I have been carrying the burden of having to tell you these things ever since I asked you to marry me. This is the reason you haven't met my parents. I finally decided I was fed up with all their secrecy and rules and I decided to marry you now, instead of waiting. There never will be a perfect time, Brea, if we are always waiting for someone else, that's why I want to marry you now."

Brea saw that Matt was really trying hard and she touched his cheek. "Matt, is your name Matt?"

Matt smiled and nodded.

"Matt, my heart knows you. I've known you, it seems, forever, but I'm very confused."

"I know," said Matt, "but know that I am the same person and you and I will still have an eternal marriage. All the things we want will come true, we'll have children, lots of children, a nice house, a dog, a garden, but because of my family's wealth, it will be easier to obtain. Everything, Brea, everything you have ever dreamed of can be yours if you just trust me and marry me."

Brea looked deeply into Matt's eyes. He was sincere. She could feel his heart aching. Hers was aching too. She knew he was telling the truth. She switched seats to sit by him, hugged his arm and laid her head on his shoulder. "I love you, Matt. I don't care if you're rich or poor, from a wealthy family, or from a farming community in Kentucky. I love you."

Matt kissed her and then said, "I know that." He encircled her waist with his arm. "This is why I want you to know as much as possible. I trust you, and in my book that's all that matters. I don't care what my family thinks or plans for me. I want you and I love you and we are going to be together."

"Your family doesn't want you marrying me?" asked Brea.

"No. They have chosen someone else for me to marry, but I refused them."

"They chose someone for you to marry?" asked Brea in surprise.

"Yes, to strengthen family alliances."

Brea was shocked. "That's positively medieval!"

"I know and I refused them. I'm kind of 'in the dog house' because of it."

"In the dog house? What does that mean in your family? Have they disowned you?"

"No, not exactly. They can't afford to disown me. I'm their only son. They are just trying to pressure me into doing what they want."

"So they don't know you're marrying me today?" asked Brea.

"No."

"No?" asked Brea, shocked and flattered at the same time.

Matt shook his head. "No. I figure that if we can get to the temple and be sealed, everything will be OK. We'll be together for eternity and no matter what happens, no power on earth can undo that blessing."

"Matt!" said Brea

"What?"

"You're talking like you did when we first got engaged. Why do you talk like that—like you and I can't be together and be happy? I get the feeling you think something dreadful is going to happen."

"No, I keep talking like I want to do everything in my power to assure that you and I are *together*. My parents are pretty controlling people and they have a way of getting what they want. I'm not quite as powerful, but I promise you that we will have the future we desire. We've worked hard to deserve it. The Lord says we can have it and he is a higher power than my parents. I trust him. He will protect our promises and our union."

"I believe that, Matthew."

"Good. Now open the second box."

"OK," said Brea as she pulled the lid off the second box. Inside was a mesh veil decorated with white pearls sewn in circular patterns. "What's this?" asked Brea as she unfolded the wide material, having to stand up because of its length.

"It's the veil that goes with this dress," said Matt as he pushed a button. A hidden closet door opened revealing a sleek white satin dress with a fitted bodice.

"*Oh, Matt!*" said Brea as she stroked the softness of the dress. "This is so *gorgeous!*" she took the dress from the closet and looked at the back. Her eyes taking in the tiny pearl and clear jewel buttons that traveled from the floor up to the neck. "I love it!"

Matt could only smile.

Brea couldn't stop the tears that sprung to her eyes as she looked at Matt. He was to be her husband. She rushed to him, and kissed him resolutely. As they embraced, she looked inside herself and reached out for Matt's soul. She believed him to be sincere. She trusted that feeling. It had never been wrong. She loved him more than she loved anything. He was worthy. He would be a good father. Most of all, the Spirit had confirmed to her that he would be a good choice. That was enough.[37] Yes, she wanted to be with him, even if he didn't have a family to offer her.

She looked into Matt's eyes and said, "Matt, although I don't know everything about you, I trust you. I know you'll protect me and care for me like I care for you."

Matt smiled and said, "Thank you for that trust. I love you, Brea."

"I love you too, Matthew Daimler," said Brea. Then their lips locked once again in an unyielding, passionate kiss, one that would last forever in both their memories.

Notes to "Enchantment"

Oh If I Were An Angel

[1] "But where is the spirit world? It is incorporated within this celestial system. Can you see it with your natural eyes? No. Can you see spirits in this room? No. Suppose the Lord should touch your eyes that you might see, could you then see the spirits? Yes, as plainly as you now see bodies, as did the servant of Elijah. If the Lord would permit it, and it was his will that it should be done, you could see the spirits that have departed from this world, as plainly as you now see bodies with your natural eyes" (Brigham Young, *Discourses of Brigham Young,* vol. 3, 368).

[2] "The brightness and glory of the next [world] is inexpressible. [Spirits] move with ease and like lightning. If we want to visit [the physical earth,] Jerusalem, or this, that, or the other place—and I presume we will be permitted if we desire—there we are, looking at its streets. If we want to behold Jerusalem as it was in the days of the Savior; or if we want to see the Garden of Eden as it was when created, there we are, and we see it as it existed spiritually, for it was treated first spiritually and then temporally, and spiritually it still remains. And when there we may behold the earth as at the dawn of creation, or we may visit any city we please that exists upon its surface. If we wish to understand how they are living here on these western islands, or in China, we are there" (Brigham Young, *Discourses of Brigham Young*, vol. 3, 380).

[3] The spirits of righteous people who have died "are not far from us, and know and understand our thoughts, feelings, and motions, and are often pained therewith" (Joseph Smith, *Teachings of the Prophet Joseph Smith*, 326).

[4] "And in hell he lifted up his eyes in torments…have mercy on me, and send Lazarus, that he may dip the tip of his finger in water, and cool my tongue; for I am tormented in this flame" (Luke 16:23-24).

[5] "What of the derelicts, the drifters, the wrecks, moral and physical, of whom scripture says, 'He which is filthy let him be filthy still.' These are earthbound spirits—stranded souls by the millions—who, until repentance shall turn them again toward spiritual growth, wander over the earth-plane and linger about the places that claimed their earthly love; the miser near his hoard, the worshiper of mammon in the whirl-pools of trade gambling, the immoral man in houses of ill fame, the drunkard in the saloon, and so on: all trying to feel by ghostly propinquity a little of the illicit thrill of sensuality that earth-life once afforded them" (Professor N. L. Nelson, "The Veil: Its Uses and Abuses" *Improvement Era*, March 1929, vol. 32 No. 5).

[6] At death spirits are still "free to obey or disobey, to live in harmony with, or in violation of, the commandments of God. If, therefore, a spirit on this side may waste time peeping through the Veil [through diviners], a spirit on the other side may equally waste time looking in this direction [the physical world]" (Professor N. L. Nelson, "The Veil: Its Uses and Abuses" *Improvement Era*, March 1929, Vol. 32, No. 5).

[7] "But if our gospel be hid, it is hid to them that are lost: In whom the god of this world [Satan] hath blinded the minds of them which believe not, lest the light of the glorious gospel of Christ, who is the image of God, should shine unto them" (2 Corinthians 4:3-4).

[8] "The Spirit of truth is of God. I am the Spirit of truth, and John bore record of me, saying, He received a fulness of truth, yea, even of all truth; and no man receiveth a fulness unless he

keepeth his commandments. He that keepeth his commandments receiveth truth and light, until he is glorified in truth and knoweth all things" (D&C 93:26-28).

[9] "Whatever principle of intelligence we attain unto in this life, it will rise with us in the resurrection. And if a person gains more knowledge and intelligence in this life through his diligence and obedience than another, he will have so much the advantage in the world to come" (D&C 130:18-19).

[10] "And they that will harden their hearts, to them is given the lesser portion of the word until they know nothing concerning his mysteries; and then they are taken captive by the devil, and led by his will down to destruction. Now this is what is meant by the chains of hell" (Alma 12:11).

[11] "If the sacred truths of heaven are dispensed in this life according to the preparation we have made, we can have every assurance that the same will be the case in the spirit world. The memory of our premortal experience will be revealed to us only as we are worthy to receive it. This means that some will never have that knowledge restored to them. The idea that at death our memory of the premortal existence is restored to us disrupts any notion that the blessings of the gospel are dispensed there as they are here or, as Peter said it, "according to men in the flesh" (1 Pet. 4:6). (Joseph Fielding McConkie, *Answers: Straightforward Answers to Tough Gospel Questions*, 107).

[12] "...That same spirit which doth possess your bodies at the time that ye go out of this life, that same spirit will have power to possess your body in that eternal world" (Alma 34:34).

[13] "But behold, from among the righteous, he organized his forces and appointed messengers, clothed with power and authority, and commissioned them to go forth and carry the light of the gospel to them that were in darkness, even to all the spirits of men; and thus was the gospel preached to the dead" (D&C138:30).

[14] "It would hardly admit of doubt, then, that the released spirit moves onward—classifies itself upward or downward by virtue of its own inner affinity. Paradise is evidently that state and place to any forward-looking soul, where it finds correspondence; the point at which it can effectually catch on—its frontier of eternal progress, as it were. Hades is probably the scriptural name for a similar, but negative, correspondence to the drifting soul; the point at which the good, the beautiful, and the true, do not pursue it to its discomfort and annoyance" (Professor N. L. Nelson, "The Veil: Its Uses and Abuses," *Improvement Era*, March, 1929 Vol. 32, No. 5).

[15] "...The spirits of the wicked, yea, who are evil—for behold, they have no part nor portion of the Spirit of the Lord; for behold, they chose evil works rather than good; therefore the spirit of the devil did enter into them, and take possession of their house—and these shall be cast out into outer darkness, there shall be weeping, and wailing, and gnashing of teeth, and this because of their own iniquity, being led captive by the will of the devil" (Alma 40:13).

[16] "Souls that gave themselves over to mere sensation while on earth, and having formed no 'hunger and thirst after righteousness' or things of eternal progress, are consequently obtuse to the spiritual promptings which call their fellow-spirits to higher spheres of achievement. Such souls are in hell—for what better characterization is there of hell than wanting to and can't? Out of hell they are reaching earthward, eager to feel again the low sensations to which they gave their lives" (Professor N. L. Nelson, "The Veil: Its Uses and Abuses" *Improvement Era*, March, 1929, Vol. 32, No. 5).

[17] "The great misery of departed spirits in the world of spirits, where they go after death, is to know that they come short of the glory that others enjoy and that they might have enjoyed themselves, and they are their own accusers" (Joseph Smith, *History of the Church*, Vol. 5, 425).

[18] "And they [the disobedient] who remain shall also be quickened; nevertheless, they shall return again to their own place, to enjoy that which they are willing to receive, because they were not willing to enjoy that which they might have received" (D&C 88:32).

[19] "For every one that doeth evil hateth the light, neither cometh to the light, lest his deeds should be reproved" (John 3:20).

[20] "Remember the worth of souls is great in the sight of God" (D&C 18:10).

[21] "Know this, that every soul is free, to choose his life and what he'll be, for this eternal truth is given, that God will force no man to heaven. He'll call, persuade, direct aright, and bless with wisdom, love, and light, in nameless ways be good and kind, but never force the human mind" (William C. Gregg, *Hymns*, 90).

[22] "But, behold, faith cometh not by signs, but signs follow those that believe" (D&C 63:9).

[23] "And now because of their unbelief they could not understand the word of God; and their hearts were hardened. And they would not be baptized; neither would they join the church. And they were a separate people as to their faith, and remained so ever after, even in their carnal and sinful state; for they would not call upon the Lord their God" (Mosiah 36:3-4).

[24] "Behold, here is wisdom, and let every man choose for himself until I come" (D&C 37:4).

[25] "Those who acknowledge God are delivered from death and the chains of hell" (See, D&C 138:23, *Guide to the Scriptures* "Hell").

[26] "For strait is the gate, and narrow the way that leadeth unto the exaltation and continuation of the lives, and few there be that find it, because ye receive me not in the world neither do ye know me" (D&C 132:22).

[27] "If God is just, then all of his children must have an equal opportunity to accept or reject the gospel before the Day of Judgment. As Latter-day Saints, we know that those who did not have the opportunity to accept the gospel in this life will have it in the spirit world before they are called forth from the grave. These, Peter said, will then "be judged according to men in the flesh" (1 Pet. 4:6). This statement means that the standard of discipleship is the same in this world and in the next. In principle it should be neither easier nor harder to exercise faith or to repent in the spirit world. Were that not the case, those in that estate could not be judged according to men in the flesh. For some it will be natural and easy to accept and live gospel truths, for that will have been the practice of a lifetime. For others it will be very difficult to do so, for eschewing the things of the Spirit will have been the practice of a lifetime. The difference is not in the gospel but in the hearts and souls of those to whom the message is being presented." (Joseph Fielding McConkie, *Answers: Straightforward Answers to Tough Gospel Questions*, 114).

[28] "Wherefore, men are free according to the flesh; and all things are given them which are expedient unto man. And they are free to choose liberty and eternal life, through the great Mediator of all men, or to choose captivity and death, according to the captivity and power of the devil; for he seeketh that all men might be miserable like unto himself" (2 Nephi 2:27).

[29] "Take [a] class of spirits-pious, well-disposed men; for instance, the honest Quaker, Presbyterian, or other sectarian, who, although honest, and well disposed, had not, while in the flesh, the privilege of the Priesthood and Gospel. They believed in Jesus Christ, but died in ignorance of his ordinances, and had not clear conceptions of his doctrine, and of the resurrection. They expected to go to that place called heaven, as soon as they were dead, and that their doom would then and there be fixed, without any further alteration or preparation. Suppose they should come back, with liberty to tell all they know? How much light could we get from them? They could only tell you about the nature of things in the world in which they live...What, then, could you get from them? Why, common chit chat, in which there would be

a mixture of truth, and of error and mistakes, in mingled confusion: all their communications would betray the same want of clear and logical conceptions, and sound sense and philosophy, as would characterize the same class of spirits in the flesh" (Parley P. Pratt, *Journal of Discourses*, Vol. 1, 12).

[30] "I have not the least doubt but there are spirits there who have dwelt [in the spirit world] a thousand years, who, if we could converse with them face to face, would be found as ignorant of the truths, the ordinances, powers, keys, Priesthood, resurrection, eternal life of the body, in short, as ignorant of the fullness of the Gospel, with its hopes and consolations," as the religious and political leaders of our day. (Parley P. Pratt, as quoted by Robert L. Millet and Joseph Fielding McConkie, *The Life Beyond*, 65).

[31] "Those who receive the gospel in the spirit world do so as if they were in the flesh. The requisite faith, obedience, and courage associated with accepting the gospel can be no less there than it is here in mortality (see D&C 138:10). There are no shortcuts to the kingdom of heaven. The price appended to its blessings remains constant from dispensation to dispensation and from one world to the next" (Joseph Fielding McConkie, *Answers: Straightforward Answers to Tough Gospel Questions*, 103).

[32] "Ask, and it shall be given you; seek, and ye shall find; knock, and it shall be opened unto you. For every one that asketh receiveth; and he that seeketh findeth; and to him that knocketh it shall be opened" (Matthew 7:7-8).

[33] "Now that the righteous spirits in paradise have been commissioned to carry the message of salvation to the wicked spirits in hell, there is a certain amount of mingling together of the good and bad spirits. Repentance opens the prison doors to the spirits in hell; it enables those bound with the chains of hell to free themselves from darkness, unbelief, ignorance, and sin. As rapidly as they can overcome these obstacles—gain light, believe truth, acquire intelligence, cast off sin, and break the chains of hell—they can leave the hell that imprisons them and dwell with the righteous in the peace of paradise" (*Mormon Doctrine*, 2nd ed. [1966], 755).

[34] "And I will bring the blind by a way that they knew not; I will lead them in paths that they have not known: I will make darkness light before them, and crooked things straight. These things will I do unto them, and not forsake them" (Isaiah 42:16).

[35] "O that I were an angel, and could have the wish of mine heart, that I might go forth and speak with the trump of God, with a voice to shake the earth, and cry repentance unto every people!" (Alma 29:1).

[36] "For behold, this is my work and my glory—to bring to pass the immortality and eternal life of man" (Moses 1:39).

Ties of Eternity

[37] "In selecting a companion for life and for eternity, certainly the most careful planning and thinking and praying and fasting should be done to be sure that, of all the decisions, this one must not be wrong. In true marriage there must be a union of minds as well as of hearts. Emotions must not wholly determine decisions, but the mind and the heart, strengthened by fasting and prayer and serious consideration, will give one a maximum chance of marital happiness" (Spencer W. Kimball, *Marriage and Divorce*, 144).

CHAPTER TWELVE

JOY IN GOD

"I do not boast in my own strength, nor in my own wisdom; but behold, my joy is full, yea, my heart is brim with joy, and I will rejoice in my God" (Alma 26:11).

**The gulf
Between Prison and Paradise**

Portal to Heaven, Earth and Beneath the Earth

"Edna Randal?" an angelic voice rang clear as a bell over the heads of the waiting crowd.

"Gregory! They called my name! *Oh, sweetheart! They said my name!*" exclaimed a woman to Dane's right. "I can't believe it!"

Dane looked to see a couple happily embracing, and then noticed similar things happen as more names rang through the crowd. Dane's attention returned to the couple nearest to him.

"Good, Edna, darling," said a man in a slow drawl. "Congratulations, my dear! Go! I'm sure they'll call my name soon, too." Right then the man broke away and prodded the woman to leave him. "You must go now or miss your own baptism."

The woman shook her head and clung more fervently to whom Dane was sure was her husband. "I can't leave you, Gregory. You're a part of me!"

"You must, darling. I'll be along soon, don't you worry. It's now that our life truly begins."

The woman hesitated, looking into her husband's face. Then a small smile began to tease her face. "We *will* be together now, won't we?"

"Yes, for always." Gregory, the husband winked and kissed his wife's forehead. "You'll never be without me darling. Just go and enjoy the moment. This is your moment."

"I'll help them find you, too." The woman promised. She lingered for a few moments more as she hugged her husband again. Then she smiled wide and moved away. Within a few steps the crowd swallowed her as she moved towards the white building on the hill.

Dane asked in a whisper, "What's going on?"

"The obvious," said Jenessa smiling brightly looking towards the white shimmering building. "Isn't the plan just wonderful? We're watching as that woman's dreams are coming true."

Dane looked around and said, "Did she win the lottery?"

"No, Dane!" Jenessa scoffed and then shook her head. "That woman, Edna Randal, is being rescued from prison! She's being reborn! She's getting a chance to enter the kingdom of heaven.[1] Someone from earth has received her name and is going through the temple for her. She'll be baptized very soon."

"Oh!" Dane smiled. "I bet that big castle-like building is a temple in front of us," said Dane as they continued to weave through the people around them.

"Yes it is," said Jenessa as she nodded. "Then she will receive her other temple blessings, which will allow her to be sealed to all her worthy ancestors as well as her husband and children!"

Dane looked up at the gorgeous golden spires and marveled at their height. "I didn't know there was a temple here! I thought temples just existed on the earth."

"Nope," Jenessa shook her head, still smiling. "We have our temple too."[2]

"Back on earth, all you do in a temple is work for the dead." Dane looked around, "Since there are only dead people here, who are you guys doing work for?"

Jenessa looked down and stifled a laugh. After a moment she looked at Dane with patience and said, "You know this, Dane. Remember? Spirits are the recipients of the work. In our temple we witness the work and attend the work. It's people who are on earth who *do* the work."

"Spirits are able to witness and attend the work done on earth? How is that possible?" asked Dane. "There are so many temples on earth, how would someone know where their work was being done and by whom?"

"Oh, believe me, *the spirits know*. This temple is a part of what is known as the 'axis mundi,'" said Jenessa simply. "It links us..."

"The axis *what*?" Dane interrupted Jenessa, wondering if he had stepped out of their conversation for a moment because he was so lost.

"'Axis mundi' is a term that means center of the world. Because our temple is linked to the ones on earth and then those are connected to the one in heaven, we are a part of an axis which identifies the *center of the universe*."[3]

Dane looked up at the blue-white sky as he continued to move along next to Jenessa. "So we are in the exact center of the universe?"

"Yes."

"How can you tell?" asked Dane looking around, expecting to see a sign saying so.

"It just is. The temple here and every one on earth is the center of the universe."

"Now you're talking gibberish. Sometimes you say things that are just too confusing," said Dane raising a hand to his head. "I thought I was beginning to understand things too…"

Jenessa's eyebrows arched as she brought her hands to her hips. "What is so confusing about the central reason for all existence?"

"Review again what that is?" said Dane grimacing.

"Us, Dane, it's us!" [4]

"Oh yeah," said Dane feeling completely stupid.

"We *are* the center of the universe," said Jenessa.

Now Dane knew he was *completely* lost. "Are you talking physically we are standing in the center of the universe, or that symbolically *we* are the center of the universe—or were you talking about the temple still?"

"Yes. All of it."

"Jenessa!" Dane stopped walking through the crowded field and frowned. "You're driving me crazy with your double talk!"

"Dane, calm down. Relax your spirit and try and perceive what I am saying. Again, you're trying too hard. Let the understanding come naturally."

Dane looked at Jenessa for a moment, unable to relax, but then Jenessa brushed his arm with her hand. With that simple touch, Dane suddenly began to feel calm again. "OK. I'm getting mellow again. What should I do next?"

"Just listen to my voice and don't try and understand. Let understanding find you."

"Again! I don't know how to do that," said Dane getting frustrated with his elementary spiritual abilities.

"Let the understanding find *you*," said Jenessa with a kind but piercing stare.

Dane bowed his head. "OK, I'll try."

Jenessa continued. "In the temple we learn things that one cannot learn anywhere else in the universe."

Dane shrugged. "Well, I hear that's true. I haven't been able to go through the temple yet, but go on," said Dane.

"Among those things we also come to know God. We learn of God, learn how to come to God, and how to be like God."

"That sounds right."

"Essentially, we learn of reality." [5]

"Right. That's a cool way of thinking of God—reality."

"Yes, God is the only true reality, but knowing of him then leads to all other realities.

"In this way the temple is symbolically the center of the universe. All things in the universe revolve around those ideas. It is the symbolic knot that spiritually and physically ties all three worlds together."

"So it's the center."

"Yes!"

"But is it the physical center?"

"Yes!"

"I thought you said that," said Dane almost to himself. "Tell me how?"

"The Lord's kingdom is infinite."

"OK."

"There is no end to his work,[6] thus the center of his universe is not measured in space or distance, but by purpose. Anything that brings his children physically to him, is the center, because he is the center."

"Oh, and in the temple we learn how to physically come into his presence after we are resurrected!" exclaimed Dane smiling.

"Yes! Good! I think you're figuring things out!"

"Yahoo! I got it!" Dane turned to people who were smiling around him, "I got it! Did you hear her?" he said as he pointed at Jenessa over his shoulder. "I finally am figuring things out here!"

"Good job, son!" said one man.

"I still have problems understanding things," said a woman as she patted his arm. "Keep it up, it will all make sense."

Jenessa and Dane began to walk again towards the temple. "Let's try something deeper."

"I don't know," said Dane. "I think I'm at my peak."

"Let's try some visual imagery."

Dane shook his head. "That sounds too hard."

Jenessa ignored Dane and began again. "The temple is a conduit to God."

"OK, what am I supposed to do here?"

"Relax again, and tell me what visual images come to you."

"Alright, do I keep my eyes open or closed?"

"It doesn't matter. You don't see just with your eyes anymore, remember?"

"Oh, yeah. I keep forgetting."

"The temple is a conduit to God," repeated Jenessa.

Dane listened to Jenessa's words and thought about them. Suddenly a picture of a thin but bright pillar of light spanning from heaven down to the top of a nonspecific temple on earth, came into his head. "I'm beginning to see what you're talking about!" said Dane excitedly.

"Good, go with it," encouraged Jenessa.

"Are you helping me see these things?" asked Dane.

"A little, but it doesn't matter, keep concentrating."

"OK."

"What do you understand by your images?"

"I see that the temple opens a real path to God—only, it's not a path like you would walk on the earth. It's a light that would lead you as a path would, heavenward. I see that it truly is straight and narrow![7] It seems like only one person can go through at a time."

"Yes, you're understanding things spiritually. Good, Dane. Tell me why only one person at a time can fit through the light you're seeing."

"Because...I think, no one can save you, but you. Heaven is obtained one person at a time. Christ paid the price, parents and prophets preach, the living do the work, but only we can choose to accept what is offered."[8]

"Good, Dane. You're right. The way is very narrow, but it is open to all who choose it."[9]

"Right, I can feel that's true, too."

"Look at that light, Dane. Does it go further than from heaven to the earth?"

Dane relaxed further and allowed his mind to search all the corners of his sight. "Yes. I see that the light actually shines through the temple, piercing the earth below it."

"Yes, good. You see the light shine into the earth to symbolize God's connection to the spirit world. The plan of salvation is for all people, living and dead."[10]

"OK."

"That light is a conduit where God, worthy men, and spirits can move along, but through it also runs the authority to bind in heaven what is bound on earth."[11]

"Ah. I see," said Dane as the picture in his head continued to expand. Now he saw the light that came from the heavens splinter and shoot through the windows of the temple. Dane saw that each golden strand of light was linked to a person, either living on the earth, or dead below the earth.

"What are you seeing?" asked Jenessa.

"I see that there are many people linked by the light from heaven."

"Yes, who are they?"

"They must be those that are sealed together, because you said the light represents authority to bind."

"Right. Good. Now, look for someone specific. Look for yourself."

"OK." Dane reached inside his mind to find himself in his vision. One strand burned brightly, and he followed it until he came to himself standing before the glorious temple. His vision then grew more specific. He saw that he was linked to his grandparents, mother, father, brothers, and sisters in their various places on the earth. Great and sudden joy burned within him. With that vision came the testimony of the truthfulness of the scriptures. He would be linked to them forever! Oh how he loved them! He was so grateful! *"I see my family!"* he said breathlessly trying to hold back his excitement.

"Good, are you connected?"

"Yes. The light connects us all!"

"That's good, Dane. Now look for that man that you saw behind us. Find him in your vision."

Dane reconfigured his thinking. He searched for the man, "Gregory Randal." Dane looked high and low. No light led his mind to him. "I can't find him, Jenessa. What's wrong? Am I doing this wrong?"

"No, Dane."

"Why can't I find him? He seemed like such a good guy!"

"You can't find him because he's not there. He hasn't been sealed to his family yet."[12]

"What? Why? He needs to be bound to his wife and children. He needs to have the blessings and the ordinances so he can traverse that light to God."

"Yes, he does, Dane. He is worthy. He deserves everything that you have."

Dane began to worry for the gentleman. "How do we fix this Jenessa?"

"We can't, Dane. Not here at least."

"This isn't fair."

"No it isn't."

"God is just—he'll work things out," said Dane trying to dismiss his worry.

"Yes, God is just—but do you feel despair?"

Dane stopped and looked inside himself. He was feeling some despair for the man who could not enter the temple with his wife. What would happen if no one could find his name to do his work? "Yes. I just don't like it that he can't be with his wife. He obviously loves her."

"Without the temple, that feeling for him would be mixed with devastation and mourning, magnified a million times. This is the feeling that all who had died without the gospel would have had. It would make the atonement unavailable for the departed, because they would not be able to access the ordinances of the flesh."[13]

"That would have stunk—big time!" said Dane amazed.

"More than that. All spirits, who had not been baptized on earth, no matter how good, would have become devils, subject to Satan himself."[14]

"OK, Jenessa, you have got to stop with that stuff because I don't want to have *those* images running around in my head."

"OK, but I do want you to consider one more point."

"Alright."

"Find out what would have happened next if we didn't have our temples."

"What do you mean?"

"What would have happened to the living?"

"What are you getting at?" asked Dane.

"Just look and see."

Dane concentrated, but then realized he needed to relax. Moving his hands slowly, he forced himself to focus his thoughts. An image of the earth came into his sight. Then a terrible thing happened. He saw it turn from a lush green and blue to a foreboding black. Then without warning the whole thing exploded leaving nothing behind but particles of rock hurtling through space.[15]

"What was that?" Dane exclaimed.

"You saw the end of a cursed world."

"Why?"

"Because without a welding link between all the righteous who have ever lived, the earth would have been wasted with a curse."

"Why?" asked Dane again.

"Because for all the righteous to obtain celestial glory, they need their righteous dead. They cannot be saved without them. All must be linked together as one righteous whole."[16]

"I didn't know that," said Dane still feeling numb with amazement and surprise.

"It's true. So the temple not only saves the dead, but it allows the living to achieve their potential, too."

"What a way to serve! Save others so that you can save yourself."

"Exactly. That is the plan in a nutshell."

"Do unto others and lots will be done unto you!"

"Good, Dane! That is very good."

"Thanks, Jenessa." Dane looked up at the building that towered before them. "Hey do we get to go in that beautiful building?"

"I think we should! Let's go!" said Jenessa holding out her hand for Dane.

Dane took Jenessa's hand. It was a perfect fit.

Thy Will Be Done

It was evening before Corrynne was taken over to the hospital by an Army helicopter. Even though they had requested nurses to go to the hospital, there was only one way to get there over the deep water that flowed down the streets. A helicopter had to be freed up from its other responsibilities to transport medical personnel who were willing to go to the hospital to help out. The delay was aggravating after tempting herself with the possibility of finding Dane and Carea there. Her mind whirled at the possibilities of things that could be happening to her lost teenagers until her mind went numb. She had to stop worrying, she told herself, because worry never changed anything.

Corrynne and about twenty others walked through the emergency entrance escorted by the police. They were met with an emergency waiting area full of people. There were people sitting on the floors and standing in the isles, filling the corridors. There were people with cuts on their heads with the blood long since dried. There were crying babies with weary mothers, and a toddler with matted hair full of blood, still with incessant energy, climbing on furniture, while his parents dully looked on.

People automatically looked up at the group, not to judge, not to inquire, only as a reflex movement from minds far beyond fatigue and shock. Corrynne suddenly felt self-conscious of her looks. Back at the tent city, Corrynne had put on dark green Army scrubs that were much too big for her, but she synched up the waist and allowed the top to just hang loose. She had no makeup on and her hair, although freshly washed in a makeshift shower, hung flat down to the middle of her back. Never, under ordinary circumstances would she show up at work like this, but what were her options? Beauty would have to wait.

Corrynne pushed some hair behind her right ear and shifted her vision to the floor, as the group approached a table with a woman who looked like a secretary.

"Where do you want us?" asked a jovial doctor in their group who was much too happy for the circumstance.

The woman smiled and said, "Are you doctors?"

The doctor smiled and said, "Yes! We're here to help out!"

Corrynne interjected, "Some of us are doctors, some of us are nurses."

The woman scanned the group quickly and then said, "Ah, there are many needs I know, but the computers are still down. I have no idea where to send you. I'm just directing patient traffic."

"Well where is the biggest crowd who needs a-looking at?" asked the doctor, looking around.

"Again, I have no idea," said the woman as she shook her head. "Why don't you try just walking around from area to area until you find a place where they need you?"

The doctor's smile ceased as he thought about what to do. "OK...I guess I'll go into the Emergency Room and start there. Maybe someone needs an OB." Then he walked over to the wall and touched an ID pad and the doors opened.

The woman turned to Corrynne, "You're a nurse right?"

"Yes," said Corrynne.

"Right behind me they need a nurse really badly."

Corrynne looked up to see a lone nurse working in a triage room, and then realized that all the people outside that room were waiting to be seen by her.

Corrynne gulped. That was such a huge job! If she began to see those people, would she ever be able to find Dane and Carea? She could picture herself getting socked in and working as she feared, until she couldn't anymore. "Ah," she began, trying to pick her words carefully, "I could help some, but I don't know how long. I really need to find out if someone is here. Is there a log book that says who has been admitted and who hasn't?"

The woman's expression changed, as she seemed to see right through Corrynne. Shaking her head she answered. "I have no idea about admissions. We aren't keeping records right now."

Corrynne tried to squelch the guilt that was creeping into her chest for coming to the hospital on false pretenses. Quickly putting it behind her, rationalizing that her children's needs came before strangers she said, "Well, it would be someone who was very sick."

The woman motioned to the closed department behind her to the left. "Maybe they would know in the Emergency Room because all severely injured people are being handled in there."

"All right," said Corrynne and she walked over to the ID pad and pressed it. Double doors opened and she walked in.

Inside the Emergency Room, Corrynne was amazed at the continued chaos that existed there too. People were everywhere! Beds were in the halls, wounded people sat on chairs and on the floor, nurses and doctors were rushing from room to room carrying bags of supplies with them. She felt guilty once again, only this time for just walking around and adding to the congestion of people.

She moved to a nurse who was measuring out some medication. "Excuse me?"

"Yes?" said the woman without looking at her.

"My son is missing and I think he was brought here."

"I'm sorry, I can't help you. It seems that everyone's sons are missing and everyone thinks they're here," said the woman as she turned away from Corrynne and headed into a room. "Half the people are here to wait for someone else that they can't find," she said over her shoulder. Turning at the last second she said, "But ask our secretary, she has been here going on twenty-four hours."

Corrynne looked around and saw another person at the desk in the center. She looked like she was going to fall over from exhaustion. Corrynne moved to her side. "Excuse me," she began again. "I'm looking for a very sick boy who's 18. He was most likely brought here by Life Flight. A girl in a satin yellow dress down to her ankles was with him."

The woman scowled with red eyes as she looked at Corrynne then she said, "I've seen a couple of 18 year olds, but no girls with yellow dresses down to their ankles. I would remember that one, although I have to admit I haven't seen *everyone*. It's been a madhouse around here. But I'll keep an eye out."

"Thank you," said Corrynne, frustrated as she turned away from the secretary and just stood by the desk as she collected her thoughts.

Corrynne was at a loss. What should she do? How could she possibly know where they were? Reflexively she began to pray a silent prayer.

Sincere and heartfelt prayers had become a real part of her problem solving processes lately. Feeling a little ashamed that this wasn't how it had always been, but thankful that the Lord was a loving and forgiving God, she hoped that he would impart to her what she should do next.

Under her breath Corrynne prayed as she walked. She moved through the back Emergency Room doors down the hall towards the operating room, stepping around people as she went. It was her intention to search every crack and cranny in the hospital to see if they had come. As she walked she said, "Father, help me," she pleaded. "I don't have anyone to lean on this time, just like I didn't when we were in the rafts on the water. I know thou wilt help me and continue to help me as thou hast throughout this tragedy. Please tell me where to find my children."

Suddenly a thought came to her as strong as her own, but she knew that it wasn't hers because it disagreed with her plan to search the hospital. She was told to turn around and go back to the Emergency Room and give them her talents and services.

"I shouldn't search?" asked Corrynne as if she was asking someone standing in front of her.

Again the feeling came to go back and help. No explanation was given, no further direction imparted. Corrynne stopped. Oh how she wanted to look! It was hard to stop walking. She looked down the long hall. It wouldn't hurt to take a look she rationalized. Surely the people who needed help would still be there when she was done. She took a couple more steps, but as she did she knew clearly that she was needed for something else and to do as she was told.

Corrynne promptly turned and went back the way she had come.

Temple

Dane and Jenessa found their way through the myriads of people gathering at the base of the mountain that rose before them with the temple sitting gloriously on top. A thought came to Dane and he turned to Jenessa. "Earlier you were telling me something, but I didn't let you finish," said Dane as he walked beside Jenessa.

"What did I say?"

"You were saying that this temple linked—and then you said that strange 'axis Monday' word and distracted me."

"*Axis mundi*," corrected Jenessa.

"Whatever. It sounds Latin to me."

"I think it *is* Latin, Dane."

"What do you know!" Dane smirked. "I'm smarter than I thought."

Jenessa smiled at him and then said, "I think I was telling you that this temple is linked to the other temples on the earth. People can actually go and watch their work done."

"Really? There are hundreds of temples on the earth. Which temple is this one connected to?"

"All of them."

"How…" Dane thought better of getting into another deep discussion. Instead he said, "More and more this place reminds me of Star Trek reruns."

Jenessa asked, "What is a 'Star Trek'?"

"Oh, just a show at home my Mom used to like. Time and space were always bent in some way by someone."

"Then there are some similarities here. The limitations of physical space do not exist here. Things do not have to mathematically add up. The Lord's ways are not man's ways."[17]

"Yes, right…I'm trying," said Dane.

"The temple here is directly connected to temples on earth, which in turn is connected to the temple in heaven. It is the one place all three worlds connect."[18]

"Really? Heaven, earth, and spirit world all connect in there?"

"Yes."

"That is way cool! Does that happen in all temples?"

"Yes it does. In every temple the spiritual becomes physical, time and dimension expand bringing the past, present, and future into one eternal 'now,'" said Jenessa easily.

"OK, hold on Bessy. You lost me there."

"Who's Bessy?" asked Jenessa as if she had missed something this time.

"No one—just a figure of speech. Anyway, explain what you just said, without going into a lot of detail."

"I said that the work done in the temple for the dead allows those departed to choose to accept the gospel, eliminating the barriers of time created through death; erasing the fragmentation of humanity and all becomes whole."[19]

Dane shook his head. "Good thing you said that in an easy, understandable phrase," he said facetiously.

"Hey!" said Dane changing the subject. Off in the distance, right outside the temple, Dane noticed a white tree with fruit that glistened in the light. "That looks like the tree Lehi described in his vision.[20] Does that tree really exist?"

Jenessa nodded. "Yes. It's a real tree and it really exists. Why would the Lord protect Adam and Eve from partaking of it in the Garden of Eden if it didn't?"[21]

Dane thought a moment and then said, "I guess I didn't know the two were the same."[22]

"They are," said Jenessa matter-of-factly.

"So, is it true that if someone who had a physical body, ate that fruit, their body would never die?"[23]

"Yes, if a physical body partook of a physical fruit of the tree of life, their body would live forever. The one before you is a spiritual tree of life."[24]

"How is that?"

"Remember, everything created physically is created spiritually too."[25]

"This place is amazing! Bending space, erasing time and now, a real tree of life!"

"Yes, these trees exist only where celestial people live."

"Why only where celestial people live?"

"Because the celestial, are the heirs of God, set apart to enjoy the love of God forever."[26]

"Oh, I see, the fruit represents the love of God, which is Eternal Life.[27] Where else can we find these trees?"

"One is here in paradise,[28] one was in the Garden of Eden[29] and there are many in the celestial kingdom."[30]

"Hmmm," Dane was intrigued. "I would love to know what that fruit tasted like. Do you think I could have some?"

Jenessa looked at Dane with a thoughtful stare. "I don't see why not. You're worthy and you're baptized. By virtue of those two things you qualify to be able to partake of the fruit."[31]

"Good!"

"Only, you would not eat it as you would with a physical body. Eating here is not a biological function. It would be a different experience."

Dane smiled and laughed. "That's OK with me!" For some reason he was almost giddy with delight. The thought of actually tasting the tree of life spoken of in the scriptures was overwhelming—body or no body!

"This is so great, Jenessa! Let's go on this field trip again tomorrow!" said Dane playfully pulling on Jenessa's hand to try and encourage her to move faster towards the temple.

"First of all, there are no 'tomorrows' here, because there is no night…"

"I know, I'm just kidding," said Dane as he and Jenessa joined the people who had been called one by one out of the crowd to go to the temple.

Looking past some of the people in front of him, Dane saw something odd. Before him there was a big black, bottomless gulf that separated spirit prison from spirit paradise.[32] It stretched as far as he could see to the right and the left of him. The grass tapered down as if it was coming up against a riverbank, but instead of a river a bottomless blackness separated the two sides.

"What is that black void?" Dane asked Jenessa. "It looks like you could just step off the grass ledge and be lost forever."

"You probably could," said Jenessa in a whisper to Dane. "It's an area that spirits cannot go. This is the gulf that separates spirit paradise from spirit prison. Lehi also saw this in his dream."[33]

Dane tried to remember Lehi's dream. Jenessa was right, but Dane was learning quickly she was always right. He remembered there was a gulf that separated the wicked from the righteous in Lehi's vision. So many things he thought were only symbolic he was finding really existed!

Two huge men stood side by side with swords of fire in front of a great thick gate that opened into a bridge that covered the black ravine of nothingness. "What are those guys for?" asked Dane.

"They are guarding the Gate of Heaven."

"Is this the gate?" asked Dane.

"This is the gate that leads to the way to heaven. Only those people who are going to be baptized can pass by those sentinels and go up to the temple."

The female spirit who had been calling the names on her list, moved to the two huge sentinels. They parted allowing the small group and Dane and Jenessa through.

The small crowd moved effortlessly up the mountain towards the gorgeous temple. As they came closer, two golden doors swung open automatically and received them.

Inside the temple the group of very excited spirits were lead down opalescent, gleaming stairs. At the bottom of the stairs was a font of pure gold that was set high on twelve pillars. Surrounding the font were veils that shimmered and moved as if they had a life of their own.

"Edna Randal," the voice of an angel called.

"Yes! I'm here," said the woman whose spirit seemed to vibrate with excitement.

"It is your turn to be baptized. Do you accept the work that is being done for you on the earth?" asked the angel who had led her to this point.

"I do! I do! A thousand times I do!" said the woman, weeping joyously as she was led down into the font.

With Edna's acceptance, a portal opened up that revealed another font directly above her. In a moment she was pulled into the adjacent dimension and time. Dane watched her go, feeling overwhelmed with happiness. He was surprised at his own emotions. This woman was a stranger, yet he felt connected to her.

Jenessa turned and looked at Dane. Then she said, "You can still see her, Dane, as she takes upon herself her promises. You can see and experience anything you wish. All you have to do is apply your desire."

Dane looked up at the portal and smiled. Yes, he could follow Edna's experience. He knew he could.

Dane focused his thoughts; suddenly he began to feel not only Edna's happiness but also the happiness of two others. His perception opened up now to ten, then fifty. His perception then grew to include one hundred, two hundred but didn't stop there. Next he began to feel the hearts of a thousand, two thousand, ten thousand—what joy! What desire! What glory to be able to progress and seek out their future!

Suddenly Dane understood what Jenessa had told him earlier. Although all the people he was sensing were individuals, they were all connected. All spirits beneath, spirits on earth, and spirits above were parts of a celestial whole, without each other, all were incomplete.

Dane's joy continued as he witnessed links completed and connections extended! He knew this was why the temples were the vortex of eternity as well as the universe! Within them all things were bound and linked as one! The glory of each spirit grew and added to the whole! Dane understood! He understood the great desire of millions to join with each other and God in eternal increase! There was no other work greater than bringing this joy to fruition!

"Dane," a voice called him from another realm. Dane felt a soft hand in his hair.

"Dane, we must go now. We must leave."

Jolted from his experience, Dane turned to Jenessa, "Why?"

"Because the others are being given the continued chance to progress through their ordinances."

Dane frowned. "Aren't we going to go with them?"

"No."

"Why not?"

"You cannot. You have not yet received your endowments, thus cannot progress past this point here. You must wait as all the rest wait. You must wait for someone to do your work."

"*I have to wait?*" A terrible pain, an almost unbearable yearning began in Dane's heart. "How can this be? I want to go on! I want to see more! How can you stop me when I have tasted such amazing potential?"

"That potential can be yours, but you must receive your progression as all others."

"*No! Please!*" Dane whispered urgently. "*Don't make me leave!*"

"We must go, Dane." Jenessa pulled gently on his arm.

Dane immediately knew he must obey Jenessa's urging, although he wished there was some way he could experience the upper chambers of the temple. "When, Jenessa? When will it be my turn? I don't have a body anymore."

"Yes, you do…"

"What? I do?"

"Yes. Remember…" Jenessa's voice seemed to fade and become a part of him as he was then transported back to the oak tree.

Dane was filled with so many emotions! So many things to accomplish! The memory of the thousands—millions seeking the same thing that he sought accompanied him, filling him with a vision of how things were to be. Dane looked around him for Jenessa but could not find her.

"*Jenessa!*" he yelled.

"What?" the soft reply came from behind him.

"Oh, you are here."

"Yes. I'm here."

"I looked for you but couldn't find you."

"Some things are not obvious the first time you look."

"I know that now." Dane was still amazed at how diverse reality was.

"Be true to yourself and seek for that which is good."

"I will."

"It's almost time."

"Time for what?"

"Just a few more lessons."

"Then what?"

"It's your choice," said Jenessa, and then once again she left him to contemplate the things he had learned.

Notes to "Joy of God"

The Portal to Heaven, Earth and Beneath the Earth

[1] "Jesus answered and said unto him, Verily, verily, I say unto thee, Except a man be born again, he cannot see the kingdom of God" (John 3:3).

[2] Speaking spiritually, "There are three temples: one in heaven, one on earth, and one beneath the earth...These three are identical, one being built exactly over the other, with the earth temple in the very middle of everything, representing "the Pole of the heavens, around which all heavenly motions revolve" (Hugh W. Nibley, as quoted in "Exterior Symbolism of the Salt Lake Temple: Reflecting the Faith That Called the Place Into Being," *BYU Studies*, 1996-97, Vol. 36, No. 3).

[3] "The temple [on earth] represents the axis mundi, the center of the world around which the earth pivots. As the axis mundi, the temple is the earthly end of a great shaft connecting the center of the earth to the center of the heavens" ("Exterior Symbolism of the Salt Lake Temple: Reflecting the Faith That Called the Place Into Being," *BYU Studies*, 1996-97, Vol. 36 No.3).

"The role of a temple as an axis mundi is well known throughout the earth and across time. For example, among the Moslems, The Kacba at Mecca is still thought to mark the exact middle of the earth and hub of the universe; it is surrounded by special shrines marking the cardinal points, and the roads that lead to it are holy, the main one being called the Royal Road. There at a set time the whole human race must assemble in one tremendous concourse, as it shall assemble on the Day of Judgment before the throne of God. It was common in the Middle Ages to represent Jerusalem on maps as the exact center of the earth and to depict the city itself as a quartered circle" (Hugh W. Nibley, *The Ancient State*, 102-104).

[4] "For behold, this is my work and my glory—to bring to pass the immortality and eternal life of man" (Moses 1:39).

[5] The temple is "the center...pre-eminently the zone of the sacred, the zone of absolute reality." The temple ultimately teaches us what is real—what is eternal and significant" ("Exterior Symbolism of the Salt Lake Temple: Reflecting the Faith That Called the Place Into Being," *BYU Studies*, 1996-97, Vol. 36 No.3).

[6] "And, behold, thou art my son; wherefore look, and I will show thee the workmanship of mine hands; but not all, for my works are without end, and also my words, for they never cease" (Moses 1:4).

[7] "O then, my beloved brethren, repent ye, and enter in at the strait gate, and continue in the way which is narrow, until ye shall obtain eternal life" (Jacob 6:11).

[8] "That every man may act in doctrine and principle pertaining to futurity, according to the moral agency which I have given unto him, that every man may be accountable for his own sins in the day of judgment" (D&C 101:78).

[9] "He doeth not anything save it be for the benefit of the world; for he loveth the world, even that he layeth down his own life that he may draw all men unto him. Wherefore, he commandeth none that they shall not partake of his salvation" (2 Nephi 26:24).

[10] "For to this end Christ both died, and rose, and revived, that he might be Lord both of the dead and living" (Romans 15:9).

[11] "And I will give unto thee the keys of the kingdom of heaven: and whatsoever thou shalt bind on earth shall be bound in heaven: and whatsoever thou shalt loose on earth shall be loosed in heaven" (Matthew 16:19).

[12] "...all the families of the earth must be sealed together. By the time of the end of the millennium, all of Adam's posterity who accept the gospel must be sealed together as one family by the power of the priesthood, which is the power to seal on earth, and it shall be sealed in heaven, and to bind on earth, and it shall be bound in heaven" (Eldred G. Smith, "Family Research," *Ensign*, Nov. 1975, 106).

[13] "...Because man became fallen they were cut off from the presence of the Lord. Wherefore, it must needs be an infinite atonement—save it should be an infinite atonement this corruption could not put on incorruption. Wherefore, the first judgment, which came upon man, must needs have remained to an endless duration..." (2 Nephi 9:6-7).

[14] "O the wisdom of God, his mercy and grace! For behold, if the flesh should rise no more our spirits must become subject to that angel who fell from before the presence of the Eternal God, and became the devil, to rise no more. And our spirits must have become like unto him, and we become devils, angels to a devil, to be shut out from the presence of our God, and to remain with the father of lies, in misery, like unto himself..." (2 Nephi 9:8-9).

[15] This representation is a literary extrapolation of the "curse" that would "waste the earth." Symbolically it is to indicate that the world would have been wasted. It would have been as if there had been no earth and no plan of salvation. The purpose of the earth, to bring to pass the immortality and eternal life of man, would have been frustrated, thus wasting the earth.

[16] "It is sufficient to know, in this case, that the earth will be smitten with a curse unless there is a welding link of some kind or other between the fathers and the children, upon some subject or other—and behold what is that subject? It is the baptism for the dead. For we without them cannot be made perfect, neither can they without us be made perfect. Neither can they nor we be made perfect without those who have died in the gospel also" (D&C 128:18, italics added).

Temple

[17] "For my thoughts are not your thoughts, neither are your ways my ways, saith the LORD. For as the heavens are higher than the earth, so are my ways higher than your ways, and my thoughts than your thoughts" (Isaiah 55:8-9).

[18] Speaking symbolically, "There are three temples: one in heaven, one on earth, and one beneath the earth...these three are identical, [in purpose and spirit] one being built exactly over the other, with the earth temple in the very middle of everything, representing "the pole of the heavens around which all heavenly motions revolve, the knot that ties earth and heaven together, the seat of universal dominion" ...Here the four cardinal directions meet, and here the three worlds make contact" (Hugh W. Nibley, as quoted in "Exterior Symbolism of the Salt Lake Temple: Reflecting the Faith That Called the Place Into Being," *BYU Studies*, 1996-97, Vol. 36, No. 3).

[19] "The temple sits in the center of time and transcends it, making time an endless eternal round. [We] can perform sacred ordinances vicariously for departed ancestors. These ordinances can seal together a family chain that goes back to the beginning of human history and forward into the future. The endowment links us with the future. The ability of time to fragment the human family is thus overcome. Past, present, and future become one in eternity. Time is collapsed into an omnipresent" (Hugh Nibley, *Meanings and Functions*, Vol. 4, 1462-1463).

[20] "And it came to pass that the Spirit said unto me: Look! And I looked and beheld a tree; and it was like unto the tree which my father had seen; and the beauty thereof was far beyond, yea, exceeding of all beauty; and the whiteness thereof did exceed the whiteness of the driven snow" (1 Nephi 11:8).

[21] "So he drove out the man; and he placed at the east of the garden of Eden Cherubim, and a flaming sword which turned every way, to keep the way of the tree of life" (Genesis 3:24).

[22] A footnote for Revelation 22:2, labeled 2a, there are three scriptures footnoted. One in Genesis describing the tree in the Garden of Eden, one describing a tree in paradise found in Revelation 2:7 and then the tree described in 1 Nephi is also footnoted. Thus it is safe to say that all of these trees are the same kind of trees that Lehi saw in his vision. See footnote for Revelation 22:2a to cross-reference.

[23] "For behold, if Adam had put forth his hand immediately, and partaken of the tree of life, he would have lived forever, according to the word of God, having no space for repentance; yea, and also the word of God would have been void, and the great plan of salvation would have been frustrated" (Alma 42:5).

[24] "And I, the Lord God, said unto mine Only Begotten: Behold, the man is become as one of us to know good and evil; and now lest he put forth his hand and partake also of the tree of life, and eat and live forever" (Moses 4:28).

[25] "And every plant of the field before it was in the earth, and every herb of the field before it grew. For I, the Lord God, created all things, of which I have spoken, spiritually, before they were naturally upon the face of the earth" (Moses 3:5).

[26] "Wherefore, the wicked are rejected from the righteous, and also from that tree of life, whose fruit is most precious and most desirable above all other fruits; yea, and it is the greatest of all the gifts of God" (1 Nephi 15:36).

[27] "And, if you keep my commandments and endure to the end you shall have eternal life, which gift is the greatest of all the gifts of God" (D&C 14:7).

[28] It is possible that the tree referred to in the following scripture grows in the Celestial Kingdom which is also termed "paradise," however, since it has been established that all things were created spiritually before they were created physically (Moses 3:5), it is very possible that the following scripture does describe the paradise portion of the spirit world. The scriptures do not define the difference. For this project, all things created physically are depicted in the spirit world to stay consistent with the creation and death process. See the following scripture.

"To him that overcometh will I give to eat of the tree of life, which is in the midst of the paradise of God" (Revelation 2:7).

[29] "And out of the ground made the LORD God to grow every tree that is pleasant to the sight, and good for food; the tree of life also in the midst of the garden, and the tree of knowledge of good and evil" (Genesis 2:9).

[30] "In the midst of the street of it, and on either side of the river, was there the tree of life, which bare twelve manner of fruits, and yielded her fruit every month: and the leaves of the tree were for the healing of the nations" (Revelation 22:2).

[31] "Blessed are they that do his commandments, that they may have right to the tree of life, and may enter in through the gates into the city" (Revelation 22:14). By this scripture we learn that the fruit of the tree of life is only available to those who are righteous Saints who belong to the kingdom of heaven.

[32] "Between us and you there is a great gulf fixed: so that they which would pass from hence to you cannot; neither can they pass to us, that would come from thence" (Luke 16:26).

[33] "And I said unto them that it was an awful gulf, which separated the wicked from the tree of life, and also from the saints of God" (1 Nephi 15:28).

CHAPTER THIRTEEN

TO LOSE ONE'S SELF

"Wherefore, whoso believeth in God might with surety hope for a better world, yea, even a place at the right hand of God, which hope cometh of faith, maketh an anchor to the souls of men, which would make them sure and steadfast, always abounding in good works, being led to glorify God" (Ether 12:4).

00:09:03, 21:20:10 Zulu
Saturday, March 26th
7:40 p.m.
Provo, Utah
Regional Medical Center

Delight in Service

Corrynne promptly walked to the triage room and the adjacent Emergency lobby that was filled with injured people. It was there the Spirit encouraged her to go. She sought out the elderly nurse that she had seen earlier working by herself. Maneuvering around the many people on the floor without stepping on anyone was tricky, but with effort she made it to the narrow door of the triage room. She stuck her head in to see the nurse attending to an overweight gentleman in his tee shirt. Moving further into the room she asked, "Do you need help in here?" with a genuine smile on her face.

"Absolutely!" said the nurse making an obvious effort to try to return the positive attitude. "My name is Sheryl. I'm so glad that you've come!" The old nurse wiped her forehead with her shoulder, holding gloved hands out in front of her. "It's been like a war zone. Just in this area of the hospital alone, we've got gurneys in the hallway, three in each room and a crowd of people waiting to be seen."

"I know," said Corrynne. "I've seen the Emergency Room as well as the lobby out here!"

Sheryl nodded, "I hope we can find more nurses that can help out, or the hospital is going to have half the staff in a few hours from *us* needing gurneys just to recover from our shifts." The nurse winked and then continued, "If you know what I mean!"

Corrynne looked at the woman. She didn't recognize her from her many years as a nurse. She assumed she was someone who had come from another hospital to help out.

Corrynne gestured to the crowd outside the triage door. "What can I do to help?"

The elderly nurse looked around as if it was hard to think where to begin. "Well" she started then she pursed her lips together. "What can you do?"

Corrynne shrugged noncommittally. To be honest, she was very interested in what the Lord wanted for her to do. She didn't want to give any hints to mess up inspiration that might be going on. "I don't know..." but then she said, "Just push me in a direction and put me to work. I do almost anything."

Sheryl's eyes brightened a little. "OK! That's great! Can you suture?"

"Yes," Corrynne said smiling politely. In this day, suturing was something even a medical technician could do. Her palms suddenly felt itchy. Was this what the spirit had prompted her to do? Was this the thing that was so important that it overshadowed finding Dane and Carea? Swallowing, Corrynne squashed her pride and said, "Sure I can suture. I can even make a quilt if I have too!" said Corrynne as she rubbed an arm in anticipation of a long night.

"Ah, here are the supplies that you'll need." The old nurse said. She reached behind her and picked up a large box filled with gauze, tape, antibiotic ointment, and other miscellaneous materials.

Corrynne looked up at the woman and frowned. "Are there doctors around to assess the patients before I go out on a medical rampage?"

The old nurse sat back down, knee to knee with her patient as she shook her head. "Nope. No doctor's orders. No doctors anywhere. You'll have to be independent and rely on the 'Good Samaritan Act.' What doctors we do have are all busy. Just don't touch anyone unless they promise to not sue you if you do a bad job," the woman said with a tired smirk.

Corrynne nodded and took the box. She looked around for some sort of gown for a barrier and found one hanging on a hook. Taking it with her free hand she stepped out into the crowded lobby.

Slipping the gown onto her right arm Corrynne balanced the box in her left as she looked around the room once again. In her mind, she tried to figure out whom she should help first. She addressed the crowd loudly; "I'm a nurse. I will care for the most emergent cases first and then eventually get to everyone else." Slipping the other side of the gown over her left arm she asked, "Is anyone having a difficult time breathing? Having chest pains? Feeling sweaty and nauseous?" Corrynne looked around but everyone continued to stare at her with dull eyes. No one volunteered. "OK," said Corrynne, "How about bleeding? Is anyone bleeding uncontrollably?" Again no one volunteered. "OK, what are you guys here for?" Corrynne said becoming increasingly frustrated.

"We were told by the Red Cross-people out there," pointed a middle-aged woman to the outside doors, "That this was where we got stitched up."

"Ah," nodded Corrynne. Now she understood why the old nurse asked her about her stitching abilities. All the patients with other injuries had already been triaged to other parts of the hospital. Continuing to feel very underutilized she took a deep breath. Resigning to the thought that if stitching was the thing she needed to do she decided she would do it. She would show the Lord she would be faithful in even the simple things.

"Alright, well if no one is bleeding profusely, I'll just start here and work my way around," said Corrynne as she knelt down on the floor and began looking at the toddler she had seen earlier.

"My finger has been cut off," interjected a young male voice, as if he was afraid he would have to wait too long for care. "But it's not bleeding anymore. Is that a bad enough wound?"

Corrynne whirled her head around to find the person who was speaking. She saw a teenage boy holding up a plastic bag filled with ice with the other hand wrapped in what looked like a sweater. "Is your finger in that bag?" she asked looking at the dripping sack as she got to her feet.

"Yes," answered the young man immediately.

A couple of people in the room could be heard gasping or groaning now that it had become public what the boy had been holding in the bag.

The boy looked around the room, obviously suddenly self-conscious.

Corrynne found a little amusement in the common response. It was only a finger!

Turning to the mother of the toddler she had been assessing, she pointed to the bathroom door. "Go wash your daughter's hair in the bathroom. It will be faster for me if you do that. Then I'll attend to your child next. Just be careful of her wounds and don't use too much water. All the water is rationed until they fix the dam and build up the reservoir again."

The woman scooped up her little girl and headed into the bathroom as she was told.

Corrynne then walked over to the young man and said, "You're lucky you could find a plastic bag and ice. There isn't anything left in the stores."

"The people at the first-aid tent outside gave it to me. Do you think that you'll be able to reattach it?"

Corrynne didn't think she could. She wasn't a plastic surgeon. However, she donned gloves and took the bag, opened it and looked in. The finger was mangled. She looked at it from a different angle, but still it didn't look anything like a finger. She shook her head as she continued to study it. "No, I'm sorry, but there is no way *anyone* is sewing *that* back on your hand."

The boy looked down as if he might cry.

Corrynne, watching the boy, felt sad for him as she realized losing his finger was very traumatic for this young man. Quickly she stumbled for something more therapeutic to say other than her clumsy statement. How unfeeling of her, she needed to have some sense of professionalism.

Corrynne took the boy around the shoulder and said, "What's your name?"

"Craig."

"Craig, I'm so sorry that we cannot save your finger. It must be very hard for you to think about not having a normal hand."

The boy was silent for a moment and then said, "I was just finishing *Rachmaninoff, Prelude in C sharp minor*. My recital was in a month."

Understanding filled Corrynne's mind. This young man was a very accomplished pianist! To loose a finger was like losing part of his life! His powerful talent was most likely woven into his identity. Corrynne felt sick to her stomach. How could she be so callus? This situation called for some real empathy.

"You know, I played that when I was a senior in high school. That's a very hard piano piece. I could never play it today! You must be very good," Corrynne said, trying to find some common ground and build some trust with this stranger.

"I was," said the boy sadly.

"Here have a seat." Corrynne said to the boy as she held her hand out to the floor.

The boy sat down in his spot.

Corrynne then got to her knees again and said in a quiet, comforting voice, "You can still play the piano without that finger," she said trying to offer some hope. "I know people who can. Anyway, the finger you lost is on the left hand which for a pianist is better than the right!"

The boy slowly nodded. "I know. That's what my mom said." Craig straightened his back a little, placed his bag on the floor and began unwrapping his wounded hand. "I can probably change the fingering in my piece."

"Yes, or even still play with the short finger," said Corrynne. "There are lots of things you can do."

The boy nodded in agreement.

Corrynne was impressed with this boy's efforts to be brave. With the kindest voice she could find, she said, "Let's see what we can do for your hand."

Craig held his hand out and let Corrynne look at it. His index finger had been severed cleanly at the second knuckle except for some dangling skin.

She looked closely at the skin. It was nice and pink. After cutting off some of the jagged edges, she would use it to cover the stub. She hoped it would heal well that way.

"What happened?" Corrynne asked as she got out some hydrogen peroxide and poured it on gauze and began to clean old blood from the intact skin of his hand. She wanted to get a clear look at the whole hand before she began working.

"Our car stalled out in the water and I tried to fix it. My hand was cut in the fan when it started again. But it was all for nothing because it stalled again after that."

"Oh, ouch! That must have hurt!" said Corrynne as she finished rubbing and cleaning the hand. She began pouring saline in the wound over a white towel that she retrieved from the box to wash it out.

"Well, I didn't really know what happened. I just thought I was nicked until my sister screamed."

"Your sister screamed?" asked Corrynne smiling at the boy then looked down into her box for her materials to suture the finger.

"Yes, she has a weak stomach," the boy said as he watched Corrynne find the items one by one.

Finally, Corrynne looked back up at Craig and renewed her smile. Then looking back down she opened a sterile towel on the floor. Next, she removed a medicine cup from its container sterilely and placed it on the towel. Being careful not to spill, Corrynne poured a small amount of Lidocaine into the medicine cup. "I have a weak stomach sometimes," she said as she finished.

"You do?" asked Craig, as if the thought was impossible.

"Yep. Everyone does at one time or another," Corrynne said as she dropped the threaded 3.0 silk with a fishhook needle, the Betadine, swabs, scissors, syringe and needle right in the center of the towel, peeling the various packaging back towards her hands and flipping the materials into the center.

The boy hesitated and then said, "Did my finger bother you? It's pretty gross, isn't it?"

Corrynne looked at Craig and saw he was grimacing. She smiled again, shook her head and said, "Nope. I think it looks cool. Your hand looks cool too. You're going to have great scars and a story to tell to your children." Taking off her contaminated gloves she now opened a package of sterile gloves and put them on one at a time. "You should keep your finger in some formaldehyde somewhere. Wouldn't that be great?" she continued as she washed the area around the end of Craig's stump with Betadine to kill any bacteria that was lurking near the surface where she needed to work. "Then when you pass on, your family will still have a part of you they can—*hold on to*."

With that statement Craig let out a little laugh. Corrynne was happy that she was helping this boy find some place in his mind where he could laugh about his injury.

"Where is your family?" Corrynne attempted to change the subject as she waited for the Betadine to dry.

The boy shrugged. "They're around here somewhere."

"Good. At least you're all together."

Craig nodded. "I'll go find my mom at the gray tent outside. She's there with my little brother who broke his foot jumping off the deck when he saw the water coming."

"How did you get away from the water?" asked Corrynne as she screwed the needle on the syringe and drew Lidocaine into its chamber.

Craig didn't answer but looked at the syringe intently.

Corrynne stopped for a moment as she saw Craig's expression. "Are you afraid of needles?" she asked.

"Do I have to have a shot?" Craig asked looking worried.

Corrynne laughed a little and said, "Only if you don't want to feel every stitch."

The young man scowled and said, "I only have to have one shot right?"

Corrynne shook her head and said, "I don't know. I will give you this numbing medication, as you need it. I'll at least have to give you a shot on each side of your finger. But look." Corrynne held up the needle. "It's practically the thinnest one we have. The prick of the needle is hardly anything, but then the medication will burn at first. After that, everything will go numb."

Craig swallowed and then said, "OK, go ahead."

Corrynne then slid the end of the needle under the surface of the skin at the tip of the wounded finger. With a press of the plunger she released Lidocaine into the tissue, making a raised bump. Then without totally withdrawing the needle she pulled back, redirected it and then advanced it to a new area and released more Lidocaine. She repeated this procedure three more times and then moved to the other side of the finger and repeated the same actions.

Craig had his eyes closed and his teeth gritted as Corrynne numbed his finger. Every so often he would let out an "Ouch!" and then breathe in and out deeply through his teeth.

After Corrynne was finished, she touched the end of his finger with her gloved hand. "Do you feel that?"

Craig opened his eyes. "No."

"Good, we're almost ready," said Corrynne as she unwound the suture thread with the curved needle on the end.

"Now what are you going to do?" asked Craig with a scrunched face.

"I'm going to even out the jagged skin on the end of your finger with the scissors, but you won't feel it."

"I hope not!" said Craig maintaining his look of displeasure.

Corrynne picked up the scissors and carefully cut off the jagged pieces from the flap of extra skin. "We want a nice clean, fresh edge to sew over the end of the stump so that it will heal quickly. The body makes a kind of glue that causes injured ends to stick together. If we can put ends of the skin together to make a straight line, it will heal even faster."

"Good!" said Craig now looking a little pale.

Next, Corrynne picked up the needle. "Now I'm going to sew the skin over the end of your finger to cover your injury. Are you ready? You're looking a little sick."

Craig looked up at her with puppy dog eyes and let his face go slack. "I'm getting a little dizzy, but I think I'm OK."

"OK," said Corrynne as she inserted the needle on one side of Craig's finger and let it come up on the other side of the injury to the healthy skin, pulling the thread through both sides until only a small tail was left. With that tail she carefully tied a knot to bring the two raw edges of skin together and then cut the thread with the scissors. Repeating this procedure, soon the end of his finger was completely enclosed.

Applying triple antibiotic ointment to the sutures, Corrynne said, "There! Now doesn't that look much better?"

Craig looked at his finger and then nodded. "That looks pretty good! You're a good nurse."

Corrynne smiled and then dug in her box to find a bunch of 2X2 gauze still in the packaging. Opening the plastic covering she said, "Be careful not to bump the end of your finger. Your blood vessels are very delicate right now. If the clots are torn open, you'll have another mess and the healing time will be longer."

"OK," said Craig as he continued to study Corrynne's every move.

Corrynne wrapped the gauze and the rest of the finger repeatedly, until the whole finger was engulfed in white fluffy material. Applying tape to secure the bandage Corrynne smiled. "You're done!"

"Thank you so much!" said Craig now with light returning to his eyes.

"You're welcome," said Corrynne as she removed her gloves and then patted him on the back. "After that heals I want to hear you play at Carnegie Hall!"

"I'll try," said Craig as he got to his feet.

"Don't forget this," said Corrynne as she handed him his leaking bag now filled with water and floating flesh that he had set down on the floor.

"Thanks!" said Craig as he grinned from ear to ear. He then picked his way through the people filling the room. Finally he walked out the door.

Corrynne took a deep breath and looked around at all the people that looked back at her with longing. She was only one person! How was she going to help all these people? It was going to take so long!

Clicking her tongue Corrynne leaned over and picked up her box. An uncontrollable and unexpected smile moved across her face and she became filled with a new sense of mission. She was suddenly very happy. She was doing something important; making a difference during a hard time. That was more important than the fact that she was tired and the work was tedious. No. She'd make sure these people got the best care she could give.

"Next!" she said boldly.

Tools for Knowledge

"Here, I have something for you," said Jenessa with a lilt in her voice. It was obvious she was excited about something. She had both hands behind her back.

"What is it?" asked Dane, as he couldn't help smiling, feeling Jenessa's exuberance.

"Try and guess. Close your eyes and see what I have behind my back. Look into my mind. You can do it."

Dane closed his eyes and tried to open his perception as Jenessa had taught him. He sent his mind out to explore the finite question before him. Dane had worked very hard in acquiring this new ability. He found that his perceptions could be flung out to find answers like waves of a sea, ebbing and flowing, sending out questions and bringing back answers. He found he could search concepts and realities that he didn't even fathom existed, just by creating the proper questions in his mind, having a desire to know and being open to the answers. He had learned that his thoughts could reach the farthest part of the universe if he desired it, but right now, he only wished to see behind Jenessa.

Dane focused his energy. He searched Jenessa's mind. He could sense happiness and joy. He could sense anxiety for his welfare. Words flowed from her mind. They said, "Maybe…someday…we could…build a future…together…but you must choose wisely…."

Dane smiled and opened his eyes, "Hey, that's not fair. You're cheating. Stop saying things."

Jenessa threw back her head and laughed, "Me? I'm cheating? But, I'm the pillar of the community."

"Pillar or not, you're distracting me. Stop teasing."

"Oh, OK," said Jenessa as she wiped the smile off her face and tried to look serious.

Dane tried again. His mind flowed past Jenessa's feelings. That was the hardest part, her emotions were so strong he almost couldn't see past them, but after a few seconds he was able to segregate her feelings from her thoughts. Still, he could not see what she had in her hands. He heaved a sigh in frustration. "Are you imagining what you have in your hands?"

"No," Jenessa answered simply.

"Why not? You know I can't see what you have unless you see it."

"Dane, are you still that simple? Look into my memory. See what I have seen. Touch what I have touched."

"Jenessa, you're making this difficult."

"No, I'm teaching you."

Dane shrugged; there was always a lesson. "OK, OK. I'll try."

"Good."

Dane started again. He sent out his perceptions and they washed over Jenessa. They surrounded her and then began to flow through her. Again he sensed her emotions, then her thoughts. Now he searched for a hidden recess, called her memory. Normally, these thoughts were hidden underneath everything else and slipped right by the observer. One could only access these recordings if the person willed it. Jenessa had invited him to explore, so he knew he would be able to if he searched long enough. His perceptions looked for the hidden entrance, exploring every charged particle that held information. Suddenly, he found it. He allowed his mind to enter.

Dane perceived a jumble of facts, figures, symbols, and faces. How was he going to make sense of this? Nothing was in order. He looked for a logic string, but nothing was logical. "Jenessa, I think I'm in, but nothing means anything."

"Try and think like I do. Try and put yourself in my position and see the knowledge I have, as I see it."

Dane began to try this technique. He aligned himself with Jenessa, being like her—feeling like her. Suddenly he felt very logical and steady, with a dimension of such purity that it took his breath away. Jenessa was so beautiful! She was intensely brilliant! His spirit body began to feel brighter and stronger. He perceived she was definitely a chosen light, a beloved daughter of God. The experience was so intense that Dane felt he might get lost in it and lose his own identity. "Jenessa...I...can't." Then he felt her arm about his shoulders.

"Dane, try. You're almost there," she encouraged him. "Keep your objective in mind. Don't get sidetracked. Refocus your question."

Oh, that was it. He needed to focus on what he was looking for. 'Ask and ye shall receive,' it was the order of all knowledge in the universe. "What is Jenessa holding? She must have picked it up somewhere, seen it before, felt its edges.... What are the sights and feelings she had when she did?" With that question, Dane's thoughts took on a wholly new dimension. A flash of memory filled his mind. He saw Jenessa's hand reach into a bag. It was a bag of purple velvet. Then she pulled out a sparkling crystal, or was it a diamond? The substance of its creation was not made known to him. Jenessa must not have ever wondered what it was made of. Whatever it was, the brilliance of the stone was magnificent. He found himself looking into the stone, as Jenessa must have and images began to swirl in his mind. Answers, upon answers flowed to him instantaneously. Were they answers that Jenessa had searched for?

238   Millennial Glory III

"Jenessa, I see a gorgeous white stone. A stone that you can look into and find answers quickly," said Dane.

"Yes, Dane, good. You are correct."

Dane refocused and came back to himself. He watched Jenessa pull the same stone that he had seen in his mind, from behind her back. Its starlight brilliance was astonishing. "So that's it, huh?" Dane exclaimed in a charged whisper. "Wow!"

"Yes, this stone is a Urim and Thummim."

Dane took the stone in his own hands. It was cool to the touch and smooth. Inside the stone were many facets, like a diamond where light bounced and played off the dimensions within it. "I didn't know that you had these things here."

"Yes, those who are worthy of the Celestial Kingdom will all receive one. You will receive a stone like this one too. It will be yours forever, to search the galaxy for all truth."[1]

"Mine?"

"Yes."

"Are you saying that you have already achieved celestial glory?"

"No. This stone is not mine. It is one that many of us share here in our research. It's beautiful isn't it?"[2]

"Yes, beyond belief," said Dane as he marveled openly. "What do we do with it?"

"Our time is coming to a close. We need to accelerate your learning."

"What else am I to learn?"

"Power."

"Power? How do you learn power?"

"Faith is the source of all power both in heaven and earth."

"So I am to learn faith?"

"Yes, and the application of it."

"Didn't I learn that in Primary when I was young?" asked Dane, half teasing.

"No, you may have learned of it, but you have never really applied the true powers innate in faith."

"Do we need this stone to learn about faith?"

"Yes, because you need to be able to ask and find answers to questions that have been impossible to find before."

"Why?"

"Because the elements of faith require that you know the nature of God."

"I thought we had that discussion before...remember? We discussed how his power was through all things..."

"No, that discussion exposed his influence in all things. To apply faith powerfully, in order to move mountains, stop the sun in the sky, and raise the dead, one must know all the characteristics of God."

"But how does one do that without meeting him?"

"Look into the stone. You will find the answers there."

"Do I just look?"

"No, you formulate the questions, and use your perceptions just as you did to search my memory."

"I see. OK. I'll try." Dane looked around, he wanted to find a place that he and Jenessa could sit together. He wanted to sit under their favorite oak. "Let's go to our place."

"Alright," agreed Jenessa.

Within a flicker of thought, both Dane and Jenessa were sitting below the large branches of their tree.

Notes for "To Lose One's Self"

Tools for Knowledge

[1] "Then the white stone mentioned in Revelation 2: 17, will become a Urim and Thummim to each individual who receives one, whereby things pertaining to a higher order of kingdoms will be made known; And a white stone is given to each of those who come into the celestial kingdom, whereon is a new name written, which no man knoweth save he that receiveth it. The new name is the key word" (D&C 130:10-11).

[2] There is no documentation that asserts that we will have such tools in the spirit world. This is a literary extrapolation based on the knowledge that all beings that are worthy of celestial glory will have a white stone of their own.

CHAPTER FOURTEEN

WHAT WAS LOST IS FOUND

"I will seek that which was lost, and bring again that which was driven away, and will bind up that which was broken, and will strengthen that which was sick" (Ezekiel 34:16).

00:09:03 19:25:40 Zulu
Saturday, March 26th
8:35 p.m.
Provo, Utah
Regional Medical Center

Works of Faith

"Corrynne!"

Corrynne looked up rapidly from cleaning a deep cut on a woman's cheek. It was Dr. Crawford, a physician she worked with often in the ICU. Sudden adrenaline rushed through her body as the sound in the doctor's voice told her there was an emergency.

Dr. Crawford was on top of a rolling gurney, kneeling and performing chest compressions on an unconscious patient. Two firemen pushed the gurney from behind. "Corrynne, come here!" he called out.

Corrynne dropped her needle on a wad if gauze and rushed to the doctor's side, moving along with the gurney. "Do you want me to take over compressions?" she asked.

"No. I need you to attend to the gurney behind us. There's a girl on the stretcher that is having an anaphylactic reaction."

"To what?"

"I don't know," the doctor said between compressions. "There's almost a total airway obstruction. She needs to be intubated immediately!"

Fear filled Corrynne's heart. "*I can't intubate!*" she yelled back at the doctor. "I'm not good at it! Get a Respiratory Therapist! The girl would have a better chance!"

"There aren't any. Believe me, you are the only one who can help her right now. You're her only chance."

Corrynne shook her head, "No, Doctor! *Please!*"

"I have confidence in you. You know what you're doing!" said the doctor as he continued the CPR and disappeared around the corner.

Corrynne turned around with great apprehension. Through the open doors she could see the girl Dr. Crawford was talking about. She was sitting up on a gurney gasping for breath with a very frightened look on her face. Her skin had an ashen color, telling Corrynne that there wasn't very much time before she would die from a lack of oxygen, if her airway closed and she couldn't breathe. She was already hypoxic.

Rushing towards the door Corrynne looked around her for other medical personnel who could assist her in the almost impossible task of intubating an alert person with airway swelling. But everywhere she looked all she saw was patients; endless patients, bleeding, broken, waiting and waiting…. The doctor was right. There was no one else to save this girl. Suddenly she understood; this task was the reason the Holy Ghost had prompted her to return. If the girl was going to live, it would be because Corrynne intervened, thwarting death.

"Father, help me!" pleaded Corrynne out loud as she rushed down the hall and out the doors. "Help me know what to do! I can't do this on my own!"

The young girl began grasping at her neck and motioning to Corrynne, as she pushed the gurney into the atrium of the building, out of the doorway. Corrynne nodded emphatically trying to communicate she understood what was happening. "I know you can't breathe. I'm going to try and help you!" she said as she eyed an emergency intubation kit on the ground, outside the door, where the firemen must have left it for her.

Kneeling on the floor, she rifled through the contents of the kit. Corrynne looked frantically for medication to give this girl. First she looked for some Epinephrine to decrease the swelling, or maybe even a sedative to put the poor girl to sleep while she attempted to put a tube down her throat, but to her dismay the kit only held instruments for intubation.

Corrynne picked out a stainless steel, lighted scope with a tongue blade. In the other hand, she grasped an endotracheal tube. Standing up and moving to the stranger's side, she held up her instruments and said, "I need to put a tube into your lungs so that you can breathe. It will protect your airway, but you have to let me do it."

The girl shook her head as she made a squeaking sound. Her eyes were filled with terror.

"I know this seems hard! It's hard for me, too!" said Corrynne, feeling her own body begin to shake. "But it is your only chance to breathe. Please, lie down and let me try."

Again the girl shook her head, but then her eyes rolled back and she collapsed. Unconsciously, her body went limp and began to roll off the gurney towards Corrynne. Luckily, Corrynne was able to break the girl's fall, without dropping her instruments by grasping the girl's torso with her forearms and using her own chest to ease the girl's her body onto the floor. Despite Corrynne's efforts to make the fall a soft one, the girl's legs fell on to the ground with a thud.

With the girl unaware, there was no time to lose. Corrynne placed her instruments on the girl's abdomen, and then stood up quickly. With one quick tug, she ripped the sheets off the gurney. She would use them to tilt the girl's head back so she could see down her airway. Bunching up the sheet, Corrynne knelt back down above the girl's head and shoved the bundle under her neck. Next she picked up her instruments and with the scope in her left hand and the tube in her right, she flipped out the tongue blade, hinged onto the scope, and turned on the light. Inserting it past the tongue and into the back of the girl's throat, Corrynne tried to peer down into it, but all she saw was swollen, purple tissue from lack of oxygen. Corrynne shook her head. She couldn't see the vocal cords! There was too much swelling! The airways were sealed shut.

Corrynne didn't give up. She pushed the tube in blindly, hoping to hit the right spot. Again and again, she tried. Finally, after no success, Corrynne threw down the instruments and looked up in frustration. "What do I do next?" Corrynne asked in an urgent verbal prayer, filled with worry. She felt so unprepared for this task! "This girl is going to die!" she told Heavenly Father. "Please fill my mind with what I should do!"

Suddenly an idea came into her mind. Looking to her left at the Emergency Room in which she was sewing lacerations, the people in it had come to life. They were watching her in great interest. Even the little children watched in silence.

"Where is my box?" she spoke out to the people she had been helping.

From deep in the crowd rose her box of medical supplies. It was passed hand-to-hand, overhead until it was brought to Corrynne. Quickly she dug into her mass of packages.

"I need needle-nose scissors, a syringe, and a large bore needle," she mumbled to herself as she picked the items out of the depths of the box one by one. Then she frantically repositioned herself alongside the girl, attaching the needle to the empty syringe. Running her fingers down the structures on the outside of the neck, she traced the Adam's apple to its base, and then with the needle at 45 degrees, she pressed the tip into the skin. Pulling the plunger of the syringe up it caused a stagnant suction against the tissue. She continued to apply pressure to the needle until she felt a "pop" and the chamber of the syringe suddenly filled with air. She was in! Corrynne assessed the puncture site. There was relatively little blood. Good! She didn't hit any blood vessels. The hole she had made was in the right place.

Withdrawing the needle, Corrynne then used the needle-nosed scissors; she made one cut to make the tiny hole larger, but not too large. Quickly rummaging through the intubation kit, she found some extension tubing and a thin, plastic connector. Taking the end of the tubing, she threaded it through the opening in the girl's trachea. It was a perfect fit!

Next, looking under the gurney, Corrynne found an oxygen tank and more oxygen tubing that always sat below the bed of the gurney in a harness. With a quick move, she connected the two sets of tubing and turned the oxygen on full blast.

Corrynne watched the girl's chest intently to see if it rose. She was significantly rewarded to see that it did! Jumping to her feet, Corrynne clapped and laughed loudly. "Wahoo! *Thank you!*" she said loudly, meaning it with every fiber of her being.

Cheering from the watching crowd followed her celebration. But then, Corrynne noticed that the girl did not wake, nor did the chest fall in normal respirations. "Oh no, we still have a problem," she said wondering what she had missed. She began to rethink her treatment. She then realized that although oxygen was now being pumped into the girl's the lungs, she wasn't able to exhale.

Grabbing the scissors, Corrynne bent down and quickly cut a hole in the oxygen tubing, about as big as the nail on her pinky. As she did, the girl on the floor exhaled. Then Corrynne put her thumb over the hole and the girl's chest rose again as oxygen filled it.

"It worked! Oh my goodness it worked!" said Corrynne as she covered her mouth with her free hand. "What a miracle!" she gasped. "I can't believe it!"

Again, the crowd behind her erupted with congratulatory remarks.

Looking around Corrynne wondered what she should do next. She couldn't get the girl back on the gurney to further help. There was no way she could lift her. Once again her eyes moved to the people watching her. She motioned with her free hand to them. "I need help to move this girl. Who will help me? Now that she's breathing, she needs to get inside to receive more help!"

Five men stepped forward to help Corrynne, even though many of them had not been helped themselves. "What do we do?" asked one.

"Everyone take a part of this girl and lift her back on the gurney," said Corrynne as she continued to time the respirations with her thumb over the hole for inhalation.

The men bent over and together lifted her effortlessly onto the gurney. Corrynne let go of the tubing momentarily to hit the ID pad to open the ER doors and then the group of men rolled the gurney and the girl into the next room.

Once in the next room, Corrynne did not stop walking. She had to find the doctor! Much more was needed to stabilize the girl. Corrynne had only momentarily put off the inevitable. The men continued to push the gurney at Corrynne's beckoning.

Then around the corner came Dr. Crawford, as Corrynne had predicted. When he saw the entourage, he began smiling from ear to ear. "Look at you!" he said to Corrynne gazing at the young girl with the oxygen being forced into her lungs. "Way to do the impossible!" The doctor looked at the set up even closer than before and then said, "I told you you knew what you were doing! Darn good job!"

"Thank you," Corrynne said to the doctor with a pleasant smile, but then her face twisted into a scolding, "But don't *ever* do that to me again! That was a little too much stress!"

"Corrynne!" a female voice called to her from ahead, "Oh my goodness! You're here!" Carol, her friend from the ICU, rushed up to her side.

"Yes, what's wrong?" asked Corrynne with her heart still beating in her throat.

"I found your daughter here last night!"

"What? Where is she?"

"She's with her brother."

"Dane? Carea and Dane are both here?" asked Corrynne with wide eyes. Tears instantly began to accumulate and fall down her cheeks.

Carol put her arm around Corrynne's shoulders and nodded. "Yes, he is. He had surgery and the doctors were able to stabilize him."

"Where is he?" asked Corrynne.

"He and his sister are in the ICU! Your daughter is asleep by his side."

"Oh Carol! The ICU? I can't believe it! All this time, he was in the most obvious place!" Corrynne hugged her friend with her free arm as she continued to hold the oxygen tubing steady for the young girl she had saved.

"I've been keeping an eye out for them," said Carol, smiling.

"Thank you! Thank you for taking care of them! You don't know how worried I've been!" Corrynne gasped huge sobs of relief.

Dr. Crawford smiled and said, "I'm the one that triaged your son, not knowing he was yours. Otherwise I would have told you myself. Carol here put me straight."

"Oh, I'm so thankful!"

"Go to them, Corrynne! I'll take over what you are doing here," said the doctor, as the young girl on the gurney began to stir.

"You will?" asked Corrynne almost in disbelief of her blessings.

"Yes. I've slept and am ready for another run at these wounded. You go."

Corrynne's eyes blurred with tears as she passed the oxygen tubing to her colleague. Wiping her tears on her jacket sleeve, Corrynne bolted for the stairs leading to the second floor with her gown flying behind her.

Nature of God

Dane, marveling, took the stone that Jenessa had given to him and looked into it.

"Ask a question, Dane. With questions, comes knowledge. Desire to know," encouraged Jenessa.

Dane continued to study the stone. Its brightness was blinding. All he could see was great intense light. The brightness was impossible to see beyond. He knew he had to focus his thoughts. Jenessa was right. He needed to ask questions. What questions should he ask? He thought he would start easy.

"What does God look like?" he said out loud only to focus his thoughts, and then closed his eyes as he tried to send his perceptions out to the end of the galaxy to find God on his throne of glory.

"See...." whispered Jenessa in his ear.

Dane did as he was told and focused his vision. As he did, he saw space and time inside the stone. It swirled and then sucked his awareness in. He began to see with a new consciousness, with unknown eyes, as if another new reality began to evolve, eliminating all the present ones that he was already aware of.

Within his vision he began to see the form of a man. It was a noble, humble man who walked in dust on thin sandals and dressed in worn, woven robes. Dane watched as this man looked upon the droves of people that reached to him. Dane comprehended miracles upon miracles that these people sought, which were rewarded by their beliefs in the simple man in whom they followed so faithfully.

"What do you see?" asked Jenessa from another realm.

"I think I see Christ," said Dane as he continued to watch the scenes around him.

"How do you know?"

"Because he is as I have always imagined him, and he is healing the sick and performing miracles upon many people."

"Is this the vision you sought?" asked Jenessa.

"No, I asked what God looked like. Did I do something wrong? Maybe I should have said 'What does Eloheim, the Father, look like?' The stone might have thought I was asking about Christ."

"Well, try it."

"OK," Dane cleared his throat and said clearly, once again, only to focus his thoughts, "What does Eloheim, the Father of our spirits look like?" Dane waited to see if the vision changed, but again, he was shown the same vision of the same simple man healing and administering to the people who followed him. "Nothing changed, Jenessa. I still see Jesus Christ. What am I doing wrong?"

"Maybe nothing. The stone shows nothing but truth, so the answer to your question must lie within the vision it is showing you. Maybe you should ask another question."

Dane watched as Christ healed a blind man and he marveled at his power and patience. So many thronged around him, hanging on him, begging him for their own needs, but he never lost his patience. He just continued to love and serve.

"You know Jenessa, maybe this is God the Father. Didn't Christ once say that he only did what he saw the Father do?"[1]

"You may be right, Dane. Continue to search until you know the full answer."

Dane nodded. Then he tried to add to his previous questions and asked, "Is this the vision of the Father or of the Son of the Father?"

Dane waited, but still there was no change. There was no clarification. Finally, he decided to ask his question a different way. "Is this vision a representation of the desire of my heart?" Maybe including the true desires of his heart would cause the answers to become clearer.

In response to his question, the man in his vision stood straight up from the child that he was bending over and focused in Dane's direction as if he could see Dane before him. Then he nodded and pointed to himself. Then a clear voice came into Dane's head, "*He that hath seen me, hath seen the Father also.*"[2]

Suddenly Dane understood the implications of what he had just been told. God was a perfect man, just like Christ was.[3] As he looked upon the face of Christ, he realized he also looked upon the face of God. In that, now Dane knew what God looked like. He looked like Christ! He had come to the earth to reveal the Father. He, just like the Father, is a personage of flesh and bones, as tangible as the exalted man, Jesus Christ.[4]

"Wow. I get it," said Dane in a breathy voice. "I guess I never realized that Christ looked and acted exactly like God. It seems so simple now. I'm amazed. I never perceived it possible, but I think I remember things I didn't before. I think I know God! I remember him and how similar he and Christ looked." Dane turned to Jenessa. "I did know him, didn't I?"

"Yes, Dane, you did know him. But the lesson I want you to learn is that even without your memory of him, you could know him. Anyone can know him. First one must love Christ. If they love him than naturally, they will obey him.[5] As they obey him they become like him. In becoming like Christ, they become like the Father also. In this way their knowledge of him grows. All can know God. Remember this and teach it."

"Alright. I will." Dane nodded. This knowledge felt so good.

"Now you know two aspects necessary for the application of faith."

"Which two?"

"First, you know that God exists."

"Oh, yes. I know for sure!"

"Second, you know his character, perfections, and attributes."

"Yes, he is a perfect immortal being, like Christ, of flesh and bones, with power that is through all things. He has power over all things and the supreme intelligence of the universe, knowing all things, being a personage of justice and love."[6]

"Right. You are doing very well."

"So what is the third element I need to understand?"

"That your life is in accordance to his will."

"My life now, or when I'm back on earth?"

"Both."

"So I need to be worthy."

"Not just worthy, but putting his will first in your life constantly, acting as he would, no matter how hard it is."

"Oh, you mean that when I go back to the earth that I make sure that my choices are the same choices he would make in my place?"

"Yes, exactly, choosing his plan over your own, having endurance and patience for others that do not know these truths, being willing to forgive and be as longsuffering as he."

"That shouldn't be a problem, I think, should it?"

"You have to decide that."

Dane set his jaw and said confidently. "No, it won't be a problem."

"Then, with this knowledge and commitment, you now can make your faith perfect and fruitful."[7]

"Explain that further."

"The Lord will constantly attend you, make his will known to you, and through your faith, miracles will surround you, because his power will be fulfilled through you."

Dane couldn't help but smile. "That is so cool!"

"It's more than cool. It is of the utmost importance. Your mission will be difficult. It will be hard for you to watch people ignore truth that is so evident to you. However, you must. You must love those people as you love obedient people, and give them many opportunities to change. Be persistent. Be brave. But above all, be true."

"Oh, I will. Jenessa, I will!"

"That will do, Dane, that will do."

Reunion

The lights flickered in the hospital as Corrynne rushed down the hall to the ICU on the second floor. She was out of breath from climbing the stairs because the elevators were out of order.

Coming to the ID pad to enter the ICU, she pressed her thumb to release the locks on the double doors, but then the lights flickered again and then went out.

"Shoot!" exclaimed Corrynne. In the dark she pressed the pad over and over again, but the energy was gone and the pad did not respond. She moved to the double doors and pushed her body weight against them to try and open them manually, but they were locked tight.

"*Let me in!*" she yelled, losing all inhibitions in an effort to get to Dane and Carea. Pounding on the door loudly she yelled again, "*I need in! Someone open this door!*"

A click was heard on the other side of the door and a man in street clothes opened the door. "Do you want in ma'am?"

"Oh, yes! Thank you!" said Corrynne as she rushed by him.

The lights flickered again as the generators somewhere deep in the hospital kicked in. Slowly lights turned back on as she rounded the secretary's desk.

"Dane Rogers, he's here right?" she asked an unknown man in a lab coat.

"Who are you?"

"*I'm his mother!*" Corrynne said, in a frantic tone.

"Oh, come this way. He's in room 220," said the man as he led her to the room.

Carea must have heard her coming because suddenly, Corrynne saw her peek her head around the corner.

"Mom!" she said, already crying.

"Carea! My sweet girl!" said Corrynne crying too as she fully embraced her daughter. "Oh, my goodness! You're OK! I can't believe it! You're alright!"

"Yes, I'm alright," said Carea with her head now in her mother's shoulder.

"I'm so thankful! I'm so thankful!" Corrynne said over and over again, holding her daughter.

"Mom, Dane is sick!" said Carea still crying into her shoulder. "He's very, very sick, Mom."

"I know, baby. It's OK," said Corrynne as she rubbed Carea's back to soothe her. "Everything will be fine now."

"Oh, Mom..." said Carea as she shook her head. "It's my fault he's like this! It's my fault!"

Corrynne pushed her daughter away from her and looked into her eyes. "*No, don't ever say that. It is not your fault!* Somehow we have been pulled into situations that we don't understand."

"But, Mom, look at him!" said Carea as she looked back toward the bed.

"I will, Carea, but I want you to know you are innocent of any wrong doing. Whatever has happened is not your fault. Do you understand?"

Carea frowning, wiped her tears with her right hand and then with her left.

"*Answer me, Carea! Do you understand?*" insisted Corrynne.

Carea hesitated but then nodded.

"Good," said Corrynne as she hugged her daughter again. "Now let's see Dane."

The man in the lab coat who had lead Corrynne to the room had backed away from the room momentarily, to give Carea and Corrynne privacy. As soon as they were finished and were heading into the room, the man said, "Mrs. Rogers?"

Corrynne looked back over her shoulder. "Yes?"

"Before you go into that room, may I have a word with you?"

"Of course," said Corrynne attempting to recover from her intense emotions, but feeling another layer of shock coming on. She assumed this man at the door was the doctor come to tell her some bad news about Dane. She could tell just by how he was acting.

"I'm Dr. Wilcox. I normally practice out of LDS hospital, but because of the flooding, I was pulled here."

"Nice to meet you," said Corrynne. "I'm Corrynne Rogers. I normally work here, in the ICU as an RN, but I was pulled to the ER."

"Oh, good. Then I can talk to you frankly."

Corrynne nodded. "Yes, please," feeling her legs tremble from the adrenaline that was coursing through them.

"I operated on your son. He has had a huge bacterial insult from a wound on his right hand."

Corrynne nodded. It was as she suspected.

"We identified the pathogen as *Streptococcus A*…"

"He has Necrotizing Facietis," finished Corrynne for the doctor.

Dr Wilcox looked at Corrynne for a moment and then said, "Ah, yes, he does. It has affected much of the flesh on his hand."

"I understand," said Corrynne as she nodded now feeling an odd numbness creep over her, as if she was short-circuiting.

"I irrigated the wound with penicillin and given large doses intravenously, but still your son is very septic."

Corrynne nodded again, she was amazed that she was not emotional anymore. When her children were in danger she was never stoic like this. It must be the shock of the moment, Corrynne rationalized. "Yes, I know how these cases progress."

"I guess you would. Wasn't there an outbreak of *Strep A* here a while ago?"

Corrynne nodded, remembering the first case six months ago. "Yes. I worked on that young man until he died."

"I'm sorry."

"No problem, I just hope I don't have to relive that experience with my own son," Corrynne said in a flat tone as all emotion continued to diminish.

"I hope not, too," said the doctor with a grim look.

Corrynne turned towards the bed. She noticed he had quite a few pumps with IV fluids. "So how does it look?"

"He's in a coma."

"I see," said Corrynne looking at Dane's supine form under a single sheet. This experience was surreal for Corrynne, as if she was now outside her own body. She recalled the many other times she had seen this happen— to others....

"We've intubated him, as you can see and we have three different pressors to keep his blood pressure up."

Corrynne responded automatically, as if she was now totally disconnected from the form under the sheet. "Are we making any headway?"

"It's hard to say. I believe his odds will improve just because we removed the source of infection."

Corrynne pulled the sleeves of her cover gown up at the elbow, like she always did on shift, so she could wash her hands. "What are the vasopressors you're using?"

"Dopa, Epi, and Neo, but I'm afraid they're at the max. We need to bring them down." The doctor folded his arms.

"What is his pressure running?" asked Corrynne as she looked up at the monitor and saw that his blood pressure was barely acceptable.

"Well it's labile; it's all over the place. We're trying to keep his mean at least around 57," said the doctor.

"57?"

"Yes, his blood vessels are very dilated. I think his body is trying to respond to therapy, but that *Strep A* that got into his blood from his wound is very aggressive."

"I know. This strain is stronger than the common type."

"How do you know?" asked the doctor.

"Experience. I've seen too many young people die from this. I also knew the guy that engineered it." Corrynne was so numb she couldn't even feel any anger for Dr. Page now.

"Engineered it?"

"Yes. It's a long story that I would rather not go into right now," Corrynne knew she was too exhausted to even attempt to re-tell it.

The doctor looked at Dane's vital signs and then nodded. "I understand."

"So what's the plan?" asked Corrynne, forcing herself to show interest. The information was essential, but her mind was growing foggy.

"At this point, we'll continue to give him penicillin intravenously and titrate the drips as per his response..."

"OK," said Corrynne nodding.

"Then we'll graft where we have removed the infected tissue from his right hand and arm later."

"Alright."

"Oh, yes, one more thing."

"Yes?"

"We found a small chip of some sort in his palm. It looks like a computer chip believe it or not."

Corrynne gave a controlled nod. "Yes, I know about that."

"Is it there for a reason? It might be adding to the source of the infection. I'd like to remove it in another surgery. We didn't this time because Dane did not endure surgery very well. We found it right underneath the necrotic tissue."

"*Don't touch it!*" Fear exploded within Corrynne, as her heart rate sped up. She was immediately reminded of the threats Dr. Page had given her about instantaneous death if anyone attempted to remove the chip. Corrynne's fear caused her to be very abrupt. "Leave it there. Messing with that might make things worse!"

Doctor Wilcox shook his head, "But, Mrs. Rogers, if we want a sterile wound, we need to remove it."

Corrynne continued forcefully, forgetting all respect and communication etiquette, "*I know what normal medicine practice dictates, but it is imperative that you don't remove the chip!*" Corrynne took a deep breath and tried to calm herself down, after a moment she continued, "Let's just continue to irrigate that area with the antibiotic."

The doctor frowned. "That's a strange request," he said then obviously tried to change his look to a tight-lipped expression.

Corrynne knew he was trying to do his best and instantly felt guilty for her outburst. Swallowing she said, "Please," as she pointed to herself. "*I'm* the patient's mother and *I* ask you to honor my request."

The doctor shrugged. "Alright, but I'll note in my dictation that you refused my medical advice and that your request was directly contrary to my medical opinion and recommendation."

Corrynne nodded. Relief hit her and she felt like she needed to sit down. "That's fine." With a little step she leaned against the doorframe for support.

"OK." The doctor hesitated as if he was trying to think of something else to say.

Corrynne interjected without waiting for him. She needed to end the conversation, so she could go sit down. She was beginning to feel sick. "Thank you, doctor."

The doctor complied. "You are very welcome. I hope everything turns out alright."

Corrynne nodded and forced a smile. "Thank you," she said again then she moved gingerly into the room and shut the door behind her. She needed time with no demands on her mind. She needed to hold her son and daughter. It seemed like it had been forever since she could.

Notes to "What Was Lost, Is Found"

Nature of God

[1] "Then answered Jesus and said unto them, Verily, verily, I say unto you, The Son can do nothing of himself, but what he seeth the Father do: for what things soever he doeth, these also doeth the Son likewise" (John 5:19).

[2] "And because he said unto them that Christ was the God, the Father of all things, and said that he should take upon him the image of man, and it should be the image after which man was created in the beginning; or in other words, he said that man was created after the image of God, and that God should come down among the children of men, and take upon him flesh and blood, and go forth upon the face of the earth" (Mosiah 7:27).

[3] "This is the world's mystery revealed. This is God manifested in the flesh. This is the Son of God, who comes to reveal the Father. Jesus Christ, for he is the image and likeness of that Father's person, and the reflection of that Father's mind. Henceforth when men shall say, Show us the Father, he shall point to himself as the complete revelation of the Father, and say, 'He that hath seen me, hath seen the Father also'" (B. H. Roberts, "Jesus Christ: the Revelation of God," *Improvement Era*, August, 1902, vol. 5, 10).

[4] "God is a perfect man. Such was Jesus Christ, and he was God manifested in the flesh. "Was," did I say? Nay, "is," I should have said; and such will he remain for ever; a spirit he is, clothed with an immortal body, a resurrected body of tangible flesh and bones, made eternal, and now dwelling in heaven with his Father, of whom he is the express image and likeness; as well now as when he was on earth; and hence the Father also must be a personage of flesh and bones, as tangible as the exalted man, Christ Jesus the Lord" (B. H. Roberts, "Jesus Christ: the Revelation of God," *Improvement Era*, August, 1902, vol. 5. 10).

[5] "If thou lovest me thou shalt serve me and keep all my commandments" (D&C 42:29).

[6] "We learn the six following things: First, that he was God before the world was created, and the same God that he was after it was created. Secondly, that he is merciful and gracious, slow to anger, abundant in goodness, and that he was so from everlasting, and will be so to everlasting. Thirdly, that he changes not, neither is there variableness with him, and that his course is one eternal round. Fourthly, that he is a God of truth, and cannot lie. Fifthly, that he is no respecter of persons; and sixthly, that he is love" (Joseph Smith, *Lectures on Faith, Q&A*, lecture 3, 12).

[7] "Let us here observe, that three things are necessary in order that any rational and intelligent being may exercise faith in God unto life and salvation; first, the idea that he actually exists, secondly, a correct idea of his character, perfections, and attributes, thirdly, an actual knowledge that the course of life which he is pursuing is according to his will. For without an acquaintance with these three important facts, the faith of every rational being must be imperfect and unproductive; but with this understanding it can become perfect and fruitful, abounding in righteousness, unto the praise and glory of God the Father, and the Lord Jesus Christ" (Joseph Smith, *Lectures on Faith*, lecture 3, 5).

CHAPTER FIFTEEN

THE PRICE

"For the word of God is quick, and powerful, and sharper than any two-edged sword, piercing even to the dividing asunder of soul and spirit, and of the joints and marrow, and is a discerner of the thoughts and intents of the heart" (Hebrews 4:12).

00:08:26, 17:05:22 Zulu
Sunday, April 4th
7:55 a.m.
Luxemburg, Germany

The Pope

Apollo Ramius stirred uncomfortably in his bed as he slowly wakened. He could hear beeping and clicking noises of monitoring systems. In growing waves, his clarity of thought and physical senses were returning from a thick fog.

His face twitched in a spasm as his throat burned with fire. Apollo attempted to swallow but the swallowing motion caused the walls of his throat to stick together. He was so parched and dry! With effort he stretched his neck and lowered the back of his tongue to open his airway. It opened and he took a few rapid, shallow gasps to catch his breath.

Apollo attempted to open his eyes, but they were crusted over with something that made it impossible. With weak muscles he struggled to rub them but his hands were restrained. His mind began to ask a thousand questions. What was the reason his hands could not move? Why was he so weak? Why was his throat so dry? What substance bound his eyes? Where was he…?

"Your surgery is over, Your Holiness," said a soothing female voice that spoke to him in German. "It was successful. You endured it very well. Your hands are restrained to protect your stitches until you can wake up fully.

There are bandages over your eyes, so you will not be able to see until we remove them. Do you understand what I am saying, Most Holy Father?"

…Yes, there was a surgery to be performed—to his face and head. Was it over already? It must be, since this is what he was told. Apollo nodded slowly to answer the voice waiting for his reply.

"Good." A hand patted Apollo's shoulder as if he was a child to be encouraged, but it did not offend him. Elementary thoughts filled his head as he continued to gain awareness.

"Thirsty," he whispered. "May I have water?"

"Not yet, Your Holiness. No drinks yet. We must wait until your body wakes up further, otherwise you may become sick to your stomach."

Apollo nodded and then whispered in a slightly stronger voice, "Ice?" He needed something to moisten the back of his throat.

"Here is a swab."

Apollo felt a cold wet sponge placed in his mouth. Immediately he endeavored to close his lips around the stick of the swab, but his lips could not close completely. They were numb—and so swollen! With his tongue he pressed the sponge against the roof of his mouth to drain every drop from its tiny chambers. He received partial relief, as he was finally able to swallow.

"What day is it?" Apollo rasped.

"It is the Lord's day, Your Holiness."

"Sunday?"

"Yes, Most Holy Father. It is nearly eight in the morning."

Apollo thought for a moment. He had gone into surgery Saturday afternoon, April the third. "I have almost lost a day." A slight panicked feeling began to stimulate the back of his mind. *He couldn't bear to lose any days…he had to hurry and enjoy—everything. Time was ticking.*

"Yes, sir, that happens," replied the voice interrupting Apollo's thought process. "Long surgical procedures steal time like a thief. Don't worry, you'll gain your bearings soon."

"Alright," Apollo said sleepily, forgetting already what he had been thinking. He allowed himself to relax back into his bed.

A vague recollection of the past week's events began to unwind in his still groggy mind. He remembered many earthquakes. One had taken the life of the Pope—yes, that was it. He had drunk wine in a meeting with the infamous MD in his elegant American mansion...and then…a visitation—his mind recoiled, and then froze. For a few moments he could think of nothing more.

A poignant feeling of choking in MD's mansion came to his mind involuntarily. Spontaneous fear filled him from his memory, as a helpless sense followed. He thought about the overwhelming power of the dark being that had visited him. How could he compete with such omniscience? There was no fighting his control. Despair followed as he came to terms with his vulnerable position. Then with a deep, stiff breath he surrendered. He knew he could blame no one else for his situation. His own choices and values had made him vulnerable and had brought him to this point. There was no turning back. His fate was sealed.

But…Apollo searched for some comfort. All of it was over. If he was going to retain his rightful place—the seat of the Pope, it seemed obvious to him there was no other way than the way he was pursuing. Yes, Apollo thought, the work had been done and his soul bought…that was OK with him. It *had* to be OK with him. It had been his choice and he was willing to deal with the consequences as well as the benefits.

Benefits—yes. Now Apollo reversed his thinking. He might as well begin enjoying the benefits. Why think about the negative when so many positive benefits would soon be his? Beneath the bandages, he felt a smile tempt him. He knew without a doubt there would be many benefits to his new position; freedom, prestige, wealth beyond anything he had ever experienced, and power…*great vast power*…power over kings and countries…. No he wasn't sorry for his decision. The price of his choices was well worth the outcomes; at least right now they were.

Powerful memories now replaced the dark ones. Apollo reminded himself that despite his plight, all his dreams *were* coming true. Just a few days ago the conclave, the group of Cardinals given the stewardship to elect the next leader of the Roman Catholic Church, had done just as MD, and the being that had visited him, promised. Miraculously, he was *now the new pope!* It had been just that easy! He never would have thought his ascension could be so quick. *But oh, it was!* The sweetness of it all was…liberating!

In his mind's eye he reviewed being ushered into the coveted High Seat in the center of St. Peter's Basilica. Hundreds of clerics had gathered around his chair. He remembered being charged with electricity as the members of the conclave rose in unison and the great hall fell silent as his name was announced to the world after a closed election process. *"Cardinal Archbishop Apollo Damon Ramius, over the reorganized Archdiocese Germania, still acting Bishop of Berlin, Germany, has been chosen by secret vote by the conclave as our Pope and Father of the Holy Roman Catholic Church. From this day forward he will be known as Pope John Paul the Fourth."*[1] An explosion of thunderous applause followed the announcement from countless clergy affirming him as their new pope.

Apollo's mind continued to recall Cardinal Franklin, one of his close friend's giddy smile and nervous, sporadic behavior as he and three other prominent Cardinal Archbishops had immediately come over to congratulate him, bowing and kissing his rings.

"Your Holiness?" A new German male voice interrupted his thoughts. It momentarily surprised him, but then satisfaction returned. *"Your Holiness…"* he had been called. Yes, what a glorious title. It was right that he be addressed in this manner. He had sacrificed much to obtain it!

The Pope moved his head as though he was looking at the man in his room, whose voice came from the right side of his bed. "Yes?" responded Apollo also in German.

"I am Doctor Gustuf. I performed the surgery on your eyes. How are you doing?"

"Well I think," said Apollo. "I'll know more after I can see."

"Ah, yes, forgive the tape and padding. Due to the delicate surgical process, it is best if your eyes remain in total darkness for at least twelve hours."

"What exactly did you do?" asked Apollo not really remembering the details of the surgery.

"We used lasers to cut away the conjunctiva, which is a fine lining that covers the outer surface of the eye, and then used new electrical technology to assure a successful splicing of the optic nerve."

"Why did you do this?" asked the Pope with only slight interest.

"So we could implant the donor eyes, Your Holiness," said Dr. Gustuf. "I assure you, within a couple of days your eyes should be feeling as good as new, but in the meantime they'll feel dry and sore until the tiny blood vessels re-grow, healing that conjunctive layer that normally secretes oils and mucus to keep your eyes moist. You'll need to use plenty of sterile eye lubricant."

"Ah, good advice, Doctor." said Apollo, not really listening now. His mind was still basking in the glory of his coronation.

A shifting of several bodies in padded chairs around him snapped the Pope out of his daze. He could sense people—how many he did not know, but they were in his room, watching him wake up! Where was his privacy? Who was accountable for this poor treatment of the *Holy anointed?*

Turning his head, Apollo moved his blind gaze from the right, steadily sweeping toward the left, as if to look at everyone who surrounded him. He wished to give the eerie impression he could see every person in the room through his thick bandages. Through the gauze wrapping his head and partially covering his ears, the Pope sensed his pointed attention was successful. He heard muffled sounds of creaking chairs weighted with nervous bodies and stirring feet on the floor as whoever was in his room seemed to attempt to escape his focused, sightless stare.

Finally, a rough, gravelly cough broke the heavy silence.

Apollo recognized the sound. He snapped his focus to the foot of the bed and slightly off to his left where the cough had just erupted. "I'm glad you're here, MD," said the Pope in a somewhat superior and perhaps toying voice as he slowly lowered his head back onto the pillow.

Subsequent whispers coming from the different corners of the room indicated his audience was duly impressed with his perceptive powers. Satisfied he thought, "Just wait!" as he remembered all the supernatural abilities and powers he had been promised by his visitor who had come in the dead of night. "I assure all of you the show hasn't even started!"

Prayers of a Mother

Corrynne looked around her in the nondenominational chapel of the hospital. It had been too many days at her son's bedside and she needed a break. Luckily, Carea had been reunited with the family at the tent city and seemed to be recovering fine, however, Corrynne was exhausted. Rubbing her neck with her hand, she realized she was very tense. She decided to take a walk and loosen things up. Ending at the hospital chapel was not her original idea, but as she walked by the doors, it being the Sabbath, going in seemed like a good idea.

Corrynne looked at the empty pews. It struck her as odd that this room was the only room empty in the whole hospital. She would have thought that Sunday would have brought at least a few people to pray for their sick.

Shrugging, she released the thought. It wasn't important. What was important was that here Corrynne could have some privacy to explore her feelings. She sat down in a pew that was in the very back row. With a big sigh she buried her face in her hands.

Corrynne's emotions turned to anger. She focused on Imam Mahdi. Her chest burned with fire as she thought of the awful, devilish man. She was glad that he was dead. The world was much better off and she hoped he was burning in Hades—wherever that was! The anger and hatred continued to grow within her. *"How dare he! How dare he hurt my son and scar my daughter!"* she said out loud.

Corrynne was so frustrated! She had requested both Dane and Carea, to be given the Prevnar shot at the doctor's office to counteract whatever Imam Mahdi could do to them. The shot was given in hopes their bodies' immune systems could develop antibodies against the deadly bacteria! She had thought she had been so clever.

Before Dr. Page had died, she remembered he had spitefully taunted her. He had said that there were millions of Streptococci in stasis around the chip in Dane's hand, ready to be released in a moment with a push of a button from some remote. She remembered him laughing as he said that no one could fight such an insult. The rash of bacteria released all at once would kill, as it was developed to kill. Now she saw he had been right. It seemed Dane did not have a fighting chance. He was dying, slowly.

"Oh, Dane!" Corrynne said her son's name wistfully out loud. She felt her tongue push off the roof of her mouth as she ended his name. It sounded so strong and emphatic to her…. Looking out across the pews in the room as she remembered watching Dane from the window just a couple days before. When she woke that day, he was out fixing the sprinkler system, getting it ready for spring. His father must have asked him to do it.

Corrynne had heard the loud clang of steal on stone and looked out to see who was shoveling. She remembered marveling at his huge structure. She had watched his back flex with every shovel full of dirt. "Wow," she had thought, "I don't remember him being so big!" It seemed like yesterday he was coming up to her with a big crooked smile and saying, "Mom, look! I'm up to your nose! I'm getting taller"…or "You're shrinking, Mom." He had laughed at his own humor like he always did when he was trying to be clever. Corrynne remembered she would tease him by scowling, which would make him laugh harder.

Now her Dane was all grown up and almost ready to go on a mission. Time was ruthless in its progression. It seemed like the world was rotating faster. It would be her third son to go on a mission. Oh how she wished she could turn back time and see Dane laughing and being silly again! But it wasn't to be.

Prayer was an obvious necessity at that moment. She needed to understand the rules of things. Corrynne promptly turned around and knelt down in front of the bench.

"Dear Father," Corrynne swallowed as her emotions began to rise. The events of the previous days seemed to compile many stresses upon her.

"…WHY?" Her choking words echoed off the walls of the chapel. "Why my son? Why the flood? Why so much pressure on Carea? She is so innocent! Why do we have to suffer like this? Where is the purpose? Help me understand!"

Emotions continued to bubble as she prayed, "Forgive me, but I feel so confused in these trials. What are we expected to do, to think? My son is— dying…. How am I to feel?"

Tears dropped on the wooden pew, but Corrynne continued, "Thou knoweth all. Please, my husband told me that Dane will return to mortality when it is time, but what does that mean? Will it be during the Millennium? Please don't let that be the case! And Carea suffers so much from guilt! Please release her! She doesn't deserve this sadness. She is a stalwart, brave young woman who stands up for your truth! Please bless her with peace!"

Corrynne was silent for few moments, then returned to her prayer; "Thou knowest that we live in a time when death is often cheated. Please…. I have served thee and this community saving lives, giving back sons and daughters to their mothers and fathers…. I wish for that myself, too. Is that not the right thing to ask for? Am I not to pray for the welfare of my son? …Help me understand what I am to want…to pray for…to expect—from thee!"

Corrynne waited for a response to her pleadings, but only quiet nothingness wafted around her. Corrynne wondered if her charged emotions and swirling thoughts were interfering with answers that had come quickly to her lately.[2]

Hot tears continued to stream down Corrynne's nose. Quietly she struggled for control. After a few minutes more of silence, Corrynne started again, beginning to feel embarrassed for what could be perceived as her lack of faith. "I'm sorry, Father…. I'm so sorry. I don't mean to be angry. I want to be accepting. Please forgive me. Thou gave me beautiful children whom I love so much. They have given my life dimension and fulfillment. They have taught me lessons that have made me infinitely better than if I didn't have them....

"I know that they are thy children too. And in reality they are not mine at all. They are yours and I have no claim." Corrynne continued, "Without thee, I would have never enjoyed life and motherhood. I see that not even my body is mine because thou hast created it.[3] Now I understand that I have no right to anything, however, I pray for thy peace to help me get through this!"[4]

For a while, Corrynne sat in silence wondering if she was strong enough to let go of her anger. She didn't think she was, but with strength through the Spirit she believed she could. With that thought she took courage and gave up her will, hoping she could trust the Lord to do what was right. "...Do as thou wish.... thy will be done...Dane is thy son and Carea is thy daughter, ...and I am sure that thou art in control. I should realize that whether in life or death, in pain or joy, the plan of salvation is the same. Christ still paid the price for our sins and in that we have eternal life.[5]

"Thank you, for thy own sacrifice—that most terrible sacrifice of thy own son for the saving of all people. Even when others scorned him and tortured him, thou still allowed his sacrifice to be applied even to them, if they repented.[6] How difficult, even for a God, that must have been!"[7]

Corrynne's pleadings to her Father in Heaven were complete. Despite this she continued to kneel. A small feeling of gratefulness mixed with peace began to replace the anger that had controlled her heart just minutes before. The feeling grew, emanating out of her chest and into her limbs, evolving into a new admiration for the endless love her Heavenly Father must have for his children.[8]

Slowly she began to have the impression that Dane, wherever his spirit was, would be fine. That Carea, through time, would be fine. Whatever those feelings meant, she did not know for sure, but for her, right now, that was enough.[9] At least she didn't have to deal with Imam Mahdi any longer. That by itself was a relief!

Holy Metamorphosis

The Pope, now keenly aware of his surroundings, remembered that he was not recovering in a normal hospital bed. He was actually recovering in the medical wing of MD's mansion in Luxembourg, Germany.

The graveled voice of MD took control of the gathering. "Ladies and gentlemen," MD began, "what you see before you is nothing less than a miracle—a miracle of technology and God-given opportunities brought together. The medical ability to perform such seemingly impossible physical transformations has been in existence for some time, but our good doctor and his colleagues in this very room have perfected it through exhaustive research, appropriate tissue matching and computer mapping." MD stopped and then added a side thought, "Having an appropriate donor, our departed Imam Mahdi, helped, however."

Apollo noticed the light, polite chuckling heard in the room. By the sound of the voices, he was beginning to have an idea of the identity of some who sat near him.

"Dr. Kran," continued MD, "the world's foremost authority in face transplantations, was our esteemed doctor on the case. He and his staff were brought here to perform the operation that will change world history and facilitate peace between all the warring factions of the world!"

The room suddenly erupted in applause from MD's inspiring comments.

When MD began speaking again, his voice came from the right side of Apollo's bed. He must have moved to the doctor's side during the excitement of the moment before.

"Doctor? Could you bless us with your explanation and take the honor of unveiling the new physical attributes of our beloved spiritual leader? Please explain the gist of what you have done—being careful to tell us in words, we simple minded, can understand."

A couple people in the room laughed in agreement.

"Yes, I would be happy to," said the doctor in English but with a thick German accent.

Apollo's interest perked. Now that he was more awake, he was very interested in all the details of the operation. He found himself sitting higher in the bed.

Apollo heard the doctor take a few scuffing steps to his bedside. The Pope wondered if this meant some of his bandages were going to come off. He hoped there would be a mirror close by so he could see himself.

"It certainly was no *ordinary* procedure, I must say," began Dr. Kran as the sound of stiff paper could be heard being ripped. "In fact, this is the first and only procedure of its kind employing so many procedural approaches at once."

There was a shuffling sound, mixed with the sound of bending paper as Apollo assumed the doctor was handing something out that had been in an envelope. Maybe it was packet of papers demonstrating the procedure, or pictures.

After the papers were handed out, Apollo heard the doctor return to the side of his bed. Next, he felt a light hand upon the back of his head as the doctor said, "We started with the recipient here...."

The Pope turned as if to look at the doctor. He was being much too casual in reference to his person. His blind gaze seemed to have the desired effect because the doctor immediately apologized.

"Forgive me, Your Holiness."

Apollo nodded graciously, then held up a bandaged hand to encourage the doctor to continue.

"MD is correct in his review of this unique surgery. Because of new microsurgical devices and anti-rejection drugs, we are now able to transplant skin, muscle and bone from a dead person and apply it to a live person. In the past this procedure was used to help burn victims or trauma victims who had suffered damage to their own face. But for us, this technology will accomplish even higher purposes that will heal the world."[10]

Statements of approval were whispered at the foot of Apollo's bed.

"If I could continue—" said the doctor quieting the whispering. "To perform this procedure, we took a micro-detailed topographical picture of the Holy Father, mapping every miniscule detail of his entire face, scalp, and neck, recording every scar, blemish and line. Then, with the same technology we mapped the *donor's* physical characteristics down to the micron. Then through complex calculations and comparisons, a computer mapped the perfect path for a compatible laser incision for both, now Pope John Paul IV and the donor. Then through advanced Fifth-Axis technology, allowing many variant angles, we were able to provide an invisible incision because it will follow His Holiness's original facial flaws and lines."

"Amazing!" said one voice.

"Yes, definitely!" Agreed another person sitting at the foot of the bed.

"The whole thing took just over ten hours," the doctor bragged.

There was a cough in the corner and then an unidentifiable person, who had a young rich voice, spoke up, "Yes, doctor, your procedure seems to be flawless, but will the Holy Pope's expressions and mannerisms match that of the donor?"

MD chuckled a little. To Apollo it sounded almost nervous. "Excuse my son's suspicions, he is a detail type of person, but I too am interested in your answer. Do you have an answer, Dr. Kran?" asked MD politically.

"It's more than OK, I welcome skeptics," replied the doctor. "Identical mimicking is my specialty. You see, because we transplanted the facial bones, maintaining facial muscles, tendons and nerve integrity, every expression and slight muscular tremor will be *exactly* like the donor's. No one will be able to detect a difference."

"Not even scientific attempts at identification?" asked the same young voice.

"Not even scientific identification," answered the doctor confidently. "Not even the finest microscopes will see any surgical lines, because as I said before, there are no surgical lines other than those natural lines that existed before surgery."

"What about dental records?" asked the young man again.

"Ah, all dental records have been destroyed," assured MD as if he was trying to salvage the doctor's promises. "There shouldn't be a problem..."

"Well," interrupted the doctor. "Even if they were in existence, they would match perfectly."

"How?" asked the young man.

"Like we said before. The Pope has the very face of the donor, including his teeth. The whole bone structure with the teeth intact was transplanted as one. His Holiness has the donor's teeth, so any dental records, destroyed or in existence, will match—by laws of 'substitution,' for those of you that took Geometry," said the doctor who suddenly was trying to be funny.

A laugh peeled around the room, easing the tension that had been building.

"And hair?" said the young man not giving up.

"The hair is simply not an issue. I assure you all DNA testing will match," said the doctor.

Apollo felt the weight of the doctor's hand on his head, but he did not sense touch as the doctor picked at a piece of tape on his head. "Dr. Kran, I cannot feel you touching my head, although I know that you are."

Dr. Kran took a breath and then exhaled as he began to unwrap the gauze on the Pope's head, but kept the face covered. "Your Holiness, you will not feel your scalp, nor your face for a while. The nerves responsible for sensation have been severed. It will be awhile until they heal. We have attempted to reattach the nerves responsible for movement, so you can move your new face however."

"I see," said Apollo feeling nervous all of a sudden. He hadn't thought about this aspect of the surgery. "You're sure the sensation nerves will be able to grow back?" he asked trying to sound confident but growing apprehensive.

"In most of the surgeries that I have done, they have. However, there is a small percentage that continue to have numbness in certain areas of their face." The doctor patted Apollo's shoulder.

"All right. I trust you doctor. It seems like you know what you are doing..." said Apollo, but he was interrupted by gasps from different parts of the room. He could feel long hair suddenly hit the top of his back that his gown failed to cover.

Apollo's good friend, Cardinal Franklin's voice abruptly called out, "He has a full head of hair again! No more combing hair over your bald spot, Cardinal Ramius—I mean Pope John Paul!"

Apollo could tell he was smiling by the sound of his voice. He didn't know if he liked being the butt of his joke, however. He was being a bit too irreverent.

"Yes!" said a regal woman's voice. "You should see it, Your Holiness. It's thick and jet-black with some natural curl. Dr. Kran, can you do that for me?" asked the woman to the doctor. "I could do with some thick locks to improve public opinion."

"Madam President, nothing could make you more beautiful," said the doctor without missing a beat.

"Oh, you'll get everywhere with those flattering words, Dr. Kran."

"I hope so, Ma'am. I hope so," answered the doctor proudly. Then Dr. Kran continued. "You see this head of hair is real hair. It is alive and still growing."

"Where did you get it?" asked MD

"You should know that, MD" There was silence as the doctor waited for some response, but there wasn't any. He continued, "We got it from the donor, of course. We had to do some repair work from his injuries but now, as you can see, all is perfect."

"Oh yes," said one person

"Absolutely!" said another.

"Isn't it true that we want all hair samples to be that of the donor's?" asked the doctor. "Hair continues to grow long after the body dies."

"Of course!" said MD "You are a genius! I knew I picked the right man for this job!"

"Now that the hair is fed by His Holiness's blood supply, it will become his," explained the doctor. "We just peeled back the entire scalp from off the bone on both the Pope and the donor, then placed the scalp of the donor like one big cap upon the Pope's skull."

"Maybe it is good that I can't feel anything yet," said Apollo out loud, thinking that the massive surgery could have been extremely painful.

The group laughed again, this time at the Pope himself.

The young man's voice that had questioned the doctor earlier spoke out once again. "Yes, all of this is amazing, I admit, but what do you say about fingerprints?"

Apollo felt one of his hands picked up off the covers in demonstration. They too were wrapped in gauze dressing.

"We have transplanted the skin, onto His Holiness's hands from the donor, just like a skin graft. Unless authorities will be examining the toe prints, which I don't think there are any records to compare anyway, I don't think there will be a problem."

Again the now jovial group laughed.

Apollo heard some backslapping. "You have thought of everything, Dr. Kran," said MD.

"*Not everything*," interrupted MD's son again.

"What do you mean, son?" questioned MD defensively. "I think we are sure that the world will look at our Pope and believe he is the donor and the donor *is* the Pope. It will be a miracle straight from heaven."

"No, Father. There is no way the blood can be changed to match the donor's. No science has been able to change the DNA and cellular markers of the blood of a person."

"Ah, you are right, my son. You have discovered the beauty of this plan. The blood does not have to match. Right, doctor? Right, Cardinal Franklin?"

"No it doesn't," said the doctor agreeing heartily with MD.

"MD is a genius! *It will deceive everyone, so they will follow us like lambs!*" said Cardinal Franklin in ecstatic emotion.

There was a sudden silence in the room as everyone automatically held their breath. The secret objective had been voiced out loud. Apollo cringed inside for his friend. It was the one rule that was not to be broken within the circle of these prominent associates.

After a moment of silence, MD ordered into the unseen recording devices, "*Erase Cardinal Franklin's statement, NOW!*"

Notes to "The Price"

The Pope

[1] When a new Pope is selected, he selects a new name to be known by. See http://www.newadvent.org/cathen/04192a.htm for details.

Prayers of a Mother

[2] "Too often we offer our prayer or perform our administration and then wait nervously to see whether our request will be granted, as though approval would provide needed evidence of his existence. That is not faith! Faith is quite simply, a confidence in the Lord. In Mormon's words, it is a 'firm mind in every form of godliness' (Moroni 7:30).

"We know He lives; therefore, we trust Him to bless us according to His divine will and wisdom. This childlike confidence in the Lord is known in the scripture simply as the 'sacrifice of a broken heart and contrite spirit' (D&C 59:8)" (Lance Wickman, "But If Not," *Ensign*, Nov. 2002, 31).

[3] "And now I ask, can ye say aught of yourselves? I answer you, Nay. Ye cannot say that ye are even as much as the dust of the earth; yet ye were created of the dust of the earth; but behold, it belongeth to him who created you" (Mosiah 2:25).

[4] "Peace I leave with you, my peace I give unto you: not as the world giveth, give I unto you. Let not your heart be troubled, neither let it be afraid" (John 14:27).

[5] "And I give unto them eternal life; and they shall never perish, neither shall any man pluck them out of my hand" (John 10:28).

[6] "For the natural man is an enemy to God, and has been from the fall of Adam, and will be, forever and ever, unless he yields to the enticings of the Holy Spirit, and putteth off the natural man and becometh a saint through the atonement of Christ the Lord, and becometh as a child, submissive, meek, humble, patient, full of love, willing to submit to all things which the Lord seeth fit to inflict upon him, even as a child doth submit to his father" (Mosiah 3:19).

[7] "At noontide the light of the sun was obscured, and black darkness spread over the whole land. The terrifying gloom continued for a period of three hours. ... It was a fitting sign of the earth's deep mourning over the impending death of her Creator.

"At the ninth hour Christ uttered that anguished cry, 'My God, my God, why hast thou forsaken me?' (Matt. 27:46) In that bitterest hour the dying Christ was alone. [So] that the supreme sacrifice of the Son might be consummated in all its fullness, the Father seems to have withdrawn ... His immediate Presence, leaving to the Savior of men the glory of complete victory over the forces of sin and death.

"Realizing that He was no longer forsaken, but that His atoning sacrifice had been accepted by the Father, and that His mission in the flesh had been carried to glorious consummation, He exclaimed in a loud voice of holy triumph: 'It is finished.' In reverence, resignation, and relief, He addressed the Father saying: 'Father, into thy hands I commend my spirit.' He bowed His head, and voluntarily gave up His life" (James Talmage, *Jesus the Christ*, pp. 612-13, 615, 661).

[8] "As we step back and try to understand this love of God, we are astounded by its profound impact. At its center is the reality of a literal Father in Heaven whose love for His children knows no bounds. All truths, wisdom, power, goodness, and love He desires to share with His children, whom He created and sent to earth. He would have us reach up and know Him as a Father, as one who forgives, as a helper, as friend, as lawgiver—as one anxious to grant to every man the full opportunity of His love and potential and ultimately the blessing to one day become like Him. This love from Father in Heaven and its effects upon one of His children or the whole world is miraculous and contagious. He is constantly and everlastingly watching over us to lovingly and gently nudge us along" (James M. Paramore, "Love One Another," *Ensign*, May 1981, 53).

[9] "With scriptures to anchor and reassure us, we, too, can 'look unto God…and he will console [us] in [our] afflictions (Jacob 3:1). We, too, can be 'supported under trials and troubles of every kind, yea,…he will still deliver [us]' (Alma 36:3, 27). Whether in tranquil or turbulent times, our best source of comfort is the Comforter" (Neal Maxwell, "Encircled in the Arms of His Love," *Ensign,* Nov. 2002, 16).

Holy Metamorphosis

[10] This procedure, although sounds like science fiction, is possible today. See the CNN article reviewing plastic surgeons in England exploring face transplantation. http://www.cnn.com/2002/HEALTH/11/28/face.transplants/index.html, or the Los Angeles Times, Feb 21, 2004, for further details.

CHAPTER SIXTEEN

SORE ADVERSITY

"O GOD, where art thou? And where is the pavilion that covereth thy hiding place? How long shall thy hand be stayed, and thine eye, yea thy pure eye, behold from the eternal heavens the wrongs of thy people and of thy servants, and thine ear be penetrated with their cries?" (D&C 121:1-2).

00:08:11, 06:40:10 Zulu
Monday, April 19th
10:20 a.m.
Provo, Utah

Condemned

Bo picked his way down the sidewalk of his once immaculate neighborhood. Stepping over the trunk of a fallen tree that lay across the sidewalk and into the street, he slipped on the other side in mud. Grabbing onto some of the branches that jutted out into the air, he was able to steady himself.

"Careful, Jax, as you cross this tree," Bo said, looking behind him at his son.

Jax carefully straddled the trunk as his father asked and moved across it without incident.

It had been almost three weeks since the earthquake and the flood. After a week of living in tents, trailers were brought in by the Federal Emergency Management Agency[1] for the homeless to live in. Donated clothing from Deseret Industries kept all the displaced families covered in the early spring chill. Bo and his family didn't complain. It was amazing how thankful they were these days for every little thing.

Today Corrynne was called again for duty at the hospital, which she accepted to be close to Dane. Soon after she left, Bo was given the go ahead by the city disaster managers to return to his home to assess the flood and quake damage. Bo left Carea to stay with the smaller children as he and Jax left to explore their home.

A city bus loaded up some of the residents of the houses in his area and took them to the vicinity where they lived. Bo and Jax had been dropped off at the corner of 3700 North and University and told to meet back at the bus in two hours. In tall rubber boots, Jax and Bo exited the bus and took off trudging through the slick, deep mud to their home a few blocks north.

"I understand the building inspectors have already been out to our house," said Bo as he took calculated steps to avoid falling.

"To do what?" asked Jax as he moved out in front of his father, being a little more nimble.

"To shut off the gas, electricity and water."

"That's good," said Jax simply.

"They also have inspected the homes to see if they are salvageable."

"Is ours salvageable?"

"I don't know. If there is a large orange 'X' on the door that means we can go in. If there is a large orange 'X' with a square around it that means our house had been condemned and it will have to be demolished."

"That would be a bummer," said Jax. "Hey look, Dad!" said Jax suddenly as he pointed in front of them.

Bo focused to where his son was pointing and saw that there was a car pile up. There were four cars bunched together. One rested on the roof of another, as a third was on its side. Bo surmised that the rush of the water must have moved them like matchbox cars into that position. "Yes, the water was pretty powerful wasn't it?"

"I'm not talking about those cars there. I'm talking about the car in the tree!"

Bo shifted his gaze a little and then saw it. There was a car in a tree! It was silver Volkswagen Bug lodged in the branches of a stark Quaking Aspen. "Boy I wish I had a camera to take a picture of that one!" said Bo smiling a little. "Ry and Roc would have liked to have seen that."

"Look what else are in these trees," said Jax as he began to look from tree to tree.

Bo also began searching the branches. "I see some boots," said Bo.

"There's a Big Wheel in that one over there."

"There's someone's trash in that one," said Bo as he pointed to a big black plastic bag with debris hanging from its mouth.

There was a pause and then Jax exclaimed, "*Sick!*"

"What's wrong?"

"I just stepped on a dead skunk!'"

"What?" said Bo quickly moving to his son. Looking down in the mud, he saw some black and white fur. Bo got down on his haunches and studied the animal. Its head was buried in the mud so he couldn't see it very clearly.

"Do you think it's a skunk?" asked Jax plugging his nose.

Bo shook his head slowly. "No, I think it's a cat or something."

Jax looked down again and unplugged his nose. "Whatever it is, that's sick that I stepped on it."

"I think there will be a lot of dead animals we'll have to get rid of from the flooding. That's just something that you find after disasters like these. Be careful where you step."

"I will," said Jax as he began to walk again.

As they began to round the corner to their home, Bo picked up the pace but began to tell Jax a story. "There was once a flood in the Washington, D.C., area in 1889, back when there were farms around there…"

"Yeah?"

"Over 50,000 hogs and over 1,000,000 chickens drowned."

"No way!" exclaimed Jax.

"They were burning those things for weeks."

"Why did they have to burn them? Why didn't people just eat them?"

"Because by the time they could clean up the area, flies had infested them."[2]

Jax gagged. "Dad! Stop! No more stories, OK?"

"Got a weak stomach, son?" teased Bo.

"No, just a vivid imagination, so Mom tells me. I gag easy."

Bo stepped off the curb into even deeper sludge to cross the street to their home. "Can you see if there's an orange 'X' on our home?" he said to Jax as he noticed the roof was sloping strangely.

Jax leaped through the mud with large steps and came quickly on the other side. "I think I do see an orange 'X', Dad."

"Is there a square around it?"

"I can't tell," said Jax leaning forward in an effort to see.

"Go closer, but don't get too close."

"OK," said Jax as he walked across the muddy lawn, slipping a little but catching his balance.

Bo continued to labor through the thick mud that threatened to take his boots off his feet every time he stepped.

"Dad, yes, there is a square around the 'X'—what does that mean again?"

Bo stopped moving and stood mid-street as he looked up at his house. His worries were confirmed. His house was condemned. That meant that they would not be able to go in to retrieve anything. Corrynne would be heartbroken. Shaking his head he said with a loud voice, "That means our house is toast, son."

"It is? It looks fine to me," said Jax as he moved up the steps to the front door.

"Stop, Jax! Don't move an inch more!" yelled Bo with a sudden edge to his voice. "There are probably things that you can't see."

"Like what?" asked Jax as he eyed the door.

Bo could tell his son was itching to try and open the door. "Wait. Let me come over there. Just stay where you are," commanded Bo in his most authoritative voice.

Jax looked over at his father with a disappointed look. "I'm not three, Dad."

"I know, but I don't want you hurt. Teenage boys are just as bad as three year olds."

"Thanks, Dad! I'd be careful," said Jax sounding hurt, as Bo finished crossing the street and moved onto the hidden sidewalk and lawn.

"Your older brother is lying in a hospital bed probably because he thought he couldn't get hurt either. I just don't want another son in the bed next to him."

Jax didn't respond as he turned away and looked at the door, obviously hiding sudden emotions.

Bo moved up the steps and to the front door. He studied it. Yes, there was a bold, neon orange 'X' with a square drawn deliberately around it. Carefully he reached out and turned the knob of the door and pushed. The door opened about two inches and then stuck.

"Why isn't the door opening all the way, Dad?"

Bo thought for a moment. He looked at the edges of the door to find the ceiling meeting the upper right hand corner of the door. It was obvious the ceiling had fallen in, or at least was threatening to. "Like I said, our house is toast. The ceiling of the living room has collapsed."

"How did it do that? Was it just the earthquake?"

"I'm sure having a water bed upstairs didn't help things," said Bo with disgust. "My bed is right above this ceiling and I think it's about to fall through."

"*Hey!*" yelled a voice from behind Bo and Jax. "*You're not going in there are you?*"

Bo turned around and met a man with a hardhat who quickly came up his steps. "No," he said, "We were just looking."

"This house is condemned. There is no salvaging it," continued the man. "You need to step away from it."

Bo frowned. Sudden frustration erupted within him as the man proceeded to tell him what to do. For some reason, Bo's patience disappeared and he lashed out. With a stern look and a deep voice Bo asked, "*I am very aware of what is wrong with my house. The question is, who is going to pay for this?*"

The man looked at Bo with sudden apprehension and took a couple steps back. "I don't want trouble, I was just trying to help. We don't want anyone hurt. This neighborhood is worse than a mine field."

Bo cleared his throat and squared his shoulders, swallowing his anger. In a more kind voice he asked, "What exactly are we to expect next?"

The man pulled out a digital display. "It depends on your insurance carrier. There are so many claims from the earthquakes and disasters everywhere, more and more insurance companies are going belly up every day."

"What?" asked Bo allowing the anger to enter his voice again. The shock of it all was getting to him. "Do you have a list of those insurance companies? I want to see the list."

"Yes, but, don't hurt the messenger," exclaimed the man lifting his hands up defensively. "My Palm Pilot has the Internet. You can access that list here." The man held out his Palm Pilot to Bo.

Bo scrolled down the names of insurance carriers until he came to the name, "Provincial." That was his insurance. Yes, it was on the long list of insurance companies that would not pay any claims for loss of property from the disasters the weeks before. "Dang!" said Bo out loud.

"What, Dad?"

Bo looked up at Jax and said, "I don't know, Jax."

"Don't know what?"

"I don't know what we're going to do."

Jax walked over to his dad and put his hand on his shoulder. "We'll figure it out, Dad. We always do. Now, give the man back his Palm Pilot."

Bo numbly handed the digital display back to the man. "Ah, sorry. I'm not normally so angry," he said in a monotone voice, feeling totally defeated.

Without replying, the man quickly took his electronic device and rushed off.

Heartbeat

Corrynne stood over Dane's body. Ever since he had come into the hospital, he had lain still in a comatose state. The only movement she could detect was the automatic turning of the bed as it rotated his body from the left to the right and back again to avoid bedsores. Corrynne marveled. No matter how many times she had to come to the hospital for her family, it still struck her as odd to see her own child in a hospital bed.

Corrynne stood still and stared at her son. She noticed that his bed shook slightly with every beat of his heart. Looking up at the monitor she watched the continuous EKG. Dane's heart was beating 130 times a minute. That was way too fast. Corrynne had seen this situation a hundred times before with other people's family members. Infection drove Dane's body to a hyperdynamic state that caused his system to struggle. Corrynne put her hand to her son's forehead, and looked at the monitor. He had a fever of 104 degrees Fahrenheit. Corrynne shook her head.

Reaching down under the side rail, Corrynne unlatched the handle. The side rail rolled back, as the bed automatically leveled itself. An alarm went off indicating the rotation therapy was suspended. Corrynne reached out and silenced the alarm. She wanted Dane to just be still for a moment so she could hug him.

Corrynne pulled a chair near the side of the bed and sat next to Dane. The bed was low enough that she could place her open hand gently on his chest from a sitting position. She watched her hand as it almost bounced off Dane's chest wall from his rapid, insistent heartbeat. Next, she laid her head on his ribs, keeping her hand in place and listened to the quick double rhythm as the heart muscle contracted rapidly, squeezing the blood to the rest of the body. She couldn't help but wonder how long Dane's heart could keep this pace. It was obvious that the infection was taking its toll.

Corrynne looked at Dane's face. It was so calm—almost peaceful. What was he feeling, as he slept so soundly? She had always wondered what a comatose patient felt. Do they feel the ache for oxygen, like they had run too quickly up a set of stairs? Do they feel trapped in their own body? She didn't know for sure, but she hoped Dane was not suffering.

Corrynne got up from her place on the chair and took Dane's chart from the counter. She had pulled it earlier on her way into Dane's room to look at the doctor's notes. It was one perk of being a nurse at *this* hospital. She had unusual access to all of Dane's records.

Standing next to the counter, she leaned against the adjacent wall and flipped through the different sections until she came to the physician's notes that outlined his care. With her finger she scanned the words that had only been written that morning. The freshly dictated words spelled out clearly Dane's circumstance. At the top of the page it said, *"condition—unstable."* The words stung her deeply. Although cognitively she knew the reality of Dane's situation, seeing it in black and white was emotionally draining.

Corrynne continued to read. Normally, there was a list of current diagnoses below the patient's stated condition that the doctor was addressing in his care. Dane's chart said, "*sepsis, adult respiratory distress syndrome, liver failure, acute renal failure.*" Corrynne knew from taking care of patients like Dane, that the sicker the patients were, the more organs would be damaged. That translated to a smaller and smaller chance of his survival.

A tear slid down her cheek and landed on the dictation, magnifying the word "*failure.*" She immediately brushed the tear off the record and wiped her tears from her face. It didn't do any good to cry. She sniffed and wiped her cheek again with her shoulder.

Looking up from the chart, Corrynne closed it. She didn't want to read any more. After placing it back on the counter, her eyes fell on the array of pumps that surrounded his bed. Beside the bed on tall poles, they were stacked upon each other like glowing Lego blocks. She reviewed and double-checked the familiar numbers that showed on their faces. Normally, when a patient had this many drips, they were at the end of their life. It really was time she accepted that this was the case for Dane, too. At least he didn't have Methicillin Resistant Staph Aureus, the antibiotic resistant bacteria that seemed to kill so many these days.[3] She didn't think he'd have a chance if he got that one. He was so weak already.

Corrynne approached the bed once again and reached for Dane's lifeless hand. With her touch she felt something wet. Corrynne quickly removed her hand to assess the source. In a second, she realized that Dane's gauze bandage, that wrapped his right hand, was soaked with pink drainage from his wounds. *Contamination*!

Automatically, Corrynne rushed to washed her hands thoroughly at the nearby sink with lots of soap and water. Panicking, her mind searched for the possibility that the *Strep*, still left in his hand, could attack her own tissue. Maybe some of the capsules that were still viable rubbed off on her skin— she couldn't afford that. She had too much mothering to do for too many people. After the soap and water, she reached for Betadine that sat in the cart and doused her skin in the cold brown liquid. It was the strongest antimicrobial substance she knew of.

Corrynne stared at her own hands as the fluid dripped from them and fell into the bleached white sink. With the sudden stress, she felt her own pulse beat at her temples. She would allow the liquid to sit for a few minutes to make sure all the bacteria, if there were any, were dead. She took a long controlled breath in and let it out slowly.

Had Dane's wound been cultured lately? With his fever, who knew what else grew in his moist wound. Corrynne rinsed off the Betadine and then dried her hands with paper towels. Next she picked up the chart and flipped through it again, looking for test results. Coming to the testing area, she thumbed through the various results until she came to the microbiology report…Yes, Dane's hand had been cultured, and no, there wasn't any viable *Strep* seen in the wound. Relief flowed through Corrynne. There was nothing to worry about—this time.

Corrynne forced herself to take another deep breath and relax. She was much too jumpy. Maybe she needed a break. She had been at the hospital too long today. Corrynne put down the chart and turned around, leaning against the sink. She reached for gloves in a nearby dispenser. "That bandage has to be changed." She said out loud, gathering her courage back. "I'll do it. It's the least I can do."

After collecting the supplies, Corrynne sat down again next to her son. She released the tape that held the gauze in place and carefully unwrapped the heavy wet material. "Boy, his wound is really weeping," she said to herself.

After unwinding for a while, she finally came to the mutilated hand. Her eyes widened in amazement. She hadn't seen it before this moment. It had always been covered, and frankly she wasn't interested in seeing the damage Imam Mahdi had caused. A breath caught in her throat—*It was so ugly….* The tissue that was left on the bones was almost all black, or gray, only showing a small amount of pink tissue higher on the wrist area, which was the source of the profuse fluid. Corrynne shook her head and clicked her tongue. "I bet this will have to be amputated. It doesn't look good."

Corrynne then turned the hand over to expose the palm. There was the chip still sitting in his palm, but totally exposed now. Corrynne looked closer at the tiny thing that only measured approximately four by four millimeters, if that. It seemed to have silver like tendrils that webbed out through the whole palm. What are those? She wondered. She looked closer. Maybe it was just connective tissue looking silver. But the more she looked, the more she realized the silver thread like webs through his tissue was not natural. They were artificial.

Seeing the silver strands made Corrynne wonder. Her mind began to file through all that she knew of the chip. She reviewed her memories of the night Dane received the chip in his palm. She didn't remember seeing anything sticking out of the chip when Ann implanted it in Dane's hand at the Rave. Yes, she had been watching the procedure on a video screen, and maybe she couldn't see that well, but the way Ann slit the skin and slid the chip in the flesh indicated that all she implanted was the chip itself.

Corrynne wondered if it was possible that the chip produced the silver strands itself. She knew that technology was advanced enough it could have. But what was the silver webbing meant to do? After thinking, she came to the conclusion that the webbing was meant to secure the chip in the hand. Suddenly, a new thought came to her mind. She wondered if the same kind of webbing was being produced from the chip in Carea's forehead. If it was, then that might explain why Carea had such headaches and signs of brain swelling before Imam Mahdi died. Now it was all making sense! If some foreign object was burrowing into the brain, but not destroying the tissue, it definitely would cause swelling and pain! That would explain the headaches.

Corrynne shook her head and looked up at Dane's blank face. "What did we get ourselves into?" she asked him, but predictably, there was no response.

Taking new thick absorbent white fluffs, Corrynne began to pad Dane's palm and then once the padding was substantial, she began to wrap it with the new gauze. With every revolution, her mind continued to make new conclusions. She wondered if the silver tendrils could conduct energy—and if they could, couldn't they use energy to stimulate parts of—the brain—like in Carea's situation, to control her somatic experiences? Corrynne knew she had studied that kind of medical science in psychology. Often in treatment for seizures, the doctors would stimulate parts of the brain for desired responses.

Corrynne held the end of the gauze bandage in place as she applied white tape to it. She turned around in her chair to look for something absorbent to place underneath the hand, and found a padded disposable sheet, known as a "chux," on the counter. Standing up to reach it, she then folded the two-foot by three-foot pad in quarters. Gently she lifted Dane's hand and placed it on the pad.

"There that's much better...isn't it, Dane?" Corrynne smiled at her son, patted his leg and stepped back a few steps.

Corrynne folded her arms and tapped her toe as she continued to think. Could her hypothesis about Carea be true? Right now Carea was acting fine, but a couple of weeks ago, Carea was a basket case of strange behaviors. Corrynne reviewed in her mind what she had seen Carea do at home. Her hunger was affected, her moods, her sleep, even her attractions...Corrynne tried to remember what part of the brain those kind of responses could be controlled from. It was somewhere deep in the brain. It was a center that controlled the basic functions of life, rather than the higher thinking centers. She would have to look in books on the shelves in the ICU, because at the moment, the exact location escaped her.

"I know that's how he did it," Corrynne said out loud continuing to talk to Dane in the bed. "He was using brain stimulation to modify Carea's behaviors. With a global positioning device, he could identify Carea and apply a punishment whenever she was surrounded by us and at home, and then he applied positive ones when she was away from home. It was just a matter of which button to push on some control pad, like some videogame...or maybe it was all programmed into a mainframe somewhere." Corrynne shook her head. "He was a sick, sick man."

Corrynne turned away from Dane's bed, and began to pace slightly. She continued her thoughts out loud. "Naturally, Carea was beginning to hate being at home. *He made her want to run away*, and you know what? I don't blame her. I would too, if I was getting sick from hunger and lack of sleep." Corrynne nodded, "I can just imagine what it was like once she reached his house. How did she resist him? All I can say is that he wasn't playing fair. Poor Carea."

An alarm went off on a nearby pump. It was Dane's maintenance fluid. There was a new bag waiting on the med cart, obviously left there to replace the empty one. Automatically, Corrynne picked up the fluid and hung it on the pole. Pulling off the empty bag, she spiked the new one and let the fluid flow into the drip chamber. Pressing the buttons to reprogram the pump, she cleared the volume.

Approaching the bed for the last time, Corrynne put the side rails back up. She reached out and touched his shoulder and continued her one sided conversation with him. "But you stopped him, Dane. You are a true hero. Because of you, Carea is free again. She doesn't have to worry about strange unwanted hungers and propensities." Then Corrynne added, "...At least for now."

Corrynne frowned. That was a troubling point. Who had control of the chips now that Imam Mahdi was gone? She hoped no one did. Corrynne bit her lip. She forced a smile as she looked down on her son, as if he could see her. "Yes, Dane, I'm figuring out all the secrets of the mad man that ruined your life. He had many dark secrets."

Corrynne pushed the nurse's button, and in a couple minutes, the nurse came in. It was someone that she was very familiar with and had worked with for years. "Lisa, I changed his IV fluid and I changed the dressing on his hand. It was soaked."

Lisa came over to the bedside and looked at the wrapped hand. "Oh, thank you, Corrynne. You didn't have to do that."

"I know, but I wanted to," Corrynne smiled.

"Well, you are definitely welcome to do anything you wish to help out."

"Thank you. I appreciate that. It lets me feel useful." Corrynne said as she moved to the counter and picked up the chart. "Here's his chart. I was looking at it."

"Oh thanks."

"I'm going to go back to the trailers for a while. I need to be with my family."

Lisa nodded. "Good, I agree. You need to take it easy."

"So I'll see you soon."

Lisa smiled. "I'll be here."

Corrynne quickly left the room.

Adversity

Corrynne looked at her watch. It was 4:30 p.m. She pulled open a latch on the side of the twenty by ten foot trailer to find Bo cooking something on a single propane burner. "Hi, Bo," she said, trying to have a good disposition.

"Hey, there's my Corrynne," said Bo over his shoulder, but then he hesitated as if he had something to say.

Corrynne waited for him to say what he was thinking about, but he seemed to dismiss his initial thought.

"How's Dane?" Bo asked visually shrugging something off.

Corrynne studied her husband for a moment. "Did you want to talk to me about something?"

Bo looked back at Corrynne. "Yes, but not right now. Later when the kids are asleep."

"OK," said Corrynne, knowing what he had to tell her was some sort of bad news. Squaring her shoulders Corrynne refused to entertain dismal thoughts. She would wait for Bo to talk to her and not allow her mind to run crazy like it normally did. One stress at a time was enough.

"How was Dane?" Bo repeated his question as he continued to make dinner.

"Not very well," said Corrynne, but then smiling she said, "But you know. Things like this take time."

Bo nodded. "Right. Were there *any* signs of improvement?"

Corrynne turned down her lip, with a blank stare and reviewed Dane's status in her mind. Finally shaking her head slowly, she said, "No not really. Actually, I think he's getting worse. That hand is a mess. I think it should be amputated."

Bo cringed. "That's not optimal, but whatever has to happen."

Corrynne took two steps and dipped the tip of her finger in the vegetable and meat filled gravy that Bo was stirring. After putting it in her mouth, she said, "Hey, have you seen Carea lately?"

"I think she's laying down back there." Bo motioned with his face to the bed end of the trailer.

"Good." Corrynne turned, "I've got to talk to her. I think I know how that chip controlled her behavior."

Bo stopped stirring. "Really? How?"

Corrynne motioned to Bo. "Come in here and we'll talk about it."

"OK. I'll just let this stew simmer."

"By the way, tastes good, Bo," said Corrynne.

"Of course it does," said Bo with a straight face. "I wouldn't have made it if it didn't. Del Monte did all the work anyway."

"Ah," Corrynne winked. "Didn't know canned stew tasted so good!" She turned and continued towards the back of the trailer, stopping a moment to pick up a stray shirt and a couple of socks off the floor on her way.

"Hey you guys, I'm going in the back with Mom. Keep an eye on the twins. They're crawling on the floor. Entertain them for me."

"OK," said Ry automatically who was playing UNO with Jax and Rocwell at the tiny dinner table.

Bo moved to the back with Corrynne who was getting ready to wake Carea, who was bundled in a red sleeping bag.

"Carea, are you in there?" said Corrynne softly as she caressed her daughter's hair.

"Yes," came a soft voice from inside the material, then with exposed fingers Carea slowly pulled the edge of the sleeping bag down. "What is it?"

"How are you doing?" asked Corrynne with a smile as she stroked her daughter's hair again.

With one eye, Carea looked at her father who now sat at her feet with her mother. "I'm OK."

"Are you sure?" asked Corrynne. "These last few weeks have been hard on all of us. You especially have been through a lot lately. It can be overwhelming I know. Not many people could have emerged from all the stress whole. You're lucky."

Carea looked intently at her mother and father again. Sitting up she scratched her bed head and then pulled up one knee and hugged it through the sleeping bag. "Lucky? I don't consider myself lucky," she said thoughtfully.

Corrynne hesitated, and then she decided to tell Carea what she had found at the hospital. "I think I've figured out the mystery concerning your headaches. Maybe you can tell me what you know and I can tell you what I know and we can come to a conclusion that makes sense. Would you like that?"

"I guess," Carea said apathetically. "I wish *something* would make sense."

Corrynne reached out and softly touched Carea's hand. "Come on, baby, try with me. Talk to me."

Carea lethargically looked at her mother and sat up a little higher. "OK, I'll try. What do you want to talk about?"

Corrynne tried to take on a more up-beat attitude, hoping it would rub off. "I think I know the secret behind how Imam Mahdi controlled your behavior, a while ago. Do you want to hear about it?"

Carea shrugged. "I know, too."

Corrynne sat back in surprise. "You do? You didn't tell me."

Carea began to trace a stitch in the material of the sleeping bag. "Well, I think I do. Tell me first what you're thinking," she said quietly.

Corrynne gathered her thoughts and then started. "Tell me what you know about your chip's capabilities?"

"The one in my head?"

"Yes," said Corrynne, wondering for a split second if there was another one that she wasn't aware of.

Carea shook her head and rubbed her eyes at the same time. "I don't know anything other than what *'The Great and Powerful Oz'* said…"

"Who's that? …Imam Mahdi?" asked Corrynne.

Carea stopped and then smiled slightly. "Yeah, that's the guy."

"That was kind of funny, Carea—good job!" said Corrynne pleased with her attempt at humor.

Carea rolled her eyes and began again. "Anyway, *that man* said that he had the chip implanted in my head so that he could *'hurry my destiny'*."

Corrynne thought for a moment. This was new information. "Destiny, huh? What was that?"

"Oh, he said I had some ability to attract people or something. He said that he wanted me to stand by his side so he could take over the world or…*whatever*. I don't really know. I'm trying to forget that part."

"Did he say anything else?" asked Corrynne, studying her daughter.

Carea shook her head. "No, but he could look at me and cause me to faint, or throw up, or be hungry, or whatever he was trying to do. I felt like a puppet."

Corrynne nodded. "That's exactly what you were. You *were a puppet*. He was controlling your experiences to try and elicit certain behaviors. It sounds like he wanted you to act a certain predictable way."

"What do you mean, Mom? Speak'a my lan-gu-age," Carea said in an Italian accent.

Corrynne smiled again. Humor was a sign her daughter was beginning to heal. She continued, "Well, get this—in medicine, it is possible for an outside source, for example, a doctor, to stimulate the brain with probes that conduct electricity and cause the patient to move his leg, or remember something without the patient wishing to."

"Yeah?"

"So in theory, with proper brain stimulation, and an understanding of which brain structures control what function, anyone could control basic physical functions of anyone else. All they have to do is wire the brain."[4]

"What?" said Carea in a dull tone with eyes to match. "Do you think that's what happened to me?"

Corrynne nodded. "Ah, yes, actually...it is the only explanation that makes sense."

"How?" Carea's expression did not change.

Corrynne held up a finger pointed to her other hand. "When I was at the hospital today, I undressed Dane's hand and looked at the chip that was implanted in his palm."

"No way!" said Carea showing some surprise now.

"Yes."

"How did you see it if it was under the skin?"

"Well," began Corrynne in a medical fashion, "all the infected and dying skin had been removed in his surgery to try and save..."

Carea cringed and covered her ears. "OK, OK! Don't tell me anymore."

Corrynne stopped abruptly. "Alright, sorry. I'm just trying to explain things to you."

"Tell me about the other stuff, not about his hand."

Corrynne nodded. "Alright. I'm sorry. Anyway, when I looked closely, I saw that there were hundreds of silver strings that went out from the chip and into the rest of Dane's tissue."

"Why?"

"I think one reason was to make it so that the chip could not be removed. There probably is a trigger programmed in the chip that causes a lysing of capsules that hold *Strep* A bacteria in stasis, pouring them into the tissue. I'll bet if the strands are cut, or disturbed, it sets off a chain reaction, resulting in mass infection of the tissue."

"That's a pretty thought—so what does this have to do with stimulating my brain?"

"I think the chip implanted in your forehead has developed silver tendrils, too."

Carea scoffed as the dull eyes returned. "Oh great! Just what I need!" she said sarcastically.

"No, listen, Carea, I don't think you're in danger as long as we just leave that chip alone, but here's another thought. I think that silver webbing has another function."

"To deliver electricity," said Carea with a contrived smirk.

"Maybe."

"I was right?" asked Carea with lifted eyebrows.

"Yes," nodded Corrynne. "It's possible that the silver webbing can carry electricity to different parts of the brain when stimulated by an outside source, to encourage behavior modification, punishment, or even rewards, like we talked about."

"What outside source?"

"Imam Mahdi probably had some kind of remote to stimulate the electrical responses to the parts of the brain that he wished to affect. That's possible with the microtechnology we have today."

Corrynne's words made Carea stop and think. Finally she looked at her mother and squinted. "Yes, but why?"

"To bend a follower's will, if need be. In your case, bend it a lot. Doesn't that make sense?"

Carea's face twisted, showing some anger now. "Oh, like making me starve, until I give in, or die?"

Corrynne nodded. "Yes, or making you nauseous, angry, friendly, or any other unexplained behavior you exhibited."

Carea hit the bed with her fist. "Oh, yes, now I get it. I don't like it, but I get it."

"And if our premise is true, all the time that you have had your terrible headaches, the chip was producing the silver webbing and it was moving through the brain tissue to its programmed areas. This would naturally cause inflammation and give you headaches."

Carea looked down at the bed for a few seconds, and then began to laugh. A giggle at first, then a hysterical cackle came from her throat.

Corrynne frowned, looked back at Bo, who shrugged and then looked back at Carea. "What are you laughing about?"

Carea threw herself back into the foam bedding and continued to laugh uncontrollably. After a minute or so, she wiped a tear that had come to her right eye. "I'm just laughing at the whole crazy thing! I mean—everything is just so ridicules. Think about it. I now have hardware throughout my whole brain! Isn't that hilarious? Do you think I'll beep at the airport metal detectors?"

Corrynne frowned deeply. "Sweetheart, this isn't a joke. It isn't funny. Truly this is an amazing find."

Carea stopped laughing and became serious. "Why is it amazing and not funny?"

"Because, don't you see? Everything makes sense now. Everything can be explained. You aren't responsible for the strange behaviors we've seen in you and you aren't crazy! Your strange hunger, illogical satiety, abrupt anger, unavoidable sleep, and tortuous wakefulness, even those crazy feelings that you had for Steve can be explained!"

"Great," said Carea.

"You see, I was trying to figure out all this stuff a while ago and I reviewed the functions of the brain. All the time I could see connections but until today, none of it made sense."

"I know that feeling," said Carea.

"Let me explain and you'll see."

Carea held out a hand, "Explain away."

Corrynne swallowed then began, "The hypothalamus, that's a part in the center of your brain, controls basic functions in the body such as hunger, moods, sexual attraction, sleeping patterns, etc.[5] There have been studies in which if these areas of the brain were stimulated in mice, the mice would overeat until they were so fat they couldn't walk, or stimulate the brain so it would sleep, or stay awake constantly. This is real stuff. I wish I had my books to show you. I'm not making it up."[6]

"I believe you. What about the throwing up?" asked Carea.

Corrynne nodded. "Yes, throwing up is a reflex controlled by the medulla in your brain stem. That part is right below the hypothalamus."

Carea looked at her mother. "So do you think the strands go there, too?"

Corrynne nodded. "I think they do now. Although earlier, I think you were just nauseous from the brain swelling."

"Oh. Well, that's nice to know. Where else do you think they go?"

"I think they go to the thalamus too. It's there that perception of pain can be controlled."

"Oh, yes." Carea nodded. "I can tell you those buggers are there too. Imam Mahdi looked at me once and caused me to have such a headache that I fainted."

"That could be the thalamus and the reticular activating system. They all are in the same approximate area."

"The what?"

"The ret..."

Carea shook her head. "Never mind, I don't want to know." A frown deepened on her face.

Corrynne looked long at her daughter. "This isn't making you feel better is it?"

"No. Not really."

Corrynne put her arm around Carea's shoulders. "I'm sorry. I thought it would add understanding to all your experiences."

Carea nodded. "Well, it's done that, but I don't see how that would make me feel better."

Corrynne continued. "I guess I thought understanding would help you release...guilt? I was afraid that you were blaming yourself for your behavior. I wanted you to know that it wasn't your fault! None of us think it was. Do we, Bo?"

"No, we don't," answered Bo.

Carea looked down at the bed and didn't say anything.

"Are you OK?" asked Corrynne.

Carea shook her head as tears began to fill her eyes.

"Why…?"

Still Carea didn't respond.

"Is it Dane?" asked Corrynne.

Finally, Carea nodded and began to cry in earnest.

Corrynne hugged her daughter and rubbed her back. "Why, Carea? His sickness had nothing to do with you."

Carea pulled away and nodded, wiping her eyes. "Yes, it did. It was my fault that he was in that stupid mansion. He was trying to protect me. If he hadn't followed me, he would still be OK."

Corrynne shook her head and hugged her again. "No, Carea," she said, "that was my fault. I told him to follow you. Please let me carry that blame."

"Excuse me," said Bo. "I would like to say something to my daughter."

"Sure," said Corrynne as she released her grip and sat back a little so Bo could see Carea.

"What is it, Dad?" asked the red-eyed Carea.

"No one here is going to carry any blame. We are much too quick to accept blame where it is not deserved."

"What do you mean?" asked Carea.

"Well, to be honest, no one here deserves any blame. Everything is working out according to plan."

"Why do you say that?" asked Carea.

"We allowed Dane to follow Carea because the angel in my dream *encouraged us* to allow him to find his mission. We weren't to be over protective. We were to allow natural consequences to occur and not interfere."

Corrynne nodded as she bit her lip slightly. "Yes, we are applying faith in the Lord's plan and allowing him to be in control."

"Wait you guys, what angel?" asked Carea interrupting.

"Dad had a dream that told him that Dane would die and that he would bring him back. When that will be, we still aren't sure."

Carea turned to her father, "What? Dad, is this true?"

Bo nodded slightly. "Well, yes, the angel told me that Dane would be saved by a priesthood blessing. There must be some lessons in this that he, or all of us, are supposed to be learning. However, I don't recall the angel saying that Dane would die."

"Oh, I thought you said his life would be *taken*," said Corrynne.

"Yes," acknowledged Bo, "but we don't know in what way that means."

"Well, I think we know now," said Carea.

Bo's focus switched to Carea. "Yes, but have faith in the Lord's abilities. He *will* come back to us."

Carea looked like she was contemplating a thought. "So, Dad, you were told you were going to be able to fix Dane?"

Bo nodded once. "Yes, in so many words."

"Through a blessing?"

"Right."

"Then why haven't you given him one yet?"

Bo leaned his torso forward and balanced his elbows on his knees "Because the Spirit has not moved me to."

"Do you need the Spirit to tell you to do everything, Daddy?" asked Carea. "I thought we were supposed to do what was right even when we aren't prompted to. Isn't giving a blessing to heal 'right?'"

Bo nodded. "Yes, ordinarily, but in this case I was told specifically to refrain from giving him a blessing."

Carea readjusted her weight in the bed. "Tell me, Dad, what exactly does that mean?" asked Carea.

"That means I am only a servant of Heavenly Father. I must do his will. Let me explain further. …The power of the priesthood comes from God and my faith in God. My faith cannot be exercised contrary to the order of heaven or contrary to the will and purposes of God. If the Lord's will is not sought after, my priesthood means nothing. In other words, if I were to try to give a blessing expressing my will that Dane be healed, against the advice to wait, it wouldn't work. It wouldn't be time. I have to follow what God wants, in the way he wants it. Even if he told me not to bless Dane, I would have to obey."[7]

Carea jumped from the bed and took her father by the shoulders. "But, Dad, he will die if you don't bless him. I know it!"

"I'm going to bless him, sweetheart. Don't you worry; we have to wait for a reason we aren't aware of. His timing is not our timing. His ways are not our ways."[8]

"What if you're wrong, Dad? What if you wait too long?" asked Carea as she sat back on the bed.

"I'm not." Bo sat back up in his chair. "Anyway the moral of the story is that we should be tolerant of our circumstances. We need to realize that this life is going to be difficult, but it will be *devastating* if we have a fatalistic attitude. We need to see through the dark clouds and see the light. We need to see reality for what it is. Everything will be fine. I promise you."[9]

Carea stared at her father and then shook her head. "I don't know if I believe in that '*everything will be fine*' bit anymore. I've been pretty good in my life and the Lord hasn't seemed to want to protect me very much."

Corrynne frowned and grasped Carea by the shoulders. "Oh, Carea, don't say things like that."

Carea turned to her mother and said, "Why? Don't we believe in honesty, too?"

"Sure, but when you say things like that, it means that you're losing faith in truth. No matter what, we can't be negative! When we have a hard life, it doesn't change the truth. You know that. The Lord still holds out all the blessings he ever has, you're just in the midst of a trial. We all are."

"Yes, we just have to change the way we look at things that happen to us. We can't take them personally," agreed Bo.

Carea looked unblinkingly between her mother and father. "Take them personally? *That's a laugh*! This chip in my head is pretty personal. How do I see this positively? You know the same thing that happened to Dane could happen to me, except my whole face would be eaten off!"

There was silence in response to Carea's outburst. Neither Corrynne nor Bo knew what to say.

"See? Pretty awful to think about isn't it? Even you guys don't know how to address it. That gives me a lot of confidence."

"Well…let me try again," said Bo.

"Whatever, Dad. I don't know what else you could say to fix things, but why not give it a whirl."

Bo smiled and then looked down. After a minute he began. "Let's talk about Joseph Smith. He was a pretty good guy don't you think?"

"Sure. I guess so." Carea crawled back into the center of her bed and folded a pillow in her lap.

"Don't you think the Lord should have protected him a little more than he did?"

Carea nodded. "Yes. For being the Lord's servant, he sure got picked on a lot, for nothing."

"Yes, he did. Let's talk about the Liberty Jail."

"Was that the jail he was in when those men starved him and then tried to make him eat human flesh?"

"Yes, I believe so. Pretty demented, huh?"

Carea stuck out her tongue. "Yes, that's sick. At least when I was starved, I was given a decent meal afterwards."

"Good, see? You already are changing your tune."

Carea shook her head. "Don't get your hopes up just yet, Dad."

"Anyway, that jail that he was in was extremely small. They lived in a total of an 18-foot square area. Much smaller than your bedroom used to be."

"I didn't know that."

"Yes, and that was without heat, or toilets, or beds," inserted Corrynne.

"Oh, harsh," commented Carea.

"There was an upstairs and a downstairs. Joseph Smith got the downstairs that was called the 'dungeon'."

"Figures."

"The ceiling was only six foot high, not even tall enough for Joseph to stand fully erect."

"What a backache! How long were they in there?"

"They were there from December 1st to April 6th." [10]

"That's a long time…that's like four months."

"Yes it was, and did you know he felt the same way you do?"

"He did?"

"Yes, he did. He was starving, dirty, sick, depressed, and frustrated. He wondered why the Lord allowed him to suffer so severely, just like you. He prayed all the time, asking for help, but for four months he was allowed to suffer." [11]

Carea bowed her head. "I don't know if I could have hung on so long. I probably would have decided life wasn't worth it and died of a broken heart."

"Maybe Joseph might have too, but the Lord answered his prayers with support. It buoyed him up and gave him strength to continue. That is what the Lord does. He makes us equal to our trials and temptations, so that we can become stronger and more wise." [12]

"Tell me what he said."

"I'll paraphrase, if that's OK."

"Sure."

"He asked the Lord where he was hiding." [13]

Carea smiled slightly. "He asked if the Lord was hiding?"

"Yes, it was his poetic way of asking why the Lord did not manifest his power in his behalf."

"Oh, that makes sense," said Carea.

"He asked how long he would allow oppression to plague him and the other servants of the Lord. He asked how long the Lord would allow dishonesty, immorality and lawlessness to reign and control them." [14]

"Good questions. What did the Lord say?"

"He said that Joseph should allow peace to come to his heart."

"Oh, great. That's a hard one."

"Next he said that his trial would be just for a moment, and then he made him a great promise. [15] Now this is key, are you listening?"

"Sure. What was the promise?"

"He said if Joseph endured his opposition well, then he would be exalted and triumph over all of his foes. [16] He also promised that the punishments to those that fought against the Lord's servants would be severe." [17]

"That's good…. So what was the key? I guess I missed it."

"How he endured his afflictions."

"What does that mean?"

"That means, we should accept afflictions as a part of this life and realize that through them we will become greater. [18] We shouldn't blame God, or become bitter. Instead we should look for things to learn, a deeper understanding, an opportunity for service. We should allow ourselves to stretch, to remember all of our blessings.[19] If we have this attitude, then we are deserving of the greatest help from a Heavenly Father who is aware of us and loves us."

Carea sat up. "Oh, Dad, I want to believe those things. How do I change my attitude? I try, I really try."

"Pray to him. Know that he is mindful of you. Realize that he has his own timetable of how things are going to pan out. Allow him the ability to apply his knowledge and infinite wisdom concerning you.[20] In the end, realize that the adversity you face is not to prove you to Him, but to open your eyes to your own strengths, so you can meet future obligations with confidence and a will single to God."[21]

Carea held out her arms to her father and he got up from his chair and embraced her. Carea was crying now. Tears sprung freely from her eyes. "OK, I'll try, but please take care of Dane. He's a good guy. He doesn't deserve this sickness."

Bo squeezed his daughter again to reassure her. "Sweetheart, let the Lord be in charge. He will handle it. You'll see."

"Alright. I'll trust you."

"No don't trust me, trust him. The Lord always fulfills his promises."[22]

Notes to "Sore Adversity"

Condemned

[1] Details from this chapter were inspired from the flood caused by Hurricane Floyd that caused damage from the Bahamas to New England in 1999. "A thousand families who were driven out of their homes by the floodwaters of Hurricane Floyd are welcoming the chance to move into two makeshift villages of trailer homes and campers by week's end. The Federal Emergency Management Agency (FEMA) distributed a total of 420 trailers to temporarily house those whose homes were destroyed. An estimated 1,500 to 2,000 evacuees were sleeping on cots in classrooms and the gymnasium at the school, and they had no running water. People bathed in shower tents hooked up to water tankers. Portable toilets were overflowing. 'What we have right now is like a small city,' said Dave Stone of the American Red Cross, the shelter's manager. 'It would be nice to have flushable toilets, but that's not in the foreseeable future. Thank God we've got power'" ("Patty Davis, Associated Press, "Some N.C. flood victims offered temporary homes," *Cnn.com.* September 21, 1999, Available: [Online] http://www.cnn.com/WEATHER/9909/21/floyd.04/index.html).

[2] The depiction of the consequences of flooding in the text is mild compared to real life. "Residents were urged to wear boots, gloves and other heavy protective gear while trudging through the thick slosh. Flood victims also were told to watch out for snakes, colonies of ants and other creatures lurking in homes. In addition, septic systems were washed away in many areas, contaminating water supplies. State officials said people should not use their wells until the water is tested. Residents of cities where the water supply was contaminated were being told to boil water and to drink only bottled water if possible. State emergency officials said flies breeding in more than 50,000 hog carcasses and 1 million dead chickens could spread disease. Caskets from cemeteries were washed away by the floodwaters" ("North Carolina provides trailers for hundreds of flood victims" Cnn.com, September 24, 1999, Available: [Online] http://www.cnn.com/WEATHER/9909/24/floyd.01/index.html).

Heartbeat

[3] "What is MRSA? Staphylococcus aureus, often referred to as "staph," is a bacteria commonly found on the skin of healthy people. Occasionally, staph can get into the body and cause an infection. This infection can be minor (such as pimples, boils, and other skin conditions) or serious (such as blood infections or pneumonia). Methicillin is in a class of antibiotics commonly used to treat staph infections. Although this class of antibiotics is very effective in treating most staph infections, some staph bacteria have developed resistance to methicillin and can no longer be killed by this antibiotic. These resistant bacteria are called methicillin-resistant Staphylococcus aureus, or MRSA" ("Antimicrobial Resistance MRSA-Methicillin Resistant Staphylococcus aureus*," Centers for Disease Control and Prevention,* July 2, 2002. [Online Available: http://www.cdc.gov).

[4] This scenario is fictional, but physiologically, it is possible. Medicine uses the implantation of probes to elicit desired responses as a normal practice. See the following article:

"Neurology researchers in Switzerland report the case of a woman who described 'floating above her own body and watching herself' while she was undergoing testing and treatment for epilepsy. The strange experience only occurred when one particular part of her brain, the angular gyrus in the right cortex, was stimulated with an electrode. And it happened every time the angular gyrus was stimulated.

"Doctors were using electrodes to try to pinpoint the origin of her seizures. Such brain 'mapping' is also used to help doctors identify critical areas of the brain, like those responsible for speech or movement, so they aren't damaged during surgery.

"While the electrodes are implanted while the patient is under full anesthesia, patients are fully awake during the testing procedure, so their comfort, language skills, and responses can be constantly monitored" (Marsha Walton, "Out of body experiences clues may hide in mind" *Cnn.com/science and Space*, Sept. 19, 2002, Available through archive search http://www.cnn.com).

[5] "The role of the hypothalamus in awareness of pleasure and pain has been well established in the laboratory. The hypothalamus regulates body temperature, blood pressure, heartbeat, metabolism of fats and carbohydrates, and sugar levels in the blood. It is thought to be involved in the expression of emotions, such as fear and rage, and in sexual behaviors. Despite its numerous vital functions, the hypothalamus in humans accounts for only 1/300 of total brain weight, and is about the size of an almond. Structurally, it is joined to the thalamus; the two work together to monitor the sleep-wake cycle" ("Hypothalamus," The *Colombia Electronic Encyclopedia.* Nov. 19, 2002. [Online] Available: http://www.factmonster.com/ce6/sci/A0824782.html).

[6] "Experimental stimulation of different areas of the hypothalamus can evoke the autonomic responses characteristic of aggression, sexual behavior, eating, or satiety. Chronic stimulation of the lateral hypothalamus, for example, can make animals eat and become obese, whereas stimulation of the medial hypothalamus inhibits eating" (Kent Van De Graaff, "Control of the Autonomic Nervous System by Higher Brain Centers," *Human Anatomy*, 395).

[7] "That the rights of the priesthood are inseparably connected with the powers of heaven, and that the powers of heaven cannot be controlled nor handled only upon the principles of righteousness. That they may be conferred upon us, it is true; but when we undertake to cover our sins, or to gratify our pride, our vain ambition, or to exercise control or dominion or compulsion upon the souls of the children of men, in any degree of unrighteousness, behold, the heavens withdraw themselves; the Spirit of the Lord is grieved; and when it is withdrawn, Amen to the priesthood or the authority of that man. Behold, ere he is aware, he is left unto

himself, to kick against the pricks, to persecute the saints, and to fight against God" (D&C 121:36-38).

[8] "For my thoughts are not your thoughts, neither are your ways my ways, saith the LORD. For as the heavens are higher than the earth, so are my ways higher than your ways, and my thoughts than your thoughts" (Isaiah 55:8-9).

[9] "Therefore being justified by faith, we have peace with God through our Lord Jesus Christ: By whom also we have access by faith into this grace wherein we stand, and rejoice in hope of the glory of God. And not only so, but we glory in tribulations also: knowing that tribulation worketh patience. And patience, experience; and experience, hope" (Romans 5:1-4).

[10] "The jail in which the group was imprisoned on 1 December 1838 was a twenty-two-foot square structure facing east. A small door led into the prison which was divided on the inside into an upper room and a lower room or 'dungeon,' which was lighted by two small windows grated with heavy iron bars. Each floor was about six feet high. The building was constructed of limestone rock. Inside the outer wall was another wall of hewn oak logs separated from the limestone by a twelve-inch space filled with loose rock. Thus the two walls made a formidable structure with walls four feet thick" (Leonard J. Arrington, "Church Leaders in Liberty Jail," 1972, 21).

[11] "It is I believe now about five months and six days [it was actually 4 months] since I have been under the grimace of a guard night and day, and within the walls, grates, and screeching iron doors of a lonesome, dark, dirty prison.... This night, we expect, is the last night we shall try our weary joints and bones on our dirty straw couches in these walls.... We lean on the arm of Jehovah and none else, for our deliverance" (Joseph Smith to Emma Smith, 4 April 1839; in *The Personal Writings of Joseph Smith*, comp. Dean C. Jessee, 425-26; spelling and punctuation standardized).

[12] "There hath no temptation taken you but such as is common to man: but God is faithful, who will not suffer you to be tempted above that ye are able; but will with the temptation also make a way to escape, that ye may be able to bear it" (1 Corinthians 10:13).

[13] "O GOD, where art thou? And where is the pavilion that covereth thy hiding place? How long shall thy hand be stayed, and thine eye, yea thy pure eye, behold from the eternal heavens the wrongs of thy people and of thy servants, and thine ear be penetrated with their cries?" (D&C 121:1-2).

[14] "Yea, O Lord, how long shall they suffer these wrongs and unlawful oppressions, before thine heart shall be softened toward them, and thy bowels be moved with compassion toward them? O Lord God Almighty, maker of heaven, earth, and seas, and of all things that in them are, and who controllest and subjectist the devil, and the dark and benighted dominion of Sheol—stretch forth thy hand; let thine eye pierce; let thy pavilion be taken up; let thy hiding place no longer be covered; let thine ear be inclined; let thine heart be softened, and thy bowels moved with compassion toward us. Let thine anger be kindled against our enemies; and, in the fury of thine heart, with thy sword avenge us of our wrongs. Remember thy suffering saints, O our God; and thy servants will rejoice in thy name forever" (D&C 121:3-6).

[15] "My son, peace be unto thy soul; thine adversity and thine afflictions shall be but a small moment" (D&C 121:7).

[16] "And then, if thou endure it well, God shall exalt thee on high; thou shalt triumph over all thy foes" (D&C 121:8).

[17] "Wo unto them; because they have offended my little ones they shall be severed from the ordinances of mine house. Their basket shall not be full, their houses and their barns shall perish, and they themselves shall be despised by those that flattered them. They shall not have

right to the priesthood, nor their posterity after them from generation to generation. It had been better for them that a millstone had been hanged about their necks, and they drowned in the depth of the sea. Wo unto all those that discomfort my people, and drive, and murder, and testify against them, saith the Lord of Hosts; a generation of vipers shall not escape the damnation of hell. Behold, mine eyes see and know all their works, and I have in reserve a swift judgment in the season thereof, for them all" (D&C 121:19-24).

[18] "Life is not always easy to live, but the opportunity to do so is a blessing beyond comprehension. In the process of living we will face struggles, many of which will cause us to suffer and to experience pain" (L. Lionel Kendrick, "Strength During Struggles," *Ensign*, Oct. 2001, 24).

[19] "No one wants adversity. Trials, disappointments, sadness, and heartache, come to us from two basically different sources. Those who transgress the laws of God will always have those challenges. The other reason for adversity is to accomplish the Lord's own purposes in our life that we may receive the refinement that comes from testing" (Richard G. Scott, *Conference Report*, Oct. 1995, 18).

[20] "Just when all seems to be going right, challenges often come in multiple doses applied simultaneously. When those trials are not consequences of your disobedience, they are evidence that the Lord feels you are prepared to grow more (see Proverbs 3:11-12). He therefore gives you experiences that stimulate growth, understanding and compassion which polish you for your everlasting benefit, to get you from where you are to where he wants you to be requires a lot of stretching, and that generally entails discomfort and pain.

"When you face adversity, you can be led to ask many questions. Some serve a useful purpose; others do not. To ask, 'Why does this have to happen to me? Why do I have to suffer this now? What have I done to cause this?' will lead you into blind alleys. It really does no good to ask questions that reflect opposition to the will of God. Rather ask, 'What am I to do? What am I to learn from this experience? What am I to change? Who am I to help? How can I remember my many blessings in times of trial?' Willing sacrifice of deeply held personal desires in favor of the will of God is very hard to do. Yet when you pray with real conviction, 'Please let me know Thy will' and 'May Thy will be done,' you are in the strongest position to receive the maximum help from your loving Father" (Richard G. Scott, *Conference Report*, Oct. 1995, 18).

[21] "Adversity will surface in some form in every life. How we prepare for it, how we meet it, makes the difference. We can be broken by adversity, or we can become stronger. The final result is up to the individual...

"Following a recent discussion on the subject of adversity, a young man who was greatly concerned about the burdens being carried by his wonderful mother asked the question, 'If God is omnipotent and knows all, why does He put my mother through the agony of continual sufferings when He already knows what the outcome will be?' Our response was, "Your mother's trials are not a test so the Lord can measure her. They are tests and trials so that your mother can measure herself. It is most important that she know her strengths in adversity and grow from the experiences" (Marvin J. Ashton, *Conference Report*, Oct. 1980, 81,83).

[22] "For the eternal purposes of the Lord shall roll on, until all his promises shall be fulfilled" (Mormon 8:22).

CHAPTER SEVENTEEN

DO NOT RUN FASTER THAN YE ARE ABLE

"And see that all these things are done in wisdom and order; for it is not requisite that a man should run faster than he has strength. And again, it is expedient that he should be diligent, that thereby he might win the prize; therefore, all things must be done in order" (Mosiah 4:27).

00:08:08, 21:30:30 Zulu
Thursday, April 22nd
7:30 p.m.
Provo, Utah

Suspended Relief

Corrynne exited the bus near her trailer, situated on Ninth East, in the evening twilight. She had worked a twelve-hour shift, thirteen if you counted the time it took for reporting. Her feet ached like they were broken in the middle. She was tired and very, *very* hungry.

The hospital was not allowing employees to eat in the cafeteria anymore because the food was saved for the sick within their walls. Employees were expected to bring food from home or starve. In her case she chose to starve. She and Bo decided that both of them carried more than their share of extra weight, and they would both forgo two meals each day in order to feed the children adequately and to store what they could on the side. In a way, she was excited to have to cut back on her calories. Her clothes were already fitting better. She had to admit, eating only once a day was looking good on her, but right now that wasn't her first thought. No, right now she thought she could eat a horse and wouldn't be the least bit shy about gaining back her weight!

Luckily, there *was* food at home, but neither Bo nor Corrynne knew how long that would last. Food was being provided by a combination of private donations, church welfare, government subsidy and what little Corrynne could buy with her income because food prices were outrageous![1] Due to the disasters worldwide and the devaluation of the dollar, oil prices had gone crazy and it seemed that affected everything else! Because gas in America was ten dollars a gallon, truck deliveries were few and far between. Food and everything else was becoming scarce.[2] At the stores there were limits on everything you could buy, and security guards were posted everywhere to ensure limits were strictly observed.

Bo had been laid off at the corporate offices of the hospital. Because of loss of revenue, corporate positions were eliminated until "further notice." Now Corrynne was forced to work way too much to pay the bills, which were overwhelming, not to mention, paying a mortgage to a house that her family couldn't even live in! To be honest, she hated being away from her family, but right now, what were her options?[3] Nurses seemed to always have employment,[4] plus she could keep an eye on Dane's care whenever she worked. She should be thankful for that instead of angry. At least they had some income and Bo could be home with the children. Carea was there to help him, too. Corrynne knew it could be worse.

Corrynne stepped off the sidewalk and onto the muddy path that lead to the rows of trailers that she and her family lived in now. She thought about her house only two miles away. They had a full year and a half supply of food sitting in their garage and their cold storage. They were only told to get a one-year supply by the prophet, but they had stored more, "just in case." She could see the rows of white buckets of wheat and rice, and the cans and cans of food in her mind. It drove her crazy that the city forbade them to go near their house. It had been almost four weeks! She was sure the water had subsided by now! She had a mind to walk down to that area herself and find out what the hold up was. Bo had gone a few days before to check things out, but had only come back with the report that their house was still off limits. How long was the city going to make them wait?

"Oh well," Corrynne thought to herself as she reached her tiny trailer and lifted the latch. Since the Roger's family was large, they received one of the coveted trailers to live in from the government. "I can't complain too much, there are some people still living in tents! Now, that would be terrible!" Corrynne reminded herself.

Opening the door, she stepped up the stairs into a trailer filled with children's complaining voices.

Suddenly Carea came around the corner with Striynna screaming and kicking in her arms. "I am so glad you're home! Take her!" she said in frustration. "She wants you. She's tired of me."

Corrynne caught her littlest girl just as Carea dropped her from the main level. In surprise Corrynne moved up the last step. "What's going on?"

"Dad left two hours ago and everyone is going crazy," said Carea as she rubbed her nose in anxiety.

"Where did he go?"

"To a city meeting."

"Oh," said Corrynne, hoping that Bo was arranging for them to begin cleaning up their house so they could go back home.

"*Stop, Rocwell!*" said Jax in a pseudo-authoritative voice from back in the sleeping area of the trailer.

"*I can't read when you do that!*" said Ry loudly.

Corrynne looked down the hall to see Jax and Ry lying on their beds obviously trying to read books, but Rocwell was jumping back and forth between the beds laughing uncontrollably as he continued to ignore his brothers' demands.

"*Rocwell Joshua!*" Corrynne called out boldly. "You may stop jumping on the beds or you may…" she was going to say, "go to your room," but he didn't have a room anymore.

Roc looked suddenly up at her and the smile fell quickly from his face.

"Or you may—sleep in the bathtub!" Corrynne finished.

Rocwell stepped down off the bed and said, "But we don't have a bathtub, it's a shower that doesn't work."

"I don't care what it is," said Corrynne frustrated now herself, and reaching for a napkin on the counter to wipe Striynna's watery nose and eyes. "You will sleep in that tiny, hard cubical and loose your bed privileges if you can't show respect for a soft place to sleep!"

"Yeah, and spiders come up that drain at night," said Jax trying to scare his little brother.

Corrynne shot a hard look towards Jax. "No they do not. Don't try and make things worse."

"I'm not!" responded Jax. "It's true, did you know that Americans swallow 200 spiders a year in their sleep?"

Carea shook her head and scoffed. "Oh, Jax, every time I hear you say that, the number gets bigger."

"Carea is right. There is no way that people swallow 200 spiders a year!" scolded Corrynne.

"Mom it's true! I heard it from school!" said Jax sitting up.

"Yeah, I did too," added Ry sitting up too.

"Which class? Which teacher?" drilled Carea.

"I don't have to tell you anything," said Jax with a scowl.

"OK! Stop!" said Corrynne suddenly. "No more bickering!" Hugging and kissing Striynna, Corrynne suddenly looked up. "Where's Strykker!"

Carea looked around at the floor with large eyes. "He was just here! Strykker!" yelled Carea.

"Ha?" said a tiny voice from the very back of the trailer, and then a little head popped from around the door of the bathroom.

"There you are little guy!" said Corrynne in her most loving voice. "What are you doing in there?"

"Potte!" said Strykker with a big smile.

"What?" asked Corrynne, "Did you say 'potty'? You aren't potty trained! Come out of there."

"Potte!" repeated Strykker as he fully emerged with a toilet brush and toilet paper strung from it.

Rocwell laughed loudly. "He's trying to clean the toilet, Mom!"

Corrynne smiled as she squatted down to receive her tiny son in her free arm.

"Well at least he's not dipping washcloths in the toilet and sucking on them like he used to!" said Jax laughing.

"That's sick!" yelled Ry.

Corrynne stood back up with both her twins in her arms, and smelled the sweetness of her babies' skin as Carea took the toilet brush from her brother and all of her children were laughing.

It was so good to be home!

Charity Never Faileth

The trailer door opened and in walked Bo smiling from ear to ear.

"Hello, Bo," said Corrynne as she and the children were eating eggs at the dinner table. Corrynne automatically smiled back when she noticed his broad smile. "What are you smirking at?" she asked.

"Hi, Dad," said Roc.

"Mom ruined the eggs again," volunteered Jax to his father half joking, but obviously half serious. "She always breaks the yokes."

"You ruined the eggs?" asked Bo as he bent down to kiss Corrynne's cheek. "I've really got to teach you how to cook eggs."

"Cook the eggs? I don't think I was even remotely worried about keeping yokes intact today! These children should be happy I cooked them at all. I was so hungry I was willing to suck them down raw!" said Corrynne smiling slightly.

"Eeewww!" said Ry making a face. "Mom, you could get salmonella from that."

Corrynne looked over at Ry who was giving her one of his superior knowing looks, as if he was educating his mother on some cosmic secret that she wasn't aware of. "I was only kidding," she said assuring him. Turning back to Bo she asked again, "So why are you smiling?"

"Can't a guy smile?" asked Bo with raised eyebrows, making the pink scar on his forehead very prominent. "How was work?" said Bo changing the subject.

"It was work," said Corrynne shrugging.

"Did you see Dane?" asked Bo.

Corrynne nodded and said, "I did."

"Is he getting better, Mom?" asked Ry with a worried look.

Corrynne shook her head looking from one child to the next. "No, I'm afraid he's not."

"Is he getting worse?" asked Carea suddenly with hidden charged emotion.

Corrynne looked at her daughter and put her hand on Carea's hand that was resting on the table. "No, sweetheart, he's still just very sick."

"How long can someone stay sick like that?" asked Carea.

"I've seen them go on for months," said Corrynne. "I know that people can stay in comas for years."

"A coma is like sleeping right, Mom?" asked Rocwell who had been learning about Dane's condition through his brothers.

Carea turned to Rocwell and answered for her mother, "Yes, that's exactly what it's like."

"He's OK, Roc," assured Jax.

Roc looked at his mother as if to verify Jax's comment.

Corrynne nodded. "He's right, Roc. Dane's sleeping just like Sleeping Beauty," assured Corrynne. "Only he's in a hospital, not a castle."

"And he's a guy," added Ry, as if Roc didn't know.

"Good," said Rocwell as he put another bite of eggs in his mouth, suddenly unaffected by the conversation and returning to the business at hand.

"So," said Corrynne, changing the topic again. Turing back to Bo she asked, "Tell me, Bo, what's the news? Do we get to go back to our house?"

"No, why did you ask that?" Bo's face was strangely flat now.

Corrynne studied Bo. Trying to keep things light, she said, "Because, Carea told me you were at a city meeting. I was hoping they had come to their senses and told you we could start cleaning our house and using our food storage."

Bo shook his head. "Well, no. Nothing like that—and I was at a meeting *in the city*, not a *city meeting*," he said clarifying where he had been in a very serious tone.

Corrynne raised her eyebrows at Bo's words. "*Whatever*. I just know you weren't here."

Bo just looked at Corrynne not offering any more information.

Corrynne continued to watch Bo for clues to what he was holding back. It was obvious he was being evasive on purpose. "*OK spill it*," she said forcefully.

"I'll talk to you about it later in private," said Bo, giving her a meaningful look.

"Private?" asked Corrynne, missing his hint on purpose by looking around the trailer. "There isn't a spot of privacy in this place, even if we go into the bathroom together—although I *doubt* we both could fit."

"You could go outside," offered Carea.

Corrynne turned quickly to her daughter. "I thought you were tired of watching everyone," she nearly snapped, unintentionally letting Bo's resistance get to her.

"I was, but now I've recovered." Carea said simply looking from her mother to her father. "It's important that you guys talk. People get divorces during stressful times if they don't talk."[5]

Corrynne was surprised by Carea's statement, but at the same time appreciated her perceptive intuition. Looking at Bo she said, "Yes, Bo. Let's go for a walk."

Bo thought a moment and then said, "OK, if you want to."

"*I want to,*" said Corrynne getting up from the table, and then moving to the door just a few steps from the table. She opened the door and Bo followed.

Out on the muddy pathway Bo shut the door of the trailer firmly. Turning from the trailer he put both hands in his pockets and began to walk in the direction of the sidewalk that bordered the trailer area.

Looking at Bo questioningly, Corrynne concluded that although Bo might have had some good news when he had come into the trailer, he must have other terrible news too. "So, Bo, I'll ask you again, what's happening that is making you so difficult to communicate with?"

Bo didn't look at Corrynne first, but kept his gaze firmly on the ground as he walked slowly beside her. He seemed to be carefully measuring his thoughts.

"I can tell there's something that's weighing on you. What is it? Does it have to do with our house?" asked Corrynne, unwilling to wait.

Bo looked up at Corrynne and then nodded.

"What, Bo?" Corrynne sought Bo's eyes with hers. "Tell me."

Bo opened his mouth, but nothing came out at first. Then as if he forced himself to speak he said, "I've kept something from you again, Corrynne."

Corrynne was taken back as a jolt of energy pulsed through her. In the next second she let her thoughts loose. "*What?* I thought we learned back when that old woman was bothering you that secrets were not good."

Bo nodded. "I know, I just didn't know how to tell you more bad news. There are just so many things that are putting pressure on you, with you having to work so much and Dane being sick...."

Corrynne stopped walking and faced her husband. "Bo, if things are going wrong, we *need* to talk to support each other, to help each other. Do not shelter me, Bo! You might think it's saving me stress but it isn't. It *gives* me stress when I've got to guess at everything you're hiding..." Corrynne stopped talking for a minute to see Bo's response, but he just stayed silent. "It isn't fair that we have to keep going over this issue. This kind of thing drives me crazy!"

"I know. I'm sorry, Corrynne," said Bo, looking defeated.

Corrynne shook her head to lessen the tension in the air. She didn't want Bo to have guilt. She only wanted him to cooperate! In a softer voice she said, "No, it's fine, just tell me what you're keeping back."

"Well…" Bo continued to think.

A few seconds passed. "*What?*" asked Corrynne pointedly.

Bo looked into Corrynne's eyes, and then something broke and he divulged his secret. With a hurt look in his eyes he said, "We don't have insurance for the house. Our insurance company folded."

A strong shock hit Corrynne. She felt like a Mac truck had hit her! "*What? What do you mean?* We have great insurance! We have been paying all this time…"

"There were too many claims," interrupted Bo. "There is no money to rebuild our house."

Corrynne was confused. She shook her head questioningly. "Rebuild? Why are you saying 'rebuild'? We just need to *clean it up,* right*?*"

Bo shook his head now in response. "No, I said it right. *Rebuild.* Our house has been condemned. The second floor fell because of the weight of the waterbed in our room. We aren't allowed to even go near the front door."

Corrynne felt faint. Unavoidable conclusions about her life began to click in her mind. This meant that they would have to live in the tiny trailer for—she couldn't even entertain the estimation. And work! Now, she would have no choice but to continue to work nonstop. She felt like her heart was failing as her mind turned to her children. What about their mother? Her children needed a mother. *She needed to be home!*[6] What about that? And what about the mortgage? Would they have to continue to pay the mortgage on a condemned home?[7] And—her mind turned to Dane who lay in the hospital. And who would care for Dane when the hospital decided to refuse his care because he wasn't getting better? They were beginning to do that to people whose bills were piling up. There was no room for a hospital bed in the trailer! Tears sprung to her eyes and flowed freely down her cheeks. She felt her life was beginning to strangle her. *How could things be so hard?*

"Oh, Bo, this is not fair," Corrynne finally said, her breath catching in her throat. "How could this happen?" She tried to keep back the anger that was threatening to take over her mind.

Bo pulled Corrynne to his chest. "I'm so sorry, sweetheart. I wish I could take it all away."

Corrynne doubled up her fists, dropped her head and then grabbed Bo's shoulders. "What's the answer, Bo? I don't know how to run faster. *I can't do more.* Surely the Lord doesn't want *this!* What are we going to do? We can't afford another house…"

Bo stroked her hair. In almost a whisper he consoled, "I know. I wish I could work instead of you, too. *It's my place.* I should be the provider!"[8] I'm not as good of a mother as you…" Bo took a great breath, hugged Corrynne firmly and then pulled away. Taking his wife by her arms, he held her out so he was looking straight into her eyes. *"That's why I did what I did."*

"What did you do?" asked Corrynne looking through her tears.

"Ever since I learned our home was condemned, I have prayed, looking for solutions. Finally, I received an answer that was difficult for me. I was told that the solution to our problems was an arms length away. I just needed to hold out my hand and accept it."

Corrynne searched her husband's eyes. "Why was that answer difficult for you? It sounds wonderful to me! We *need* help, Bo!"

Bo thought for a moment and then said, "Well, you know I hate taking help from *anyone,* sometimes even from the Lord. I just want to be self-sufficient. *I* want to help myself. It's my duty."[9]

"Yes," Corrynne nodded. "You are obstinate that way," but then she added quickly, "But ordinarily we are! We've never needed help from anyone before."

"Well, I know but I'm still not comfortable with the 'dole,' under any circumstance."

Corrynne looked briefly at the ground and said, "I know, so am I. That's why we're working so hard."

"Right. Anyway, I was told this time we needed help, just as you said. Then I was told that *I* must humble myself and be willing to accept it."

Corrynne smiled demurely. "I'm glad I didn't have to tell you that."

Bo continued. "I came to understand by my praying that *I* would be the barrier to the aid that is available, because my weakness is acknowledging my flaws and weaknesses.[10] At first that message was challenging. How could I be responsible for such a burden? I didn't cause the earthquake or break the dam!"[11]

"Right," nodded Corrynne.

"Then I was reminded that sometimes the Lord fulfills the prayers of some by others on the earth. It is our responsibility to be open. We need to bend and receive or stretch and give, depending on the circumstance."

Corrynne then understood. "We are to accept help from someone? Who?"

Bo looked kindly into Corrynne's eyes. "Yes, we are. That part kills me. I HATE that I can't pull us out of this situation by myself but my hands are tied, as yours are. Again, I need to realize my limits and lean on others for help if I am told to."[12]

"Yes! I agree!" Anticipation was growing in Corrynne. "So did you find help?"

"Well, I didn't quite know where to start looking. I decided to start in the city. I began going to the city meetings to figure out my options, thinking maybe there was a program I could apply for."

"Did you find one?"

"Yes. The government is rebuilding many homes in parts of Provo."

A thrill of hope pulsed through Corrynne. "So the government is rebuilding our house?"

Bo shook his head. "No."

Corrynne felt like stamping her feet and screaming like a child, but she contained herself and asked, "Why not?"

"Don't get me wrong. I applied, but we were denied."

"Why?"

"Because…" Bo paused and then said, "You make too much."

"What? I'm being punished because I have a job?"

"No, it's just that there are so many that don't even have that."

"But, Bo—so I have a job! I almost would rather work less and lose everything, than continue killing myself and not be a mother to my children!" said Corrynne with large eyes.

Bo nodded and said quickly, "I know. I agree. That's why I went to the Bishop."

Corrynne took in a great breath. Bo had sworn repeatedly in the past that he would rather die of starvation than go to the Bishop! "Bo, that was a good move," Corrynne said still surprised. "I'm impressed."

"I have to admit, the Bishop was so great. But listen…I learned an amazing lesson that I hadn't realized before."

"What?"

"The Lord makes some prosperous, not because they are more worthy, or more choice, or even more talented, but because there are those that need to be lifted. They act in God's stead to bring about miracles!"[13]

Corrynne smiled and said, "That's beautiful, Bo!"

"Yes, the Law of Consecration[14] was given for that purpose, to lift the body of the church and sanctify the giver. It takes humility for all parties to make the law profitable as each seeks to improve the lives of their fellowmen. All participants are edified by the transaction. Do you see the wisdom?"[15] Bo's face was almost glowing.

Tears of joy now began to fill Corrynne's eyes. A feeling came over her that was so peaceful and beautiful. Suddenly, all the problems that weighed her down, were melting away.[16] After trying to gain control over her emotions again, she said, "Tell me what's going to happen, Bo."

"Did you know among brother DeVine's businesses he owns a log home manufacturing company?"

Corrynne shook her head. "No, I didn't."

"The bishop told me that he had a goal of donating the material for 100 homes."

"What? Material for one hundred homes? What does that mean? Do you mean logs?" Corrynne was amazed.

"Yes, all the logs, hardware and expertise. He'll even use his machines to help us remove our house so we can start building. Isn't that great?" Bo was expectantly searching Corrynne's face.

Corrynne gave a small smile. She wondered if her little family could build a house out of logs. They had never done it before. None of them were good at that kind of thing. "Do you think we can build a house by ourselves?"

"Of course we can! But the bishop had another idea. He said he was issuing calls for all the unemployed men in our ward to help all those with condemned homes, build."

Corrynne thought for a moment. "Wow! How wonderful!" She allowed her mind to entertain the process of building a home and then living in it. A sudden thrill filled her. It would be an adventure she welcomed! She was sure that with the help of others, they could build a house. Her mind returned to Brother DeVine. "How in the world can Brother DeVine afford this? Aren't his businesses hurting right now, too?"

Bo thought for a moment. "I'm sure they are, but I was told that every one of those homes he is donating will be built from excess stock of logs."

Corrynne shook her head. "Oh my goodness! How can that be possible?"

"The bishop told me that a couple of years ago Brother DeVine felt impressed that there would come a day in which he would be called upon to furnish some homes to the Saints, and to prepare for that service. He felt that since he had promised in the temple to give everything he had in building up the kingdom of God, that this disaster qualified in his mind as the moment he had been waiting for."

Suddenly, the promises Corrynne had made in the temple to the Lord took on new meaning. Now she realized those promises would ensure the Saint's survival in the last days![17] "Yes. We do make those promises don't we? So often we just say the words without thinking about their meaning. I don't think I'll ever do that again."

"Right," agreed Bo. "Neither will I. Luckily for so many, Brother DeVine took his promises seriously and he listened to that prompting long ago."

"I am so thankful!"

"The Bishop went on to tell me that there are many stories just like his happening all over the world, and many wealthy LDS people are stepping up to the need of the people by giving millions of dollars in resources to help out their communities. He said it was the best example of the law of consecration that he had seen in his whole life."

Corrynne shook her head in continued amazement. What a blessing! What a miracle! The Lord was so smart! How thankful she was to belong to an organization that was truly "for the people." Corrynne searched for words, but all she could say was, "Oh my goodness..." again and again.

"So see, sweetheart? Through adversity we see blessings that we never would have under other circumstances.[18] There *is* help. The Lord *is* mindful of us."

"You're so right! I see it now!" said Corrynne with joy flowing through her.

"So, the bishop asked me if I would be interested in a home, under the condition that we would help build it."

Corrynne held her breath. "What did you say?"

Bo smiled. "The words, 'we would be eternally grateful' came out of my mouth before I could stop them."

Corrynne couldn't help but jump for joy and then kiss her husband's cheek! "I'm so glad! Oh, Bo, I am so glad!"

"It will take about four months."

"Of course, but my boys are good workers!" Corrynne said, still smiling. There was nothing right now that could stop her happiness. "We can do anything for a few months!"

Bo hugged Corrynne hard. "Now all we need is for Dane to get better. Things are working out." Bo kissed her forehead.

"Yes they are, Bo. Thank you for being so wonderful!"

"It's not me, Corrynne, it's the Lord. I'm just his servant trying to listen to advice."

"Well thank you for listening! Thank you for being humble. Thank you, Bo, for being you." Corrynne reached up and kissed Bo's lips gently.

Bo smiled. "Whoa, so much love…I like it." He then reached down and kissed Corrynne again, with passion this time.

Notes to "Do Not Run Faster Than Ye Are Able"

Suspended Relief

[1] There will come a time in which food will be difficult to obtain by going to the store. The exact circumstances are not available to outline why this will happen and most likely will be caused by different reasons in different areas of the world. Today we can look in the news and see that it is already beginning. The Lord desires us, his servants, to survive the times ahead so we can fulfill his work to prepare for his coming. This is why he has warned us for a couple hundred years plus to preserve food for our families. "Remember the counsel that is given…Store up all your grain, and take care of it! …And I tell you it is almost as necessary to have bread to sustain the body as it is to have food for the spirit; for the one is as necessary as the other to enable us to carry on the work of God upon the earth." (Orson Hyde, *Journal of Discourses*, Vol. 5, 17).

[2] Food is not the only thing that will be scarce in times of turmoil. Apparently all commercially manufactured items will disappear and we'll have to do with what we have. "Let every head of every household see to it that he has on hand enough food and clothing, and, where possible, fuel also, for at least a year ahead. You of small means put your money in foodstuffs and wearing apparel, not in stocks and bonds; you of large means will think you know how to care for yourselves, but I may venture to suggest that you do not speculate. Let every head of every household aim to own his own home, free from mortgage. Let every man who has a garden spot, garden it; every man who owns a farm, farm it" (J. Reuben Clark, Jr., *Conference Report*, April 1937, 26).

[3] "An important aspect of preparation that women cannot afford to neglect is career readiness. It would be desirable for every woman to have a marketable skill—one that can help her get a job that will provide for her needs and bring her as much satisfaction as possible. A few compelling facts about Latter-day Saint women support this need: Fact 1. Ten percent of LDS

women who are between the ages of eighteen and thirty will be widowed before age sixty. Fact 2. Thirty-five percent will be divorced before age sixty. Fact 3. Three percent will never marry. Fact 4. Forty-five percent will be the primary breadwinner in their homes before age sixty-five" (See *Church News*, 6 Nov. 1983, 4).

[4] The nursing profession is one example of a profession that women can seek after to fend off economic disasters that might come in the future. It is a profession of high demand. It is marketable, flexible for families and provides excellent compensation and benefits even for the part-time employed. President Hinckley made this point in addressing the Young Women of the church. "I was in the hospital the other day for a few hours. I became acquainted with my very cheerful and expert nurse. She is the kind of woman of whom you girls could dream. When she was young she decided she wished to be a nurse. She received the necessary education to qualify for the highest rank in the field. She worked at her vocation and became expert at it. She decided she wanted to serve a mission and did so. She married. She has three children. She works now as little or as much as she wishes. There is such a demand for people with her skills that she can do almost anything she pleases. She serves in the Church. She has a good marriage. She has a good life. She is the kind of woman of whom you might dream as you look to the future" (Gordon B. Hinckley, "How Can I Become the Woman of Whom I Dream?" *Ensign*, May 2001, 93).

Charity Never Faileth

[5] "The biggest rise in the divorce rate has been among couples married 10 years or longer. It's not uncommon today for couples 25 and 30 years into their marriage to seek and obtain a divorce." The number one cause, he states, "is the [couples'] inability to talk honestly with each other, bare their souls and treat each other as their best friend. ... They [talk] about mostly superficial things in order to impress one another." He goes on to say, "I find that too many people talk right through each other rather than to each other." He concludes: "The lack of communication brings on drinking, infidelity or physical or mental abuse. ...For many, there is a lack of tolerance, an inability to bear discomfort or to recognize that they're not perfect and neither is their mate" (Herbert Glieberman, "Why So Many Marriages Fail," *U.S. News & World Report*, 20 July 1981, 53-54).

[6] "...Mothers are primarily responsible for the nurture for their children..." (The First Presidency, *The Family: Proclamation to the World*, September 23, 1995).

[7] A scenario like the one in the text may be one reason we are admonished to pay off our mortgage. "...Let every head of every household aim to own his own home, free from mortgage" (J. Reuben Clark, Jr., *Conference Report*, April 1937, 26).

[8] "...By divine design, fathers are to preside over their families in love and righteousness and are responsible to provide the necessities of life and protection for their families..." (The First Presidency, *The Family: Proclamation to the World*, September 23, 1995).

[9] "No true Latter-day Saint, while physically or emotionally able, will voluntarily shift the burden of his own or his family's well-being to someone else. So long as he can, under the inspiration of the Lord and with his own labors, he will supply himself and his family with the spiritual and temporal necessities of life" (Spencer W. Kimball, The Teachings of Spencer W. Kimball, 366).

[10] "And if men come unto me I will show unto them their weakness. I give unto men weakness that they may be humble; and my grace is sufficient for all men that humble themselves before me; for if they humble themselves before me, and have faith in me, then will I make weak things become strong unto them" (Ether 12:27).

[11] It is natural to become angry when things are difficult, but if we put off that first impulse and yield to the Lord, he will shape us through adversity to be great! "For the natural man is

an enemy to God, and has been from the fall of Adam, and will be, forever and ever, unless he yields to the enticings of the Holy Spirit, and putteth off the natural man and becometh a saint through the atonement of Christ the Lord, and becometh as a child, submissive, meek, humble, patient, full of love, willing to submit to all things which the Lord seeth fit to inflict upon him, even as a child doth submit to his father" (Mosiah 3:19).

[12] "Come unto me, all ye that labor and are heavy laden, and I will give you rest" (Matthew 11:28).

[13] "When this people are prepared to properly use the riches of this world for the building up of the Kingdom of God, He is ready and willing to bestow them upon us. I like to see men get rich by their industry, prudence, management and economy, and then devote it to the building up of the Kingdom of God upon the earth" (Brigham Young, *Journal of Discourses*, Vol. 2, 114-15).

[14] "Consecration is the giving of one's own time, talents, and means to care for those in need-whether spiritually or temporally-and in building the Lord's kingdom" (Spencer W. Kimball, *The Teachings of Spencer W. Kimball*, 366).

[15] "...The highest achievement of spirituality comes as we conquer the flesh. We build character as we encourage people to care for their own needs. As givers gain control of their desires and properly see others needs in light of their own wants, then the powers of the gospel are released in their lives. They learn that by living the great law of consecration they insure not only temporal salvation but also spiritual sanctification. And as a recipient receives with thanksgiving, he rejoices in knowing that in its purest form-in the true Zion-one may partake of both temporal and spiritual salvation. Then they are motivated to become self-sustaining and able to share with others" (Spencer W. Kimball, *The Teachings of Spencer W. Kimball*, 365).

[16] "Peace I leave with you, my peace I give unto you: not as the world giveth, give I unto you. Let not your heart be troubled, neither let it be afraid" (John 14:7).

[17] "The fate of humanity and all civilization hinges on whether man will use his free agency to govern himself or ignore eternal laws at his own peril and reap the consequences. The real issues of today are, therefore, not economic. They are spiritual—meaning that man must learn to conform to the laws which God has given to mankind" (Ezra Taft Benson, *The Teachings of Ezra Taft Benson,* 83-84).

[18] "Ye cannot behold with your natural eyes, for the present time, the design of your God concerning those things which shall come hereafter, and the glory which shall follow after much tribulation" (D&C 58:3).

CHAPTER EIGHTEEN

DECISIONS

"Wherefore, beware lest ye are deceived; and that ye may not be deceived seek ye earnestly the best gifts, always remembering for what they are given," (D&C 46:8).

00:08:08 15:45:56 Zulu
Friday, April 23rd
1:15 a.m.
Provo, Utah

Phone Call

Out of the silence the cell phone rang, playing Bach's Two-Part Invention.

"Corrynne?" asked Bo, "Isn't that the phone?"

"Huh? What? What's wrong?" Corrynne lifted her head off the pillow and looked around.

The music of the phone continued, but it sounded muted, as if it was under a pile of clothes.

"Who would be calling at this time of night?" asked Bo, digging for their alarm clock from between the mattress and the wall of the trailer.

"What time is it?" asked Corrynne squinting to see the clock in Bo's hands.

The music continued through the second cadence.

"Ahhh, it's quarter after one."

"Oh, no, Bo…" Corrynne sat up quickly, accidentally pulling the covers off the twins that were sleeping between them.

The music stopped. "We missed it!" Corrynne said with an edge.

"What?" Bo jumped out of bed and fished for the phone on the counter.

"It's Dane! See who called! I bet it's Dane!" Corrynne said as she jumped out of bed too and re-covered the twins.

Bach's Two-Part Invention began again as another call came through.

"What do you mean?" asked Bo as he lifted clothes off the kitchen counter in search of the sound.

"I think it's the hospital calling!"

The sound continued into the second cadence once again.

"Can't you find it?" asked Corrynne, putting on her glasses and now looking too. "It's right here! I hear it!"

Bo found the glowing phone in the pocket of his sweats. "Here it is!" He hit the on button, *"Hello?"* he said urgently.

"…Yes, this is Mr. Rogers. …Yes, I understand. We have to find a ride, but yes, we'll be right there. …Good-bye," Bo said and then disconnected the phone.

Corrynne was already dressed and pulling on a jacket. "It was Dane wasn't it?"

"Yes, they say he has become unstable. They said something about MERSA. What is that?"

"Oh, no! That's Methicillin Resistant *Staph Aureus*. We really have no treatment for it. Where did they say that the MERSA was?"

"They think it's in his blood."

"Noo, No! No!" Corrynne hit her head with the palm of her hand.

Bo became alarmed. "Corrynne! Settle down and tell me what it means!"

"Oh, Bo, *Staph* is something that's found on the skin, but often in the hospital there are resistant forms that can be anywhere. Because of IV lines, it can get into the blood. A sick person can't fight it off and it's lethal. Do your remember that machine that Dr. Page had installed in the ICU break room?"

"The silver one?"

"Yes."

"Yes, I remember," said Bo as he slipped on his jeans and buttoned the top button.

"That machine took the blood from people who had developed antibodies against MERSA, spun it down and separated the antibodies, so it could be given to people like Dane. Often, nurses have antibodies for that bacterium. Remember how much they were paying me for my blood?"

Bo thought and then nodded as he pulled on a sweatshirt. "Oh yes, I knew it was too good to be true."

"No, Bo, it wasn't too good to be true, it really worked! Dr. Page was giving our serum to the highest bidder, without us knowing it. We had thought the FDA was reviewing the machine, but in actuality, it was saving the lives of the rich. We just didn't know it."

"Well then, as I understand it, that's good news! We can do that for Dane. You have the antibodies, he needs them, seems pretty straightforward. Is the machine still in the hospital?"

Corrynne shook her head. "Yes, it's still in the hospital, but it's against the law to give that serum to anyone because it hasn't been approved for that use yet."

"What? How was Dr. Page doing it?" asked Bo as he threw on a shirt.

"He was doing it illegally. He knew how to work the system to cover his tracks. It wasn't until after he died that we found out what was going on, and that he would label the antibodies as an antibiotic and we would give it to the chosen, paying recipients."

"Did it work?"

"It worked wonderfully! We had wondered how some of these patients were surviving, but later we found out it was because of nursing staff's blood contributions."

"So where in the hospital is the machine?" asked Bo.

"It's still in the break room."

"Why? If it's illegal, why haven't they removed it?"

"Because, the administration knows how valuable it will be once it is approved. It's the only one in the world. They will be the sole source of MERSA antibody production. I guess they have investors, and marketers all set up," said Corrynne as she looked for her shoes, found sandals and slipped them on.

"So when is this supposed to happen?" asked Bo as he sat down and pulled on his athletic shoes.

"We were told, 'any time now,' but that's the last we heard."

"Maybe we can get a variance for Dane. I'm sure when they hear Dane is doing poorly, they won't fight against you giving your own antibodies to him."

"I hope not. I'll make some phone calls when we get to the hospital. I'm sure someone will listen—they have to!"

"I'm sure they will," assured Bo. "So, how are you doing?"

"Terrible! *There is too much stress around here*," said Corrynne as she headed for the back of the trailer to tell Carea where they were going.

Bo picked up the phone again and began dialing.

"Who are you calling?"

"Our neighbors behind us."

"The Stows?"

"Yes. Their son gave them a car I think they'll let us use, under the circumstances."

"Good idea," said Corrynne as she disappeared around the wall.

Rejection

Dane lay on the grass under his favorite tree, gazing at Jenessa who knelt nearby.

Jenessa fidgeted with her hair, pulling the front to the back and then said, "OK, Dane, it's time."

"What is time in a timeless sphere?" Dane asked dreamily.

"Dane, stop teasing, you *know* what time it is."

"Yes, I do know what time it is, because time has stopped for me. I have eternal bliss, because I'm with you." Dane reached a hand out to Jenessa who was getting to her feet. "I say, it's *time* to be happy."

Jenessa flicked Dane's hand down. "Dane, remember your calling."

"What calling?" Dane played dumb.

"Aren't you going to show up for your review in front of the council?"

"Do I have a choice?"

"Of course you have a choice! We all have choices for everything."

"Well, then…*no.*"

Jenessa put her hands on her hips and frowned. "Dane."

"What?"

"We've worked so hard. You're ready now. Come-on, get up and let's go. The council will be convening soon."

"What will you give me if I do?" asked Dane, raising a hand to Jenessa again.

"I will give you nothing. This is your choice to make alone. I can't have anything to do with it." Jenessa hit Dane's hand down again.

Dane rolled over and began to get to his feet. "But, Jenessa, you do have something to do with it."

Jenessa shook her head. "No, I don't. We've been over this before."

Dane got up from his spot and moved toward Jenessa. He attempted to take her into his arms. "Yes, don't you see? Now that I know you, the mortal world seems so dark and lonely. Why would I want to go back?"

Jenessa continued to retreat. "But your family is back there. They are waiting for you."

Dane shrugged and nodded as he continued towards Jenessa. "I know. I love them, but I'll see them again. It's you that I can't bear leaving."

Jenessa held one hand out firmly to hold Dane at a distance. "You won't leave me. I'll be there with you."

"What do you mean?" said Dane with soft eyes.

"I'll be one of your guardian angels. I've already received my call. Yes, they normally only like blood relatives to do that job, but I was approved because I was your tutor. They know about our bond and they know I will be helpful in your mission."

Dane's eyes lit a little. "Will I be able to see you?"

Jenessa shook her head. "No, Dane. You know that."

Dane shook his head in response. "Well, then how will I know you're there?"

"When you feel the sunshine on your face, you will remember me and our lesson about the great love of God who allows you to exist and grow through his power. That has to be enough."

Dane turned away. "No, Jenessa, I don't think that *is* enough."

Jenessa lifted a foot as if to stomp it, but she just readjusted her weight. "Dane, it has to be. Refocus! Recommit! The Lord knows your heart. You must not have any other desire than to serve him."

"How do I do that?"

"You know how. Remember how you used to feel. Remember how you wanted to serve the Lord. Remember that in giving me up, you will gain eternity."

Again Dane shook his head. "I had those feelings so long ago." He put his hands to his chest. "I think you have taken over my heart."

Jenessa shook her head emphatically and took two steps backwards. "No, Dane. *That can't be*. It is not time. *Let—me—go!*"

Those words pained Dane beyond comprehension. He couldn't do it unless he had some sort of promise to hang on to. "Jenessa, if I give you up, will you wait for me so I can take you back again?"

"I will follow the Lord. Whatever he asks of me I will do."

"Tell me what that means!" pleaded Dane.

"That means I can't promise you anything."

A hole was ripped in Dane's his heart. *"Why not?"*

"Because my life is not my own. I love the Lord more than anything in this world or the physical world. If he wishes me to be single forever, then I would be single."

Dane rushed forward and took Jenessa's hands. "He would never require you to do that! You must marry to achieve your glory. I want you to marry me!"

Jenessa looked very sad. "I know that, Dane, and I want to marry you too, but only after you become what you can become."

"I'll work hard here! We can work together! I can reach my potential here," Dane begged. "I don't need the world."

Jenessa pulled her hands away from Dane's grasp and turned slightly away. "No, that is not how it works, it wouldn't be the same. You need the experience that lies before you to refine you. That kind of refinement takes eons here."

Dane got on one knee. "Please, Jenessa, I have eons now."

Jenessa turned fully away and shook her head. "No, Dane. My heart belongs to God. I'll tell you again. If the Lord asks me to be single, I would do it. If the Lord asks me to marry another, I would do it. If the Lord wants me to wait for you, I would do it."

Dane held out his hands in frustration. "What does the Lord *want* you to do? Doesn't he see we are good together?"

Jenessa shrugged. "I don't know. I haven't asked him yet."

"Why not? Why haven't you asked him about me?"

"Because it's wrong to give my heart to you right now. You have things to accomplish. You have a mission to fulfill, you must prove yourself worthy of such a mission." Jenessa whirled around and faced Dane once more. *"Go forth and serve!"*

Dane clasped his hands together, still on his knees. "Please Jenessa, *give me something to cling to!"*

Jenessa shook her head and began to retreat again. "No, it would be unfair. I release you, as you should release me. Nothing should hold you back."

Dane got to his feet and followed. "What is so wrong with us being together?"

"In another time, it might be right. But I will not be held responsible for you failing your promises. I am now stepping away from you, Dane. You give me no alternative. You now must be independent. Make your choices. I can no longer be a part of your life." Then she was gone.

"Jenessa!" Dane yelled into the breeze. He tried to follow her like he had learned, but she was blocking his perception of where she went. He couldn't sense her. It was useless.

Dane kicked the grass, "Jenessa, please let's talk this out!" There was no response and he knew there wouldn't be.

A Mother's Choice, a Father's Dilemma

Corrynne and Bo rushed into the hospital room where Dane's body was quickly sinking away from the world. With one glance Corrynne could tell that he was in terrible trouble.

The doctor on-call, was standing by the bedside. "Dr. Cross, his oxygenation is so low! His heart rate is through the roof! How long has it been 180?"

"It slowly has been creeping up during the night."

"With a heart rate like that, what is his cardiac output?"

"It's four," said the doctor in an unemotional tone.

"Four? It used to be much higher than that! He's beginning to decline!"

"Yes, that's because the filling time for his heart isn't long enough. We have to slow down his heart so it can pump more blood with every beat."

"That blood pressure stinks," said Corrynne as she looked up at the monitor and touched Dane's chest to feel the heart beat.

"I know. We've tried a beta blocker to slow his heart rate, but now his pressure won't handle it. We're giving Neo boluses just to keep the mean above 60."

Corrynne shook her head. "Well, without oxygen, a mean above 60 means nothing."

"You're right, but still, we're hoping that he'll turn around."

Corrynne's mind panicked, searching for more information. "Have you done a PH?"

"Yes, it's 6.9."

"Oh, Doctor, he's so acidotic!"

"We're doing our best, Corrynne, you know that. You've been here before with your own patients."

Corrynne nodded and bit a nail. "Yes, I have, many times and I know what comes next!"

"Well, we're trying to avoid *that*, but there is only so much we can do.

"I know," said Corrynne with a fallen look.

"His FIO2 is what I'm worried about," said the doctor.

"What is it now?"

"It's 100%. His lungs have almost no compliance. His peep is 18. We don't dare go any higher, we're afraid we'll blow a hole in a lung."

Corrynne's eyes grew wide as she looked up at his saturation. It was 75%. "On 100% his sats are only 75? This is crazy!"

"Yes, that's why we called you. His heart cannot keep up with the pace that it has. There isn't enough oxygen. We've already begun to see some ectopy. Lots of radical beats, telling us that it's suffering for oxygen."

"Have you done a troponin level to check for cardiac enzymes in the blood from damaged heart cells?"

"Yes, it's on the rise. It's gone from 10 to greater than 30."

"He's beginning to have heart damage," said Corrynne more to herself than anyone.

"Yes, and I'm afraid they're an indication of what is to come, if we can't help him in any other way. Do you have any ideas?"

Corrynne pulled on her lip, "What is Dane's temperature?" She squinted at the monitor. "Is that number up there right? Tell me that there is something wrong with the thermister."

The doctor shook his head. "Nope, it's right. It is 105. We double checked it with a tympanic measurement."

"I'm sure you've tried Motrin and Tylenol, a cooling blanket and ice to bring it down."

"Yes, Lisa has given alternating doses and he's on a cooling blanket right now. Corrynne, at this point, the only thing that will bring it down is a cure for MERSA, and I'm afraid we just don't have it. We have to kill the bacteria."

Corrynne's eyes began to tear. "And why can't we use that machine of Dr. Page's?"

"Because if I did, I would lose my license."

"What if I did?"

"You would lose your license."

"No, but I'm his mother. Things that I do as his mother are different than what I do as a nurse, right? I mean, I can't administer my antibodies to any of my patients, but I could to my son, couldn't I?"

The doctor stopped for a second and then said, "Corrynne, I don't know...I wouldn't suggest it. You could get fired for using hospital equipment without permission."

"Does the hospital own Dr. Page's machine? I bet they don't"

"I don't know that."

"This can't be any different than parents all over America using alternative medicines for their dying children. It's a last ditch effort after everything else has failed. You hear about those stories all the time."

Dr. Cross looked hard at Corrynne and then said, "You know I can't authorize you to give Dane anything, but if you choose to do it as a mother, I can't stop you. As his parent, you are ultimately in charge of choices concerning his care. I can, however, advise against it, which I do, but again, *you can do whatever you see fit.* Do you understand me?"

Corrynne watched Dr. Cross for a moment, and then he smiled. He was telling her to go ahead, without putting himself in jeopardy. She understood that clearly. "Yes, Dr. Cross. I do understand you. Thank you."

Corrynne looked down at her son again. His face was flushed red and emotionless. "Dane, sweetheart, hang on. Do what you can to get better. We need you here! Now, I'm going to go out for a while, but your dad is going to stay here with you. Talk to him a little. Tell him you need a blessing." Corrynne whirled from the bedside and glared at Bo. As she approached him, she grabbed his coat and pulled him out into the hall.

Corrynne half whispered and half cried as she talked to her husband, pleading, yet angry that her words were even necessary. "You know, I've been patient with this little game to 'wait as long as you can,' and I understand that you are trying to be obedient, but let me tell you, time is running out, Bo! You need to tell Heavenly Father what is happening here and that we need to hurry up with healing this boy, or there will be no boy left to heal."

Bo blinked and asked, "Have you been telling Heavenly Father?"

"*Of course I have been telling him.* What do you mean, isn't it obvious?"

"Well, then he knows."

"Bo! This is driving me crazy! My son is dying in there and I feel like we have been just sitting around doing nothing! We have power! We have abilities! I have my nursing knowledge and you have your priesthood power! Between us both, we should be able to do something here!"

Bo looked down at the ground. "I agree, and if the Lord wills it, then it will happen."

"When? When he's dead?"

"If necessary," said Bo as he looked back into Corrynne's eyes.

Corrynne shook her head. "No! I don't accept that! What about all the organ damage that he receives as he dies? What about the anoxia that is stealing his brain cells as we speak? Please, Bo, there has to be a better way!"

"I'm sorry, Corrynne, I don't know of any."

"OK, all I know is that a blessing is needed! Accepted practice in medicine can do no more. Priesthood power is the only power on earth that can save him. I can go do my part, but at this point, even killing the bacteria, will not restore him to his previous functioning condition. I'm sure there has been too much damage already."

Bo looked into Corrynne's eyes, "Corr, you know that you do not have to go do what you are about to do, and put your profession in jeopardy. You know that all you have to do is be patient a little longer."

"No! *That is not an option!* I know that I am supposed to do all that I can do and then after all that, lean on the Lord. Well, there is one more thing I know I can do, and I'm going to go do it! In the mean time please, Bo, pray. Please beg Heavenly Father to save our son!"

Bo nodded. "I have been praying, Corrynne. Every day, every night, while awake, while asleep. I get the same answer, and that is, 'not yet.' I'm sorry. I can't summon the Lord. It must be on his timeline, or not at all."

Corrynne's jaw dropped. "What do you mean '*not at all*'?"

Bo took a deep breath and then said, "There is still the possibility that Dane is supposed to die today."

Corrynne was instantly furious. "*How can you say that? I thought you were told that he would be healed!*"

"I was, but as I pray, I get the impression that Dane has a choice in this matter. I don't think he wants to come back here."

"*Why not?*"

"Well, why should he? Mortality is hard. He has served a good life and maybe, he's satisfied with that."

"No, Bo! *Tell him he has to come back!*"

Bo looked at his wife with tired and sad eyes. "Corrynne, I can't. It's not my place anymore. He is under the direction of Heavenly Father. You have to trust in that."

Corrynne stomped her foot and said, "Oh, I can't stand this! How can *you* stand this?"

"The Lord blesses with peace during hardships. You can feel the peace too, if you want to. I feel satisfied that what is supposed to happen is happening."

"What?" Bo's statement was too much. "*You feel satisfied?* That thought makes me *nauseous*! How can a son dying in a premature deathbed be OK? There is something seriously wrong with this picture. No, I don't want to feel peace. *I want to be angry.* I want to feel whatever it takes, to do whatever I need to, to save our son. *Is that clear?*"

"How can it not be? You're very clear."

"Fine. I will be right back. In the mean time, *do your part!*"

Bo shook his head. "I have been. I'm sorry you haven't seen it."

Corrynne walked briskly away from the ICU, leaving Bo standing alone outside Dane's room.

CHAPTER NINETEEN

LIFE AND PROGRESSION

"To him that overcometh will I grant to sit with me in my throne, even as I also overcame, and am set down with my Father in his throne" (Revelation 3:21).

Heavenly Spirit Council

Council

Dane walked around the beautiful city. He soaked in the light as it emanated around him. He looked at the jewels in the structures, and the brightness of the fountains as the light bounced through and off the water. How could he leave this place? There was nowhere that he felt so loved and so satisfied. Even without Jenessa, there was the satisfaction of knowing who he was and that the Lord loved him. That feeling was ever present. Imagining returning to a place in which he would have to deal with peer pressure, pimples, and ignorance of this sphere, caused him unwanted pain.

Somewhere in his consciousness, he could feel that the council was waiting for him. They were convened for his review. Dane kicked around the idea of not showing up, like he had told Jenessa, but then he wondered how that would affect his progress and learning. He didn't want to be held back in any way. There was too much to know, and too much he wanted to do. No…he would go. It was the right thing to do. Dane was used to doing the right thing.

Dane closed his eyes, and thought about the council. He knew right where they were meeting. When he opened his eyes, a council of twelve was sitting in front of him.

"Hello, Dane. We are so glad you decided to come talk to us," said one man on the right.

"Yes, we are. We are aware of your struggles and want you to know that those feelings are normal," said another directly in front of him.

Dane smiled, it was nice to not be pressured. "Thank you. It is hard. I love it here. I have learned so much."

"And you love Jenessa," said another on the left.

Dane nodded and smiled. "Yes, that's true. With all my heart."

The gentleman right in front of him said, "Yes, we know that. Your love is pure. We like to see that."

"Good. So I can be with her?"

The same gentleman shook his head slowly with a smile. "No, I'm afraid that she has rejected you, despite your desire to be with her."

Dane took a step forward with his hands open and out in front of him. "Why? I'm good, I'm learning fast. Why does she cut me off from her?"

"Because, you can become better," said the man to the left. "You can learn more, you can be great, one of the great ones on earth. She desires that you fulfill your potential. She is a noble and great one. She will seek a mate that is her equal."[1]

"Yes, I believe you are cutting yourself from her, not the other way around," said the man in the middle.

Dane was so sad. "I am?" he asked in a soft voice.

"Yes. See life from the eternal perspective. Look down the path of time and see the consequences of your actions," suggested the man to the right.

Dane shook his head and stared at the white marble floor. "I haven't learned how to do that yet."

The man in the middle said, "Well, if you have a desire, you can do it. Just focus your thoughts and you will see how things become reality through time. Your choices dictate those realities. You have many to choose from. Choose wisely."

"So just focus? Then I'll see what my choices bring?"

"Yes," nodded the middle gentleman.

"Should I try now?"

The man on the right answered this time. "Yes, time is growing short for your choices to be valid. Soon, no choice will be your choice. You will have to stay here. Then you will live for an eternity with the consequences of that choice. Any other reality will be eliminated."

"Your body is dying on earth. Your mother is sending many prayers for you to be healed. Your father is waiting for further instruction. Look now so you will know the best path," continued the man on the left.

"Alright. I'll do what you say." Dane closed his eyes and focused on what would happen if he stayed in the spirit world. Suddenly a new perception opened before him.

Struggle

Corrynne felt totally drained. She wondered if she had enough energy to even get out of the chair. She had gone way overboard and spun six units of antibodies for her son. It was more than she had ever done before and her body was being pushed to its limits. She was surprised how tired she was. It didn't make sense. It wasn't as if she was taking out the red blood cells, she was only giving antibodies.

She shivered then she shrugged. She decided she didn't care. She would go through discomfort for her son. It was no big deal.

Corrynne changed her thoughts to Dane. Her theory was if she could flood him with her antibodies, maybe they could fight the MERSA, until she could make some more.

Corrynne lifted the arm of the machine and removed the needle from her arm. She put gauze over the puncture site and held pressure for a minute.

Suddenly a nurse rushed into the room. In an urgent voice she said, "Corrynne, Dane is bradying down. His heart rate is 50!" then the nurse left the room.

"Oh, no! Please no!" said Corrynne, she knew the radical change from a fast heart rate to a slower one meant that Dane's heart would not last very much longer. She dragged herself from the chair and stood up. As she stood, blackness filled her vision and she became very dizzy. Her face felt cold. She knew she was about to faint. Quickly she sat back down and hung her head down, to make the blood return to it. After a few moments she felt better.

Another nurse came to the door, "Corrynne, come quick, your son is going to be gone soon, do you want us to begin a code?"

Corrynne, nodded as she slowly got to her feet again. "Do everything," she said with a gasp.

The nurse nodded and then left to deliver the message.

Slowly, Corrynne began to walk around the machine to retrieve the units of antibodies. She was shaking so badly. What was wrong? Was she going to make it to her son's side in time?

"Corrynne, what is taking so long?" It was Bo's voice this time. "You have to hurry. You have to make these medical decisions. I don't know anything about codes."

"I—I can't walk, Bo. Something is wrong. I have no energy and I feel like I'm on the verge of fainting."

Bo rushed over to her and put his arm around her. "What did you do?"

"I spun six units."

"Corrynne, aren't you only allowed to do two?"

"Yes, but I thought Dane needed more."

"But you can't give that much."

"Well, I thought that since the red blood cells were being returned to my body, I could."

"Oh, Corrynne, what am I going to do with you?"

"Bo, I'm so sorry. I just tried to do what was best."

"I know."

"Bo..." Corrynne began to cry. "I feel so helpless. I tried so hard, but I can't do this. I can't do this on my own."

"I know. I'm here. We'll get this stuff to Dane. I'm here to help you."

"Thank you, Bo. Thank you! I love you."

"I love you, too. That's why I'm here." Bo looked around. "Where are the keys to open this thing?"

Corrynne pointed to her pocket. "I knew where Dr. Page hid them."

Bo fished them out of her jeans. With a quick flick, he positioned the key in his right hand and opened the silver case. There hanging on a hook was six clear bottles of antibodies.

"Oh! They are so beautiful, Bo!"

"Yes, they are a gift from you."

"I just hope they help."

"I do too." Bo pulled them off the hook and turned to go. "We have to get back to Dane. They've already started the code."

Corrynne was loosing her ability to think. She didn't even hear Bo tell her the code had started. Instead she focused hard to maintain logic. She noticed that one of the bottles had long tubing still attached. She looked into the machine and saw something red begin to flow from its insides. "Bo, what is that?"

"What?" Bo turned back around.

"It looks like blood is coming out of somewhere in there."

"Blood?"

"Yes, doesn't it look that way to you? Look, it's beginning to pour out."

"I hate blood. I don't know." Bo began to walk again, pulling Corrynne along.

Corrynne stopped hard, "No, look at that bottle that has the tubing still attached. I bet that tubing was hooked to something that had blood in it, and when you pulled it away, it came loose."

Bo stopped and focused on the red liquid that was beginning to form a puddle on the floor, "Whose blood? That looks fresh."

Corrynne looked at it closer, it did look fresh. She knew that it was hers. It had been collected along with the antibodies inside the machine. Suddenly she knew why she didn't feel good. The blood wasn't returned to her! The machine had taken whole blood, spun it down, but didn't return anything! "Bo, *I bet it's my blood!*"

"Yes, I bet it is. No wonder you feel so faint. You don't have much blood left." Bo handed the bottles to Corrynne. "Here you carry these and I'll carry you. I think you're too weak to make it to Dane's room any other way." He then picked up Corrynne and began walking out of the room. "We have to get to Dane. We'll fix *you* in a few minutes."

Corrynne continued to think about the blood, feeling not quite like herself. "Dr. Page lied!" She continued, fixated on the blood issue. "He said the blood was returned!"

Bo continued to walk briskly, despite carrying his wife. He was becoming short of breath, "And you believed him?"

"Well, I never felt like this when I gave before. I had no reason to doubt he was telling the truth."

"He was probably—selling the—blood too," Bo said with difficulty under Corrynne's weight.

Corrynne frowned. "He probably was. *That scum!*"

Bo rounded the corner where many people had filled the hall outside Dane's room. "Excuse me, let us through. We need to be with our son."

Corrynne noticed familiar faces. Her father and brother, Darren, stood next to the door waiting for her. "Hello, sis." Darren said calmly. "I came to help out." Turning to her right she noticed her sister, Melynda, smiling widely. She had come too! Next to her sister was her mother who was crying, but was reaching out to Corrynne as if to strengthen her.

Tears sprung to Corrynne's eyes. Oh, how she loved her family! It was so wonderful for them to come right when she needed them. Blinking twice she then realized she hadn't seen clearly. Her imagination must be taking over her mind. Yes, Darren was there, but he was alone. Melynda and her mother were in Washington state. It was impossible for them to be in two places at one time. Her father wasn't there either! What was wrong with her? She was losing it.

A passage was cleared for Bo and he entered quickly, still carrying Corrynne. He sidestepped around the bed, as others were compressing Dane's chest rhythmically. Putting Corrynne down next to Dane, he said, "OK, Corrynne, *hang those antibodies.*"

Corrynne looked at Dane, then looked at the monitor that showed no heart rhythm. Then she looked at the antibodies that Bo held out for her. For some reason she couldn't think of what to do. She just stood there by the bed.

"Come on, Corrynne," encouraged Bo.

"I can't," Corrynne said helplessly.

"Why?"

"I don't know. I've done this a hundred times, but right now I can't think of how to do it."

Bo looked around at all the nurses and doctors in the room. "Can anyone help my wife hang this fluid?"

No one responded, but continued to go through the code. A couple of nurses looked at him with wide eyes, but none attempted to help him. Finally Bo walked over to the nearest nurse. "How do I hang this?"

She looked at him with tear filled eyes. "This won't help your son."

"I don't care. If my wife wants Dane to have it, he will have it! Even if I have to give it to him."

Slowly the nurse reached into a drawer and pulled out some tubing. "Spike the bottles with the pointed end, fill the tubing with fluid and then attach it to one of his lines."

"Which one?"

"The one that's attached to the blue tubing coming out of his central line will be fine."

Bo quickly did as the nurse instructed and hung the bottles on a nearby pole. The golden fluid began to flow into Dane's vessels. "There, Corrynne, your antibodies are being given to our son."

Corrynne broke down and cried. "Thank you, Bo. Thank you."

"Now sit down so you don't fall. I have some more praying to do."

Time

Dane allowed his mind to go down the corridor of the future. In his mind he made the decision to stay in the spirit world, then he allowed his mind to follow the path that carved itself in time.[2] He saw himself happy, content with his environment and his responsibilities, but sad at the same time. He saw Jenessa every once in a while, but she wasn't ever herself. She wouldn't communicate with him. He saw himself approach her many times, and each time she rejected him.

The Millennium came and his reunion with his family was wonderful. He had missed them so much, but one ache replaced another. It was time for temple work to be done for those who had passed on. Dane wanted more than ever to be sealed to Jenessa. There was no one else he wanted to build worlds with and create life with, but to his dismay, she chose another. The person she chose was a glorious being full of power. Dane marveled at his brightness. How did he become so bright? Dane looked down at his own hand. It was bright. He was glorious, but in comparison, he was dull and lacked intensity. What had happened? What made the difference? It seemed like he would always be behind, and not quite as good as he could have been. How could he have been so blind?

An eternal heavy anguish began to bear down on his soul. It wasn't from unworthiness, or sin, but it was lost progression that could have been his. He could have been so much further and offered so much more. Jenessa was right! She was right. Why didn't he listen to her? Dane let out a deep, painful moan.

Suddenly he was back in the room in front of the council.

"Dane, have you decided?" asked a council member. In his pain, Dane wasn't sure which one. "You must decide now. There is no more time. Your body has died. By the efforts of others your organs are still live."

Dane looked around him at the beautiful structure that vaulted high above him. He was back in time, before his decision to forgo his earthly mission had been made. Oh he was so thankful! He still had a chance to take back his future! He didn't have time to explore his choice to go back to the earth, but he innately knew that it would lead him to higher realms not possible any other way.

"Yes, I have made my decision. I want to go back," said Dane earnestly.

The middle council member stood and said, "Alright, this is a prudent choice. However, be aware that there will be intense pain, and you will not remember this time, except for moments of wisdom decided by your guardians. Do you still agree to go?"

Dane nodded. "I understand. Send me, it's the only way."

Within a flicker of light, he was gone.

Power to Raise the Dead

A great power filled Bo. He felt like every part of him was energized. A moment ago, there had only been emptiness and the feeling of waiting, but suddenly he knew. It was time to bless his third son who was dying.

"How long do you want us to continue to revive your son?" asked Dr. Cross who was running the code. "Normally, if we can't get these young people back by now, there isn't much chance."

Bo looked up at the doctor and said, "You may stop now."

The doctor responded by talking to the medical team. "Alright, guys, we're done. Time of death, 0320."

The team of medical personnel stepped back from Dane's body, and began to clean up.

Bo took the doctor by the arm. "Before you clean up, do you mind if Corrynne and I having a moment alone with our son?"

The doctor immediately nodded. "You bet. That's the least we can do for you fine people." The doctor turned and motioned to everyone in the room. "We need to leave. We'll clean up later." The group of nurses left the room.

"Darren?" Bo called out into the hall.

Darren, Corrynne's brother, cautiously moved into the doorway. A grieved look filled his face as he looked at Dane's lifeless body on the bed. "Yes?" he said quietly.

"I need your priesthood, brother," said Bo confidently as he motioned to Darren to come to the head of the bed.

The doctor who must have heard Bo, stuck his head back into the room and said, "Mr. Rogers, your son cannot be brought back. I'm sorry. To bless him now would be useless."

Bo smiled patiently at the doctor and said, "Thank you."

The doctor nodded and then closed the door behind him as he left the room once more.

Bo motioned for Darren to come to the head of the bed once more. "I'm going to ask you to assist me in a blessing. I need you to do the anointing, then leave the rest to me."

Darren looked from Bo to Corrynne, who sat motionless on the chair Bo had sat her in earlier. "I would love to assist you," said Darren managing a smile.

Bo turned to his wife, and called her name. "Corrynne."

Corrynne had been sitting with her eyes closed. As she opened them, a flood of tears continued to flow down her cheeks. "He's gone isn't he? We didn't help him at all. We won't have our son—he's gone."

Bo shook his head, "No, he's not gone. He is very close."

Corrynne frowned, "But his heart has stopped, and they called the code."

Bo reached down and kissed his wife's forehead. Then in a soft low voice he said, "With God anything is possible."

Bo then turned to the bed with Dane's lifeless body and took his place at the top of the bed, ducking under IV lines that continued to pump medications into Dane's vessels.

Bo reached into a pocket in his shirt and pulled out the oil vial that was attached to his key ring. He passed the vial to his brother-in-law. "Would you please anoint Dane?"

Darren took the vial and smiled. "May I do it in Spanish? To me it is much more beautiful than in English."

Bo nodded. "That would be fine."

Darren opened the vial and poured some on Dane's head, near the crown. Then he placed his hands on Dane's head and all in the room closed their eyes as the anointing prayer was said eloquently.

After the anointing, both the men placed their hands on Dane's head and another prayer would be said, only this time by Bo.

"Dane Russell Rogers, in the name of Jesus Christ, I command you to *live...*"

A piercing cry filled the room, then the words, "Bo! Look!" Corrynne had begun pointing at the monitor. There were unmistakable electrical forms that broke the consistency of the flat lines that had crossed the monitor before.

"...I command you to be whole..." continued Bo without stopping.

Next Dane's chest began to rise and fall as he drew in his own breath, despite the ventilator. "Oh, Bo, it's working!"

"...I command your body to be strong, without injury, so that you may fulfill the missions and responsibilities you were sent back to do..."

Corrynne lifted herself from the chair and pulled herself to the bed. She put her head down on Dane's chest. Yes, there was a heartbeat. She was so unbelievably happy!

Then Bo firmly ended the blessing.

"Amen," Bo, Corrynne, and Darren all said in unison at the close of the prayer.

Darren looked up at Bo and Corrynne. Uncontrollable tears streamed down his face. He shook his head. "I have never seen anything like that before in my whole life!"

Bo smiled. "Neither have I. But unquestionably, it was the Lord's will."

Darren patted Bo on the back. "You are a good man, Bo Rogers. You have the faith of ten men. Won't the doctor be surprised."

"I'm so sorry to have questioned you," said Corrynne in a shaky voice.

Bo bowed his head and shook it. "No, the Lord was right."

"Amen," said Darren shaking his head too.

"Yes, amen to that," agreed Corrynne, then she hugged Bo tight.

The door of the room flew open. The nurse, Jane, looked at Corrynne from across the room and pointed at the monitor. *"Look, Corrynne! Something is happening! It looks like Dane has a heartbeat again!"*

Corrynne smiled. "He's back." She said to herself. And it was true.

Notes to "Life and Progression"

Council

[1] Despite the scriptures that state, people are not married in the resurrection (D&C 132:16), it seems obvious that this scripture applies to those who have chosen temporal marriages verses celestial. For those who die as infants, before marriageable age or without a chance to marry, LeGrand Richards states those, "who are worthy of Celestial glory (D&C 137:10), will be given the chance to marry vicariously through temple work and receive the blessings of the Celestial kingdom which includes Celestial marriage and eternal increase. See the following quote. "'Neither is the man without the woman, neither the woman without the man, in the Lord." (1 Corinthians 11:11.) That being true, the Lord must have a plan so that these children [who die before they have reached maturity] can ultimately enjoy that great blessing.... Then I think of the revelation concerning those who will inherit the celestial kingdom, and the Lord said: "... which glory shall be a fullness and a continuation of the seeds forever and ever' (D&C 132:19). And so I expect some day to see the bride that my son has selected over there in the spirit world...just think what a glorious day that will be" (LeGrand Richards, "What After Death?" *Ensign*, Nov. 1974, 5).

Time

[2] It is a literary extrapolation to assume that righteous spirits have the ability to peer into the future. There is indication that this ability will be ours at some point in time as we continue to become like God and gain his abilities and attributes.

"The angels do not reside on a planet like this earth; But they reside in the presence of God, on a globe like a sea of glass and fire, where all things for their glory are manifest, past, present, and future, and are continually before the Lord" (D&C 130:6-7).

We do not know when this ability will be given, but apparently, it is possible when we are in the Lord's presence.

CHAPTER TWENTY

MIXED BLESSINGS

"Behold, I have refined thee, but not with silver; I have chosen thee in the furnace of affliction" (Isaiah 48:10).

00:08:05, 10:01:11 Zulu
Sunday, April 25th
6:59 a.m.
Provo, Utah

Great Refinement

Bo's eyes opened as he woke up early in the morning. It was Easter. He had been planning Easter dinner ever since Dane came home from the hospital. Luckily he was able to find a small ham at the store. It would be good enough to add to their celebration. He hoped the day would be relaxing and peaceful. It would be a true time of renewal.

Bo turned off the alarm that was threatening to go off any moment. He didn't want to wake Corrynne, or the twins who lay almost perpendicular to each other, taking up most of the bed between their parents. Bo smirked as he saw how Corrynne hugged the edge of the bed so that she would not disturb the twins. It was obvious who ruled the roost in his house.

Bo found some sweatpants in his tiny clothes closet that bordered the kitchen and slid them on. He then pulled out a shirt from another compartment in the same closet. He unfolded it and pushed his head through the neck. Automatically, he twisted his wrist to check his watch. Almost nostalgically, in memory of his business days in Salt Lake City, he pushed the button that displayed Zulu, or England time. He watched the time flip to a new hour. The seconds continued to tick beyond that. "Can't stop time," Bo said to himself.

Looking up, at the windows that were shaded, Bo couldn't help wondering if the death of Imam Mahdi had changed the future of America, in which he bragged he would cause fire to come down from heaven. New Year's Eve was only seven months and five days away now. Then the words of the angel came quietly to his mind. He remembered being told that Satan had a host of leaders, ready to fulfill his desires. As one passed away, another would fill his spot. Bo scratched his disheveled head of hair. Innately he knew that just because Imam Mahdi was dead, it didn't mean that the rest of what was prophesied wouldn't still come to pass.

Shaking his head, Bo took a deep breath. He decided he wasn't going to think about all of that today. Today was going to be a good day, free of adversity and trials. There had to be moderation in all things, even in the trials of the just.

Bo surveyed the tiny kitchen. The counters were relatively clear. Jax had cleaned the kitchen the night before as his chore, but he had forgotten to wipe the stove and the counters. Bo shrugged, picked up a washcloth, and turned on the water. Passing the washcloth through the stream, he then squeezed out the excess water. With powerful strokes he wiped the counter surfaces quickly. He wouldn't wake Jax to do such a simple thing, although next time he would remind him that wiping the counters was part of cleaning the kitchen.

Getting bread these days was almost impossible, so Bo decided it would be a treat to make rolls for their dinner that evening. He retrieved a large white storage bucket full of flour from under the counter. Next, he pulled a tiny bit of yeast he was able to obtain at the store, from the freezer. He found the salt, sugar, oil and dried milk from the cupboard, and took out a large bowl from a cupboard.

With well-practiced expertise he began by pouring the flour, yeast and warm water, into the bowl. Then he added the other ingredients by rough proportions combining all the ingredients into a sticky mass. He never measured anymore. It was quicker to just estimate. Next he began to stir the mixture, immediately missing his Bosch mixer. He added more flour until the ball of dough did not stick to his hands.

Bo flipped the bowl over and peeled the large ball from inside. He then kneaded the dough on the breadboard, flipping it over and over, punching the center and then flipping it over and over again. Finally, after being satisfied that the dough was the consistency that he desired, he retrieved the only flat pan he had from a tiny drawer under the oven. He sprayed the surface with a non-stick spray someone donated from their food storage, and then began to divide the bread into segments that would become rolls when he was finished.

Taking the first mass, he rolled it between his palms causing the dough to be molded into a perfectly round ball. It wasn't until all the imperfections rolled away that he placed the ball in the corner of the pan. Over and over he repeated this process, creating many perfectly shaped balls, arranged in a symmetrical order on the face of the pan. Next he got out another pan and repeated the process.

A soft brushing noise moved to Bo's left. Bo looked up from his work to see Ry at the corner of the tiny kitchen.

"Hi, bud. What are you doing awake?" asked Bo.

"I wasn't tired anymore. I heard you and wondered what you were doing," said Ry.

"Well, as you can see, I'm making rolls."

Ry licked his lips. "Mmmm, I love your rolls. I always eat three or four."

"Oh, that's why they seem to disappear so fast," said Bo nodding and hiding a smile.

Ry nodded and smirked. "Yep, that would be my fault."

"Well, take it a little easy today; I'm not making a double batch."

"Why not?"

"Because it takes a lot of work."

"But, Dad, that's my favorite part."

"I thought the candy from the Easter Bunny was your favorite part."

"Nope, not mine," said Ry as he shook his head, but then as if suddenly reminded of something, he began to look around the room for a hidden treasure. "Where are our baskets anyway?"

"No baskets this year. Candy isn't in any of the stores right now."

"That's OK," said Ry nodding, "I'll be fine with rolls."

There was silence in the room, as Ry continued to watch Bo roll the dough in his hands. Then he asked, "Why do you have to roll that dough around so much?"

"So they look nice," answered Bo.

"Why? We're just going to eat them. We chew them up."

"I know," nodded Bo.

"Then why do you take so much time? Maybe you should just throw the whole thing into a big pan and make a lump of bread. Wouldn't it be easier?"

"Well, yes, it might be easier, but I wouldn't be happy, at least not today."

"Why? It tastes the same."

"Yes, but I am the creator of these rolls. I know what they can become and the happiness that can result from their creation. I have an idea of what I want to make and I know how to make them. Because of that, I add the proper ingredients, pound them, work on them, shape them, doing whatever it takes to create the most perfect rolls I can. That is my satisfaction."

"Why's that your satisfaction?" asked Ry.

"Because I won't be happy until the flour, water, oil, sugar, salt and milk have been transformed into something wonderful. It's my job. That is what I do, take raw materials, and work with them until they become something else, much greater than it began."

Ry shrugged. "I see, but I still don't understand."

"OK, let's take you for an example."

"OK."

"When your mom and I had you, you were only a lump of a baby."

"Thanks a lot, Dad."

"No, really. You didn't do anything special. You just slept all the time. But as you grew and became you, we molded you, formed you and worked with you, and still are working with you, in hopes that you become much more than even the cute kid that you are now.

"Heavenly Father does the same with us," continued Bo. "We have so much that he wants us to accomplish. Through trials and hardships, he rolls us into perfect shapes that are in his image. Sometimes it is painful to get the beatings, the rolling and the pinching he does to us, but in the end, we become something much better than we were before. We become heirs to his kingdom."

"Hairs?"

"No *heirs*. Like royalty."

"Oh, you mean I'm going to be a prince some day?"

"No, you are a prince now, after you become married in the temple, you'll be given a promise to become a real king."

"A king? With riches, a castle, and everything?"

"Yes, you'll have worlds without end, with all the riches that exist in them."

Ry's eyes were large. "Wow. That is cool!"

"Yes, 'wow'."

"Well, that's worth it, Dad. I can be beaten up a little, if I get a kingdom in return."

"You can?" asked Bo.

"Heck, yes! That's much easier than fighting an 'end-guy,' like in my old video games. I died too much." Ry shook his head.

"Well, there still might be some 'end-guys' we have to fight, but the Lord will help us in those battles."

Ry's eyes became bright as a smile exploded on his face. "I don't think that will be a problem. The Lord has special powers. No one can beat him."

Bo smiled back. "Nope, you are right. No one can beat him. We just have to remember that and trust his plans."

Ry folded his arms and nodded once. "I will, that will be *easy*."

Bo chuckled to himself and said, "I hope so, son, I truly hope so."

Easter

Smells of fresh baked bread and ham filled the air of the small trailer. Carea was setting the table, while Bo checked on the ham one last time. Corrynne was feeding the twins bread and cooked carrots early so she could sit with the rest of the family at dinner. Ry and Roc were cutting up leftover raw carrots someone had given them and a rare head of lettuce their father found at the store, while Jax made ranch dressing from a mix.

Dane lay on the twin bed in the adjacent sleeping area at the command of his mother, under a thick goose down sleeping bag. He flexed his muscles in his legs and then in his arms. He could feel his strength coming back. He lifted his right hand out from the covers and looked at it in the light. The flesh was healing very well. It surprised all the doctors that had assessed him in the hospital. They had thought he would lose it if he lived, but here he was a week later and all the pink healing tissue testified that he wouldn't. Yes, it was a miracle.

Dane rummaged deep in his robe pocket and felt for a plastic bag. He pulled it out and looked at the object inside the plastic. It was the tiny chip that had been implanted in his hand. It had hundreds of silver strands that stuck out of it and woven around the other strands, making a mesh-like pattern. The nurse had found the thing in his bed when she was changing the sheets the day after his resuscitation. She asked Dane if he knew what it was. He had been surprised that the chip was outside his hand snatched it quickly from her hand to save it. He didn't know how it came lose from his flesh, but he was grateful that it had. It must have been part of the marvel that changed all the cells of his body from dead, to living once more.

Dane put it back into his pocket. He didn't want anyone to see it. He knew Carea would be sad if she realized he had been set free and she hadn't. He wanted to do everything he could to restore her to her previous state of happiness—before Imam Mahdi.

Dane smiled. Today, life was good. Today was a new day. Today, everyone received a chance to enjoy their time together and the blessings of heaven. Blessings...that thought made him think of sunshine and...soft wind. A glorious smiling face flashed in his memory. It was a beautiful face. He was in love with that face. Where did he know it from? Dane thought hard but could not recall the memory. Maybe it was an imagined fairy or princess leftover from too much sleep and too many dreams.... Oh well...he couldn't be concerned with useless fantasy infatuations. Dane cleared his throat and changed his focus. "Is it time to eat?" he called out.

Carea poked her head around the doorway and smiled, "Yes, Dane. For you, it's always time to eat."

Dane smiled back and nodded, "That's my sister! I'm so glad that you're back."

Carea took a step and kissed Dane's cheek. "No, I'm glad that *you* are back."

"You better be," said Dane with a sparkle in his eye, "Because I'm back and better than ever! Life will never be the same!"

"I hope not," said Carea with a wink.

"Time to eat," came the musical call of their mother.

Yes, it was a very good day, thought Dane, as he pulled his heavy body from the bedding. Shakily he made it to the table, bracing himself with every step.

"I'll say the prayer today, if you don't mind, Dad," said Dane as he squished behind the tiny table. Dane wanted to give a prayer publicly, in front of everyone that had fought so hard for his life. He was indebted to his whole family, and he planned to pay up.

"Be my guest," said Bo as he placed the little ham that looked perfectly matched for the small table.

After Bo took his seat and as everyone bowed his or her heads, Dane's baritone voice began to ring beautifully. He voiced praises to a Lord that was aware of them. A tear came to more than one person's eye. It indeed was a day of many, many blessings.

THE END...

The Ascension,
Millennial Glory IV

Braun, the eldest son of the Rogers family, is directed by the Spirit to fulfill an internship as an aide to the Secretary General of the United Nations. Through his dreams and visions of beasts and monsters he is able to act as Daniel of old, to Secretary Klump, to warn him of things to come. Together they uncover an ancient secret design as it unfolds. The man who is one of the richest on the earth plots to take control the world through manipulating its leaders. Braun feels a great responsibility to stop his ascension to total and complete power, but what can he, a lowly aide do? Conrad, the second oldest in the Rogers family, is on a mission in Israel. At first, he has limited success among the Jews, but as time moves on, the Spirit of truth rests heavily upon him. He's able to be instrumental in the conversion of a group of Rabbis which bring Jews to the church in droves as they begin to believe in Christ.

Hanging by a Thread,
Millennial Glory V

Braun Rogers travels to America and takes on a position at the White house in an effort to warn the President of the danger that awaits the nation. He finds the country in a political disarray as the constitution hangs by a thread. Through his visions, he sees the outcome of the present chaos as it spirals toward destruction. The country must return to the values that inspired its beginnings if it hopes to be protected from the secret combinations that are designing its downfall. Brea Rogers, the eldest sister of the family is trapped in an unholy web of deceit as she unravels the truth about Matt's family. The facts are too horrible to believe and too deadly to ignore. She must make some difficult decisions to protect her unborn children. Just what will that do to her love for Matt and the marriage they share? Elder Conrad Rogers becomes a hostage to the country of Israel but his burden is made light through participating in prophesy. The long awaited Jewish temple rises. The Jews know their Messiah is coming. Do you?

It is the End of Days and all is in Commotion!

WENDIE L.EDWARDS
AUTHOR

Wendie L. Edwards, the author of the "Millennial Glory" series, grew up in Edmonds Washington. At Brigham Young University she met her husband Ted and they were sealed in the Seattle Temple. She taught early morning Seminary for the Lynnwood Stake in Washington. After five children, Ted and Wendie felt inspired to return to Brigham Young University where Ted received his Master's degree in Tax Accounting and Wendie graduated Cum Laude with a Bachelor's degree in Nursing. Wendie has been an Intensive Care nurse for 10 years and holds a CCRN certification. Ted and Wendie reside in Cedar Hills with their seven sons and two daughters.

TIM HARTMAN
CO-AUTHOR

Tim Hartman was born in Kansas, and raised the youngest in a devout, non-denominational Christian family. Tim went on to become a Musical Pastor of a large Christian church after a career as a singer, song-writer in the music industry. Tim was baptized a member of the Church of Jesus Christ of Latter Day Saints in 2003. Having a vast knowledge of the scriptures and a hunger for missionary work, Tim demonstrated an interest in the "Millennial Glory" series and has been instrumental in developing new and exciting storylines in volumes 2-4, as well as co-authoring parts of book three. Now Tim is a financial professional, dedicated husband and proud father of two children, living in northern Nevada.

KATHRYNPACKER
HEAD EDITOR

Kathryn Packer, the editor of Ascension, is a BYU-Hawaii graduate with a B.S. in Information Systems and Computer Science. She is a technical writer and trainer by day and uses her memberships in the Society for Technical Communication and the American Society for Training & Development to keep her updated in current trends. Kathryn spent most of her growing up years on a small farm in Idaho raising sheep and other small animals with her 5 siblings. She currently resides in Bothell, Washington. Her true passions include traveling, music, quilting, reading, and fine art; not necessarily in that order.

TERIE WIEDERHOLD
CONSULTANT

Terie Weiderhold grew up in Wyoming, Utah and Oregon. Her teenage years were spent in Portland, Oregon. She is a graduate of Brigham Young University with a doctorate degree in psychology. Her emphasis is in learning and in parenting skills. For the past five years, Terie and her husband, Paul, have written a weekly parenting column for Central Utah's Daily Herald. Terie enjoys working with youth and is currently the owner and director of a Residential Treatment Center for troubled teenagers in Spanish Fork, Utah.

She is the mother of six children and a niece. They currently live in Provo, Utah.

LORI CHRISTLER
INTERN EDITOR

BYU Intern Editor: Lori Christler Chase grew up in a family of eight girls in Cody, Wyoming. She loves to read classic books and play the piano. She also enjoys working with children to improve their reading skills.

Lori and her husband Seth live in Provo, Utah where they are attending college. She has received college scholarships for being an "Outstanding English Student." Lori is working towards her degree in English with an editing emphasis. She hopes to become a professional book editor.